A Baby's Bones

REBECCA Alexander

TITAN BOOKS

A Baby's Bones
Print edition ISBN: 9781785656217
E-book edition ISBN: 9781785656224

Published by Titan Books
A division of Titan Publishing Group Ltd
144 Southwark Street, London SE1 0UP

First edition: May 2018
1 2 3 4 5 6 7 8 9 10

A CIP catalogue record for this title is available from the British Library.

Printed and bound in Great Britain by CPI Group (UK) Ltd.

Did you enjoy this book?
We love to hear from our readers. Please email us at
readerfeedback@titanemail.com or write to us at
Reader Feedback at the above address.

TITAN BOOKS.COM

For my parents,
JILLIAN ALEXANDER
who taught me to read and love books, and
JOHN ALEXANDER
*who told me stories of history that
still fascinate me today.*

1

Monday 25th March

It was a bone from a baby's arm. Like a twig on Sage Westfield's glove, the ends crumbled away by the action of the sieve, it was still distinctive to a trained eye.

'I'll get a second opinion as to date,' she said, pushing a handful of dark curls out of her eyes with the other hand. 'I'm certain the bones are contemporary with the spoil filling the well. Sixteenth century, Tudor.'

The police officer pointed at another small heap of finds. 'You're sure they aren't animal bones, then? Cat, maybe?'

'These are human.' The afternoon breeze blew across the garden, shivering the evergreen hedges that crowded Bramble Cottage. 'I think we have at least one adult and a baby, probably newborn or up to a couple of months old. We'll need an expert to be sure. It's surprising they've survived this long.'

'And you found them yesterday?'

'Actually, one of my PhD students found the first one. Elliott Robinson.' Sage pointed to the finds table where Elliott was crouched on the ground examining the spoil pile, watched by Steph, her undergraduate student. Elliott didn't look up, but Steph waved. 'I just labelled the bones as they brought them out.'

The policeman made a note of the find numbers on the containers. 'I'll let the Home Office know it's historical.' He looked at her swollen belly on her otherwise slim frame. 'Sad, really, a baby. Have you seen many like this?'

'I've never seen anything like it.' Sage placed the bone on a pad of bubble wrap. 'It's really unusual to have a burial outside consecrated ground. But to put two bodies down a well, and cover them with the contents of a midden – that's very rare.' Her phone beeped but she ignored it.

'Midden?'

'Medieval rubbish dump. We're finding broken pottery, cooked bones, probably mixed with manure. That's what's so disrespectful about it. It does suggest the need for a quick or secret burial. Maybe even murder.'

The police officer paused at the word, looking down at the handful of dark brown fragments. 'Care to hazard a cause of death?'

Sage smiled at him, shaking her head, then glanced at the house. The windows reflected the yellowed, late afternoon clouds. Her smile faded. 'The owners aren't going to like this.'

He followed her gaze up to tiny dormers embedded in

the thatch. 'The house must have cost a packet. They're new to the Isle of Wight, aren't they?'

'Yes. They needed listed building consent and an archaeological survey before they could start an extension. Then we found the well, and they had to foot the excavation bill. Now we have bodies—' Her phone beeped again. She glanced at it. Marcus. *Lunch?*

The officer put his notebook away. 'We'll get back to you. But for now, please treat the site as limited. Any remains to be recorded, held together, and secured for further examination. At least until we confirm it is historical.'

'Of course.' Sage watched him walk around the side of the cottage, on the tarpaulins she had laid down to save the lawn. Little chance of that, now the dig had to be extended. She wrote a message back to Marcus. *Busy*. She really didn't have time for his drama today.

She looked at the blank eyes of the cottage. They stared over the hedge and across fields that ran west, up the slight hill to the ornate chimneys of the manor house beyond. Banstock village sat on a promontory with the sea on three sides, and she'd loved to come here as a child. She had never been to the manor house; perhaps she was too young to appreciate it before they moved off the Island. She glanced up back at the stone walls of the cottage. Under its thick coat of thatch it should have been picturesque, but the place gave her the creeps. The yawn of the well drew in the darkness that had gathered under the hedge, and she pulled her coat around herself. She could only hope the baby had been dead when it was thrown into the water. She touched her bump. Her emotions were definitely getting the better of her nowadays.

'Hello?' Sage called in the front door, left slightly ajar despite the cold weather. 'Mrs Bassett?'

The owner of the cottage padded into the flagstone hall. She seemed insubstantial in a sweater that hung from bony shoulders. 'Come through to the lounge.' Even her voice was thin.

Sage considered her splattered boots, sat on the step to unlace them and went into the hall in her socks. The staircase beside her was blackened oak, smoothed to a pale brown on the treads, curved by five hundred years of feet. A child's coats hung on brass pegs, the bright colours incongruous against the reproduction coffer and pine hall table. A wicker dog basket under the stairs held a tartan blanket, clean and folded.

She followed Mrs Bassett into the plainly furnished living room, where an unlit woodburner sat in the inglenook fireplace. The beam over the opening was blackened by hundreds of years of open fires. Sage ran her hand over the timber, feeling tool marks along its length. Her host looked through the French doors to the havoc wreaked on her garden.

'So, it is actually a well,' the faded woman said. She turned to look at Sage with an assessing expression. In the half-light she appeared older than the thirties she probably was, shadows gathering in the hollows of her face and her eye sockets. 'I'm sorry, I didn't mean to stare.'

'It's OK. My mother's from Kazakhstan. No one believes I was born on the Island.' Wide cheekbones and almond-shaped eyes had always given Sage's Turkic heritage away.

Mrs Bassett sighed. 'Is the well recent or old?'

'We think it's an original Tudor well, very rare and brilliantly preserved. It's been filled in with material from a rubbish pit, that's why we're getting so many bits of old pots and glass. Wonderful finds.' Sage let her enthusiasm colour her voice. She knew, if she could get the site's owner motivated, the knotty problem of funding the dig would become easier. 'But there's more to it than just the pottery. We'll have to dig deeper.'

'What you're saying is, it will cost more money. Tea?'

'Yes, please. Milk, no sugar. Mrs Bassett—'

'Judith.' The woman twisted a smile, which quickly sagged. 'You'll need to be here longer, I suppose. Come through to the kitchen.'

Like the living room, the kitchen was bland: white walls; a cream Aga that wasn't lit; and plain oak cupboards. A draught blew in from the door to the hall. Judith filled an electric kettle, the water splashing into the silence.

Sage decided that there was no good time to break the news. 'I'm afraid there is a problem with the well itself.'

Judith's shoulders tensed but her voice was level. 'What kind of problem?'

'When we sifted some of the spoil from the excavation, we found bones. Some of them appear to be human.'

The woman froze, a teabag suspended between finger and thumb, for several seconds. Then, as if the music had started again, she dropped the bag into the mug. 'Human?'

'It appears that at some point, probably centuries ago, someone buried two people in the well. There appears to be at least one adult and a baby. I asked the police along to document the finds but they are happy it's historical.'

Judith placed a mug decorated with bright cartoon robins onto the granite work surface in front of Sage, then surveyed her over the rim of her own cup. 'Is this going to be a big problem?'

'We'll be in contact with the Home Office,' Sage said. 'Then we can definitively establish that these are historical remains. I'm afraid we'll have to excavate the rest of the well, to ensure we have recovered all of the bones.' She softened her tone, but Judith appeared unmoved. When she spoke, her voice was harsh.

'My husband's in the hospice. They say there's little chance of survival. I can see he's dying. Eight months ago we were a normal family, looking forward to moving to the Island, changing schools. He's only forty-three.'

That explained the woman's remoteness. She looked overwhelmed.

'I'm so sorry. I didn't know.' Sage wrapped her cold hands around her mug. 'This must be dreadful for you.' She shivered as a draught brushed her neck, and she found it hard not to flinch.

'I hate this house,' Judith said. She looked out of the front window, to the drive and the road beyond. The whole property was bordered by a yew hedge, gnarled and twisted with age. 'I hated it from the day we moved in. It's cold, it's dark. Maybe it's haunted.'

'I'm sorry?'

'The house. Everything started to go wrong when we moved here.' Judith sat on a kitchen stool. 'It's like what happened to the dog.'

'I noticed the basket—'

'He ran out into the road the day we got here. He was killed by a delivery van. We didn't tell Chloe, she thinks he ran off. I couldn't tell her the truth.' Judith's voice wobbled, and she swallowed hard. 'It was also the week James was diagnosed. I had to tell her Daddy had cancer. She's only nine.'

'I wish I didn't have to add to your burden at such a bad time,' Sage said. No wonder Judith thought the house felt haunted. 'Do you think you'll try and move?'

'James is too ill. He's the one who wanted a conservatory in the first place.'

'I'm sorry,' Sage said. 'We'll try to get the work done as fast as we can.'

Judith turned, and the smile on her face was distorted into a grimace. 'I don't care what you do outside. We aren't going to bother with the extension now, anyway. Do your excavation, write your reports. Will it cost us a lot more?'

'More than we originally anticipated, I'm afraid. Your planning application fee covers the basic excavation uncovering the well. Your home insurance may help, and some costs may be borne by the Home Office as we've found human remains.'

'Human remains,' Judith said. 'How long will it take, with just the three of you?'

Sage drained the last of her tea. 'We'll work as fast as we can. In the meantime, I have to ask you not to go near the excavation – it isn't safe. I'll board it up before I go. I do hope you get some good news about your husband soon.'

'Me too.' Judith switched the hall light on as she escorted Sage to the front door. In the yellow glow she seemed younger, but ill and exhausted. 'Maybe when the bones go, our bad luck will stop.'

Sage looked around. The cottage did seem like the archetypal haunted house: dark passages; lots of odd corners; creaking timbers; and bone-scouring draughts. She shivered as the wind from the open door found its way down her collar.

'There's an evil presence here,' Judith said. 'I can feel it.'

Sage stepped into her boots, and stood up, laces trailing. 'I don't really believe in ghosts, Mrs Bassett.'

Judith leaned forward. 'Neither did I.'

2

29th June 1580

Two yards of fine linen for a baby's shroud, for
Lady Banstock ——————— *two shillings and four pence*
Wages for Mistress Agness Waldren, who nurses the sick of
red pox at Banstock ——————— *four shillings*
Quarter's wages for Mistress Isabeau Duchamp, for
embroideries to your lordship's daughter Elizabeth's bride
clothes, of three loose gowns and two kirtles
◦ ——————— *eleven shillings and nine pence*

Accounts of Banstock Manor, 1576–1582

It is a pious woman that sews her baby's shroud while it still kicks within her. Baron Anthonie Banstock tups his second wife each spring and she brings forth a stillborn lamb each autumn. He has more hope this time; the last one mewed like a kitten for a day before it succumbed. Five babes lie in the vault, each in its hand-sewn winding sheet, at the will of a merciful God.

It seems to me that Elizabeth shall never wear her bride clothes, as she raves in delirium within her chamber. Already Lord Banstock has come to me to hint at a new betrothal to the younger sister, if the elder perishes. I am concerned. Fourteen years makes a poor bed-mate for nine-and-twenty, and the man Solomon Seabourne has a reputation for being a radical, perhaps even a papist. He waits at Ryde and his manservant, Edward Kelley, rides over each day for news of Elizabeth. The man Kelley is young and as sharp around the manor as a fox, asking this and that of the men, and the maids.

Mistress Agness, the rector's sister, adds spinster's vinegar to her tongue as she scolds our Viola: her hair should be bound and covered; her skirts are too short; she laughs immodestly.

When she was born, the travail took away Viola's mother, Lady Marion. The baron might have cast the seven-month babe aside, but instead he ordered the whole castle to rally unto her. I first saw her by the kitchen fire, at the breast of a wet nurse. She was tiny, a red face in loose swaddling, for she was deemed too weak to risk tight wrapping. She stopped her suckling, and beheld me, as I leaned in curiosity over this daughter of the manor. We stared at each other, and I swear she knew me. They say babies are as blind as kittens, but wherefore are their eyes open? She gazed at me, then lowered her gaze to the milky nipple and fed as heartily as a lamb upon the ewe.

From that day, I found times to observe the child, and she grew accustomed to me. The baron carried her around the manor, so devoted was he, that we often sat over the accounts while she babbled on his lap or mine. As she grew older, she was confined to her nursery more, but still found hours to visit me in my office and play with my seals and keys. As she grew older she learned letters and numerals in my office, and traced her first words in ink on scraps of vellum from the rent rolls. Now fourteen, she is the darling of the castle, except for sour Mistress Agness.

It is she who chides Viola for visiting me, and none was more argumentative in the matter of Seabourne's betrothal to Elizabeth. But a betrothal does not a marriage make.

Vincent Garland, Steward to Lord Banstock, His Memoir

3

Tuesday 26th March

'Good morning.' It was a deep voice, and it made Sage jump back and slip on the muddy edge of the excavation. She barely regained her balance. The morning had already been full of problems, and now she had a streak of clay down the inside seam of her jeans.

'Shit. You startled me—' Her words faded as she took in a dog collar on a tall man, late thirties maybe, with dark hair and round glasses. 'Oh. You must be the vicar. Sorry, you surprised me.'

He smiled at her, which made him look younger. 'Dr Westfield?'

'Sage. County archaeologist.' She stretched out a hand, before realising there was mud on her fingers.

He took it anyway, with the smallest of grimaces. 'Nick Haydon. I'm the vicar of St Mark's, Banstock church.' His skin was warm, his grip firm.

Sage wiped her hand on her jeans, which made him smile wider. 'Are you here to see the Bassetts?'

The smile faded. 'Mrs Bassett doesn't want me to visit. Actually, I'm here because the diocese has just been told about the bones. It's likely any human remains will be interred up at the churchyard, once your investigation is complete.' He looked towards the two students working under the flapping awning. Steph was working with a flotation tray, and Elliott was picking through the sievings from the day before.

Sage walked over to the folding tables. 'Would you like to see what we have? Be careful, it's slippery. Can we see what you're working on, Elliott?'

The vicar followed her over to the tarpaulin, and Elliott carefully opened one of the bone boxes. 'Don't touch,' the student warned. 'They're fragile. I'm cleaning them so they can go with the others.' Leg bones from an adult: a tibia snapped like a twig; a kneecap; and about a dozen foot bones all laid out on bubble wrap. Elliott closed the box, and Sage moved to the table where she had started to lay out the cleaned bones. She removed the covering tarpaulin.

'This is more of the adult's remains.' She found her voice naturally dropped. 'The body seems to have been bent up, at least one leg forced above the head, fracturing the femur and lower leg bones. We've just uncovered the top of the head and a hand as well.'

'The broken bones – did that mean he suffered some

violence?' The vicar's face was animated by some feeling she couldn't read.

'Maybe. And we don't actually know whether the bones are male or female. It wasn't necessarily a violent death; the fractures may have been post-mortem. We'll know more when we finish excavating the skull and pelvis.' She picked up the sandwich box that sat next to the bone box and opened it gently. 'These are bones from the baby we found with the adult.'

The bones were tiny, a handful of ribs, vertebrae and a few long bones.

'No skull?'

'We haven't found it yet. The baby seems to have been buried upside down.'

The vicar looked back at her. 'Would you mind if I said a prayer over these remains?'

'Of course not.'

Sage stepped away, watching as he lowered his face and closed his eyes. He had long eyelashes the same black as his hair, and he seemed genuinely grieved for the people dumped in the well with the rubbish. Elliott stared at Sage; she wondered if he was offended by the ritual. He didn't say anything, but Steph lowered her head.

After a quiet 'amen', echoed by Steph, Elliott carefully covered the bones. Sage glanced up at the house, remembering the overshadowed woman from yesterday.

The vicar walked over. 'Thank you. When will you be

able to release the bones for reburial?'

'First we have to prove definitively that they are more than a hundred years old. Then we have to make sure we have as many as have survived – it's likely a lot of the baby's bones have just dissolved away. I'm surprised we have so many. We also need to make sure there aren't any more bodies down there.'

'Why would someone bury a body in a well?' His voice was strained.

Sage shrugged. 'It's too early to tell. Wells are valuable resources, they are expensive to dig out and line. We occasionally see burials in wells in disease events like plague. It was an easy way to dispose of remains. Other reasons include war or even murder. Sometimes bodies were used to foul the water and make the well unusable. But the pottery we are finding is too late for that. There were no wars being fought on the Isle of Wight at the time.'

'Horrible.'

She nodded towards the boxes of bones. 'I can't imagine why they would deny these people a Christian burial.' She felt awkward talking to a vicar about faith, especially since she didn't have any. 'I mean, almost everyone was a believer at the time.'

'Maybe it was murder, then.'

'Perhaps.' Sage wrapped her arms around herself against the wind. Even with the sun out, it was going straight through her fleece.

'Will you be here for the whole excavation?' He nodded at her bump. 'I mean, you seem to have your own deadline.'

'I'm not due until June. I'll let you know as soon as we finish with the bones. It will be some time, months rather than weeks.'

'Thank you.' He leaned towards her and lowered his voice. 'The Bassetts. Do you know anything about them?'

'I know her husband's very ill. And Mrs Bassett, Judith, she—' Sage couldn't find the words to describe the wraith that she had spoken to the day before. 'She seems frozen, you know?'

'In what way?'

Sage zipped up the fleece over her bump and pulled up her collar. 'She didn't react. I mean, we find the body of a baby in her garden, and she's worried about how much the recovery will cost. Obviously, her husband's illness is more important. Then she said the house is haunted.'

The vicar smiled grimly. 'Maybe it is. There are at least two bodies down the well. Ghosts are supposed to be associated with violent deaths or being denied Christian burial.'

'You have to be kidding. You can't believe in ghosts.'

'I don't "believe" in ghosts, it's not a faith thing.'

Sage folded her arms. 'I just thought vicars wouldn't be great fans of the supernatural.'

He smiled, apparently with genuine amusement. 'On the contrary. We're all about the supernatural.' He reached into a pocket and pulled out a dog-eared card. 'Here's my number, if you need to get in touch about the burial. The woman who used to own Bramble Cottage, Maeve Rowland, she knows all about the house's history. She might be worth a visit. She always said the place was haunted too.'

Sage took the card and stuffed it into a pocket. 'Haunted? By what?'

His forehead wrinkled. 'I was never sure whether it was just a voice or she actually saw something. You should ask her. She moved into a local residential home, the Poplars, but she lived here for several decades.'

'Thanks, I'll do that if we have time. The Poplars.'

'It's set back from the road at the top of the high street. She would love a visitor.' The vicar smiled again, which changed his whole face, she thought, from long and serious to warm and friendly. 'She's had a stroke but is still sharp as a pin. Anyway, I've got visits to do. I expect I'll see you again.'

'We'll be retrieving evidence for a few weeks. Possibly longer,' Sage said.

'Maybe we can discuss the procedures involved in burying these poor lost bones. I've never done anything like this before.' He stared up at the sky, as a few spatters hit his jacket. 'It's really starting to rain.'

'The forecast did say heavy showers.' Sage scrabbled in her pocket for one of her own business cards. 'Call me if you need more information. Oh, and, vicar—'

'Nick, please.' That smile again, curving up the corners of his mouth.

'I'll be speaking with Mrs Bassett. If I can help in any way, let me know.'

He thought for a long moment. 'If the opportunity arises, tell her that the support we offer is pastoral and practical, as well as spiritual comfort. Lifts, babysitting, someone to talk to. That sort of assistance. I promise not to overwhelm her with beliefs she doesn't share. But I'm pretty handy with a lawnmower, and we have volunteers who do the school run.'

'I'll tell her if I can.' Sage could feel her smile pulling at her cold cheeks. She watched as he walked away, and felt a little warmed, especially when he turned at the corner of the house and smiled back at her.

The late morning brought heavier rain, whipped around the garden of Bramble Cottage by a wind that slapped the awning against the poles that supported it. Sage kept most of the delicate finds locked in the van.

The adult's skull slowly emerged, crown first, like it was being slowly born from a womb of clay. The face was strong; she was unsure at first whether it was male or female. Elliott and Steph, invigorated by the jawless face overlooking the dig, redoubled their efforts to find more vertebrae, more ribs, more of the baby's crumbling bones including half a tiny pelvis by lunchtime.

Sage suggested they decamp to the village pub, the Harbour Bell, for a chance to warm up and dry off. Even in a padded jacket, Steph's teeth were chattering. She treated Elliott to a soft drink, bought Steph a shandy, and ordered herself a large decaffeinated coffee while they waited for their food.

The dig seemed to have made Elliott even more taciturn than usual, but Steph got up to look around the panelled walls and beckoned Sage over enthusiastically. 'Have you seen these pictures?'

Sage looked around the pub, which was perhaps as old as the cottage. The walls were decorated with old farming implements, harness for heavy horses, and leather buckets were sat on shelves. Between them were a series of sepia photographs.

'Are they Friths?' she asked. A Victorian photographer named Francis Frith had recorded thousands of scenes across Britain in the 1800s.

Steph leaned in to examine one more closely, standing on tiptoes. 'No – these look like they were taken by an amateur.' She turned to the woman at the bar. 'These are great,' she said. 'Are they pictures of houses in the village?'

The landlady nodded. 'They are. Some old rector of St Mark's took loads. His widow left them to a previous landlord.' She nodded at Sage and Elliott. 'Are you the people digging up Bramble Cottage?'

Steph smiled, flicking long blonde hair out of her eyes. 'We're looking into the history of the place. Are there any photographs of the cottage?' Sage was impressed by her people skills, as Steph waved at the pictures. 'I see there's a *lovely* one of the pub.'

The landlady lifted up the hinged end of the bar, and took down a framed print near the door. She placed it carefully on the table in front of them, and dusted it off with a tea towel tucked into her waistband. 'That's Bramble Cottage, I think.'

The cottage looked different, the thatch thin and the chimney leaning at a perilous angle. A woman in an apron and holding a baby stood beside the house, at the side where the main door was now. She stared ahead with the serious rigidity of the Edwardian subject, but the baby was a blur of movement.

'Oh, God, it could even be them,' Steph breathed. Then she shook her head and grinned. 'Of course not, I'm being stupid. No photography in the sixteenth century.'

'It's most likely the bodies are contemporary with the fill,' Sage pointed out. 'You're also jumping to the conclusion that the baby in the well is buried with its mother.'

The landlady stepped back. 'A baby?'

Sage winced. The last thing she wanted was speculation while they had so few facts. 'We haven't finished our investigations yet. But we have found a few bones. It would be better if we didn't broadcast it until we have all the facts, though.' That cat was probably well out of the bag; gossip ran around the Island like electricity. It was one of the things she disliked about coming back here to live. The Isle of Wight had less than two thirds the population of neighbouring Southampton on the mainland, spread over a hundred and fifty square miles, but it had a village mentality.

The woman's eyes were wide. 'Oh my God, there have been rumours about that old cottage for years. It's supposed to be haunted, you know.'

Sage smiled up at her. 'Old houses are always thought to be haunted. I've seen a lot of old houses in my job but I've never seen a ghost.'

Elliott drained his drink, put his long forearms on the table, and frowned. 'I wonder if we could look at the back of the photograph? There might be some useful information.'

Sage turned it over, but it was sealed with paper tape.

The landlady shook her head. 'I don't know if Den would want us messing about with it.'

'Den?'

'That's the old landlord, Dennis Lacey; he's my husband's father. He lives with us since we moved in to help run the Harbour Bell. He's very protective of all the old stuff.' She pursed her lips, as Elliott brought out a hand lens to study the picture. 'I'll ask the old bugger, but he's grumpy today.'

As she left, the food arrived from the kitchen: toasted sandwiches and a bowl of chips to share. Sage, Elliott and

Steph were halfway through their meal when the landlady returned, this time with an elderly man leaning on her arm. His slight frame produced a surprisingly hearty voice. 'You them history folk, Carol tells me.'

Sage stood up, and offered her hand. 'Dr Sage Westfield, sir. These are archaeology students from South Solent University, Elliott Robinson and Stephanie Beatson. We were admiring your collection of local pictures.'

'Don't you "sir" me, young lady. Den'll do.' He glanced at the picture on the table. 'You want to know about that old cottage, do you? What's your interest, then?'

'It's a listed building. I've been asked to check there aren't any archaeological features before allowing the building of an extension.'

Den grunted something and settled in the seat beside Elliott. 'You should have talked to me first. I could have told you to watch your step over there. That house is haunted, shadowed with evil my gran used to say. She should know, she lived in the village all her life.'

Steph's eyes were round. 'Is there really a ghost?'

Sage couldn't help rolling her eyes but Den laughed, a crackle of sound that started him coughing. When he got his breath back, he explained. 'Ghosts ain't no trouble, girl, at my age you sees them all the time. No, there's a nasty atmosphere over there. Bad luck.' He paused. 'You know about the grave in the woods?'

Sage looked at the students. Steph stared back at her,

Elliott shrugged. 'We haven't heard anything about it,' she said.

'When I was a boy, Bramble Cottage's garden extended right to the boundary of the manor. Now it's partly common land, because the Banstocks donated some of it to the village, and they sold the rest off for housing.' He stretched in his chair, folded his arms. 'The old grave was past the stream. We used to think it was haunted, a burial like that. We thought old Damozel – that's what's written on the stone you see – must be a witch, buried so far from the church. The headstone might even still be there.'

Sage could see the conversation getting derailed as Elliott opened his mouth to ask more questions. She beat him to it. 'We were wondering whether we could take a look at the back of this photograph,' she said, holding it up. 'We're just looking for more history on the cottage.'

He stared at it for a long moment. 'No problem. Cut it off.'

'Thank you. I'll be careful.'

Sage turned the picture over in her hands and brought her mobile kit out of her pocket. She removed a small scalpel, gently slit the modern framing tape, and lifted out the card backboard. The reverse of the photograph had something written on it in pencil. 'I can't read it – have either of you got a light?'

Both students offered pencil torches. Illuminated, the elaborate letters became clearer.

Well House.

* * *

The afternoon brought relief from the rain for the archaeologists, but their work was interrupted by a small girl rushing around the side of Bramble Cottage. She careered towards the excavation and Sage had to grab her before she hit the flimsy barrier.

'Whoa! Careful, it's deep.'

'Can I see?' The child was pretty, blonde hair restrained in plaits. She stared at the mess they had made of the ground. 'You made our garden really muddy.' She strained to see down the well, already a hole seven or eight feet deep.

Sage smiled at her, but subtly waved at Elliott to cover the human remains. 'We're learning about the history of your house. Of course you can come and have a look while we're here, but I want you to promise you won't come into the back garden on your own. It's not safe. OK? Promise?'

The child peered into the hole. 'I promise. That's really deep. I can see it from my bedroom.' She scrutinised Sage. 'You're really pretty. Are you Chinese?'

'My mum's from a country a long way away, called Kazakhstan.' She glanced at Elliott, who put up a thumb. 'So, what's your name?'

'Chloe Eloise Bassett. What's yours?'

Sage introduced herself and the students, and showed the child the stones at the top of the well. Chloe soon lost interest and Sage handed her over to Steph, who got some of the pottery shards out, and started talking about Tudor history.

Judith Bassett walked around the side of the house, trudging over the mud in unlaced shoes. 'Chloe! Stop bothering these people, they're working.' Her face was pale, her lips pressed together.

'It's OK, Mrs Bassett,' soothed Steph. 'We were just looking at some pots.'

'Steph says I can borrow some things to take into school to show them.' The child held out a fragment of earthenware. 'Look, this is a bit of a jug. It's really old, like Henry the Eighth.'

'Just artefacts from the well,' Sage added. 'Nothing upsetting.'

Judith was shaking, her arms wrapped around herself. 'I don't want Chloe involved with the well. I don't want her upset in any way.' She reached out and grabbed her daughter, snatching the pottery out of her hand and throwing it to the ground. Before anyone could respond, she swung the child up into her arms, walking quickly back towards the house. Chloe stared over her mother's shoulder, holding Sage's gaze until she was carried out of view. Her fingers dug into her mother's neck, leaving little red welts.

Elliott scooped up the pot shard. 'Are you OK?'

Sage nodded, watching the door close, hearing a lock

turned. 'Just a bit surprised.' She rummaged in her pocket and found her spare set of keys. She dropped them into his hand. 'Can you two put the bones in my van? I want to be prepared in case she orders us off the property.' Then she took out a pen and one of the find record cards. She jotted down an apology and her mobile phone number and dropped it through the letterbox of Bramble Cottage.

4

5th July 1580

Stones to be cut for the new well, two masons and a master, at five pence each day and ten pence for the master mason
———————————— eighteen shillings and eight pence to date

Accounts of Banstock Manor, 1576–1582

The masons have started lining the new well. The old one, being at the back of the house, is only convenient for the use of one property, and brackish at best. Banstock stands on a promontory surrounded by the sea: it creeps into the soil and shallow wells. This one is but thirty years old and is already useless for drinking, built as it was from bits of stone from the abbey. Some say it was cursed by the abbot as he was chased from his own church, beaten and left for dead in his herb garden.

The new well will be for the use of all the houses in

the village of Banstock. It will be at the side of the road. The water man advises it is fed from a natural spring. The mason, Master Clintock, having much knowledge of wells but no longer able to go down the ladder, supervises the men as they set the stones into the shaft. Already the base, a great slab of limestone cut for the purpose, is covered with two feet of water, which makes the mortaring difficult. Boys heave up buckets filled by the masons each morning, and tip them into the pond in front of the church, with a choir of lamentation from the resident ducks and geese. Only then can the work resume.

As the steward of the Banstock estate I shall be asked to account for the bill for this second well, and already the masons are disputing the figure. I have told them I shall pay no more than five pence a day hire to each man but I know I would pay six for fast work, and they would manage with four. They are working fast to race the water, and so far are winning, but each night gives the spring the advantage, so I have authorised the use of extra lamps to extend the day through the whole length of the well. It is nearly two rods deep and we tasted the water before the mortaring began and found it sweet.

Viola, the youngest daughter of Lord Banstock, is with me. Her father and I deem it better that she be out of the house as her sister lies mortally affected by the red pox. Viola teaches a group of children to write their numbers in the road with a long pole. The hem of her dress is dusty, her hands are yellow with clay from helping to dig and she looks nothing like the daughter of a baron. Yet I admit I do not wish to stop her, for the long days of childhood are passing faster than she imagines, in her fifteenth year.

Five years ago the succession was assured, with two adult sons and a clutch of married daughters. Now bad fortune and illness have left us with just one male heir, and him on a perilous journey with Drake. At the manor my Lady Flora's women are a-twitter at her belly, and Lord Banstock, yet again, prays for a healthy son.

Vincent Garland, Steward to Lord Banstock, His Memoir

5

There was no sign of Judith Bassett or her car when Sage arrived at the cottage to set up the following morning. As Elliott was setting up the tables under the awning – Steph was at the university, attending classes – a car pulled onto the gravel drive behind her van. A young man in torn jeans and a graffiti-covered jacket jumped out.

Elliott strode over to meet him. 'Can I help you?' His tone didn't sound very helpful.

'It's OK, Ell, I'll deal with this.' Sage watched him walk back to the table, still scowling. The man fished in the pocket of his leather jacket.

'Hi. Dr Westfield, right?' He flashed her an ID card. 'Paul Turpin, structural engineer. I'm here to have a look at the well.'

She shook his hand. 'Sage. It's over here.'

Turpin stopped just short of the edge, and scanned

the hole. 'Bloody hell. It's way too close to the house. If it collapses, it could take the foundations and back wall out.' He touched the top of the ladder. 'Tell me you haven't been down there.'

'OK,' Sage lied, 'I haven't been down there.'

'You can't just climb down into a well that old. It's likely to collapse on you.'

Sage smiled at him. 'It seems in such good condition.'

'Of course it's in good condition, it's been filled in. But if you take out the stabilising fill, you have a circular five-hundred-year-old garden wall.' He leaned over, looking down into the void. 'You've gone down, what, three metres?'

'Almost. The thing is, two metres down – easy reach with tools – we found a human bone.'

Turpin looked up at her, his fringe flopping over a row of studs in one eyebrow. If she hadn't seen his credentials, Sage would have taken him to be an art student.

'Wow.' He knelt on the tarpaulin surrounding the well, and peeled it back from the edge. 'That's good masonry,' he said. 'I mean, for a five-hundred-year-old death trap. Well mortared, dressed to fit tightly.'

'So it's safe.'

'Ha.' He started scraping away at the top stone. 'No. Have you seen this?'

Sage bent to look. The top ring of stones was flat, but Turpin's scratching had revealed what appeared to be intentional tool marks.

'I thought the well would have a little wall around it for safety, and might have been levelled at some point,' she said.

'Some wells are like that, mostly to prevent injury, but flat wells are also fairly common. This one probably would have had a capstone or wooden cover, with a hole big enough to take a bucket, but it would stop people and animals falling in.' Turpin stood, and put one foot onto the top of the ladder they had been using to bring up buckets of spoil.

'I thought you said it wasn't safe?'

'Not for you, but I'm a professional.' He carefully climbed a few steps down the ladder, and started scraping the algae and mud away from the walls. 'I think this was always meant to be a shallow well.'

'How do you know?' Sage could see his hands moving over the stones, in the light of the rigged lamp.

'The stones are mortared very solidly at the top, well fitted together. Down here,' his voice echoed in the tight space, 'the mortar isn't complete. I don't think it was designed to be. The water table's high in this area of the Isle of Wight, over Pleistocene clays on top of marls and limestones. The looser fit of the stones allowed water to trickle in.' He was momentarily illuminated by a flash from his phone. 'The water must have picked up salt at high tide. There are a lot of crystals down here.'

Sage waited until Turpin had climbed out before

she spoke. 'We need to get the infill out to completely remove the skeletons and hopefully, establish the history of the interment.'

'Of course.' He leaned forward and showed her the image on his phone. 'Look at this.'

One of the blocks had a carving in it. The algae had clung to the inscription after he had scraped at the surface. The shapes were crudely scratched but complex, curves and squiggles that looked intentional. It reminded her of ancient Greek, but she couldn't quite place it. 'What is it?'

'Absolutely no idea. It looks like there are other inscriptions down there. Creepy.'

'Why creepy?' She leaned over the edge.

'Well, someone had to go down the well to carve them. That's good limestone, so it would have taken some time. They would have had to do it by candle or lamp light, and the well would have had to be empty.'

Sage studied the carved shapes, brushing more mud off the stones. Curves would have been much harder to carve than straight lines; someone had gone to a lot of trouble to put them in a circle around the well. 'I've never heard of a well being decorated like that. Maybe it's for luck, or some sort of religious blessing.' Sage called Elliott over to show him the picture. 'Or possibly the stones were carved before they were used for the well,' she speculated. Then her memory threw up an image. 'I think there might be something similar on a beam inside the cottage. Over the fireplace.'

Elliott stepped forward. 'Can we get a copy of that photo?'

'Sure.'

'Good idea. Could you send it to my work email, please?' Sage considered the engineer's words. 'You said "good limestone". What did you mean?'

'Definitely not quarried on the Island.'

She reached for her project bag, and unfolded the laminated 1866 map of the area. 'The old abbey, here, was broken up after the dissolution of the monasteries.' She tapped the map. 'Apparently, the site's completely cleared now, but a lot of the local buildings have some of the blocks. I wondered if some of the stone for the cottage came from the abbey.'

'That could be it.'

'So maybe it was already carved, like I said.'

'I doubt it, this isn't fine work.' Turpin shrugged. 'Empty it out and have a look. There's a contractor, Rob Greenway. He's a caver, and he also digs and drills wells. Give him a ring. He can dig out that lot quicker, and probably more safely, than you can. But no more exploring. Just put out a tarp next to the well and Rob will bring the fill up for you.' He pulled a colourful scarf from a pocket, and wound it around his neck. 'It's cold, isn't it?'

Sage knelt down to examine more of the symbols. 'These carvings don't look ecclesiastical, they're just deep scratches. They look like folk symbols, superstitious shapes for good luck. They would be well worth another look.'

Elliott bent over the image on Turpin's phone. 'I'll look them up, see if I can find anything similar on a database.'

'We've got dead bodies, weird carvings and ghosts,' Sage said. 'I'm a scientist. I just want to work out what happened here. People are already telling me the house is haunted.'

Turpin smiled. 'Dead bodies, spooky carvings, old houses. Of course it's haunted. Or it will be, if you go down the well and it collapses on you.'

An hour after Paul Turpin left the excavation, Sage was surprised to see Judith Bassett carrying out a tray of tea and biscuits. She handed it to Sage. 'I'm sorry about yesterday. I just saw the well, and Chloe – I didn't want to make her sad or frightened. The idea of those poor people down there, it upset me.'

Sage smiled, put the tray down on a worktable. 'We understand. It must be incredibly unsettling to find bodies in your garden, especially with the other stresses you are under.'

Elliott stuffed his phone into his pocket and took a mug, nodded his thanks, then turned back to cleaning pottery.

'He doesn't say much, does he?' Judith said quietly, handing Sage the second mug.

'He's very focused. He's doing a PhD, and takes it

very seriously.' Sage could see Elliott turn to Steph. She immediately came over, wiggling her fingers in her nitrile gloves.

'Ooh. Tea.' Steph wrapped her hands around the mug. 'Thank you, my hands were freezing in that water. I'm washing off pottery,' she explained. 'Some of it's late Tudor, which is quite unusual for this part of the Island. Normally we'd get this quality of finds at big sites like manors and churches.'

'Have you found anything new?' Judith looked across at the tables where trays were laid out with finds. 'No more bodies, hopefully.'

Sage answered. 'Well, nothing we've found suggests a third person. It looks like one baby and one adult, probably female. The skull is neither classically male nor female, but the bits of pelvis we found suggest the remains of an adult female.'

'So a mother and baby?'

'Maybe. We'll be able to tell more when we have the rest of the pelvis.' Sage sipped her tea. 'The sixteenth century was a time of high infant mortality, deadly diseases. Maybe the well was useless; the surveyor said it was very salty. So in an emergency, people might have used a disused well to dispose of bodies, although it seems unlikely.'

Steph chimed in. 'People cared deeply about burial practices, they still do.'

Judith shuddered in the fresh breeze. At least weak

sunshine was breaking through the clouds. 'It's very sad.' She wrapped her scarf more tightly around her neck.

'But a long time ago,' said Sage. 'Steph, where's that jug piece you found?'

Steph showed Judith the handle of a jug she was cleaning up. 'Some of these pots were imported from Europe. Good quality. The owners of the cottage were prosperous.'

Judith smiled faintly, but didn't look interested. She followed Sage over to the awning as a few spots of rain fell, and nodded at Sage's stomach. 'This can't be an easy job for you, being pregnant.'

Sage shrugged. 'Baby's bones are always sad, but this all happened four hundred odd years ago, going by pottery. Some pieces date from around the middle of the fifteen hundreds.'

'How far along are you?'

Sage felt slightly uneasy at the probing. She wasn't sure how she felt about the pregnancy herself. 'Six months.'

Judith smiled a little more warmly, moved her hand as if to touch Sage's curved belly, but seemed to think better of it. Sage stepped away anyway. She hated it when people thought pregnant women were public property.

'I remember being pregnant with Chloe. James and I were so happy. Just starting out together, selling our flats and buying a house together, planning a wedding.'

A stab of yearning shot through Sage, quickly suppressed. *Marcus.* 'The father and I… we don't live together.'

'Oh. I'm sorry.'

Sage was aware that the students were listening, then Steph turned her head away. 'No, it's fine. He didn't want a baby. It's my choice.'

Judith turned to go into the house. 'Don't get too cold.'

When Sage put her bag in the van Elliott followed her.

'I was wondering if I could get a lift into Newport?' He looked back at the cottage. 'Steph's finished already.'

'I'm sorry, Elliott. I'm going straight home to Ryde. Do you have my spare keys?'

He rummaged in his jeans pocket. 'They're in my bag, I can get them—'

She waved a hand. 'Don't worry, I'll get them tomorrow. Sorry about the lift.'

'No problem.' He nodded to her and turned away. 'See you.'

The van started first time, and she drove around the village to get onto the harbour road. Most of the houseboats had their lights on, and there was a drift of woodsmoke over the road from a couple of them. It was only twenty minutes or so drive to Ryde, but the road was narrow and wound through several villages. This was the Island life she liked; the different communities had their own character. Her mother had often said that each village was like its own island. Many older people only went onto the mainland once or twice a year. The isolation was one of the reasons Yana, Sage's mother, had wanted to leave, but her father was an Islander and missed it. He wasn't just an Islander, he was a West-Wighter, from a tiny hamlet called Five Houses.

Sage slowed down to join a couple of cars following a tractor. Finally she came over the hill and glimpsed the sea again, before driving down to Ryde seafront. Her flat overlooked the sea beyond the hovercraft terminal, and it was a relief to park beside her own car and trudge up three flights of stairs to the flat. *This isn't going to be easy when the baby is born.* She shouldered her work bag for the last climb.

Marcus was there, of course. Sprawled on her bed, leafing through her five-year diary.

'There you are.' He stood up, naked and unembarrassed because his body was beautiful. *It should be, the amount of time and money he spends on it.* He kissed her hungrily, insistently, and it sparked an immediate response in Sage that made her annoyed at herself.

'I thought we split up,' she grumbled. 'I remember throwing you out.' She pushed him away, his skin making her hands tingle.

'Lovers' tiff.' He lay on his back and picked up the diary again. 'Is this some kind of scoring system? Am I doing well?' He grinned up at her with an air of possession rather than humour. 'Silly question. Why are you still dressed?'

She snatched the diary off him. 'That's my menstrual

cycle. *Was* my menstrual cycle, which you saw to. Does your wife know you're here?'

The grin slipped. 'She's at her mother's. Her sister's got some family crisis. So we have all night together.'

Sage took off her fleece and walked to the window. Her top-floor flat had a good view over the Solent, and ferries and ships passing between the Island and the south coast of the mainland. She had been born on the Island but her parents had moved to Hampshire before she started secondary school. Years at university at South Solent had left her feeling like a stranger when she was home. At least here she could see boats constantly coming and going; it made her feel less stranded. She leaned her forehead against the cold glass for a moment.

'Marcus, I was serious. This has got to stop. Before the baby comes.'

'Why?'

Sage turned to look at her lover, displaying himself on the bed. It was as if he was always saying 'look at me'. He seemed genuinely puzzled. 'It's just sex, and great company.'

For you, maybe. The emotion she had carried, ignored by Marcus, was fading. 'I need to get a real life, a real partner one day. Now I need to concentrate on the baby.'

He spread his hands out. 'I think we have something special. Come here.'

She hugged the fleece to her as a barrier against his charm. 'I want to live with someone, bring up my baby with someone. I'm twenty-nine, Marcus. At my age you were married. You had had your first baby.' The word caught in her throat as she remembered the tiny, fragile bones in the well.

'This is just the hormones speaking. Christ, Fliss thought about chucking me out at the end of the last pregnancy, she was so ratty.'

As usual, he reduced everything down to something simple, like her hormones, like her job. 'And then you met me.'

'Exactly. And that worked out well, until, you know…' Until she realised he had gone back to his wife.

'Marcus, I'm not joking. It's over.'

He stood, walked over to her and stopped mere inches away. She could feel the warmth of his body fill the space between them. His face was hard, angry. 'Tell me you don't want me. Push me away.'

All their encounters usually ended on his agenda, in bed. This time she stepped back. 'I mean it, Marcus. I need to end this. If you stay, it'll just be me and the baby waiting for the next hour you can spare from your real family.' She looked down at her hands. 'I think I'm happier being on my own than just having the occasional moment when you can spare it, the constant excuses.'

He turned, pulled on his jeans, then his shirt, and started doing up the buttons. 'You are serious, aren't you?' His voice changed. 'Did you meet someone?'

'Look, we'll always be friends—' she stopped mid-sentence. They were never friends.

'No, we won't.' Marcus walked over again, disturbingly close, and as she dropped her eyes she could see hair poking out of the top of his shirt. His scent was intoxicating and she had to resist swaying against him, despite his aggressive stance. His hand touched her hair, pulled one dark curl lightly through his fingers. 'You and me, we're not friends, we're lovers. If you had got rid of the baby—'

She wondered if the baby could hear his words, hear the acid in his tone. 'I didn't want to.' Her voice was more sure than she was. The pregnancy had cleared away the certainty she had had about the future: career, house, relationship.

'Don't I have any say?' His voice was soft now but she wasn't fooled. 'I love you, Sage, in my own way.'

'It's not down to you, Marcus. It's really over.'

He shrugged, half smiled. 'Fool yourself if you like. You wait until the baby comes. You'll want me then, and I'll be here.'

'You are so arrogant.'

He turned at the doorway. 'That's what you like about me.'

There was a bit of truth in that. He was so confident, so sure of her, it had been attractive. But he had responded to her refusal to have an abortion at first with reasoned argument, then with anger. She didn't want that hanging over her baby. 'It's my life, Marcus.'

'You can fight it, but I'll win in the end. We're perfect for each other.' He opened the door and she ran after him, catching him before he closed the door.

'Key.'

'Really?' He twisted the key off the ring he kept at work, so his wife wouldn't find it. He pressed it into her hand, his fingers warm against her palm. 'You're determined tonight.'

'I have to be.'

'And I thought you were pleased to see me when you came in.'

She remembered how pleased she had been, and warmth spread up into her face. She hoped her olive complexion and the low light in the hallway concealed it as he headed down the stairs.

6

10th July 1580

Fine oak coffin, for your lordship's daughter Elizabeth upon her decease ———— two pounds, three shillings and four pence

Accounts of Banstock Manor, 1576–1582

Few grieve the young Lady Elizabeth except her family. Even the bridegroom Solomon Seabourne, here for the funeral, looks no sadder than he did at the betrothal. But he had hardly known the lady, their betrothal having been arranged by their fathers.

Lady Flora is much preoccupied with her belly. She has cramps and fears miscarrying the babe as she has so many before, so has retired to her chamber. Viola sits on the high stool in my office, writing notes for me and counting up the entries in the ledgers. I shall add them up for myself, of course, but Viola is rarely mistaken now.

Sitting at my knee she learned to read before she was six.

She has taken her cap off again and her hair, the colour of a young fox cub, is so thick and full of curls it spreads over her shoulders.

'Eighteen pounds, three shillings and ninepence farthing,' she calculates, 'before the rents from Springate farm, of five guineas.' She sharpens her pen, slivers of quill dropping onto the desk and my papers. I sweep them away.

'If you are to help me, make a list of the extra meats for the dinner,' I say. 'Cook calls for a dozen fowls, and an ox calf for our honoured guest.'

She bends over the list, the pen scratching in her quick hand. 'My lady stepmother wants eels. Mistress Agness says they strengthen the womb.'

'What would that old spinster know? Anyway,' I grumble, 'where will we get eels from, in this season?' My old back creaks from sitting still so long. 'Come, child. Let us walk around the garden, and stretch our legs.'

We go out through the side door, past the yard with the stench of the stables and a cloud of black flies that follows, and into the rose garden. It is at its best, and the scent of the blooms hangs in the air and fragrances shirts spread over the bushes to dry. A figure ahead leans over some work, seated on a bench, but I cannot see who it is.

'It's Mistress Isabeau.' Viola scampers ahead, holding her cap.

The Frenchwoman stands and makes a respectful bow.

I'll say this for her, her manners and style are impeccable, raised as she was at the French king's court. She murmurs something in French, and Viola answers, versed as she is in language.

The seamstress is beautiful. I have never wanted to clutter my life with a woman, and have been accused of having a cold nature, but even my heart is stirred by Isabeau Duchamp. She seems to glow from inside; her skin is the colour of fresh cream, her eyes are blue as lapis lazuli. Her hair is confined in a heavy caul, but the escaping curls are almost white, they are so fair. Her lips are very full, and the maids accuse her of colouring them. She has been at the manor for eight months, embellishing the silks for Lady Elizabeth's trousseau. I wonder her fate, now.

I persuade Viola away, through the garden towards the orchard where, at least, there might be some blessed shade. The child babbles: do I not think Isabeau is beautiful and kind? Do I not like the panel she is working on, no doubt now to be altered for Lady Banstock, as Elizabeth has no need for it? The child is rarely tedious like this, but I suppose a girl of fourteen is full of such romances. As we pass through the archway from the gardens, a figure in plain velvet dress approaches with his man. Solomon Seabourne, the bereaved groom, the youngest son of Lord Seabourne. The marriage would have benefited both families. He is attended by his servant Kelley, who bows low then steps back.

'Master Vincent.' Seabourne bows to me then to Viola,

and smiles at her. He is a well-made man, tall, handsome enough. His hands are his weakness: a true gentleman does not have the blackened fingers of a clerk or perhaps would hide the stains with gloves. He notices my gaze.

'Ah, you see my fingers, Master Vincent. I have been exploring the qualities of spirits of silver. The silvery metal turns black upon exposure to light. Silver is closest to gold in purity, and if we can understand its corruption we may find the impurity that keeps silver from being gold.'

Viola's blush has faded. 'So, if silver were purified, it would form gold?'

'We believe so, although it is mercury that most alchemists consider most able to make the transformation.' His face is quite animated, and I see a similar interest in Viola's features. 'My man and I are engaged upon such work. We hope to achieve full conversion at the full moon.' Viola hangs upon his words, but my gaze is caught, instead, by the servant, Kelley. He wears the oldest of clothes, yet of good quality and well patched. His boots are very fine, and new, and have a heel raising him above what must be a mean stature. Despite the heat he wears a leather cap over his ears, and his dark hair is longer than the fashion. He looks like a tinker, gypsy dark, and his eyes are sharp with interest at Viola and Seabourne's discourse.

I break in upon the talk, make my bow and Viola and I walk on, leaving Master Seabourne to his enjoyment of the roses.

Vincent Garland, Steward to Lord Banstock, His Memoir

7

Thursday 28th March

The Poplars residential home was a large Victorian property with a modern extension, but along one side it had an original orangery, with cast-iron supports and window frames. As Sage slipped her muddy boots off a care assistant told her that Maeve Rowland, former owner of Bramble Cottage, spent her days there overlooking the gardens. Sage passed a pot-bellied woodburning stove, and saw an old woman dozing in a padded wicker rocking chair. Her body was hunched forward, and to one side. She opened her eyes at the clunk of the care assistant's shoes on the tiled floor.

'Nathan? That better be the bloody chocolate biscuits.' Her voice was loud, and made Sage think of crazed china, full of tiny cracks.

'Yeah, yeah, just the best ones for you. That's why you're getting so fat.' The care assistant put a plate at her elbow, along with a cup of tea. 'Don't forget to share – you've got a visitor. Dr Sage Westfield, this is Mrs Rowland.'

What Sage could see of the old woman was sparrow-thin, the skin creped and blotched with age. When Maeve Rowland looked up, her eyes were faded blue, almost lost in nests of wrinkles. One eyelid drooped, the corner of her mouth sagged.

'Dr what?'

'Dr Sage Westfield. She's an archaeologist.' Sage smiled at Nathan as he pulled a chair over for her.

The old woman gazed out of the window for a long moment. 'You're the one digging up the garden at Brambles.'

'How did you know that?' Sage asked.

'Everyone knows; all of Banstock is talking about it.' She dabbed the slack corner of her mouth with one hand.

'The new owners wanted to build an extension. They had to do a survey first because it's a listed building, and I was called in when they found Tudor pottery. The house is very interesting.'

'Draughty old rat trap, you mean.' Maeve wavered a clenched hand. 'I'd still be there if it wasn't for this bloody stroke.'

'I'm sorry.' Sage watched the woman's shaking hand reach for a biscuit.

'Don't be. I'm eighty-six. It's time. I just thought I'd die there, become one of the ghosts.' The sun came out, casting the shadow of the windows onto the tiled floor, bleaching

the throw over her legs. Maeve squinted and Sage got up
to adjust one of the blinds.

'Thanks.' Maeve waved a hand towards the plate. 'Do
you want a biscuit?'

Sage refused, and the old woman seemed relieved. 'Once
I could eat what I bloody well liked, now I have a care plan
written by a dietician. So, what have you found?'

'A well in the garden. We think it's about the same age
as the cottage but it's been filled in.'

'We thought there was something like that out there;
it used to leave a ring in the grass in dry weather,' Maeve
said. 'Why would someone fill a well in?'

'Usually because it's falling down, but we think this was
filled in for another reason,' Sage said. 'It's full of rubbish
and soil from a midden. We've found broken pottery, glass,
ash, that kind of thing from the Tudor era.'

The old woman stared at her. 'Is that all?'

Sage hesitated. 'And some bones. Mostly domesticated
animal bones but some human.'

'Isabeau.' Maeve breathed the word, her gaze intent on
Sage.

'Isabeau?'

'A young woman who went missing back in the time of
Queen Elizabeth the First.' She waved a hand. 'My husband
and I did some research on the period when we first moved
into the cottage.'

'Well, we can't identify the adult bones, beyond saying

that they are mature. And, we found a child's bones.'

'Isabeau's baby.' Maeve sat back, nodding.

Sage fumbled in her bag for a notebook. 'Can you tell me more?'

'Just a local legend. She was a French servant who supposedly got pregnant by the Devil, who then came and stole her child. But I don't believe in the Devil; no doubt the poor girl got into the family way and was hidden with her baby, to save embarrassment.' Maeve looked at Sage sideways. 'There's a headstone, in the woods behind the common. She was supposed to have been pregnant when she died.'

Sage nodded. 'The previous landlord of the Harbour Bell – Dennis Lacey – mentioned a stone. But why would there be a gravestone in the woods if she was put down the well?'

'I have no idea. I always knew there was something wrong at the cottage, though.'

'What do you mean?'

'Little things. The smell of lavender water in the front bedroom. And sunlight soap, horrible stuff, in the utility room – the old back kitchen, where some poor little Victorian dogsbody did the washing. I think it's the atmosphere.'

'Atmosphere?'

Maeve ran her tongue slowly over her lips to remove the crumbs. 'My husband used to wake up at night saying he could hear a sort of moaning, as if from an animal; he was a light sleeper. He went outside with a torch once, thinking a cat had been run over, but he could only hear it indoors.'

'Did you ever hear it?' Sage asked.

Maeve's hand shook, and she dropped the remainder of a biscuit onto her blanket. 'Yes. The last time was the day I had the stroke. I felt dizzy and fell to the floor. I just couldn't stand up. Then it started, like a noise in my own head.' A tear streaked down the weak side of her face. 'Six hours of lying there, listening to it. The moaning was— for a while, I wondered if it was *me* moaning, if I was going mad.'

'I'm sorry.'

'Don't be. My neighbour knew something was wrong when I didn't put the bin out. She got the police and ambulance. The moaning stopped once someone else was in the house, or at least, I couldn't hear it anymore.' She brushed stray crumbs off her lap. 'I never went back. Good riddance to the place. I got a good price and it pays for all this.'

Sage glanced down at her notebook. 'Can you tell me anything more about Isabeau?'

Maeve shrugged. 'Some legends say she was a witch, that the Devil appeared at one of her coven's black masses in the ruined abbey. She ran to the church, but the Devil caught up with her at the gate. There was a clap of thunder, and he ripped her baby right out of her belly.' She munched on the last biscuit, spraying crumbs.

Sage looked across the garden, her mind struggling with the horrible image. The orangery looked over a landscaped garden, lush with grass and shrubs, and someone had hung a bird feeder from a tree. The stove pushed out a lot of heat, and Sage took her jacket off.

'That's a horrible thought.' She smiled at Maeve. 'I'm pregnant myself.'

'I can see that. Well, people leave unexpectedly and myths build up. Maybe she died in childbirth, but the Devil makes for a much better story.'

'You're right. But sometimes there's an element of truth,' Sage said. 'Like you mentioned Isabeau was French. As I said before, we're not even sure whether the adult is female, though it is looking that way.'

Maeve nodded. 'It would be nice to find out what really happened to Isabeau, if she existed. Maybe she was the one making all that moaning.' She laughed self-consciously, embarrassed. 'The last time my husband Ian heard it, eighteen years ago, he had a heart attack. They said he'd been over-exerting himself, but he was strong as an ox, sixty-eight years old, and a country auctioneer. He was used to moving heavy furniture around.'

'That must have been very hard.' Sage folded her hands in her lap.

'It was, but I'll see him soon enough. Anyway, for all we know it could have just been wind through the weather vane or coming down the chimney.' Maeve rubbed her slack hand with the good one and uttered a harsh chuckle. 'I was volunteering up at the big house then, Banstock Manor. I created a walled orchard. All the espaliered apples and pears up there are mine.' Her voice was touched with pride. 'The owners were looking into the history of the Banstock family, and they found a link to the cottage in the deeds. That's when they told me about the memorial stone in the woods.'

'I'd love to go and see it.'

'Not much to see, now. It's just a tumbledown old marker, leaning over, a bit like me. Take the footpath across the common towards Marten's Farm. There's a big track; the locals walk their dogs down there. Take the other path, down to the stream. It's just on the other side.'

'Thank you,' Sage said. 'You've been very helpful.' She closed her notebook. 'Are there any papers about the history of the cottage? And it would be helpful to look at the deeds.'

Maeve struggled to push herself up the chair. 'The new owners, they have them all.'

Sage held out her hand to Maeve, who clasped it. Her skin felt like warm paper, her fingers curved with age.

Maeve leaned forward. 'You come back and tell me what you find. You promise.'

'I will. I really will.' Sage smiled as she gathered up her coat and bag.

'And you be careful, girl. There's something odd about that house.'

* * *

It was a relief to get out of the hot conservatory, and Sage walked towards the village of Banstock, enjoying the breeze. She meant to go straight to Bramble Cottage, but her eye was caught by the church. It was squat with a tower at one end, a solid nave in the middle and a small extension at the western end. It looked like it was built in the Norman style, clearly pre-dating the Tudor and Jacobean buildings that had sprung up around it by some centuries. She walked across the road to the oak lychgate, a wooden structure covered with old thatch that led through the churchyard wall. She creaked open one of the silver-grey gates.

'Hello. Sage, isn't it?'

She turned at the deep voice and saw the vicar walking towards her. He was dressed in muddy jeans and jumper, and carrying a strimmer.

'Vicar.'

He smiled. 'Nick, please. Have you come to see me?'

'I was just passing,' Sage said. 'I went to see Maeve Rowland like you suggested. She mentioned something about there being local stories of a witch in Banstock, perhaps around the same time period as the bodies ended up in the well behind Bramble Cottage.' She paused. 'You don't know anything about that, do you?'

Nick grinned. 'I haven't been here that long, but it's

virtually the first thing they told me. The story is, the Devil took his baby back from a French witch, right here at the church gate. Apparently, she ran here for sanctuary, but the consecrated ground wouldn't let her demonic baby in. So she turned, and the Devil reached into her womb and snatched the baby.' He ran his hand down the massive limestone gate post. 'These are the marks his claws left, apparently.'

Sage ran her fingers down one set of parallel grooves. 'That's what Mrs Rowland told me. How do you think these marks were made?'

'I think maybe the old gates were once hung forward of their present position and the wood marked the stone when they were moved.' Nick started to walk towards the church.

Sage crunched up the gravel path after him. 'It looks Norman. In design, anyway.'

'Some of it is. In fact, the foundations of the nave are Saxon. But most of it is fourteenth century, built on a Norman foundation. Come and look inside.'

She hesitated. 'I shouldn't really. I'm supposed to be working.' Something about churches made Sage uncomfortable, and her boots were incredibly mucky.

'We have instant coffee and a range of teas.' When she shook her head Nick added, 'And I need to talk to you about something anyway.'

He really did have nice eyes. 'OK, but just a few minutes. I need to get back to my students.'

A florist's van was parked outside the church. Sage was grateful to see an outside tap by the door. She rinsed off the worst of the muck from her boots, dribbling icy water into one of them by accident, then sloshed her way into the porch. Nick was laughing with a young woman inside.

'There you are, Sage,' Nick said. He gestured at his companion. 'Kayleigh's our local florist.'

'Nice to meet you, Sage.' Kayleigh was about her own age, and carrying a huge bunch of carnations. Her hair was a shade pinker than the flowers. 'I'd better get back to work. We've got a big wedding on Saturday.'

Sage nodded at Kayleigh, and followed Nick into the church proper, and down the limestone flagstones of the nave. The worn stones were patchworked with light from the stained-glass windows.

'Wow. Lovely.' She leaned back to study the timber crucks of the roof. 'That's beautiful work.'

'The timbers are original, from the 1100s. Some have the carpenters' marks on them.'

Sage studied the stone floor. Many of the slabs were covered with curly lettering, smoothed by generations of feet. 'You have a lot of burials inside the church. These ones look old.'

Nick nodded. 'There are a few seventeenth-century ones. Some of the Banstocks, the local landowners, are buried in the Lady Chapel.' He guided Sage off to the side of the nave where there was a forged iron screen with a door. There was a substantial iron lock, painted black. Nick pointed through the bars. 'Banstock family burials from the fourteen hundreds until about 1720 are in there. Then they built a stone mausoleum outside.'

Sage peered through the narrow bars. She could see three raised tombs with figures on them, and the floor was paved with different-sized memorial stones, all with carved inscriptions.

'I'd love to have a good look at those. Medieval memorials are rare.'

'Just call the vicarage when you've got more time. I'll show you around,' Nick said. He turned as the florist called his name. 'Be right back.'

For a long moment Sage stood alone in the nave, looking around. She couldn't guess at the date of the windows but they were rich with stained-glass images that painted the pale limestone walls with colour. Between the windows and pillars were panels, inscribed with memorials and donations. She hadn't been to church for years, except to go to the odd wedding or funeral, but this one had a feeling of calm, of permanence. Wars and plague and murders will come and go, it seemed to say. But I will still be here.

Was the woman married here? Was the baby baptised in that font?

She turned as Nick walked back to her. 'You said you wanted to ask me something?'

'It's Judith Bassett.' He led Sage down into a small

kitchen in the extension at the western end of the church. 'I know she's struggling with her husband's illness – well, anyone would. But she's upsetting some of the local mothers at the school.'

'How?' Sage nodded when he waved a teabag at a mug.

'She shouted at me in front of the school gates yesterday morning. Milk?'

Sage was surprised. 'She did? She seems so bottled up. But she did have a go at us, too.' She watched his profile as he poured hot water into two cups. He smelled like cut grass, and had a smear of green on one cheekbone. 'What happened?'

'It's my job to go into the school from time to time; it's a Church of England primary,' Nick said. 'We were talking about raising money for our sister school in Ethiopia. Chloe Bassett asked me a question about infant mortality. How many babies die in Africa compared to here.'

Sage's hand faltered as she reached for the mug he held out to her. 'Do you think she heard us talking about the baby in the well?'

'I don't know. I just thought I should warn you. Anyway, Judith ran up to me at the school gate, shouting at me to leave Chloe alone.' Nick stared at the floor for a moment. 'I can understand she's angry and frightened, but she won't let me help. She's somehow focused her anger on me. And on the church.'

'She got really upset when Chloe asked us about the

dig.' Sage looked around the kitchen, at the rotas on the wall, safety notices, a corkboard covered with clippings of cartoons. 'I suppose you see a lot of bereavement in your job.'

Nick leaned against the sink, which creaked. 'I do, but I'm speaking from personal experience. I lost my wife.'

'Oh. I'm sorry.' She wasn't sure what else to say. Amongst the awkwardness was a little spark of interest. *He's single*.

'Cancer, like James Bassett, fifteen months ago. That's why I moved to this parish. We didn't have any children but... I got pretty irrational by the end. Raging against God and fate, that sort of thing. I understand Judith's anger. But she is alienating the people who can help her, and who can help James and Chloe.'

'I really am sorry.' Sage watched lines on his forehead deepen at remembered pain. 'That must be awful.' She couldn't imagine what it would feel like. She had never lost anyone except very elderly grandparents.

'It's not how you expect it. Some days are OK. Some days are harder.' Nick managed a lopsided smile. 'The worst days are agonising. But the next day is usually better.'

Sage stared into her mug. 'To be honest I don't know what to say.'

'There isn't anything to say. There isn't a magic, comforting phrase. But when you see Judith Bassett, it would be good if she knows you care, that you would listen to her if she needed to talk. Since she won't accept my help.'

Sage nodded, and looked up. 'I'll try.'

Nick smiled, and she felt a warm feeling spreading in her chest.

'Thanks for the tea. At some later date, I'd like to have a look at your memorials. I love early inscriptions, and it would be nice to get a snapshot of the parish around the time the well was filled in. Although we don't have any firm dates yet, we think the burial was after about 1550 but before 1650. There's no Stuart pottery yet anyway, it seems solidly late Tudor.'

'We have written records, too, if they would help. Baptisms, burials, that sort of thing.'

She put the cup in the sink. 'Thank you. Anything you have on Isabeau would be great, if she was a real person. So far she's the only name I have.'

'Sage——' He shook his head, as if changing his mind. 'Let me know what you find out about the people in the well.'

'Of course.' Sage did up her coat as they walked back down the nave towards the porch. 'What were you going to say?'

Nick shrugged, and pushed open the door for her. 'Nothing that can't wait. See you later.'

As Sage walked down the path towards the lychgate a movement caught her eye. A man, turning away to talk to someone – his posture, the movement of his shoulders looked familiar. Marcus? For a moment she started to raise her hand to wave, opened her mouth to call out, but she managed to stop herself. He was an estate agent, he travelled all over the East Wight. He disappeared into a house, clipboard under one arm. She felt disturbed at seeing him, even though it was over.

Sage walked across the road to Bramble Cottage. The students had felt uncomfortable after Judith Bassett's outburst about Chloe, and she didn't like to leave them too long.

When she entered the garden they were standing over the bone boxes, talking in hushed tones. She realised Steph was teary-eyed and Elliott appeared at a loss as to how to comfort her. He looked relieved to see Sage, and walked over to her carrying a plastic box.

'We found the baby's skull,' he said, and Steph uttered a sob. Sage opened the box and gently lifted a layer of bubble wrap.

The baby's brown skull was pathetic, lying in several fragments like a pile of porcelain leaves, the jaw laid beside them in two parts. The cartilage had gone, leaving the separate face bones to be laid out. Like all babies, it had disproportionately large eyes, like an alien. Steph walked over, sniffling.

Sage patted Steph's shoulder. 'I know it's sad, but we knew it might be there. Skulls seem so much more real than just odd bones. But it all happened many years ago.'

Steph pulled herself together, and wiped her eyes with a handful of tissue. 'I know.' She sniffed loudly. 'It's just horrible. Elliott—'

'I found a cut on the lower jaw.' He traced a dark line on the remains of the bone. The cut was deep, on the left-hand side, about halfway along. It had obviously been made by a sharp edge. 'It's just a nick. I wondered how it got there.'

Sage leaned over for a better look. The scratch was disturbing; the thought of someone putting a knife to a baby's face was horrible. 'That's weird. I mean, possibly it happened when they were put in the well, but I suppose it could be deliberate.' Maeve's story about the Devil tearing a baby out of its mother popped into her head.

Steph's voice was now less wobbly. 'Maybe someone killed the baby.'

Sage nodded slowly. 'It's a possibility but really unlikely. I do have a suggestion of an identity for the adult in the well, though. I spoke to Maeve Rowland; she moved into the cottage in the seventies and sold it to the Bassetts. There's a local myth relating to a Frenchwoman, Isabeau, who might have died while pregnant, or lost her baby; it's not very clear. And then there's Den's story about another possible burial in the woods behind the cottage, with a stone from about the same period. It's been linked to Isabeau too, although she couldn't have been buried in two places at once. Of course, the stone in the woods might just be a memorial stone.' She turned to Steph. 'I thought I would check it out. Fancy a walk through the woods some time?'

Steph shook her head. 'Too creepy. I'm having so much fun digging up dead babies.' She rolled her eyes. 'Take Ell.'

Elliott, however, declared that he was in the middle of cataloguing pottery finds, which now numbered in the hundreds, and was collecting pieces of curved glass. Sage went over to him, where he was taking pictures with his phone of gleaming shards of glass. 'What is that?' The curved pieces looked like a blown bowl that had been shattered. They had caught her attention because Elizabethan glass was very rare. 'Wineglass, or decanter? Surely it's too thin for a bottle.'

He put his phone in his pocket. 'I have a theory. I'll let you know when I get more of it. There's loads in there.' Elliott turned over another fragment with his forceps. 'I'm trying to work out how to piece it together. Perhaps you can help me with it when you've got time.'

Sage examined the fragile glass, turning over fragments with a paintbrush. 'It's very thin. Blow up a balloon, and clamp off the end. You can get the right curve then. If you glue it with water-based paste you can dissolve it again when needed.' She turned to Steph. 'Any problems with Mrs Bassett?'

'Not really.' Steph glanced over her shoulder at the cottage. 'She's ignoring us.'

'I'll go and see her. Thanks, guys. You're doing a great job.'

Sage walked around to the front door and knocked, half hoping the woman was out, but Judith Bassett answered, looking even paler, if possible, than usual. 'Mrs Bassett. I just wanted to check you were all right. I'm sorry again about Chloe, we didn't mean to upset her.'

Judith waved a hand. 'Don't. It was my fault. I just get protective; Chloe's going through a lot. Come in, please.'

Sage slipped off her boots in the hall and followed her into the kitchen. The Aga was on, creating a bubble of warmth at the end of the room.

'We'll be finished as soon as we can.' Sage leaned against the granite work surface, which chilled a cold line into her hip.

'That's good.' Judith lifted the kettle and turned it on. 'My daughter is becoming morbidly interested in the dig. James – my husband – is coming home soon, and I just want her less focused on death.'

'Does she know about the skeletons?' Sage asked.

Judith shook her head. 'Not yet. But as soon as she heard about the well, she assumed someone must have fallen down it.'

'I'm sure, being a child, she would be fascinated rather than horrified. Chloe seems very bright.'

'She is. And that reminds me: her teacher wrote me a note. She wondered if you could find time to talk to Chloe's class for a few minutes one morning. Maybe even her whole year group?'

Sage's heart sank. This was one aspect of her job she knew she wasn't good at. 'I'm sure we can put a few bits together. We have found a few mutton bones and teeth, and there's loads of pottery. But Steph is much better with kids than I am, so I'll get her to help. Interpreting the past to the public is part of the job she's training for.'

'Tea or coffee?'

'I've just had one, thank you.'

While Judith clattered a spoon into a cup, Sage had a closer look at the kitchen. It was a long, L-shaped room, with a work surface that had been plastered into the walls. They were so uneven none of the furniture fitted squarely, so the builders had adapted the cupboards to fit. 'This is nice,' she said, politely.

'I hate it all. If James... I'll sell, when I can. I've even spoken to the estate agent that sold it to us. Is that awful? I'm planning to sell the house before he's even...'

Sage wasn't sure how to reply. 'You must have liked the house when you first moved in.'

Judith sat at the scrubbed pine table. 'I thought it was lovely, buying a place with so much history. When we first came to the Island, we – me and Chloe – tried to find out who lived here, on the census for 1901. We couldn't find any mention of the cottage though.'

Sage sat down with her. 'We found out the name changed; that would have made it more difficult to locate on the census. It used to be called Well House.'

'Oh.' Judith grimaced. 'Because of its history? Did people know about the bodies?'

'I doubt it.' Sage pulled her tablet out of her bag and

switched it on. 'The Harbour Bell has a picture of the cottage on the wall. Elliott scanned it in for me—' she skipped through the images of bones, to the photograph. 'See the wide front wall? I think the cottage had one of the village pumps in front of it. It's ideally suited. When piped water came in, the land was given back to the cottage.'

'Not another well.'

'I'm sure the pump well was all filled in innocently, and in public.'

Judith turned away, cradling her cup. 'I feel like I'm going mad, sometimes.'

'It must be hard,' was the only thing Sage could think to say.

'I feel better with you outside all day.' Judith's voice was distant, as if she were talking to herself. 'But there's the crying...'

Sage looked up. 'The crying?'

'Well, maybe not crying. More like howling or wailing.' Judith took a sip of her tea. 'James heard it first. That's how we knew the house was haunted.'

Sage thought carefully how to phrase a response. 'I don't think...'

Judith's lips twisted into a smile but somehow it looked as if she was in pain. 'I tried to explain it away as a neighbour's TV, an animal in the garden...' Judith's hands were trembling. 'Oh, God.' Her thin shoulders started to shake.

Sage spoke gently. 'Judith, are you getting enough

support? I mean, you've got such a lot on your shoulders, and now this...' She rose and tore a couple of sheets of kitchen towel from a cast-iron holder, then handed them to Judith. 'Here.'

Judith mopped her face and got her composure back. 'I'm fine, really. Well, not fine.' She managed a wobbly laugh. 'I have help if I need it. My mother's coming to stay in a few days. Chloe's been difficult.'

'Let me know if we can do anything. I'll contact Chloe's teacher if you give me a number. I suppose the discovery of the bones will become common knowledge soon, but I'll explain to the children that it was all a long time ago.'

Judith tore a piece of paper out of a notebook and jotted down the names of the school and the teacher. 'There. Thank you.'

She turned her back on Sage to walk into the hall. Her shoulder-length hair was twisted up into a ragged bun, her pale neck emerging from a cardigan. It was covered with red marks that hadn't quite breached the skin.

Sage hesitated, but she felt compelled to say something. 'Judith – you have some nasty scratches on your neck. Is everything OK?'

Judith wrenched open the door. Her voice was colourless, and her eyes were fixed on Sage's chest rather than her face. 'Everything is fine. Thank you for stopping by.'

The door clicked behind her, and a key grated in the lock.

8

31st July 1580

Indenture made on the last day of July, in the seconde and twentieth yeare of the reign of our soveryne lady Queene Elizabeth, between Sir Solomon Seabourne of the county of Sussex, and Lord Anthonie Banstock, Baron of said manoir. Being the lease of the Well House, one garden, one orchard, six acres of good pasture in nine fields, let to Richard Arnesley of Newport, and fourteen acres of woods. The sum of thirty guineas per annum, to be paid upon the first day of July, each yeare. Signed by the hand of S. Seabourne and V. Garland on behalf of his lordship Anthonie Banstock.

Accounts of Banstock Manor, 1576–1582

The women make much of Viola since her betrothal, which is little to her liking. She is forbidden childish pursuits such as visiting the farms, or fishing in the river with her father. Instead, she must learn the arts of the kitchen, still room, scullery and the laundry, that she might command her servants. Not that Seabourne has a great household, merely three menservants and a few rooms in a house in London. But here he has arranged with Lord Banstock that he will rent the Well House until the marriage. Then the couple will take up residence in a wing of the manor itself, at least for part of the year. I am glad, for Viola is its heart, with her laughter and singing, and she lightens all our tasks.

The harvest is going to be a poor one, and taxes are still heavy, but Viola turns account after account into people for me. 'Ah, Master Collins, he has a bad leg,' she tells me. 'But his son is sending him money from his draper's business in Southampton.'

Another snippet. 'Andrew Mattock,' she says, with the wisdom of a matron, 'has got Mary Fitton with child and must marry her. My father has promised a dowry.' She pauses in her calculations, a frown upon her brow. I see that all the women's potions have not prevented the sun bringing out her freckles. 'Why does my father dower a poor girl?' she asks.

To sweeten the contract, thinks I, *as the Fitton girl has been turned onto her back by half the scythemen and shepherds on the Island.* Better she be wed before she bears another bastard child. At least her fertility is proven, unlike our sad mistress, who is now plagued by a rash that makes her tear at her skin. She also suffers sharp pains that send her attendants into a panic many times a day. But the babe at least kicks well.

'In charity, as he does for other poor girls on occasions.' I underline a total in my ledger and turn to the new page. 'And a few pounds are nothing to a man like his lordship.'

She turns to me. 'Will you account my dowry, too, in your ledgers?'

'Indeed.' I look at her, sat suddenly quiet and shy on the high stool. 'You shall have clothes as well as gold for your marriage. And my Lord Seabourne will settle monies upon you as his son's wife.'

'It is a good connection for us, isn't it? The Seabournes are rich and have many ships and holdings.' Viola's voice is small, and she stares at her hands.

'And we have friends at court. Indeed, your father has already introduced Lord Seabourne to a number of lords and merchants who might use his fleet of ships in their own enterprises.' I look at her, seeing the childish fears. 'And he will love you for your own sake, for who could not?'

When Viola smiles it is as if the sun warms my old bones. People tell Viola things. They trust me, their steward. They will bow to me, answer my questions with a few words, but Viola opens their smiles, and they babble like children. All except her bridegroom. He is kind but talks to her as if she were a child, or a puppy. She is tongue-tied. I can see she is dazzled by him, his cleverness, his handsome face and good figure, but his eyes stray too much towards our reclusive seamstress for my liking.

The embroideress grows pale, and whispers gather in the laundry and stables that she is not virtuous. I wish Viola was not so enamoured of her.

Vincent Garland, Steward to Lord Banstock, His Memoir

9

Friday 29th March

Sage brushed her wet hair out of her eyes. It was a bit drier under the awning they had put up, but not much. The wind fled from the sea and whistled between Bramble Cottage and the hedge. It fluttered papers and chased plastic pots across the two tables she had put up. They now had forty-six adult bones, including a skull, half a jaw and most of a shattered pelvis, arranged in one container. The baby's bones fitted into the large sandwich box: half a femur, the arm bones, most of the skull, three ribs, a clavicle, a few fragments of one tibia and a number of vertebrae.

Professor Yousuf Sayeed was looking through the finds with Steph. The forensic anthropologist had jumped at the chance to come to the Island, and Sage knew him well. He had been one of her lecturers a decade before.

'These are remarkably well preserved,' Yousuf said. His

camera flashed. 'So often we lose infant remains altogether. Do you know if they were dropped in the water itself, or just buried in the loose debris after it was filled in?'

'We assumed they were covered along with the infill. The bodies were only a few metres down.'

He turned a tiny vertebra over with forceps. 'If the bodies were dropped in the bottom of the well the water may have allowed them to float up through what would be liquid mud. I'm surprised at the condition of the bones. Of course, the water is quite alkaline here, which would aid in preservation.' He turned the arm bones over. 'You saw the scratch on the left humerus, I suppose?'

'No. Where?' Sage and Steph leaned over the sandwich box, and Elliott looked up from his sieving and sorting.

There was an incised line, deep into the tiny humerus, close to where it would have joined the shoulder. Sage felt her own baby flutter like a bird. 'Why would someone injure an infant?' She felt sick. It was bad enough to imagine the baby drowning, let alone wounded. She touched a hand to her bump.

Yousuf glanced down at her belly before he answered. 'It might not be ante-mortem. Maybe someone wanted to disarticulate the body to conceal it, and changed their mind. Dropped it down the well.' He shrugged. 'In forensic work we see quite a few concealed or discarded babies.'

Elliott, who had come over to the table, pointed at a piece of the small jawbone. 'We were wondering about the nick in the jaw. I thought I might have scratched it getting it out, but Sage thinks it could be a cut.'

Sage pointed it out. 'It could be deliberate, I suppose.'

'It is very straight. And there's something else,' Yousuf said. 'The bones of the skull aren't completely fused, they are separate plates. Most of the bones are poorly ossified. This was a baby who died very soon after, or at birth. From the last month of pregnancy to a month after term, shall we say.'

'Oh, God.' Steph pressed her hand to her mouth for a moment. 'Was it even born, Professor? I mean, it might have been inside the mother. Could it be a coffin birth?'

Yousuf went over to the adult's bones. 'That's a reasonable idea; post-mortem foetal extrusions are incredibly rare, but possible. But I don't think so in this case.'

'Post-mortem whats?' Elliott's face was screwed up.

Sage explained. 'During decomposition, gas and fluid build-up in the abdomen can put pressure on an unborn foetus and force it out of the mother.'

Elliott looked nauseated. 'But that isn't what happened here.'

'The skeletons were found separately, the baby wasn't close to the adult pelvis.' Yousuf pointed to the adult bones. 'This was unlikely to be the mother of the child. If a woman had gone through a full, or almost full-term, pregnancy and birth, I would expect dorsal pubic pitting in this area. There are no grooves that I would associate with pregnancy or childbirth. This is probably a female skeleton, but I can't be sure. And obviously I can't guess at the gender of the baby.' He sighed. 'You possibly have a woman with someone else's child buried here. I doubt if you would get useable DNA, and the cost would be prohibitive, but that would be the easiest way to confirm it.'

Steph leaned forward. 'Can't we be certain of the adult's gender?'

He shrugged. 'Eighty, ninety per cent maybe. It's not a typical pelvis for a female, and we can only be sure in ninety-five per cent of cases anyway. The femur also suggests an unusual height for a female of the era. Maybe five nine or ten. It's an anomalous picture.'

Elliott, who towered over the group, brushed the dirt off another tiny bone and laid it on the table with the baby's bones. 'Here's a collar bone – I mean a clavicle. Now we have both.'

Yousuf gently arranged it into position, then leaned forward to look more closely. He picked up the dry clavicle already in place. 'You know, I think there was a more extensive injury. Let me show you.' He picked up a ruler used for scale. 'You are a small baby. If I cut on this plane, in a slashing motion—' He placed the edge of the ruler against Sage's collar bone diagonally onto the top of her arm. 'Here, we find a cut on the humerus, a deeper one in the clavicle, and another nick terminating at the jaw. A single slash.'

The four stood under the flapping tarpaulin of the awning, taking in the awful implications of Yousuf's words. Sage struggled with the image his words created, and looked at Steph and Elliott, who were both silent. She was the first to speak. 'Thanks, Yousuf, I really appreciate this.'

'Anything else while I'm here?'

'Any estimate as to the woman's age?' Sage pointed to the skull. 'I'm thinking mid-thirties.'

Yousuf held up the skull for Steph to see, ever the professor. 'This area, the spheno-occipital synchondrosis, is fused in ninety-five per cent of people by twenty-five.' He traced the line with his finger. 'How would we further examine the skull?'

Elliott leaned over Steph's shoulder. 'We could score the sutures for the degree of fusion to get an estimate of the age.'

'Exactly. It's much easier to estimate the age of young adults but my feeling is this—' he ran his finger down the lines wiggling across the skull, 'suggests someone over thirty rather than under. See? These sutures are smoothing out altogether. Thirty to forty, maybe more.' He looked again at the pelvis. 'I think female, on balance, but it's unusual. Maybe there's something pathological. I have an idea. Send me photos of the bones and I'll look into it. Anything else?'

Sage shook her head. 'No, we're— actually, maybe there is something. What do you make of these?' She scrolled through pictures on her phone. 'They were carved into some of the stones at the top of the well.' She handed the phone to Yousuf.

'Interesting.' Yousuf peered at the pictures. 'I have no idea what they are. Probably superstitious or religious. But it's not really my area.'

'There are more carved into the beam over the fireplace in the cottage.'

Yousuf looked intrigued. 'I haven't seen anything similar before; they are quite elaborate. And curves are harder to carve than straight lines. The man you need to talk to is Felix Guichard — that's G-U-I-C-H-A-R-D. He's a social anthropologist based in Exeter; I know him because we both work for the World Health Organization. He loves all these folk symbols, warding off bad luck and so on. Send the pictures to him, see if he recognises them.'

Sage took the phone back and made a note. 'Is he French?'

'Not as far as I know. Nice guy, got divorced a couple of years ago if you're interested.' He laughed when she frowned at him. 'OK, OK, back to your burial. Which is fascinating.'

Sage couldn't stop herself smiling. 'Can you confirm a date?'

'Looking at the degradation — although I'll do a chemical analysis for you on my samples — I think you are safely in the historical area of 1400 to 1800, at first sight. Burial inside the well prevented animal scavenging, weathering, that sort of degradation. The midden may have been high in bacteria and insects, which would have stripped the bones quickly, if they are contemporary with the infill. The archaeology suggests 1500s, maybe a little later, but you know that already. Keep me informed. It's an interesting case. I'll inform the Home Office it's definitely historical.'

Sage followed him to his car. 'Thank you, Yousuf. Don't think I'm being completely hysterical, but this place creeps me out. It makes it difficult to be objective. We're all behaving a bit strangely. Steph's tearful, Elliott's in a world of his own. I can't be as objective as I'd like about the baby.'

'Of course. It's an occupational hazard of working with crime scenes, I'm afraid. I do two or three a year, this is your first.'

'Crime scene? But it's centuries old.'

'Something evil was done to that child, and probably to that woman. It's natural to be appalled, upset. But one thing is certain, and it should give you comfort.'

'What's that?'

'At least the killer is dead and buried.'

Sage decided to take a walk at lunchtime, to see if she could find the gravestone the pub landlord had mentioned. Steph and Elliott were full of morbid speculations about what had happened to the people in the well. It was understandable but unsupported by the evidence, and it was good to be on her own. Seeing Marcus near the church yesterday had shaken her a bit. She was still attracted to him, still flattered that he was interested, even at more than six months pregnant. She couldn't shake the idea that he was checking up on her.

She lengthened her stride, her work boots getting purchase on the wet grass of the common. A field left for Banstock village to use for recreation, it was bordered on two sides by a wall of dressed limestone blocks. The Victorian map had shown the site of the old abbey only half a mile away, now levelled, probably the source of the well stones. A low mound towards the south had a few trees on it, rabbit paths widened by dogs and walkers criss-crossing the slopes. Sage thought it was the right size and location for a plague burial. She shaded her eyes from the low sun, which lit up celandines peppering the grass, along with a few early daisies. An older woman marshalled four fluffy dogs on an assortment of extending leads, like a mobile maypole weaving some spring dance.

A footpath sign led through a gateway in the wall from the High Street, and the landscape changed. The ground ran downhill, the scrub trees and bushes giving way to dense oak and beech coppicing maybe two or three hundred years old, a tiny pocket of ancient forest. The path forked into two, and Sage took the less worn one. It meandered, found a muddy patch that might become a stream in wet weather, and disappeared into brambles up the other side of the dip. She saw several fallen trees, one of which appeared solid enough to take her weight, and used it to get halfway over the mire, jumping the rest.

The trees on the other side of the dried-up stream were closely packed, the undergrowth encroaching onto a rough path. The wood was strangely quiet. A few distant calls from robins and blackbirds staking out territory echoed from the common, but she could no longer hear the road.

The crack of a twig underfoot made her jump. Something rustled through the brambles to her left, and she twisted around to follow the sound of scrabbling. It faded away and after a few moments of hearing her own heart beating uncomfortably in her ears, Sage took in her surroundings.

She almost missed the stone. Partially obscured by a fallen bough, the limestone block was half jacketed with green moss. A straight edge caught her eye. She took her camera from her pocket, photographed the greenery in situ, and then started to tug at the branch. It was tied down with brambles and had been partly sucked into the muddy ground. She was sweating despite the cold in the shade, but finally she tore the bough loose and dragged it aside.

The revealed marker leaned back about forty degrees, and she photographed it from different angles with her glove for scale. Then she took a flexible tool from her pocket and started scraping at the vegetation covering the stone.

It was difficult to remove, mosses grown onto lichens, some of which could be as old as the carved inscription. Gentle scraping gave way to more vigorous work, and finally Sage could clear out the lines of the writing with a pick. D – A – M gradually emerged from the left-hand side, followed by an O or a C, then Z – E – L. Damozel, the word Dennis Lacey had used? More photographs, then she found a heap of dryish leaves to kneel on, to tackle the thinner words underneath. Isabeau. Finally Deschassee. There was no date, no cross. DAMOZEL ISABEAU DESCHASSEE. She explored the ground around the stone, looking for any other evidence of the burial, like a sunken area or a grave mound.

'Who the hell are you?'

Sage jumped to her feet, spun around at the voice and flinched at the sight of a shotgun. The man holding it was tall and heavy, his checked shirt falling in a curve over his waistband. He scowled from under thick white hair, some of it standing on end. He waved the gun in her direction.

'Well?' he snapped.

'I came on the footpath.' Sage put a hand up. 'Don't point the gun at me, please.'

'Who are you and why are you trespassing? This side of the stream isn't common land.' The man dropped the tip of the gun towards the ground. 'That's criminal damage, right there, scraping at the stone.'

Sage stood tall, though her heartbeat was thudding uncomfortably in her ears. 'I'm Dr Sage Westfield, and I'm from the county archaeologist's office. Did you know you have a gravestone here?'

'Damozel? Certainly.'

'Well, this might be what we call an irregular burial. Do you know anything about this Isabeau?'

The man broke the gun open, and hooked it over his arm. 'Bessie! Bessie, girl!' He whistled loudly, which was answered by a bark somewhere in the scrub. 'Bloody dog.' He looked at the stone, and bent to read the rest of the cleaned-up inscription. 'Isabeau. Funny name. I don't even know what the word underneath means. We knew about the stone of course. My brother and I used to play here as children, dam up the stream, that sort of thing. We thought Damozel was either a suicide or a witch. We made up all sorts of stories about her and her ghost.'

'Why a witch?' Sage asked. 'There weren't any witch trials here around Banstock, were there?'

He waved up towards the slope and the trees at the top of the rise. 'Behind the windmill is an area called Witch Hill. Local legend is that witches used to gather in the ruins of the abbey.'

Sage vaguely remembered hearing about Witch Hill as a child. She looked at the stone again in its mossy coat. 'Then who left a gravestone in the woods?'

His manner seemed to soften and he half smiled. 'To be honest, my father always thought some servant girl got herself into trouble and topped herself.'

She tapped the stone. 'This is an expensive grave marker, but in unconsecrated soil. That's unusual.'

He scowled at her, all warmth gone. 'Maybe so, but you just can't come barging onto private land and deface gravestones.'

'I can assure you, I haven't damaged it, and I didn't know this was private land,' Sage retorted. At that moment an elderly golden retriever bounded up to the old man, then to Sage, frisking around her and splattering her waterproof jacket with mud and hair. She patted the dog, reducing her to ecstasy by scratching the middle of her back.

'You know dogs.' The old man looked at Sage appraisingly.

'My mum and dad have two Labradors.'

'Bloody idiotic dogs, worse than golden retrievers. They're even worse than spaniels.' He appeared to make a decision and held out his hand. 'George Banstock. Lord of the manor and all that rubbish. So, what put you onto Damozel's grave?'

She gripped his big hand. 'Please call me Sage. The landlord of the Harbour Bell pub mentioned it. I've been working on Bramble Cottage for the new owners. We found some human remains in an old well, possibly from around the same era as this marker.'

George Banstock raised his eyebrows until they were lost in his bushy hair. 'Bloody hell. Like a murder?'

'It would be a very old one. Between 1500 and 1600

we're guessing, from artefacts found with the bones. Although it might be a plague burial or an accident.'

The lord of the manor stroked his chin. 'Well, the cottage wasn't even there until the mid-1500s. My family owned it until about 1860. It was a farmhouse then, and we owned all the land backing onto the church. Actually, this was all part of the original farm; my great-grandfather kept the woodland when he sold the house off.'

Sage ran her hand over the headstone. 'This style of burial marker is unusual for the period, if indeed it is from the same time as the bodies in the well. Would you mind if I at least do a survey of the site?'

'Do you want to dig her up?' George folded his arms, the gun dangling between them. It hadn't been loaded, she noticed. She wondered why he had been carrying it, although the dog had disturbed a few pigeons.

'If there's actually a body here it would be fascinating from an archaeological point of view. That would be for the Home Office to decide, though.'

'The museum applied once before, but nothing came of it,' the old man said. 'There wasn't any funding. My wife will love all this mystery. We open the house and gardens to the public, and she has a team of volunteers looking into the history of the manor and the village. We have a lot of old documents, you know, though the local records office has most of the originals. All written in gobbledygook Latin.'

Sage stroked the dog's soft head, as it gazed up at

her adoringly. 'I would love a look, at some point. I have a couple of students with me; they could help look for mentions of Damozel or Isabeau. Or anyone else who went missing at the end of the 1500s for that matter. They are used to reading old English and Latin.'

'Well, come up to the house and talk to my wife. How about Sunday morning? Her ladyship's got a meeting of the history society after lunch, so if you come around eleven there'll be cakes. Give her a ring, we're in the phonebook.'

Sage watched the old man stamp across the woodland, the dog jumping up until he threw a stick for it. She slid down the slope towards the stream, and waded across the driest patch, her boots sticking in black mud that was over her ankles.

Sage was just packing the latest finds into the back of the van with Elliott when she saw Nick, this time in black shirt and dog collar under a long coat, approaching the cottage at a brisk walk. She went out to meet him.

'Hi. Wow, you really look like a vicar today.'

'Well, I really am a vicar. All dressed up for evensong.' He looked down at her. 'Finished for the weekend?'

'Yes, finally.' The sky was deepening its blue minute by minute.

'Are you going home now?' He seemed tense, his face tight.

'Not straight away. I have to go to the office first and find somewhere to put all these bags and boxes. We've catalogued more than two hundred finds today.' Sage paused. 'Is something wrong? I got the impression you wanted to talk to me yesterday.'

'I went to visit James Bassett at the hospice this afternoon.' Nick put his hands in his coat pockets. 'He's coming home tomorrow. He wants me to pop in after the weekend.' He looked down, his eyes striated by long, black lashes. It occurred to Sage that he was handsome in a 1950s, knitting pattern way. His lower lip was caught between his teeth for a moment. Then he looked up, straight at her. 'Do you have a minute?'

'Of course.' Sage reached out a hand and touched his sleeve. 'What's wrong?'

Nick sighed, then ran his hand through his dark hair. 'It's Judith. She's been going through hell. Her husband is dying, she has a young daughter. I feel like I'm letting them down by not being able to convince Judith to let me and the church help her. The child isn't responding very well, either. She's been very aggressive at school. At home too, I suspect. I'm not sure if Judith is coping with her. Judith's got some nasty scratches – the school mentioned it – and Chloe has thrown a couple of tantrums at school. Have you had a chance to talk to her?'

Sage didn't know what to say. She turned to get a glimpse of Bramble Cottage, visible through the shrubs in the front garden. 'Judith? She just seems so broken.' She hesitated before lowering her voice. 'Is there anyone else there? I did see the scratches on Judith's neck.'

'I don't think so,' said Nick.

Sage stepped closer, into the lee of his body, keeping her voice low. Out of the corner of her eye she noticed Elliott, scowling at her. 'Have you talked to her husband about it?'

'I tried to.' Nick sighed again. 'But I don't want him to worry about her when he isn't there. Could you have a chat with Judith and James on Monday? You could sit down with them to talk about the well. Maybe gauge her reaction to me visiting him?'

Sage rubbed her upper arms with gloved hands. 'I'm the last person you should be asking.' She looked over at the tall figure of Elliott, standing by the van, frowning impatiently at Nick. Over his head, she thought she saw a hint of movement at one of the cottage's dormer windows. Maybe Chloe. 'I'm the opposite of diplomatic.'

'That kind of openness creates trust. If you could just pave the way for me it would help. Tell them I'm interested in the dig, I'm going to help re-inter the remains. Anything that will make it easier for me to visit James.'

'I'll try.' He was so close, Sage was drawn towards his warmth. 'Nick, I really was sorry to hear about your wife.'

'I know.' He managed a crooked smile, then gestured towards her stomach. 'Are you and the baby's father getting married? I noticed you weren't wearing a ring. I could do you a deal, probably get you a discount on the flowers too.'

'The father's out of the picture. He never wanted the baby anyway.'

Nick grimaced. 'I'm sorry.'

'It's fine. Really.' Sage stroked her tummy. 'I have the baby, that's enough.' She smiled at the vicar. 'In a way the baby has forced me to end a not very healthy relationship with a very egotistical man.'

'Good for you.' He paused for a long moment. 'I'm glad for me, too.' He half waved at Elliott. 'Looks like your student wants you.'

Sage didn't know how to answer. Why was he glad for himself? She looked over at Elliott, who was still waiting by the passenger door of the van, arms crossed. 'I'm giving him a lift to Newport.'

'Well, have a great weekend.'

Sage watched his tall shape, a little hunched against the cold, walk away. She felt a pull. Ridiculous. Maybe there was some sort of biological instinct to secure a father for the baby. She shrugged it off and turned to Elliott. Steph was already on her bike, lights on.

'I'll be glad when the clocks go forward,' she said, before she wobbled into the road and disappeared onto the High Street.

10

3rd August 1580

Basket of eels from Yarmouth river for my Lady Banstock
◦———————————— one shilling and three pence farthing
Four pence for the boy to bring them to the manor
◦———————————— one shilling and seven pence farthing

Accounts of Banstock Manor, 1576–1582

The man Seabourne has moved his traps and servants to Well House. He has just two men in the house, one Allen Montaigne and Edward Kelley, and a lad in the stables. There are fine horses, three, including a high-stepping mare. I gave him the direction of Mistress Ashdown, who takes in laundry, perhaps not to a gentleman's standard, but he does not want a woman in the house. The new well forward of the house is almost finished, and the villagers plan to celebrate its opening. Seabourne will have to be on good terms with his neighbours, since they will be frequent visitors to the new well, which gives sweet water with no trace of salt, despite our closeness to the Solent shore. His servants will be glad of the good water, since the old well behind the house is vilely brackish.

I ride over with Viola, to welcome him to the village. At my knocking upon the door we are greeted by the servant, Kelley. It is a humble cottage for a man of Seabourne's resources, I think, but he has a fine walnut chair Lord Anthonie himself would not have despised, and a cupboard of oak, carved abundantly and covered with books. His table, scarred and scorched, holds a number of boxes and a pile of papers much inscribed. A good fire warms all against an early frost, and despite the hour, two lamps are lit against the dull day.

His man is sent off for wine and it is carried in fine glasses. We sup, Seabourne in his chair and Viola and I on a good settle, and talk about the journey.

'Master Seabourne,' I finally ask, 'what lies in these boxes?'

His eyes brighten and he smiles at us. 'Kelley,' he shouts, and the man appears. 'Fetch the alembic,' he says, and the man vanishes, to return with a leather case, much embellished.

'Shall I get the Paracelsus, my lord?' he asks. At Seabourne's nod, he carries one of the larger tomes over, reverently in his arms, and lays it upon the table. As he turns pages it is clear he is familiar with the work, and able to read.

'Now, let me show you,' Seabourne begins, opening the wooden box, packed with hay. 'This still, or alembic, is used in France for the distillation of spirits. But this has been made to my specifications by a glassmaker in Bohemia.' A large glass bottle, elegantly blown, emerges in his tender hands. 'This is the base vessel, the cucurbit, and there is the cap in the case. This retrieves the base metal, in this case, mercury.'

Kelley searches under papers for a stand, and his master carefully sets the vessel upon it, and fits the lid on top. It looks like a hat with a long glass spout, which he fits into a fat bottle.

Viola leans forward, and I see her eagerness to learn light her face. 'Is this alchemical equipment, Master Seabourne?'

He steps away from the fragile construction. 'It is a tool in understanding what we call "chrysopoeia", the transformation of base metals into gold.' He frowns at her like a teacher. 'In doing so, we understand the quality of metals and of all nature.' He strokes the page Kelley has left the book open to. 'I am a student of Paracelsus, and have studied with the great natural philosopher Tycho Brahe in Vienna. "The same stone which the builders refused, is become the head stone in the corner. This was the Lord's doing, and it is marvellous in our eyes."'

I am interested, but worry about the interest that Viola is showing in what, in the wrong light, could be seen as heretical. Quoting the psalms did not make it less so.

'You speak, I gather, of the philosopher's stone?' I stand, picking up my coat from the arm of the settle. 'Dangerous work, my friend.'

Seabourne opens his mouth, but it is Viola who answers. 'Important work, Master Vincent! What could be more important than understanding the mysteries of God's own creations?'

I meet Seabourne's eyes. 'A man may explore within the confines of proper scholarly investigation, but a woman may not be tainted by any suggestion of impiety.'

'You told me that knowledge is for all, Master Vincent,' Viola says. I turn to see if she is being impertinent, but she is serious. 'That truth is to be sought.'

'Knowledge, yes. But some questions are best left to the scholars and clergy, lest we are led off the righteous path.' She looks so downcast that I add, 'And, perhaps, artists and poets. We shall leave Master Seabourne to his work.'

The man himself steps forward with a handful of pamphlets. 'If you deem them seemly and suitable, Master Vincent, perhaps Viola may enjoy these poems from the court.'

His humility in approaching me as if I were Viola's father flatters me, perhaps, for I glance cursorily over them, and allow Viola to take them.

Vincent Garland, Steward to Lord Banstock, His Memoir

11

Saturday 30th March

The car ferry to Portsmouth had a rhythm of its own. Drivers waited, were waved on and directed inch by inch to the spot the ferry man chose. Finally, they were allowed to park their car. Sage had a booked slot, so she could visit her parents in Petersfield. Stepping onto the car deck was a blast of the quay air: brine, oil, spray.

Sage grabbed her laptop bag from the passenger seat, locked her car, and clattered up metal steps to the passenger deck. Not queuing for a coffee gave her a good choice of seats, and she selected one by the salt-crystalled window.

Opening her laptop and letting it load up, she watched the other passengers taking their seats. Many were probably Islanders like Sage, at least on her father's side. There was a certain tongue-in-cheek snobbery about being a local with a good Island name. The picture of the well woman's skull slowly loaded on the screen. She wondered what features the woman's face would have had, and whether she looked like a 'good Islander'. Most of the skull was intact, so it should be possible to get at least an approximate reconstruction done.

She looked away as someone, a man by his shoes, sat down opposite her, at the end of the seat. When she glanced up, she saw Marcus smiling at her. She jumped.

'What—?'

'Do you mind if I sit here?' he said.

'No. I suppose not.'

'I thought you might be on this boat. Going to visit your mother?' He dropped his voice, murmuring over the engine grinding below decks. 'It's nice to see you. You OK? How's the baby?'

'I'm fine. We're fine.' She stopped and did an internal audit. She was tired; she was wrestling with strange dreams; the bodies in the well, though fascinating, represented months of work for which she had no budget. And she was missing the contact, the familiar touch of Marcus's body. 'And I'm really busy.'

'Me too. I'm going to an auction in Tunbridge Wells on behalf of a buyer.' His eyes dropped to her cleavage. 'God, you're beautiful.'

She knew it was true for him. Some things he couldn't fake.

'Just stop, OK? I'm trying to move on.'

'I hear you are digging up the garden at Bramble Cottage.'

She sat back, staring at him. 'So it was you I saw.'

'Possibly. I've got a few clients in the village at the moment. Don't spoil the garden at the cottage, it was always a great selling point.'

'Was it you who sold it?' Stupid question really: Marcus had a good reputation on the eastern side of the Island and it was just the sort of property he liked in his portfolio.

'It's a great cottage. If people keep dying there it's going to be a real money-spinner.'

Sage couldn't believe what he'd just said. 'You are disgusting.'

He shrugged, half smiling. 'Just looking for the silver lining. I liked Bassett, he seemed like a nice guy. But the wife – she used to be some sort of bigwig artist. Not my type.'

'Look, Marcus, I've got work to do before I get to the mainland.'

'Well, I'm just saying, if you need anything, you let me know.' His smirk killed the warmth growing inside her like a slap. 'You look tired. You should make sure you get enough rest. When Fliss—'

She cut him off with a wave of her hand, as if to push him away. '*Fliss* had a husband when she was pregnant. She also didn't have a full-time job just to pay the mortgage.'

'I just meant—'

'I'm really busy, Marcus, and I'd rather not sit with you. OK?'

She pulled her headphones out of her pocket and

plugged them into her phone. She checked her emails and was pleased to see one from Felix Guichard, the social anthropologist recommended by Yousuf. *Divorced*, the echo seemed to reach her. *Nice guy, divorced.*

Dear Dr Westfield,

I've had a quick look at the images and see some similarities with known sigils. Intriguing puzzle. You might like to look at a book by Solomon Seabourne in the British Library from around 1580, *Casting Out Devils leading Good Women to Witchcraft*. You're welcome to come and see me – I'd love to talk over these photos and put them in the context of what else you've found. Contact my research assistant Rose Billings for my schedule and I'll clear some time for you.

Felix Guichard
University of Exeter

Sage typed his name into a search engine and a stack of hits came up, mostly relating to his work with the World Health Organization, as Yousuf had mentioned, but one result stood out: 'Professor publishes sorcery manuscripts!' It was from a tabloid newspaper, a pretty lurid piece, detailing Guichard's work on symbols that were supposed to be involved in magic, not just from the past but from the recent inquest into the death of a teenage girl. A photograph showed him to be a tall man, tanned and relaxed-looking.

Sage sent Guichard an email confirming she'd make an appointment. When she looked up, Marcus had gone. She wasn't sure if she should be relieved or hurt, but either way it was painful.

Leaving the ferry had its own rhythm too. Again, the blast of sea air, the smell of seaweed growing off the dock, the slap of waves against the fishing boats moored alongside. Sage climbed into her car and waited to be beckoned forward, to bounce up the ramp onto the road. The familiar route through Portsmouth led to the A3, and off to her parents' house in Petersfield.

Her mother met her at the door, the dogs barking and bouncing, and Sage couldn't get a sentence out until they had been patted, shoved in the dining room and commanded to go in their baskets. It wouldn't last, they would slink out again, but at least they would be quiet for a few minutes.

Yana put the kettle on and leaned against the table looking at her daughter. They were a similar height, Yana more rangy although heavier in the hips, but their features were very similar. 'Straight off the Steppe,' Dad would say.

'You look thin,' Yana announced, her accent more pronounced than with strangers. 'Are you eating enough? For baby?'

'I've been really busy.' Sage looked around the room,

seeing a few spaces in the familiar clutter. 'You've had a clear-out.'

'It was time. Actually, that's what I wanted to talk to you about.'

Sage smiled. 'Decluttering?'

'We're selling the house.'

Sage's smile froze on her face. 'What? But you've been here nearly twenty years. I thought you both love this place.'

Yana pushed open the back door, which led into a large conservatory. 'I do. But some things have changed.' She carried a tray with teapot, strainer, spoons and mugs on it into the conservatory and put it down on a low table next to a sofa and armchair.

'What?' Sage could hear her own voice had squeaked up. 'What's going on?'

'Your father and I have decided to separate. Divorce, sell house.'

'Dad?' Sage sat down on the wicker sofa, feeling it creak under her. 'Why? What happened?'

Yana shrugged. She turned her head towards the garden, and Sage saw that there were dark shadows under her eyes, new lines on her forehead, and her dark hair was growing longer than she would normally let it.

'Mum? *Sheshe?*

Her mother turned to Sage and held out her hand. Taking it, Sage could see the stains in the creases of her mother's palm and fingers. *She must have been making tinctures, herbal medicines for her practice.*

'Your father has met someone else. You mustn't be cross.'

Sage struggled to find the words. 'I thought you were happy.'

'It isn't his fault. Really.' Yana let go of Sage's hand and settled into the armchair. 'So I am selling house, and buying something smaller. Is only fair.'

'He's been cheating on you—'

'Well, we can't judge him for that, can we?' Yana looked meaningfully at Sage. 'Neither of us are innocent in that respect, are we?'

'What do you mean?'

Yana smiled, as she stirred the contents of the teapot. 'Well, your man is married, isn't he? Why else would you not move in together? Why else would I have never met him?' The spoon clinked musically.

Sage could feel a blush building in her face, and for one horrible moment, felt a wave of shame. 'That's all over. He's staying with his wife and he doesn't want the baby. But I can't believe Dad is like that.'

'He had one affair. I had several. Your father was patient and forgiving, but then he met someone who really understood him.'

Sage could hardly breathe. 'You had affairs? When?'

Yana leaned over and patted her hand. 'A long time ago.

I love your father, of course I do – who could not? But the truth is…' She paused for a long time, as if trying to find the right words. 'I fall in love with women, Sage. We weren't free to think like modern women back then. We were told to fall in love with nice boy, get married, have children. But I never felt with David—'

Sage rubbed her forehead. 'I can't believe this. You fell in love with women, plural, and Dad just put up with it?'

Yana nodded. 'I tried to keep it secret, but he's my best friend and he could always see. I think it broke his heart each time – I know it did mine. So when he met Karen, I couldn't stand in his way. She is good woman, kind woman. You will like her.'

Sage slumped into the old cushions, releasing the musty smell they had accumulated over the winter. 'So my mother's a lesbian and my dad's shacked up with someone else.'

Yana smiled at her. 'And my daughter's a pregnant ex-mistress. Grown-up life, yes?'

Sage managed a pained smile of her own. 'Please tell me Rosie's still happily married.'

Yana chuckled. 'Your sister has her own dramas. Work, children, husband – she imagines she's living in a soap opera.'

Sage studied her hands for a moment. They were big hands, like her mother's, worker's hands, Yana had always called them. The soil had stained the creases of her palms, like her mother's. 'So, you'll be on your own.'

'Like you. And with a baby coming in the summer, and no man.'

'I'm OK, plenty of women bring up children alone.' Something bubbled to the surface before Sage could stop it. 'Actually, I met a nice guy this week.'

'Oh?' Yana poured out the herbal tea through the strainer. 'Come on, now, you need a tonic.'

'Oh, Mum!'

'It would be terrible if the herbalist's daughter got anaemia, and ended up having a caesarean, wouldn't it?' She dropped a slice of lemon in the reddish brew. 'Tell me about this "nice guy".'

'Oh, I didn't mean—' Sage sipped the tea, grimaced, and added a spoonful of sugar. 'We're just working together. He's the vicar of Banstock. The people who own the cottage where I'm working are going through a lot, and I'm keeping an eye on them. We found some bones in the old well, some of them from a baby. The vicar's been able to give me some information on the history of the village.'

'Well, vicars do hear all the gossip.' Yana stroked one of the dogs, who had ambled in and slumped its head onto her lap. 'Is he single? This man?'

'Mum!' Sage took a bigger gulp of the brew, which wasn't so bad now. 'Actually, he's widowed.'

Yana smiled. 'At least single, yes?'

'He was just nice, friendly. He told me about this legend

of a witch called Isabeau, back in Tudor times.'

'It was so easy to call a woman "witch" in those days, huh?' Yana crossed her ankles. 'She was probably sleeping with someone else's husband. Maybe wife.' She laughed.

'And she was French.'

Yana spread out her hands. 'There you are. Probably a wise woman who knew all about herbs, and a foreigner as well. Burn her, she must be witch.'

Sage smiled wryly, and finished the tea. The baby wriggled, and she rubbed her tummy. Yana stood up from her chair to kneel beside her daughter. She rested both hands over Sage's belly, the warmth in her palms spreading through her. When the baby kicked again, Yana's face broadened into a huge grin. 'Ah, *bobek*!'

Tears filled Sage's eyes as she saw the strong hands holding the baby, and herself. '*Sheshe*, it's sad. The baby in the well – I can't help thinking about it.'

'Of course, of course.' Yana leaned over, lifted her hands to cup her daughter's face, and kissed her cheeks. 'You are a mother now, yes? You will always care more. But it isn't your baby in the well. Yours is warm and safe. And in June, I will hold her, yes?'

'Or him.' Sage smiled, and wiped the dampness from her eyes.

12

6th August 1580

Lavender from France and sweet flowers for bedchambers,
to Master John the Apothecary ⸱——————— six shillings

Accounts of Banstock Manor, 1576–1582

t is a sad day and a merry day together, when Viola and I visit the church to remember her mother. Lord Anthonie used to join us for prayers for her soul, and her rest in heaven, but since his remarriage it is just we two. After the service, we sit together by the tomb in which her mortal remains lie, reading the sharply engraved words.

'Lady Marion Banstock, died in her twenty-ninth year, beloved wife of Anthonie, Lord Banstock, 1566.' Viola traces the ornaments along the edge of the stone. 'She had so much life in those years. Marriage, seven children and death, all before she was thirty.' She twists the woven posy of lavender stalks between her fingers, releasing the scent. 'And she died giving birth to me.' The child contemplates her own journey.

'Indeed.' This day of all days, my mind runs on Lady Marion, the first wife of Lord Banstock, as I first beheld her. She was being lifted down from her horse by a groom, and I, a simple clerk to the old steward, was fresh from university. She was dressed for travelling, her face pink with the heat, her copper hair creeping from under her hood. She looked around and her eyes met mine. My heart was taken in one glance, and it was only when my brother stepped forward to take her hand and welcome her that the true story was revealed. I believe still that in that one moment she too beheld a mate, but we were never to speak of it.

I read the other stones to Viola, as she has asked me to do since she was a small child. She starts with the effigy of her grandfather.

'Lord Anthonie, second baron, child.'

'He has a stern face.' Indeed, the old lord, my father, was remembered on his tomb as a knight, with a dog crouched at his feet in old tradition. His face was as harsh in real life.

'He was a strong man,' I say, as a compromise. 'Fair.'

'He came, and took you from your mother to place you in a school.'

'He did.' I had no warning that at the tender age of ten my father, whom I had never met but who sent money to us each quarter day, would wrench me from my home. My mother died that winter, from plague, and I spent every holiday at the manor thereafter. I was neither lord nor peasant, guest nor family, but boarded with the steward so I might learn my craft. I was then sent to university. Old Lord Banstock never, by word or glance, acknowledged me as a son. Yet I was known as his bastard over the whole Island, named base-born son in his will, and given the place of agent to the young lord and his bride. Lady Marion and Lord Anthonie became my closest friends as well as kin.

Viola crouches down on the freshly carved stone where her tiny half-brothers and sisters are interred. 'Cecily. I liked that name. I wonder if Lady Flora will use it again.' She rises, rubbing her hands together where the stone has chilled them. 'The babe was sweet, like a doll.' She sighs in a moment of sadness.

'There will be another baby.' I lay my hand upon my lady's tomb, as if I could warm her bones within. 'And a marriage. Your mother would be pleased, I think.'

We look down at the newest stone, still plain. The slab that lies above Viola's sister's remains. The master mason who carves the tombstones at Banstock is employed as stonemason at the church at Brading and cannot be spared to inscribe her name for several more months.

Viola smiles, but it is a sad twist of her mouth. 'I do miss Elizabeth. And I wish I had known my mother, as she did.' Then the smile comes out, that warms me, always.

'But then, I would not have two fathers.'

When we return to the manor, we find the household in a storm. The rector's sister, Agness Waldren, who had attended my suffering lady upon the opening of divers sores upon her skin, had whispered a scrap of hearsay of Mistress Isabeau. She accuses her, as I feared someone would, of being papist. Lady Flora is so distressed that her women have sent for my Lord Anthonie to soothe her.

Since the lady swoons and the midwife has been called, we can do no more than direct Mistress Duchamp to my office, and we question her. The rector's sister insists on telling us that she knew the Frenchwoman was a Catholic and as such her presence was putting the babe at risk. Myself I think it is rather the relish of the pious woman shrieking such accusations above the head of her afflicted mistress that is dangerous. I have to eject Agness from the room with force, no mean feat as she is as tall as a man and filled with spiritual zeal. I tell her to moderate her tone and avoid any such gossip in my lady's rooms but she is defiant and, she says, doing the Good Lord's work. Christ's mercy save us from such burning piety.

'Moderate the words of the Lord himself?' she asks, as I bundle the woman down the main stairs. Mistress Agness is of much of the same bony make as her brother, and were I less generous, I would say about as comely. She is a bitter woman. Such I believe is the temperament of some spinsters, for marriage and children soften many a shrew.

'We must show forbearance, and forgiveness, madam,' I warn her. 'For our forefathers were Catholic.'

'She is an evil influence.' The woman is so angry, she spits the words at me. 'She bewitches the men of this house, even Master Seabourne.'

'Madam, calm yourself.' I am stern, for I know where such rumours can go. 'I will have no talk of witchcraft where there is none. What spells are needed where a maid is pretty and unmarried?'

'She should be beaten from the door.' The woman is red-faced with fury. 'She should be stoned as a papist.'

I am forced to shout over her strident tones. 'You forget yourself! Go back to the rectory, and pray for guidance. For Mistress Duchamp has done no more than be born to a Frenchwoman.'

Vincent Garland, Steward to Lord Banstock, His Memoir

13

Sunday 31st March

Sage drove out to Banstock Manor along the sunny road from Ryde, daffodils swaying along the banks. She took the turning into a gravel drive with an impressive Queen Anne gatehouse. When she'd called to arrange an interview, Lady Banstock had been eager to invite a 'real live archaeologist' as if she was a rare monkey.

The manor house itself was tempered by the centuries. It had a grand Jacobean frontage but the central part of the house looked older. The walls were made of a light stone, each block a separate entity, the mortar partly weathered away. Two rows of mullioned windows stared out below octagonal chimneys in red brick. The house nestled into a hillside that put its back to the prevailing winds. Trees had been sculpted into shrubs that hunched along the ridge, offering skeletal fingers to the west side of the Island. The portico, built out from the front of the house, had an arched doorway shielding the massive oak door. An older woman, beautifully dressed in patent leather shoes, wool suit and a string of pearls looped to her waist, stood in front of the entrance. Sage parked her car and walked across to greet her.

'Dr Westfield! How lovely to meet you. George has told me all about you. I'm Phyllida, Lady Banstock, but everyone calls me Lady George.' Her handshake was warm, and her enthusiasm infectious.

'It's very kind of you to talk to me,' Sage said.

'Not at all. We're having a little meeting of the historical society this afternoon anyway, I expect George told you. You're very welcome to stay for it.' She led the way across the tiled floor of the portico. 'We don't open properly until Whitsun, so we're busy with conservation work. It's a constant battle to keep on top of damp, deathwatch beetles, woodworm and moths. We have some eighteenth-century carpets, you know.'

Sage made impressed noises, as Lady George shut the massive door with a clunk that reverberated around the hall beyond. The floor was laid with tiles, but the original great hall had been divided by panelled partitions. It was still a large room, with a huge fireplace at one end. The walls were hung with portraits of people in all sorts of costume from the 1500s onwards.

Lady George followed her gaze. 'Oh, them. Some are of the family, some we bought at auction, a couple are copies. Death duties when George's father died forced us to sell the really valuable ones. That and the insurance; it costs a fortune each year. We had a couple of portraits by Godfrey Kneller, you know, we had copies done. Visitors expect a lot of memorabilia. The armour we got at a house sale in Wiltshire, it's always a hit with the school parties.'

They walked through an arched doorway into a much cosier room, created by the partition, furnished with three mismatched sofas. Sage looked up the panelled walls to the carved wooden ceiling. 'Is that original?'

'The wood is chestnut. It's the original roof, which was built between 1529 and 1533. Lovely, isn't it? No one ever asks about it except historians. Most visitors would much rather fall over the armour or photograph the big table. Now, do sit down. Olivia will bring us some tea – she wants to meet you too.'

For a moment Sage imagined a Victorian housekeeper. 'Olivia?'

Lady George walked to a smaller door in the panelling and opened it. 'She's our site manager and archivist. She markets the place so we can afford to go on living here. We're ideal for weddings and photo shoots. We're even available for costume dramas, although we haven't landed one of those yet. Here she is. Olivia, this is Dr Westfield.'

A slight woman in her thirties pushed the door open, carried a tea tray in and set it on a massive side table. Once Lady George had poured them all a cup, Olivia nodded to Sage.

'So, how can we help you?' Her voice was soft, with a Scottish Highland accent.

Sage sipped her tea. 'As you probably know, I was called in to do an evaluation of a property in the village. Our investigation has revealed two bodies, in what we call an irregular burial. One of an adult, one a newborn baby.'

Lady George dropped her voice. 'Down an old well. It's like a murder mystery. Do you think it ties in somehow with the memorial in the wood? George said he found you looking at it.'

'One irregular burial is unusual, that's all,' Sage said, 'then people started talking about another one. I suppose it made me curious about the stone in the woods. The pub landlord told me about it.'

Olivia started making notes. 'This could be good for our publicity. Are the burials from the same time as the stone?'

'Not necessarily, but two irregular burial sites in unconsecrated ground may be related,' said Sage. 'They are extremely rare from this era. To have two in the same village – well, it suggests there might be a connection. Which was why I wanted to get as much local history as I could.'

The three women looked at each other. 'You mean the gravestone in the woods is a burial too?' Olivia said. 'We just assumed someone moved the stone, not that someone was actually buried there.'

'You're probably right, but it may be a grave.' Sage took

a deep breath. 'I'd like to apply for an exhumation order from the Home Office and find out. There were various reasons burials were done outside a churchyard.'

'Suicide?' Lady George's eyes were round.

'Or religious difference, accusations of witchcraft or—' Sage was beginning to catch Lady George's tendency towards the dramatic and dropped her tone '—possibly murder.'

'But then why would someone put a headstone up?' Olivia brought out a computer tablet. 'I had a look through the records from the 1580s. We have the financial accounts from the third baron's time. One of them has always puzzled me. It seems to be a payment to the sexton to dig a hole in the land associated with the home farm. He got paid twice as much as usual. Here we are: "To dig the hole commissioned by your lordship, though the ground be frozen, four shillings for Wm. Grove, sexton." But I thought people didn't put gravestones in until much later.'

'Of course, someone may have put the memorial stone there later. They were rare in Elizabethan England.' Sage took the tablet and enlarged the image. 'And of course, most of them just didn't survive that length of time. These are from the manor's accounts?'

'The third baron, Lord Anthonie Banstock, had a steward called Vincent Garland. He kept minute financial records in ledgers. We've scanned most of them in, so you're welcome to have copies. The originals are at the County Records Office; there are about two dozen of them.'

Sage decoded the first few sentences. 'These are amazingly detailed. This Garland guy was meticulous.'

'He was the illegitimate son of the second baron.' Olivia took the tablet back. 'He has a memorial in the church with the family tombs. I can put the records on a memory stick for you. And if you find anything else, we'd love to know about it.'

'That would be great.' Sage looked around. 'You've already done so much work. If you have some time, I'd love to ask you more questions.'

Lady George put her hands on her knees. 'Funding the manor costs a fortune. We run at a loss some years and struggle just to keep it standing. Something like this could be really helpful to our publicity.'

'But the well isn't at the manor...'

Lady George leaned forward. 'Oh, but it was. All the land around here was attached to the manor, as far as Nettlecombe.'

'Bramble Cottage – Well House as it was – was built in the 1500s?'

Olivia consulted her records. 'About 1550, as far as I can remember. It was built to house a woman called Jennet Garland. I suppose she was related to Vincent Garland, the steward.'

'The latest finds in the well are maybe late 1500s,' Sage said. 'We do have a few bits of glass but the pottery is just ordinary sixteenth century, nothing that dates more specifically.'

'Can you date pottery that accurately?' Lady George asked. 'I mean, a pot is a pot.'

'You can date some very specifically.' Sage smiled. 'Commemorative items are very helpful. There were cups made to celebrate the defeat of the Armada, for example, and the queen's various birthdays, but we don't have anything like that from the well. Sometimes there's a popular style that can help. We're looking for a coin to help narrow it down, but during that period coins from Henry the Eighth's reign were still in circulation. But I'm intrigued by the story of Isabeau. If she went missing…'

Olivia spoke softly, as if revealing a secret. 'There's a reference in the records to the younger daughter of Lord Anthonie Banstock, Viola. An Isabeau Duchamp was employed to embroider her wedding clothes.'

'It's an unusual name for the period. It could really be her in the woods.'

Lady George's more vigorous voice lightened the atmosphere. 'If you can prove some human interest angle why she was buried up there, maybe you can link it to the well. We could put on a nice display, with Viola's picture, and what's left of Solomon's books.'

'If she is actually buried up there,' said Sage, trying to stop the flow of enthusiasm. 'Solomon?' That rang a bell. Professor Guichard had mentioned the name. She pulled up the email on her phone.

Lady George nodded. 'Solomon Seabourne lived here

when he was betrothed to Viola. There's our publicity angle, you see. He wrote several books about science, although we only have the covers now.'

Olivia nodded. 'A previous lord moved the old pages out and stuck pages of his own in. We can sell the idea of Solomon living here, his romance with Viola, even the mysterious seamstress. Viola was quite a celebrated poetess, in her time.'

Sage finished rereading Felix's email. 'Actually, Seabourne's name has already come up. I'm going to talk to a social anthropologist called Felix Guichard about the carvings in the well. He mentioned Seabourne too. You said there is a picture of Viola?'

Olivia stood and walked to one of the portraits on the wall. She beckoned Sage over. 'This is believed to have been done when she was in her twenties.'

Sage stepped towards the portrait. Despite being in need of some cleaning, the picture was vivid. A woman with white skin, long neck, and rich auburn curls clustered around her head in front of a lace ruff. A prosperous woman, shown holding a pen in one hand and a book in the other. Not beautiful, perhaps, but striking with a heart-shaped face and pointed chin.

Something about the border caught her eye, and she leaned in for a closer look. In the background were scattered delicate designs. The shapes were familiar; they were similar in style to the designs scratched into the stones lining the well. She held up her phone. 'Do you mind if I take a photograph?'

'Not at all,' Lady George said. 'And there is another connection.'

'Connection?' Sage turned to look at Lady George.

Olivia spoke instead. 'Before he married Viola, Solomon rented Well House.'

14

10th August 1580

Ink pot with black ink for your lordship's daughter Viola

— ten pence

Accounts of Banstock Manor, 1576–1582

Viola is in a melancholy mood, matched by soft rain spattering the windows. The spiteful Agness Waldren made it her business to spread her accusations about Isabeau throughout the manor, and when I find Viola, writing her poetry in the solar, I see her reddened eyes.

'Viola—' I begin, but the words crowd in my throat. 'What ails you?'

'I make rhymes for "queen" but none are quite right.' She turns her paper to the grey light creeping into the long room. 'I write for Her Majesty's accession anniversary, of course,' she says, looking down. 'My sister Anne read my poem in celebration of her birth to Her Majesty's ladies-in-waiting, and it was well received.'

'Child.' I hold out a hand, but she looks away.

'Why do people believe such things about Mistress Isabeau?' she asks, picking up her pen.

'Perhaps they are jealous of her.' I think about her beautiful face. 'Also, she is paid much more than the other women at the manor and has the freedom to go and work wherever she wishes. She has worked for ladies of the court, you know.'

'Yet she came to embroider my sister's bride clothes here, on the Island. And now mine.' Viola crosses out a word, and writes another above it.

'She has a freedom few women possess. Her artistry gives her that.'

'I would like that freedom, sometimes.' Viola tucks the paper into her sleeve. 'To marry whom I choose, to travel anywhere I please.'

'To starve anywhere you please, more like. When Mistress Isabeau is not employed she is prey to robbers and ruffians, and she is at the mercy of her sponsors.' I cannot but laugh a little, perhaps unkindly. 'Mistress Isabeau is in the worst of situations. If she is found to be a Catholic, she will be cast off and will find it difficult to find employment with any family.'

'She is no more papist than you or I. I have seen her at her devotions in the chapel.' Viola places her cleaned pens and ink bottles in her writing box. Her voice has a snap in it that reminds me of her mother or even, perhaps, myself.

I follow her through the hall, along the corridor to the women's quarters, and immediately hear the scolding of one of Lady Banstock's women. All voices fall silent as Viola pushes open the door to the room where the Frenchwoman works. She ignores the two waiting women.

'I have heard sad news, Mistress Isabeau.' She speaks with a softness I had not expected. 'That you are the subject of tittle-tattle. Nay, slanders.'

The Frenchwoman speaks in her own language, so fast Viola frowns. 'Please, in English.' She reaches out a hand to the woman but does not touch her. 'You need only assert that you are Protestant, and none will challenge you again.'

The woman bows her head, then raises it again. 'I worship God as you do, in your own chapel. Who invents such stories?'

I intervene. ''Tis Mistress Agness Waldren,' I say, 'who is something of a zealot.'

'Master Vincent,' Isabeau says, calmly. 'That rumour stains not just me, but Lord Banstock and his family. They do not harbour a papist.' She says the words, yet the slightest flicker of the eyes leaves me undecided. She bows her head.

I wonder what secrets she holds.

'Then,' I say, 'the matter is easily resolved. If you are willing to be examined by the rector in your faith, then we can put this rumour to rest.' I glance at the other women. 'After all, you were brought to England and grew up in a Protestant age, like many others.'

She bows her head in acquiescence. 'I am happy to be questioned by Reverend Waldren.'

I only wish she had not retained so much of her mother's accents, or perhaps her beauty. Jealousy breeds such vile mischief.

Vincent Garland, Steward to Lord Banstock, His Memoir

15

Monday 1st April

*H*ope you find time to see Mrs Bassett. Thanks for all your help. Sage smiled as she read the text from Nick Haydon, then tucked her phone into the glove compartment. She appreciated the comfort of maternity trousers, but they didn't have pockets. Elliott held the van door open for her.

'Good morning,' he said, smiling.

'You're in a good mood,' she said, turning to pull out the first container of specimen boxes and bags.

'I've been working on the glass fragments over the weekend. I think it's Tudor scientific glassware, what they called an alembic.' He hefted the heavier tools out of the back of the van and shouldered them, then the two of them walked around the side of Bramble Cottage to the garden. 'I can't be sure, it could be some sort of drinking vessel, but it is so fine I doubt it.' His enthusiasm made Sage smile. 'It's very delicate but I think we should get most of it.

Some of it's stained with this black stuff. Do you think we could analyse what was inside it?'

Sage nodded. 'I suppose we could. Analysing the glass itself might tell us where it was made. An alembic is a kind of still, isn't it?'

'Yes,' Elliott replied. 'I think there are possibly metal oxides lining the thickest part of the bowl, which must have been the base. They look fused into the glass.' He laid out the sieves and spades on the tarpaulin workspace they had created. 'This could tell us more about sixteenth-century beliefs around magic and alchemy.'

'Which would be fascinating. But we may not be able to safely get it all. The contractor the engineer recommended is coming this morning, so we might be able to get the bigger pieces.'

'No way!' Elliott's voice shot up an octave when he was agitated. She watched as he mastered his reaction. 'I mean, we can't just send someone with a shovel down there. We need to excavate carefully, over time. I don't mind going down.'

'Well, the university minds about your safety and we don't have enough time anyway. I'm sorry, Ell, but we'll make the guy take as much care as possible.'

'Can I at least have a look for any big bits that are exposed now?' he pleaded. 'This is so important.'

Sage hesitated, but they had all been down over the past week and it seemed daft that they now had to wait for an 'expert'.

'Look, stay on the ladder, pick up what you can but no digging, OK? Remember what the engineer said, it's just a garden wall held up by the infill we're removing. It could collapse.'

Steph walked into the garden, pushing her bike. 'Hi, guys.' She smiled at Elliott. 'Sage, Mrs Bassett just asked if you could pop in for a chat?'

The two students set up the table and Steph started filling the plastic boxes they used to wash specimens from a garden tap.

'Keep an eye on Elliott,' Sage said. 'He's got to stay on the ladder, OK?'

'OK,' Steph answered with a glance at Elliott. It didn't look like it would be a huge chore for her.

Sage walked around to the door and knocked. Judith answered and stared at Sage without blinking for a long moment. Her skin was pale, and her arms wrapped around herself as if she were cold. 'James is home. My husband.' Her voice was flat, and she didn't return Sage's smile.

'Oh. Good.'

'He wants to talk to you.' Judith made no effort to move out of the doorway.

'Well, if it's convenient for you.' Sage raised an eyebrow and waited.

Slowly, Judith took a step back, and lifted a hand a few inches. 'He's in the living room.'

'Thank you.'

The room was warmer than before, the woodburner glowing and flickering. The sofa was occupied by a thin man with blue eyes, who stared at Sage as she entered. A huge bunch of daffodils sat in a vase on the coffee table, vivid in the plain room.

'She said you were a stunner.' He held out a hand. 'I'm James Bassett. I understand you've been trashing my garden?'

Sage shook his hand, feeling the strong bones in her palm. He retained a vibrancy that made his wife look even more insubstantial.

'I'm so sorry we've made such a mess of the grass.'

James Bassett smiled, his long features twisting unevenly. 'It's more of a pain for Judith, I think. Chloe's very excited. She's hoping you'll find a secret tunnel or a sleeping princess.'

'Did your wife explain about the human remains?'

'You found the bones of at least two people down the well, put there in the distant past.' He waved to a chair. 'I'm guessing this is really unusual?'

Sage sat down, noticing Judith flit past the kitchen door. 'Very. We have to respect the burial, while finding out as much as we can.'

'Nick, the local vicar, said he'll do a proper funeral when you've finished.'

She nodded. 'He mentioned that.' A shadow across the kitchen doorway suggested a figure standing, listening. 'We'll do a reasonable amount of research to put a name to the bodies first. I have been given a few ideas by Lady Banstock.'

'Oh, good.' James rested his head against the cushions of the chair. 'Sorry, weak as a ninety-year-old at the moment.'

'I'm sorry. If there's anything we can do to make this easier—'

'Actually, it's fascinating to me. I used to go metal detecting with a friend at university. Famous battlefields, that sort of thing; we used to go looking for musket balls and military buttons. Ju said this house is older than we thought?'

'The Banstocks think it was built around the mid-1500s, as part of their estate. It used to be called Well House.' She watched as the shadow flinched.

'So Judith said. She and Chloe have been looking up the census returns for the house.'

'We have a picture of the house from about 1900. I've brought a copy for Chloe.' Sage rummaged in her bag for a folder, and passed over the page. 'The 1901 return probably records their names.'

'Thank you. Chloe will love this. Keep us informed, we'll be interested.'

Sage stood. 'I would be happy to go over the information with you, and maybe include the vicar? It would be helpful since he will be involved too, with the reburial.'

James looked at her, and a twitch of his features suggested a smile not quite realised. 'My wife isn't very keen on God at the moment.'

'Oh, I understand. I just thought – Nick's a community figure with access to church records, the history of the parish, that sort of thing.'

James glanced past Sage to the kitchen door. 'I would really like that. Set it up, will you? You do a bit more digging, and if I'm still here, call a conference.' He winced a smile. 'Would the house itself be of any interest to your investigation? You're welcome to have a look around.'

'Actually, I did wonder about the original timbers and stonework in the house.'

'There are some odd carvings in that beam over the fire. Are they initials?'

Sage stood up to inspect them. 'I don't think so. They're too elaborate.' The low light in the room didn't help, and she looked around for a light switch. 'Do you mind?'

'Go ahead.'

Between the lights and her pocket torch she could make out eight curved marks and one area in the middle of the beam – charred from previous fires – where one might have been. The single piece of oak had twisted along its length, successive owners replastering around it until the whole chimney looked lopsided. There was easily enough room for a chair within the fireplace opening itself. 'As I said, I spoke to the owners of Banstock Manor,' she said, crouching down to see the underside of the beam. More deeply carved figures were cut into the surface, under layers of soot. She reached for her phone to take a few pictures. 'They have more information of who was living here in the 1500s. I'd like to show these to an expert. There are at least a dozen in here.'

She stood up, which made her catch her breath. The pregnancy had fitted somehow into her tall body until the last few days, when it seemed to distort her and change her centre of gravity. The baby wriggled and she rubbed her belly.

'Do you know what you're having?' James smiled, leaning into the cushions, his eyelids drooping. 'We knew in advance with Chloe.'

Sage grinned. 'They say it's definitely a baby but couldn't be sure of the gender at my last scan. I was wondering if it was a calf, myself, it kicks so hard.'

James laughed. 'Is the father excited?'

'It's just me and the baby.' Sage picked up her bag, not keen to discuss the intricacies of her love life any further. She gestured at the beam. 'They remind me of some odd shapes that we found in the well. I'm following them up with an expert, a social anthropologist.'

'Great. Let me know what you find out.' He grimaced as if in pain for a moment as he clasped her hand. 'If I'm here, anyway.'

For a second Sage didn't know how to respond. 'It's good to finally meet you, and I hope we don't disrupt your home for too much longer.'

'Sage?' Elliott popped his head around the door. 'I've got the glass ready for you.'

'Elliott, this is Mr Bassett.'

While the two men shook hands, her eye was drawn to a few toys on an armchair, one of them a cloth doll. Its black hair had been inexpertly hacked short, and something was stuffing the toy's jumper. James followed her gaze and laughed.

'Chloe has really taken to you. She adapted a doll into an archaeologist, complete with baby bump.'

The eyes had been inked in with black. They looked disturbingly like empty sockets.

'Oh.' Sage turned to go, but paused when James spoke again.

'To be honest, I've been worried about Chloe. Judith, too. This place seems to make them more – well, gothic. When Chloe has a tantrum – which she didn't really do, before – I almost expect her head to spin around.'

Sage turned back to him. 'It's a terrible time for you all. I'm so sorry.'

His eyes held hers. 'I know you are. Thank you.'

As she left, Elliott held the door into the hall open for her. Sage could feel tears prickling in the corners of her eyes.

Two hours later, Sage was turning over fragments of pottery with a finger. Most large Tudor households used earthenware jugs, as well as tableware. Broken pots would end up in the midden, along with food waste. She had plenty of green glazed shards and the curved grey of an imported Bellarmine jug, which would probably be worth reconstructing. It would be a good project for her first-year students, especially as she could see the edge of the characteristic face pressed into the clay before firing. She dropped another handful of spoil in the tray, and she could immediately pick out a star-shaped bone, almost blackened. She washed away the soil that clung to it, and put it on a piece of kitchen paper to dry. It was a perfect human vertebra in miniature, no bigger than a cat's but less spiny.

She checked the message on her phone again. *I was wondering if you would like to drop by the vicarage this afternoon? I have someone coming who might help with your historical puzzle. Come about 3 if you're free, Nick Haydon.* She wondered if he really was interested in her. There was something about the first time they met... She texted him back with an acceptance and got back to recording potsherds.

The sun had moved during the morning, warming the work area. From the occasional muffled comment from Elliott Sage guessed that he was finding more glass, and Steph was photographing and cataloguing, preparing specimen codes and labels ahead of the finds. They already had over three thousand.

'Dr Westfield?' Sage jumped at the voice, and looked up to see a stocky man in filthy clothes addressing Elliott. He turned and gave her an appreciative glance, and she could feel colour starting to move to her cheeks.

'Yes?' Sage said.

'I'm Rob Greenway, well specialist. Your boy shouldn't be down there.'

'Elliott is conserving extremely rare and valuable Elizabethan glassware.'

He shrugged, tucking his thumbs into the top of his jeans. 'He'll be buried along with them if he's not careful.'

Sage laid out the ground rules. No feet in the bottom of the well, all material to be laid out on the spoil tarpaulin, and not disturbed more than necessary. Greenway was to respect the fact that he was digging up human remains. He listened and nodded, but clearly didn't understand or value the work.

Sage suddenly had an idea. 'Follow me.'

He stumped after her around the cottage, calling out for 'Harry' as he walked to the road. Sage unlocked the back of the van, and pulled out one of the bone boxes. She gently unwrapped the baby's skull pieces, moving the face into position. When she looked up, Greenway and Harry seemed stunned.

'This is what we're working on. This is a baby, dumped down the well like rubbish. One of the local children. He or she may have been murdered.'

Harry cleared his throat. 'My granddad, he came from Banstock, way back.'

Greenway reached out a finger, but didn't touch the

bones. 'Poor little bugger. How old was he?'

'Newborn, we think.'

Greenway hitched up his jeans. 'So this is, like, a historical crime scene?'

'That's how we need you to treat it. We need you to think like detectives rather than just clear out the well.'

Satisfied that the message had gone in, Sage explained that some of the baby's remains and half the woman's bones were unaccounted for. Once she had got Greenway and Harry working, with Elliott standing over them fussing, she felt able to walk through the village to the vicarage.

The vicarage was a large Victorian building opposite the church, with a gravel drive filled with cars. Sage walked in through the open door, into a long tiled hallway with doors leading off to left and right. A large handwritten sign pointed one way, towards 'Mums and Babies'. The other way led to a heavy door, and a brass plate that read 'Reverend Nicholas Haydon'. She knocked.

'Come in.'

Sage's first impression was of a solicitor's office. Hardback books in colour-coded rows were arrayed on built-in bookcases. A heavy oak desk covered with piles of paperwork was surrounded by several mismatched armchairs. One was inhabited by a compact older woman, white-haired, with a colourful scarf knotted around her neck. She watched Sage with dark eyes, as Nick stood to greet her.

'Glad you could make it, Sage. Mrs Jordan was coming in to talk about raising funds for new books, so I asked her to join us. She has some insights into Bramble Cottage's history. Kate is our local historian and runs the library.'

Sage smiled, and reached out a hand to the shorter woman, who didn't smile in return. 'Nice to meet you. Any help you can give me...' Her voice faded as the woman continued to stare, then took her hand briefly.

'I think we've met before,' she said, 'when you were at school. Is your mother Yana Westfield?'

'Yes,' Sage said, cursing her distinctive features. 'I'm told we do look alike.'

Mrs Jordan looked at Nick. 'Yana was a medical herbalist on the Island, before your time. I knew her years ago.'

Nick looked surprised. 'Tea or coffee?' Nick's hand hovered over a coffeemaker, half full, and an electric kettle.

Sage nodded. 'Tea would be great.' She turned to Kate Jordan, who was still staring at her. 'What can you tell me about the cottage, Mrs Jordan?'

'Call me Kate, everyone does. It has a reputation for being haunted.'

Sage smiled her thanks for the tea, and sat on the nearest chair. 'I've heard the stories. I'm more interested in the history.'

'That's the thing about the truth,' Kate said. 'It's bound up with the mystery.' She turned a bracelet on her wrist a few times. 'Solomon Seabourne lived there in the 1580s. Do you know anything about him?'

Sage shrugged. 'All I know is his name – oh, and that he wrote some books that are kept in the British Library. Lady George has the covers at the manor.' Nick silently pantomimed cutting a slice out of a golden cake studded with fruit, and she nodded at him. He handed her a large wedge on a plate.

'Well, you know he was a famous sorcerer.' Kate's words hung in the startled atmosphere of the room before nodding vigorously. 'Black magic, alchemy, all the dark arts, right here in Banstock. He became engaged to Viola Banstock when her older sister died. Viola was only fourteen.'

'That wasn't very unusual at the time for women of high status.' Sage took a bite of the cake. 'This is delicious,' she mumbled through the crumbs.

Kate ignored her. 'Solomon was a student of famous sorcerers. He was present when Dr John Dee raised a man from the dead.'

Sage swallowed, trying to find a subtle wording for *what a load of bollocks.*

Nick stepped in. 'What Kate is saying is that there's a lot of mythology about Seabourne.'

'The spells he performed are supposed to haunt Bramble Cottage,' Kate said. 'Have you met Maeve Rowland, the previous owner? She says bad luck affects whoever hears the ghostly wailing.'

'I do wonder where these stories come from.' Sage eyed Nick again, then shrugged. 'I'm a scientist. What I have is tragic enough without talk of ghostly voices or black magic. I'm looking for the possible identities of a woman in her thirties or forties, and a tiny baby.'

Kate spoke in a flat voice. 'Solomon Seabourne seduced a servant up at the manor, a seamstress. It's a local legend. There's your woman and baby.'

Sage sipped her tea. 'The problem with that theory is that the woman's skeleton has no signs of ever having been pregnant. The baby seems unrelated. It is possible it was an emergency plague deposition, but there are suggestions of injury to the child. People in that time took Christian burial very seriously and this feels like an illicit dumping of bodies.'

Kate leaned forward. 'Something else you might not know. Solomon paid for the church tower, as penance for an unknown sin.'

'I was told that when I first got here,' Nick said. 'I looked him up.' He pulled out a piece of paper from a pile on the desk. 'There are entries in the church records, the previous vicar had the originals copied and bound; I looked it up. Three hundred and forty pounds for the building of the tower, and eighty-eight pounds and seven shillings for the casting of two bells. Nothing about penance, though.'

He held out the photocopy. 'I can just about read the entry itself, but the notes are a mystery.'

Sage took the paper and held it up to the light. Beside the main entry, there were some heavily inscribed notes in Early Modern English. "'That the bells be inscribed with names..."' she read out. 'I can hardly read this.' She felt around in her pocket for her hand lens, and peered at the letters. "'...and that the smaller be named Isabeau, and the larger Viola.'"

There was a long silence. Nick broke it. 'Why two bells? I know Isabeau's name, was she his mistress?'

'It seems a bit inappropriate to name one after his wife and one after his mistress, if that's what they were,' Sage interrupted, with a note of scepticism. 'Kate, does the legend you mentioned explain how this seamstress died?'

'Well,' Kate began, 'you've heard the story. Her ghost – the book calls her Isabelle – is supposed to wander through the village looking for her baby.'

'What book? Nick told me a story about the Devil attacking her at the gate of the church.'

Kate pulled a book out of her bag and opened it with a flourish. 'I brought this over from the local history collection at the library. The vicar of Banstock in the 1800s transcribed some of the parish documents and published them. He added a lot of his own speculation and local gossip.' The modern reprint was called *Banstock Tales*. Sage took it, leafed through it. There was very little from the

Tudor period except a bit about the dissolution of the local abbey. Then a startling page.

'Listen to this. "And we received the dread news that his lordship's son, George, did die at sea upon Drake's great undertaking, being the last male heir. Then did his lordship announce the betrothal of his youngest daughter Viola to Master Solomon Seabourne, a scion of that great seafaring family. So did the sea deliver as it has taken away."' She squinted at the date, written in a footnote. 'This was written by the rector of the church in 1580. And we know Isabeau lived here and had a bell named after her by Solomon.'

'Look at all the witnesses to the betrothal.' Kate squinted at the page. 'I could do with my glasses. It's like they invited everyone with a title in the south of England. Lord... Thomas Seabourne, is that right? The father-in-law?'

'I'll have to look that up.' Sage sat back, glancing up to see Nick smiling down at her.

Kate scanned the next few pages. 'He doesn't write about the wedding.'

'Maybe it happened in London or at the Seabournes' estate. Or maybe,' Sage shrugged, 'those documents were just missing by the 1800s. There must be a load of gaps.'

Nick leaned forward. 'It's mostly gaps. No mention of Isabeau?'

Kate shook her head. 'Just the story of the Devil coming

for her at the church gate. I thought it would make a great ghost story for Halloween at the library a couple of years ago. I couldn't back it up with any hard facts.' She smiled faintly. 'I still used the story of course.'

Sage finished her lukewarm tea. 'That's all great information but there's no evidence that links to the woman or the baby in the well. I doubt if they would be mentioned in the parish records if they ended up dumped like rubbish.' The baby kicked inside her, as if in protest, and she rubbed her belly to comfort it. She noticed Nick watching her hand.

'We'll keep looking. We've got all sorts of parish records held at the library and the county library,' he said. 'This seems like something the historical society will want to work on. It would be nice to bury the skeletons with names, at least. More tea?'

Sage looked at her watch. It didn't seem fair to leave Steph and Elliott for too long. 'I'd love to stay, but I'd better get back to work. Thanks for the cake. Nice to meet you, Kate.'

'I'll see you out.' Nick put a hand under her elbow, and the warm pressure stirred something in Sage. He guided her through the door.

At the porch Sage turned to him. 'Nick—' she didn't know what to say. The weight of his bereavement and the baby stirring stalled what she was going to say. 'I spoke to Judith and James – well, James really. He said he'd be OK with a meeting to discuss the excavation and the burial, just to get you in the door.'

'Thank you. That would be a start. I'll phone him, set up a meeting.'

Sage nodded. 'It's all very sad. The dig, I mean. I understand the locals are going to be upset. If we can put out information about the dig it will be better for everyone.'

'Thank you for all the care you're taking over this.'

'Of course. Now I've really got to get back to work; I've left Elliott defending the dig from two builders.'

'Will you be around tomorrow?' Nick asked.

'I'm off to the mainland for a couple of days. I'm going to consult with an expert tomorrow, then I've got a chance to do some research and maybe look at ways to get funding. I'll be back on Thursday.' She turned away, wrapped her coat around her in the sudden chill and stepped onto the drive. Parked illegally in front of the church was a red car that looked exactly like Marcus's. Before she could make sure, it was gone, accelerating down the hill towards the harbour.

16

14th August 1580

Dowry for Mary Fitton at your lordship's beneficence
ten pounds

Accounts of Banstock Manor, 1576–1582

It is a time of whispers and rumours, thanks to the wagging of Agness's tongue. The Reverend Matthew Waldren, her own brother, gave a lesson upon the dangers of spreading malicious rumours that kept even Lord Anthonie awake. It left the men of the manor whispering, and I am afraid to say, gazing at Mistress Isabeau. The seamstress always worships with the rest of the household, sitting aside from the men and with my lady's waiting women, as is proper. She makes all the right responses and gives no hint of popishness, yet she must have been brought up a Catholic, being a Frenchwoman

147

raised in the heart of Queen Catherine de' Medici's court. She quietly performs her duties, working in the sewing room on exquisite gold embroideries and embellishments. There are more whispers in the village, I hear.

So I take myself to the alehouse, and there make myself comfortable by the empty fireplace. I buy a few jugs of beer and we toast our fine harvest until no man is steady of foot or tongue.

As the landlord pours more cups of his strongest ale, the men begin to speak. They turn to me to ask if the French maid be a papist and they tell me rumours of a priest hidden at a manor near Newport. I disclaim all knowledge of any such, but the men and boys at the manor are like to make a spark into a bonfire. I chide them, as the seamstress is closely chaperoned by Lady Banstock's waiting women. They tell stories of her creeping out of doors after dark, when my Lady Flora and I were in London with Lord Anthonie. The tittle-tattle told of lights seen at the ruined abbey, late at night. This gave me a little disquiet, but I rubbished such talk, and if it were after dark, how could anyone see who attended such meetings? But I admit, I was worried. There is, they say, no smoke but from fire, and gossip is blowing on those embers.

I finish my ale when the servant Kelley from Well House enters. Voices die away, as they are wont to do before a stranger on the Island. I take pity on the man, and wave to him, a little curious myself.

'Master Vincent.' He touches his cap, but does not remove it.

'Fetch young Master Kelley one of your fine cups of ale, Beatrice,' I call out. 'How go your master's experiments?' I ask him.

The youngling, for he seems barely a boy and has little beard, bows his head respectfully before he seats himself upon a bench. 'More questions arise than answers, Master.'

'Then tell me of your travels, for you are not an Islander, with your fair speech.'

'I am lately from Cambridge, sir,' he says, nodding his thanks at the landlord's wife for the ale. 'I was assisting a Lord Robert Dannick with his studies and gained my education there. He introduced me to Master Seabourne.'

While he drinks of his ale, I wonder at his cultured words. 'And of what stock do you come, Master Kelley?'

He hesitates, glancing into his cup before he looks up at me, very direct of gaze. 'I am the youngest son of an Irish landowner recently fallen upon hard times, sir.' Catholic, I imagine, and reluctant to recant. 'My family name is Talbot, but I go as Kelley, which was my mother's name.' Ho, I think to myself. A bastard making his own way upon the world, no doubt, and I like him more for it.

My gaze is drawn again to his hat, and the ale loosens my tongue. 'What do you hide beneath that cap, young man?'

He colours quickly, with a comical look between embarrassment and anger. 'Vanity only, sir.' He drains his cup, stands, and bows to me. 'A baldness that is unseemly in one of my youth.'

I know he is lying. In truth, I suspect almost every word he speaks, yet I like him. One such as he, born with the stain of bastardy, must necessarily make his own story. But I still wonder about the hat.

Vincent Garland, Steward to Lord Banstock, His Memoir

17

Tuesday 2nd April

Sage crept into the back row of Professor Felix Guichard's lecture five minutes after it started. The social anthropologist looked just as he had in the newspaper photograph Sage had seen, a tall man in his forties in a fisherman's jumper and paint-spattered jeans, holding forth with some enthusiasm. She hoped Professor Guichard wasn't the type to heckle latecomers.

As she took a seat, Guichard was introducing the ideas of magical belief and how they overlapped with early science. As he was an amusing lecturer, she settled into her seat.

'Who believes in magic?' he asked. The question surprised his audience, prompting a rustle of papers. 'I'm serious. Who believes that you can say some magic words, and they will come true?'

No hands went up, but there was a small wave of laughter.

'No one? I'm going to prove to you that most of you

do believe in magic.' Whispering and giggling suggested the students weren't taking him very seriously. He lifted his arms to get their attention. 'This is a serious point I'm making, people. I need you to think of a person you love, the person you would miss the most if you lost them. OK?'

For a few moments a current of murmurs circulated.

'Now, stand up. Magic is easier when you stand up. All you have to do is repeat after me. I wish—'

There was an awkward mumble. Guichard laughed. 'Come on now, big voices! This is a magic spell, remember.'

Sage added her voice to the next attempt.

'I wish—'

'With all my heart and every fibre of my being—'

'With all my heart and every fibre of my being—' The room had sobered, as if they were actually giving some sort of oath.

'That my loved one called—'

Here the words became a jumble.

His voice resonated like a bell across the room. '—gets cancer, and dies.'

The voices faded away, into gasps and mutters. Only Sage finished the incantation as a wave of nervous laughter came from the students.

Guichard lowered his arms, gesturing for his audience to sit down. 'Now, most of you decided not to say it. But you – the young lady in the back – you did. Can I ask why?'

Sage grinned. 'I don't believe in magic,' she said.

'I'm sorry, I don't know your name?'

'Sage Westfield.'

'Ah! Dr Westfield is a visiting archaeologist, ladies and gentlemen; a scientist, a natural sceptic. But those of you who didn't finish the spell, why not?'

The students gave various reasons for their reticence, some angry, some confused. Professor Guichard used them to support his theory that belief in magic predated scientific explanations in young children, creating an overlap and the retention of early belief systems in superstitions and quasi-religious ideas. Sage liked his theories. It had felt strange cursing her mother with cancer, and at the end of the session, she was happy to join in a sixteenth-century sorcerer's 'dispelling ritual', which had the students stamping their feet and calling out blessings in Latin.

At the end of the lecture she walked down to the front of the hall to meet Guichard, whose long face creased into a lopsided smile. 'Sorry to put you on the spot like that, but you were the perfect exception that demonstrates the rule.' He put out a hand. 'Felix. Nice to meet you, Sage.'

'I enjoyed the lecture. I'm looking into a sixteenth-century sorcerer myself.'

'Yes of course, Solomon Seabourne.' He lifted a pile of papers and nodded to the doors. 'Let me dump these in my car and we can find somewhere to talk. Would you mind if we combined it with lunch? There's a nice bistro just off campus.'

Sage held the doors open for him. 'That would be great. As I said in my original email, we're excavating a well on the Isle of Wight, and have found two bodies, a woman and a child, likely from the late 1500s. The pictures I sent you – of the carved symbols – are from the inside of the well, and there are similar shapes carved into a beam in the nearby cottage.' She paused. 'What's really interesting is that you suggested I look into Solomon Seabourne's book, and as it turns out, the cottage was actually *rented* by Seabourne in the 1500s.'

'Incredible.' He led the way across the foyer to the car park. 'Have you brought more pictures?' He sounded as if he was hoping she had brought sweets.

Sage tapped her rucksack and grinned at him. 'Lunch first. I am eating for two.'

Once they had ordered food, Sage handed over her computer tablet with the photographs.

'These are fascinating,' Felix said, looking at the images of the well stones. 'Are these limestone?'

'Yes, we think they're from Banstock Abbey, broken up after the dissolution of the monasteries,' Sage replied. 'They aren't religious symbols, then?'

Felix peered at them, magnifying details. 'Definitely not. Besides, the abbey would have employed masons who would have carved them perfectly, whereas these are just scratched in with something like a chisel. Forty-eight of them?'

'At least. They are the ones we've found. As I said, there are similar carvings in the house.'

'Show me.'

Sage was able to show him the enlarged images. 'These are from a beam over the fireplace, original to the cottage, as far as I can tell. But I don't know when they were carved. Maybe they were just decorative.'

Felix shook his head. 'No. Decoration in this period was very deliberate and loaded with symbolism. I recognise some of these symbols. They are sigils used in magic – sorcery.'

Sage couldn't see what he was talking about; the squiggles looked like graffiti to her. 'You are sure they were deliberate?'

'The beam looks like it's a hardwood. Slow-grown hardwoods were a lot harder to carve than modern fast-grown imports. That wasn't a bit of whittling. They look like deeply incised marks.' Felix leaned back. 'Tell me more about the bodies.'

Sage sipped the fruit juice he had insisted she try. 'A woman and baby, unrelated, dropped several metres down a well, and then a midden dug out and thrown on top to fill it in. We have late Elizabethan pottery shards and artefacts at the bottom of the shaft, covered with earlier pot fragments. That's consistent with someone having dug down to deeper layers in the midden to fill in the hole.'

'Cause of death?'

She hesitated. 'It's just speculation, but the woman had a number of fractures that could have been sustained in the fall. The baby had a slashing wound across here.' She drew a line from her chin, down her collar bone, to her arm. 'If the injuries were sustained in life...'

'Horrible.' Felix's eyes were full of sympathy. 'I do recognise some of these symbols. Seabourne wrote extensively about summoning and banishing spirits and evil influences.'

Sage was surprised. 'How many of his books survive?'

Felix smiled, then sat back as his lunch arrived. 'Thanks.' He waited until she had been served. 'The British Library has some of Seabourne's books and pamphlets. The bestseller was the one I mentioned, *Casting Out Devils leading Good Women to Witchcraft*, used against women through to the 1700s.'

Sage's stomach was growling. She remembered she had left the Island at seven. 'Banstock Manor has the covers of several of his books, but someone ripped out the pages.' She took a big bite of pasta.

'I'd like a look at that. Solomon was a bit of a mystery. He was always suspected of being a Catholic, and that adversely affected his career. Of course he was born in King Edward the Sixth's time, grew up during Bloody Mary's reign and died in James the First's. Whether you were safe to be Catholic was more a matter of timing.'

'I suppose being titled helped a bit.'

'He wasn't titled until later in his life.' Felix sipped his own juice. 'He was a youngest son who struggled to survive after his father virtually disowned him. At least until his thirties.'

Sage eyed him as he ate. He had dark curls, over his collar, tinged with grey. She could imagine him in a Tudor doublet. 'So, what were the symbols in the well for? Some sort of blessing? Banishing evil?'

'I need to do more research. But I don't think they were for banishing anything.'

'Oh?'

'I think the symbols were intended to confine something. A kind of trap.'

'Trap?'

Felix nodded. 'People like Seabourne were looking for proof of the existence of angels and demons. They treated sorcery as if it were – I don't know – quantum physics today. Just because you haven't seen a quark doesn't mean you can't predict what it will do then demonstrate it, which helps support your theory. By his thinking, if you can summon a demon, it would prove the existence of other dimensions. And you could question it about the underpinning beliefs of Christianity. God, heaven and afterlife – they were the big scientific questions of the sixteenth century.'

Sage sat back in her chair and put her hands on her stomach. 'I'm staying in the hotel down the road. Do you have any time tomorrow to talk about the symbols?'

'Come to my office in the morning, I'll look out what I have on Seabourne. I have a family thing tonight – it's my partner's daughter's birthday. Otherwise I'd have more time for your strange carvings. So. What else was down this well? Apart from a woman and a baby.'

'We found some glass. My PhD student thinks it's from an alembic. A sort of chemistry still.'

'Seabourne claimed to have managed to transform some metals into gold, in small amounts, with help from Edward Kelley.'

'Kelley?'

'He went on to be Dr John Dee's assistant. Dee was the queen's sorcerer and astrologer, and a famous alchemist,' Felix said. 'Kelley later exceeded his mentor's knowledge in many ways, certainly in sorcery. He met Seabourne, they may have collaborated on chrysopoeia – making gold out of other metals.'

Sage laughed. 'That's a hell of a claim. You'd think he would have died a very rich man if he had managed to make gold.'

Felix smiled over the rim of his glass. 'He did.'

18

Two pairs of silk hose for your daughter Viola's
wedding clothes ——————— eight shillings and four pence

Accounts of Banstock Manor, 1576–1582

The seamstress Isabeau has been examined for her faith by the rector and has been found as observant as any of us who have lived through the great changes. Mayhap she does cling to beliefs from her childhood in the French court and mumbles the Protestant creed when it is politic to do so. But who has not? Even the queen, when princess in the reign of her sister Queen Mary, took Mass.

The rector's sister has been physicked and is confined to her room. Agness's intense dislike of Isabeau seems more than just suspicion of a foreigner. Her reason seems disordered.

I sit in my office for it is rent day, and each of Lord Anthonie's tenants has their own tales to tell of why their rents are light. Each also seems to have a curiosity about the Frenchwoman, and I quell some rumours. I fine two, give others more time to pay, and caution many against the spreading of vile rumours about an innocent and hardworking woman. I shall be glad to see her leave; she has been much troubled and caused discord and suspicion.

So I find myself much surprised when the last visit to my office is the woman Isabeau herself, much distressed.

'Master Vincent, I beg you to help me.' She sinks into a curtsey, her kirtle splaying out around her in a pool of fine brocade.

'I am trying, Mistress, the lies will abate——' but she is shaking her head, sinking her face into her hands until she is kneeling on the floor.

'I wish to go back to the mainland,' she mumbles into her fingers.

'But why? Any doubts as to your faith must have been allayed, at least for now,' I say.

'*Je suis mariée* – I am a married woman,' she confesses, blushing and ashamed as if it were a sin. 'My husband is *un tyran*, he is jealous. He beats me, so I run away to places far from London. If people talk, he may find me.'

I hold out a hand, and after a moment, she takes it, and rises to her feet. 'You haven't told Viola any of this?' I ask, sternly.

She blushes again, and turns her face away from me for a moment, as she pulls her hand from mine. 'Of course I have not. Lady Viola is a child, still.'

I study her averted face. So beautiful, so secretive. Her little teeth nibble her lip, as if trying not to say something. 'What else, Mistress?' I ask, but she shakes her head, and turns that sad face to me. 'Well, I can tell you news moves very slowly off the Island. You will have finished your work in a few months, you say?'

'Just after Christmas. Before *le mariage*, the wedding.' This time I cannot mistake the tremble in her voice.

'Mistress, something else troubles you sorely.'

Her eyes are full of tears. 'I have sinned.' She speaks in a low voice. 'I have sinned in my marriage.'

'What sin?' I can see her tremble.

'I left him. I feared for my life.' She turns to me and wipes away tears. 'He cannot find me. He would kill me.'

I am perplexed. The law says that a man may beat his wife if he finds fault, but no one would condone murder. 'If that is so, we will protect you.' I am reluctant to assist a woman to break her marriage vows but there is such sincerity in her voice, such grief in her face that I am moved. 'No man shall harm you here.'

I stand and open the door for her. As she walks past it occurs to me that she moves with less grace than usual, bowed down with her sorrows.

Vincent Garland, Steward to Lord Banstock, His Memoir

19

Wednesday 3rd April

Sage spent a good night at her hotel and wasted an hour shopping in Exeter, treating herself to a baggy T-shirt and a tiny outfit for the baby. She walked up to the university and spent an hour or so looking at the books in Felix's office, a copy of odd pages of what seemed to be magical potions and a sketchbook of Solomon Seabourne's. His research assistant, a mature student called Rose, showed her a number of references from people like Robert Fludd and others, as they attempted to control an unseen world of good and evil influences and beings.

'Before you go home to the Isle of Wight,' Rose said, 'it might be worth looking into his wife's work too.'

'You mean Viola Banstock?'

Rose ran her finger over a photocopy of the front page, badly damaged, of a manuscript titled *Philosophy of Man and the Natural Science of Light and Darkness*, by S.

Seabourne. 'I typed up a transcript of the first few pages of each of the fragments and the copies we have. This dedication just caught my eye. I wondered if we could find out more about it.'

The dedication was written, by hand, under the main title, with strong, slashing letters. 'To Lady Viola Banstock, thatt shynes a light upon the mysterys of grate darkness, thatt almost had me enthralled and destroyed by madness.'

Sage sat back. 'Viola again. I hadn't thought about looking at her writing, though now I think about it, the historian at Banstock Manor did tell me that she was a celebrated poetess.'

'There are three books of her poetry in the British Library, and a few pamphlets.' Rose, a motherly-looking woman in her late forties or so, frowned. 'It's so horrible, a baby in a well. Do you think it was someone from the manor?'

Sage shook her head. 'No, I don't think so. I doubt someone from the manor could have gone missing or been buried so ignominiously without there being a fuss at the time, and local knowledge of it.'

Rose sat back in her chair and nodded. 'Anyway, Seabourne might have been quite a bit older than Viola.'

'What makes you think that?'

'It wasn't unusual. He was born about 1551 and died in 1604, but she lived for much longer. She published some poems on the birth of Prince Charles, who became Charles the Second, in 1630, under the name Viola Banstock, not

Seabourne.' Rose shuffled a pile of papers into some sort of order. 'I'd love to find out more. It's a real mystery, isn't it?'

Sage examined the folders lining one wall of the room. *Death Curses, Weather Spells, Water Witches.* 'This is a weird subject to study. Does Felix believe any of this stuff? I mean, does he actually have any evidence?'

Rose's smile was more of a wince.

Sage grinned. 'I bet you get asked that a lot.'

'All the time. The answer is, I started out completely sceptical. I think he did, too.'

'And now?'

Rose shrugged. 'Now... I'm not so sure.' She started writing on a notepad. 'You heard his lecture. Belief in magic is still ingrained in us from early childhood: tooth fairies, Father Christmas, ghosts and goblins, witches and wolves. It's hard to completely shift it. When strange things happen, we interpret what we see through layers of beliefs. Take ghosts. Nearly half of all westerners claim to have seen or heard a ghost of someone they loved.'

'It's strange but—' Sage hesitated, reluctant to give credence to Maeve Rowland's story. 'The cottage, where the well is. The owners think it may be haunted, they've heard wailing noises.'

'Wails are common, so are babies crying.' Rose tore off the paper and handed it to her. 'These are the names of books by Solomon that you might like to look up. You can find them at the British Library. And Viola's.'

'Seabourne was quite well known, then?'

'Yes, but the real occult stars like John Dee didn't agree with some of his work. They were looking for a unifying glimpse of heaven, to heal the fragmentation of Christianity. Seabourne was much more interested in the dark arts and alchemy. He may have been consulted by Christopher Marlowe before he wrote *Doctor Faustus*. They probably knew each other.'

Sage read the titles on the list. *The Nature of the Elements. The Deep Realms. The Invocation of Spirits and Binding of Souls,* and the book Felix had mentioned, *Casting Out Devils leading Good Women to Witchcraft.* 'I know it's a horrible thought, but would he ever have used sacrifices in his rituals?'

'It's possible,' Rose said. 'Human sacrifice is supposed to be the most potent. Nowadays, murder in magical rituals is actually on the increase in places like Uganda and Namibia. Felix has consulted with government agencies and NGOs in several African countries about it. Dozens of cases of people mutilated or killed for their body parts. Some of the victims are just babies, some are disabled people.'

Sage looked around at the crowded bookshelves lining the room. 'I had no idea it was that serious.'

'You'd be surprised. Hundreds of people are killed each year in India alone because they are suspected of witchcraft. I don't know if Seabourne ever did dabble in sacrifices, but there are texts that suggest it was possible.'

Sage tucked the paper into her messenger bag. 'Human sacrifice,' she said, only half joking. 'That was one possibility I hadn't considered when I was digging.'

Rose pulled a face. 'Welcome to my world.'

20

22nd August 1580

Bread and meats for the midwife
————————————— three shillings and tuppence
Wines and meats for the gossips
————————————— three pounds and sixteen shillings

Accounts of Banstock Manor, 1576–1582

ife at the manor progresses, as we wait to see if Lady Banstock can hold her child longer than any other. Gossips have arrived, matrons of status from our side of the Island, and the lady of the lord governor of the Isle of Wight has visited. The midwife has advised the household not to unlock or untie any lock or knot except the main door. This is especially tedious, because I need to look at the old rent rolls and they are tied up with ribbons. It's probably a foolish superstition but we want a healthy child.

The one person who seems to be too distracted with her own problems to worry about the baby is Mistress Isabeau. Many times she takes to the chapel, and I hear her sobbing there. Even Viola cannot comfort her.

Viola seems much taken with Master Seabourne's ideas, and he is to pay us a visit today. I have decided to act as chaperon for a while, to learn more of the man.

Seabourne bows low, and the plumes on his hat sweep against the floor. Although in his usual black, his clothes are richly decorated and his hands adorned with several rings. Viola bows back formally, and I bend my knee. We are all very proper in the solar.

'I hear the Lady Flora, your stepmother, prospers?'

Ah, I think, *we are going to have that conversation.* But Viola has other ideas.

'She does, thank you. I have some questions for you, if I may?' She leaps into passages from the pamphlets he lent her, and he, half laughing, struggles to explain them. Some of the topics are a little indecorous. The male and female qualities of substances in nature, depending on whether they yield or otherwise, is one I judge suspect, but their interest seems innocent. Both are so involved in their discussion of the properties of different humours, I confess, my mind wanders.

I let my attention travel out of the windows, where I can see the smith walking one of the farm horses up and down the drive, while a man scythes in the distance. His silent sweep must have been mesmerising, for when I look up again, the horse is gone and the scytheman is halfway down the front field.

'—but surely, there must be some sort of balance?' I hear Viola say, her hands clenched in her lap as she leans forward on the settle.

'Balance, indeed. There must be energy, to place in the transformation, to fuel it. This is drawn in by the magician, the agent, as he calls upon natural spirit to aid his work.'

Viola is too absorbed by the man to notice my attention. 'Is that why the Romans sacrificed animals to strengthen babies?'

I stare at her, the bright expression of her need to learn softened by something. Seabourne nods, but notices my attention. 'I was explaining the principles of alchemy to the lady,' he explains.

'Sacrifice smells like sorcery to me,' I grumble, much troubled by an ache in my lower back. 'A short step to witchcraft, indeed.'

He hurries to correct me. 'We are merely examining the nature of the world around us, Master Vincent. In the way that we discover that if we do not water a plant in a pot, it withers. For example, take the commonly held belief that spiders' webs prevent festering in arrow wounds. This has been proven by many soldiers, but they observe that only fresh webs work. Thus we understand more of the nature of spiders and their gift from God.'

I found I was interested myself. 'How might a sacrifice be used?'

Viola explains, Master Seabourne nodding and adding a few words of correction as she does. 'In – is it *lustratio*? Yes *lustratio*, the Roman sacrifice blessed the new child with good health and strength, by drawing the weaknesses into animals, then destroying the beasts.'

Seabourne leans forward. 'Such life energy was believed to influence the child's growth and fortunes, even its destiny.'

I stand, stretching my back. 'Well, maybe we should do that *lustr*— sacrifice for my Lady Banstock's baby.' I look at Viola, who stands, and Seabourne joins us. 'Now, I have accounts to do and no one can be spared to keep Lady Viola company, so we must bid you farewell, sir. I hope you are comfortable at Well House?'

'Indeed, very comfortable.'

Viola swings around to me, swishing her best kirtle over the rushes. 'Oh, Master Vincent! Can we show Master Seabourne how the work is progressing on the East Wing?'

The wing that the newly wedded couple will share as married man and wife. There is a slight pause as both the betrothed look uncomfortable.

'Another time, child, when John Carpenter is there to show us around.' I speak to Seabourne directly. 'There was some rot in the roof beams from a few loose tiles that needed repair, no more. But the rooms have not been occupied since Lord Anthonie brought his bride there.'

'I shall be honoured to look at the rooms when there is more time.' He bows, Viola bows, I bow. We are all very polite. I resolve to take a closer look at these radical ideas he is feeding Viola.

Vincent Garland, Steward to Lord Banstock, His Memoir

21

Thursday 4th April

Sage stopped in at Banstock village's small library before starting work at the dig, hoping to have a chat with the librarian, Kate Jordan.

The lights were still off, the door propped open by a bag. 'Kate?'

The lights flickered on, and Kate smiled when she saw her, no hint of the slight guardedness of their first meeting. 'Hi there. Could you bring the bag in? I'm sorting out lists of children's books to buy. The deadline for my budget is today.'

Sage lifted the bag. 'I'm familiar with budgets and deadlines. The joys of working for the local authority.'

Kate waved her to a table. 'Village libraries are hanging by a thread, thanks to cutbacks. Sit down. I suppose you're looking for more about the cottage?'

'I was told that Solomon died a rich man. If he was

renting Well House – Bramble Cottage – he wasn't to start with.'

Kate disappeared into a cupboard. 'I can still hear you,' she called.

Sage raised her voice anyway. 'Lord Banstock's steward kept very detailed accounts. I just wondered if anyone kept similar records on Seabourne's finances.'

Kate returned with a bulging box file. 'Banstock's steward was Vincent Garland. Olivia Mackintosh is the historian up at the manor, and we've been copying his ledgers for the local history group. Here.' She pulled out a large sheet of paper and unfolded it.

'I don't understand,' Sage said. It wasn't a ledger entry, but a legal document with seals. A bill of sale.

Kate pointed out the lines at the bottom that detailed the terms. 'To ensure the succession to Viola and her male children, the old Lord Anthonie sold the estate to Seabourne, although he continued to live in it for the rest of his life.'

Sage squinted at the tiny words. 'Wouldn't they have lost the title?'

'The family petitioned later to get the title restored when it lapsed for lack of male heirs. The estate gained land and money: Seabourne paid eighteen thousand pounds for the whole estate and bought another two hundred and thirty acres.'

'Which leaves the question,' said Sage. 'Where did

Seabourne get all that money?' She glanced at her watch. 'I better get to the site.'

'Indeed.' Kate hesitated for a moment. 'How's your mother? I meant to keep in touch when she left the Island but...'

'She's fine. Well, actually, she's separating from my dad.'

'Oh.' Kate looked like she had a lot more to say, but in the end she just smiled lopsidedly and turned back to her books. 'Well, I'm glad she's OK. And looking forward to the baby, I imagine. When's it due?'

'Fifteenth of June. It seems very soon. I'm not ready for this.'

Kate laughed. 'No one ever is.'

'Good morning.' James Bassett leaned against the doorframe of Bramble Cottage, smiling at Sage. She hadn't appreciated how tall or how thin he was. 'Are you incredibly busy today?'

'Not really, just more of the same.' She smiled. 'Lots of pottery.'

'It's just that Judith's out. I wondered if you could drop me round at the vicarage? I don't want to wear myself out walking across the green, and I'm a bit wobbly these days.'

Sage smiled at him. 'Put a warm coat on, I'll take you round now. Just let me sort Elliott and Stephanie out.'

The now empty well was secured with a heavy cover,

and the students were busy with sieving and examining as much of the spoil as they could in the time they had left. When Sage got back, James eased himself carefully into the seat of her van, his hands shaking with the effort so much she had to help him with the seatbelt.

'Sorry.'

'Not at all.' She started the van, checked her mirrors. 'I assume you've arranged to see Nick?'

James sighed, leaning into the seat. 'Yes. Judith doesn't want him in the house.' He stretched his long legs out in front of him with a grunt. The back of his hands were purple with bruises, perhaps from the hospice treatment. 'The story of the cottage has really caught my imagination. I know this sounds a bit strange but it's as though the house is trying to tell me something. I wasn't surprised when Ju told me about the bones.'

Sage drove around the one-way system and into the vicarage's drive, opposite the church. 'Your wife said something similar.'

'She seems to feel there's something sinister there, but for me it's more... cerebral. As if someone is trying to explain something, telling a story.'

Sage parked, and unlocked both seatbelts. 'The story of the people in the well? Stay there, I'll give you a hand.'

Nick came out of the porch in time to steady James's other arm.

'So sorry, weak as a cat.' James was white around the

mouth by the time Nick settled him into an armchair in the study. Sage moved towards the door, but James waved a hand at her. 'Wait. I need you here too.' He coughed, and relaxed into the chair. 'OK. Breath back. Now, Nick, tell Sage what you told me.'

'I've been getting phone calls late at night. Anonymous calls.'

James rolled his head against the back of the chair. 'The police, very nicely, asked us if we knew someone at the house was phoning Nick late at night from a mobile. I didn't recognise the number but they said it came from the village, and they triangulated it to the cottage or its immediate surroundings. It's an unregistered phone.'

'Oh.' Sage sat on a leather office chair. 'Do the police know who—?'

'Well, it started while I was in the hospice, so they couldn't blame me.'

Nick folded his arms. 'I never thought it was you, James.'

'I know. They think it might be my wife, but I know, with all my being, it isn't Judith.'

'Maybe it's a wrong number?' Sage said.

'At first, it was just silence,' Nick said. 'But last night, it was a string of obscenities shouted down the phone. It was very personal – not a wrong number.'

James looked at Sage. 'That's not Judith's style at all.'

'Anyway, the last call was definitely from a man. It was such a deep voice, even if he was trying to disguise it. The calls are changing, becoming threatening.'

Sage pulled a notebook out of her pocket, and filched a pen from a mug on the desk. 'Let's approach this scientifically. How many calls?'

'It's been going on five days now. At first, two or three a night, between eleven and about two. I don't like to turn the phone off in case I'm needed by a parishioner. I thought they were just wrong numbers at first.'

'And then?'

'I had thirty-two calls last night, some just a few seconds, a single word. I won't repeat the word in the present company. One lasted about twenty minutes; I just left the caller rambling.' Nick rubbed a hand over his face. 'Honestly, I'm exhausted. I had to turn the phone off eventually, around three.'

Sage stopped writing. 'That's awful.'

James covered his eyes with a hand for a moment. 'Well, if it was a man's voice the police won't think it's Judith anymore.'

Nick shrugged. 'I think the police only considered her because she got so upset with me outside the school. But when she was shouting at me, her voice was high-pitched, and the caller's voice is really low.'

Sage dropped her voice into the lowest register she could manage. 'How low?'

James managed a chuckle.

Nick smiled. 'Very good. But I bet you can't shout like

that.' He sighed. 'I get the impression the police think I'm being a bit hysterical but honestly, I'm exhausted. They just tell me to record them in case the caller leaves some sort of clue.'

James leaned forward, and caught Sage's eye. He tapped his fist on his knee. 'If I had the energy, I'd come over this evening and listen, see if I could help.'

'I'll do it.' Sage surprised herself, but then turned the idea over. 'I mean, I'm only filling out endless bits of paperwork for the one billion artefacts we've found in the well. I could do that here. Give me a ring when the calls start, if they do, and I'll come over and you'll have another perspective on the voice. At least you can get a bit of sleep.'

James smiled. 'Excellent. Now, I did have a useful thought. Take my mobile number and give me a ring when this crank calls Nick and I can have a look around the cottage and the garden. I'm a bit fuzzy after I've taken my medications, but I'm OK to have it a bit late.'

'Are you sure?' said Nick.

James grinned at them, suddenly looking younger. 'I know I've got cancer, but I'm actually dying of boredom. This will be the perfect antidote.'

Sage had managed to do a couple of hours of paperwork at home before Nick called.

'I've had the first call.'

'I'm on my way.' She glanced at the clock; it was later than she had expected, nearly ten. 'Put the kettle on and I'll be there in twenty minutes.'

'I'll make coffee.'

'Make it tea. Decaf if you have it.' She cut off any attempts at apologies. 'See you soon.'

Sage snatched up work bags and her tablet, grabbed a warm jumper and headed for the van. As she drove through the town streets into the quiet of the countryside, she slowed for foxes and a badger, her headlights picking up the sudden white swoop of a barn owl. She pulled into the silent village, past dark-eyed houses and the gleam of cars. The scrunching of gravel under her tyres sounded loud as she pulled up on the vicarage's drive. She got out of the van and turned towards the road, looking over the village green to the thatched house hunkered down in its nest of yews. She had the strangest feeling, as if someone was watching. She stood still, just her own breath hissing in the silence. Bramble Cottage was still and black, and Sage had to ignore the feeling of malevolence creeping from it, as if the darkness was somehow deeper around its limed walls. She shook the idea off. The whole situation was becoming far too fanciful.

A wedge of yellow light stretched across the vicarage drive as Nick opened the door.

'You've got me spooked, now,' she grumbled, walking over to him.

Nick stood looking down at her, dressed in a sweatshirt and worn jeans. He opened his mouth, then paused, as if he couldn't say the words that first came into his head. He settled on, 'Thank you.'

Sage brushed past him, following the light into the kitchen. The room was more modern than his study, with new worktops and a decent cooker, though the high ceiling was dusty with old cobwebs. The kettle was hissing next to two mugs. Sage made tea as Nick followed her in, glad to see that he had found decaffeinated teabags, and sipped hers slowly. She missed coffee; it was like a physical loss some days.

'Tell me about the phone call,' Sage said.

'More obscenities. The usual.' Nick flopped onto a kitchen chair, resting his arms on the table. The landline handset lay on it. 'I am so tired. I don't like to turn the phone off in case... it's part of the job. Especially with James Bassett at home at the moment.'

Sage sat down next to him. 'Let me hear the next call. Then we'll call James, and he can have a look around, confirm it isn't coming from inside the cottage. Then I'll take over recording the calls for a couple of hours and you can get some sleep.'

Nick rested his forehead on his arms before looking up. 'I really appreciate this.' Then his body jerked as the phone rang.

'God, you are really wound up.' Sage reached for the phone.

'Wait! The calls are horrible. They're my responsibility really.' His voice faded as she answered.

'Hello?'

A long hiss was the first thing Sage heard, followed by a silence as whoever was on the other end reacted to her voice.

'Hello? This is the vicarage.' Sage was rather enjoying herself, and added, in a hollow voice, 'Is anybody there?' Nick rolled his eyes.

A growling sound began to come from the tinny speaker. Then the words started, screamed so loud it took her a few seconds to work out what he'd said. 'What are you doing there?'

Sage was chilled at the tone of the voice. She glanced down at her forearms, exposed when she had rolled up her sleeves, to see goosepimples lift the skin. The voice repeated the words in a deep rolling tone, as if the speaker was drunk, forcing Sage to pull the receiver away from her ear. 'What are you doing there? Get out! Get out!' She grimaced at Nick as she forced her suddenly cramped arm to put the handset down. With a mundane click, the snarling voice was abruptly stilled.

'Shit.' Sage was shaking, and wrapped her arms around her cold body. Nick was half smiling in sympathy. 'Who *was* that? That's mean.'

'At least I can tell the police I'm not imagining the rage in the caller's voice. Did he recognise you?'

'Maybe.' She felt in her pocket for her mobile. 'He thought so, anyway, but he never mentioned me by name. I'll call James. How long is it between calls, usually?'

'It won't be long.' Nick's voice was tense. 'They keep coming until I give up and switch it off.'

'How do you record them?'

He demonstrated the buttons to press. 'The memory filled up in the first few nights. I put a bigger memory card in for the police to look at.'

The phone rang again, an annoying jingle, a contrast with the strange voice Sage had just heard.

'OK.' She pressed the button to record, then called James from her mobile. She tried to ignore the tinny voice coming from the landline handset, shouting obscenities.

'James, we're getting a call. Anything going on over there?'

'Nothing.' James's voice sounded even weaker over the phone. 'And Judith and Chloe are both asleep in our bed.'

'OK, I'll speak to you tomorrow.'

Sage ended the call as Nick hung up the landline.

'I'm sorry,' he said. 'It's bad enough him having a go at me but now he's shouting at you.'

'Well, it's definitely not Judith and it's obviously male.' The strange voice was so filled with frenzied rage it stayed with her, teasing at the back of her mind. 'It reminds me of something. Maybe someone. It must be someone who knows you and recognises my voice. That narrows it down a lot.'

The next call was longer, and Sage let the recording run. Maybe the caller would let some detail slip that would help identify him. It was horrible listening to someone who sounded so deranged. Eventually he started howling 'whore' down the phone so repetitively she cut him off.

Nick yawned. 'He sounds mad. Why would he have a problem with me?'

'And me, now.' Even as she spoke the words, Sage shuddered inside. *What are you doing there, you whore?* 'It sounds personal, as if he knows me, too. I don't think you're safe. You have to talk to the police again. At least we have a recording.' She shook herself. 'God, that bloody cottage. Judith keeps going on about it being haunted.'

'Maybe old houses just make us speculate about the people that have lived there over the centuries. You have just been excavating the well with the tragedy of a dead baby. Or maybe we're picking up on the Bassetts' pain.' Nick leant on the edge of the table. 'I've always thought places pick up emotions. After a great service, for example, the church feels as if it's still full of people, long after they've all gone home.'

The phone rang again and Sage pressed record, burying the handset under a tea towel so she couldn't hear the invective.

'Do buildings make people insanely angry?'

Nick smiled. 'Not normally.'

Sage looked up at him. 'Go to bed. I've got this for a

couple of hours. It'll give you a bit of time, anyway. I can unplug the phone before I leave.'

'I feel bad leaving you with… that.'

'Don't worry about me. I'm a night owl.' The baby moved, and she patted it. 'We both are.'

Nick yawned again. 'OK. Just for a couple of hours, though. But I don't like the idea of you driving home too late. Not at this time of night.'

Sage laughed. 'You are kidding. "This time of night" – do I look like I can't party until dawn?'

He smiled in return. 'Sorry. I'm a bit old-fashioned. But you are pregnant and it's late.'

'Then I'll crash on your sofa. Go to bed. I'll be fine.'

By twelve o'clock Sage had recorded eighteen calls. She had relocated to Nick's study to use his desk, and had written up eighty finds and labelled them. Then she had wandered around the room looking at Nick's books and pictures for three nosy minutes. There was a picture of Nick with a laughing woman hugging a dog. She was young, maybe early twenties, and her blonde hair swung in the breeze like a shampoo advert. Sage didn't feel she could compete with that freshness, while she was carrying her lover's baby. Nick looked younger, too, and happy. She wondered if he was interested, for the hundredth time going over the few times they had met. She checked her mobile occasionally. Marcus was still texting her, inviting her to meet – which probably meant much more than just lunch – as if she hadn't ended it. She pushed the problem of Marcus to the back of her mind as another call came in, setting it up to record.

The caller was now screaming down the phone, she assumed with frustration since she wasn't saying anything back. When she did, he shouted at her to get out of the house. Clearly he was very disturbed. It was easier to keep her archaeologist's hat on and just make notes, make the recordings.

At half past twelve Nick appeared in the doorway, his hair sticking up at the back like he'd at least managed to get a bit of sleep.

'Has it stopped?'

Sage looked up from the desk where she was leaning her head on her hand. The find numbers were starting to blur even as she wrote them. 'Not yet. I just turned the ringer right down.'

Nick unplugged the phone's base, and placed it on the desk next to her. 'I think that's enough for tonight.'

She yawned. 'Who have you pissed off so badly?'

'I have no idea. I've been here less than a year and everyone's been really friendly. It makes me feel sick, to be honest. He's also starting to repeat himself.' He leaned over her to switch his computer off as it idled in the background. 'Except his reaction to you, that was new.'

His breath was just tickling Sage's neck, where a few stray hairs were drifting across her skin. It was distracting. She turned her head to find his face disturbingly close. 'So far, it's just phone calls. Let's give the police tonight's recordings.'

His gaze dropped to her lips for a second, and she could feel warmth spreading up to her neck. 'I'm really drawn to you,' he said, in a low voice. 'I don't know why you should be interested in me... I mean, you're obviously not available, and I'm... well, not available, either.'

Sage leant back in the chair, looking at him. He *was* attractive, in a brooding, dark way.

'Nick...'

He took a breath, and stood up straight. 'You're right. Sorry. I'm tired, it's late.'

'No problem.' She curled her legs under her in the chair. 'I could stay.'

He raised one eyebrow. 'I'll make up the spare bed.'

'I'll sleep on the sofa, if it's all right with you. It looks comfortable.' She rose and went over to the overstuffed leather sofa with fabric cushions. 'Just get me a blanket, I'll be out like a light. The baby's finally asleep.'

His smile was crooked. 'If you're sure.' He seemed confused by her matter-of-fact approach to staying over.

'Go. Just show me where the bathroom is.'

It was strange. Nick found a new toothbrush, lent her his extra minty toothpaste, and put a soft blanket and plump pillows wrapped in floral cases on the sofa. He saw her tucked in before saying goodnight.

'Are you sure——?'

'Go to bed! For goodness' sake.' She sank into the pillows, and her aching back immediately eased. 'Oh, that feels good.' She let him turn off the lights, leaving only a bulb lit in the hall. The strange voice on the phone seemed to echo in her head for a few minutes then the ticking of a clock somewhere and the creaking of his movements in the bedroom overhead lulled her towards sleep. 'You may not be available,' she whispered to herself, 'but I am.'

22

6th September 1580

Axe to cleave firewood ————————— *two shillings*

Accounts of Banstock Manor, 1576–1582

s the month progresses I have cause to ride past the abbey grounds, gifted to the first Lord Banstock for his services to good King Henry when he set aside the monasteries. I turn in at the old gate, hanging open by one hinge, the postern wall mostly levelled to ground level. I ride over the old track, the grass sweeping my horse's belly and my legs to both our displeasure, until we come into the clearing before the abbey itself. Little grows in front of the buildings save short sward. The villagers declare it cursed, but I recall the drive to the abbey being dressed with crushed stone, and therefore there is little to sustain the plants. The abbey itself was mostly burned out ten years ago after some of the roof timbers and panelling were taken, no doubt for the building of the new inn. It had been robbed, and perhaps the thieves sought to cover their crime, but no one tried to douse the flames when they came, the reputation of the place making the villagers fearful. The inferno heralded a new age, where the people are ruled by English princes, not the foreign pope.

Beyond the main building the cloister cells remain, and as I pass one I see a doorway. Being a curious man, and a custodian of the estate, I look inside. A simple pallet within is covered in simple blankets, the windowsill bears evidence of many candles lit upon its ledge. A posy of dead flowers rests in a cup, long dry. Someone has used it as a trysting place, perhaps many times. I cannot think who would do so, as the local girls seek quiet barns and fresh haystacks for their lovers. I cannot imagine a girl of Viola's rank having such liberty that no one knows their whereabouts, and my lady's waiting women are either too old or too pious. My thoughts jump to Isabeau, much attended when we are in residence perhaps, but when we are in London… Isabeau, who said she has sinned against her marriage vows. Not just by deserting her brutal husband perhaps.

I consider the men of the manor. Has she lain with one of them? Then my mind flies to my suspicions of Seabourne, who visited Banstock for the betrothal. When we left for London, he made an excuse to visit Dr Fell in Newport.

I leave the little room, and ride back to the manor house with my mind in a turmoil.

The narrow cell, in a place that for four centuries was one of veneration and worship, has been defiled. It disturbs me with its ritual of seduction, as if the stench of sin lingers.

Vincent Garland, Steward to Lord Banstock, His Memoir

23

Friday 5th April

Sage had woken on Nick's sofa when she heard noises in the room above. She squinted at her watch. *Shit.* Eight fifteen, and she had to meet Steph to walk to the school to give the presentation to the children. She pushed the blankets off, and as she put her feet on the floor, the door opened.

Her smile faded as she took in a woman, about her age, blonde hair bouncing. The woman stared at her, her mouth compressing into a thin line. 'Sorry. I was looking for Reverend Haydon.'

Sage pointed to the ceiling. 'I think he's upstairs.'

'I didn't know he had a guest.'

Sage shrugged. She wondered how close Nick and this woman were, if she just came and went as she pleased. 'Excuse me, I need to get washed and dressed.' She dragged her trousers on and squeezed past the unmoving woman.

She met Nick at the top of the stairs. His expression changed when he saw her, and she became acutely aware of her raggedy hair and rumpled clothes.

'Sorry, I'm a bit scruffy.' It sounded lame even as she said it.

He smiled at her. He looked younger without his glasses. 'I was thinking how lovely you looked, actually.' She smiled back and he stepped closer. A footstep in the hall made them both look down the stairs.

'You have a visitor. A woman, she let herself in.'

'Oh. Right. It's just Mel, who co-ordinates the parish volunteers. Work begins early around here; I'm already late for a prayer meeting.' He made a tiny grimace, and tucked his shirt in. 'Help yourself to breakfast, I've got to run.' There was an awkward moment when she almost felt he wanted to kiss her, then he clattered down the stairs.

Sage escaped into the bathroom and leaned against the door. The baby moved lazily and she stroked her bump. 'Morning, Bean. Mummy's getting very silly.'

By the time she was washed and tidied up, Nick had already gone to the church. The blonde woman was sitting in the study, writing in a big planning diary. She didn't look up when Sage came in. 'Nick says there's bread by the toaster, if you want it, butter in the fridge.'

'Thanks.' There was an uncomfortable silence, so Sage headed for the kitchen. Eight forty-five. *Loads of time.* She switched her phone on. There was a text from Marcus, asking where she was. She didn't have the patience to soften the blow and typed: *We split up, remember?*

After being greeted by an enthusiastic headmaster, Sage and Steph were shown to a classroom and introduced to Mrs Hodgkins, Chloe's class teacher. After a welcome from the children, Sage stood at the front, feeling as if she was glowing with nerves.

'I'm an archaeologist,' she began. 'Does anyone know what an archaeologist does?'

It appeared most of the kids had a good idea, so she ran through an introduction to the Tudors and started handing out the more robust finds from the well. The children oohed and aahed very satisfyingly over the pottery, especially the pieces of the Bellarmine jug with its little face, reconstructed by Steph. The student showed them pictures of the excavation, from lifting the turf, to the dark hole that was left after the infill had been dug out. She also had pictures of the reconstructed pieces of the alembic Elliott had slaved over.

It was when Sage asked for questions it all started to come unstuck.

'Miss, Miss!' She smiled at one spiky-haired little boy, who was in danger of dislocating his shoulder. 'Miss, my gran says you found a dead baby down the well. Is that true?'

'Ah.' Sage caught the teacher's eye, as she shook her

head. 'We did find a lot of bones. We think some are even cat bones.' Over a chorus of sentimental reaction, she added, 'We are going to look at them more closely in the laboratory. We will then be able to tell the difference between animal and human bones. But they must have died hundreds of years ago, long before you were born.'

Another child called out, 'My dad says there's a baby and his mum stuck down the well that was put there under loads of rubbish. My Uncle Harry helped dig it up.'

'Really?' *Bloody Harry.* 'I'm afraid we won't have all our results for a little while. But Reverend Haydon says we can put a report in the parish magazine, so we can let you know.' Sage glanced at Chloe, who was looking pale. 'This all happened far back in history. Everyone from that time has been dead for hundreds of years. So even if someone did die then, which would be sad for their families, it wouldn't be so sad for us now.'

'I still wouldn't want dead bodies and skulls and stuff in my garden.' The first boy looked over at Chloe, and the teacher intervened.

'Thank you so much, Dr Westfield. I'm sure we will all look forward to seeing that report. So, can we give all the specimens back to our visitors, and show them how much we appreciate their visit?'

Over the round of applause, Sage and Steph repacked the specimens, and the teacher set the class a new activity.

Before they got to the door, Mrs Hodgkins stopped

them, Chloe at her side. 'Dr Westfield, Chloe wanted a word. Is that OK?'

'Of course.' Handing Steph the van keys, Sage looked down at the child. 'What did you want to know?'

'You didn't tell me about the dead people.'

'I'm sorry, Chloe, but we really couldn't be sure what had happened at first.' The child hunched up one shoulder, looking down at her shoes. Sage dropped to one knee, so she could look up into her face. 'If I tell you everything, will that make you feel better?'

'I'm not a baby.'

'I know.'

Chloe lifted her gaze to Sage's. 'Nobody is telling me about my daddy, and my mummy is acting really funny. People are lying to me all the time, even my nana. I know Daddy is really ill, he keeps going away to the hospice.'

'I'm really sorry, Chloe.'

'Mummy says I might have to go and live with Nana for a while. But I won't go.' Expressions raced over her features like clouds across the sky. 'I want to be here when you have your baby.'

Sage didn't know what to say. She couldn't imagine having a parent die, even now. 'I'm sorry it's so tough for you at the moment. All I can tell you about is the dig, OK?' She stood up and led Chloe out of the classroom into the corridor, where they sat side by side on two child-sized chairs outside the head's office.

'Tell me about the baby in the well,' Chloe said. 'Is it a real baby?'

'It was a very long time ago.' Sage thought carefully about her wording. 'Yes, it was a real baby. But now there's just a few bones, like in the graveyard by the church. We've taken all the bones away now, there aren't any left in your garden.'

'Oh, good.' Chloe swung her feet, squeaking the edge of her soles on the shiny tiles. 'I get scared sometimes. There's a ghost in my cupboard.'

'Ghost?' Sage was startled.

'The ghost that whispers to me at night.'

Sage sat back; the matter-of-fact delivery was spookier than the suggestion of a ghost. 'How does this ghost talk to you, Chloe?'

'It just does.' Chloe stared up at Sage.

'What does it sound like?'

The child pressed her chin onto her chest. 'Like a scary man.'

24

9th September 1580

Candles for the seamstress ———— *one shilling and five pence*

Accounts of Banstock Manor, 1576–1582

I can find no pretext for speaking to Isabeau privately for several days. She seems tired, and my lord's chamberlain reports that she has asked for extra candles to work late. Finally, I manage to catch her one morning as she steps into the garden.

'Mistress Isabeau.'

She does not turn, but stands frozen, as if she knows what is to follow. Her hair fills her fine caul, which covers it almost completely. Her long neck curves forward, and I know a wish to spare her pain.

She turns, her face paler than usual, her hands trembling until she clasps one with the other. 'Master Vincent.' Her lips tremble, her eyes filled with tears.

I am loath to distress her but I have to consider the reputation of the manor and its daughter. 'I must ask you—'

'I am with child. I cannot conceal it indefinitely, so I must confess.'

I am shocked and saddened. She looks down, closes her eyes, then looks at me. 'And this is not your husband's child?'

'No. Do with me as you will.' She stands tall, and lifts her face up, like a great lady. 'When my husband finds me, he will surely kill me.'

'I must know, who is the father?'

She shakes her head, and smiles a little. 'It is my sin, and my burden to carry. I will finish my work and then I must leave.' There is such dignity in her bearing, as if she were not just a servant caught by lust, but some imprisoned princess.

'Madam.' I take a deep breath. 'The father must bear some responsibility, and help you. You will find it difficult to support yourself with a bastard child.'

'He is… I cannot ask him.'

'He is married, perhaps?' I look over the roses, seeing the last heads are blown to rags by the late winds. 'My mother, too, found herself in your position, though widowed.'

She looks at me with calm conviction. 'I shall not tell him, and soon I will be gone.'

I shake my head and step closer. 'Mistress Isabeau, let

me be your go-between. I shall negotiate on your behalf and mayhap get you a pension for the child.'

Her smile fades. 'I cannot, Master Vincent.' She shakes her head, but slowly, as if she is not convinced herself. I think again of Master Seabourne, who was here when the family was away.

'Then let me guess. The man you lay with was then betrothed, and is again.'

Her hands tremble, and she covers her mouth with a hand for a moment, as if to prevent a cry. 'Master Vincent,' she says, 'he is betrothed to Lady Viola, and I would not hurt her.'

Nor I, I think, but it is hard to know how to keep it a secret. 'I shall speak with Master Seabourne and he shall devise a safe place for you and the child. Far away, where you will never meet again.'

This brings tears to her eyes, already bright. I am not a hard man, and the woman is love-bitten. But a man must be firm in such cases and this isn't the first servant I have arranged to have taken care of. Why, even my Lord Banstock supports a few bastards in a quiet way.

'Better I were dead,' she says, in a low voice.

'To think so is a mortal sin, and with a babe, murder besides!' I allow my anger to show, and she covers her face with her hands and weeps in distress. 'Come, Mistress,' I say, but gently. 'Sit upon the bench and have your tears before we are observed.'

She curbs them in a few painful sobs. I wait, the scent of bruised rose petals and drying lavender filling the late summer day. 'I would not upset Viola,' she whispers.

'Too late to consider Viola's feelings,' I say, perhaps more harshly than I intended. 'If we are discreet, she may never know,' I add, more gently. *Besides*, I think, *the offence was against her sister, newly betrothed and now dead.*

I look at the seamstress, but her wide skirts conceal any evidence. I think back to Elizabeth's betrothal. The woman must be more than six months with child, but her tall slenderness and her heavy clothes do not yet display her shame.

Vincent Garland, Steward to Lord Banstock, His Memoir

25

Monday 8th April

Sage walked into the back garden of Bramble Cottage, already nervous. She hadn't been able to put Chloe's description of a 'scary man voice' out of her mind over the weekend. Clearly the family weren't coping very well with James's illness and the excavation was making it worse.

Elliott met her at the well, which he had already uncovered. 'I've got to talk to you.' He was fidgeting with one foot, tracing circles in the mud. He looked away, took a deep breath.

'OK.' She was wary; he looked even more awkward than usual. She handed the boxes to Steph. 'Put these in the van for me, will you? It's not locked.'

'The alembic — which it is, by the way — was an incredibly expensive piece of scientific equipment, possibly made in Bohemia,' he said. 'I've got some emails out to museums.'

Sage nodded, her gaze drawn to the blackness in the well. 'Great.'

'I sent a sample of the glass over to a friend who's doing a PhD in analytical chemistry, and they found out what was in the bottom of it.' He dug some sheets of paper from his jeans pocket. 'Look.'

Sage unfolded them carefully, allowing Elliott his moment of drama. It had taken a while to take to the shy young man, but he was growing on her. It was good to see some passion for his subject.

'Lead, gold, mercury – there's a lot of mercury,' she read. 'Professor Guichard said Seabourne was trying to make gold from mercury, maybe he succeeded,' she joked.

Elliott shifted from one foot to the other. 'Look at page two.'

Steph joined them. 'What are you so excited about?'

'Uranium?' Sage stepped away from the well involuntarily. 'There's uranium down the well? How much? Is it dangerous?'

Elliott waved away her concerns. 'No, hardly any, microscopic amounts. There's a tiny amount fused into the glass.' He grinned at them. 'It may be evidence of what they were doing. Actual proof of the experiments alchemists carried out.'

'Uranium's dangerous stuff. How *much* is on the glass?'

'Barely enough to trigger their alarm,' Elliott said nonchalantly.

'What?' Sage gave him the results and held out her hand. 'I want the phone number of the lab, now. And you are to leave the glassware alone until I am certain it's safe.'

Elliott scowled at her, but pulled out his mobile. 'Seriously, it is safe, it was a minute amount.' He read out the number and Sage entered it into her phone.

She made the call. 'Hi, I need to speak to someone in charge?' She watched Steph read the results over Elliott's shoulder and waved at them. 'Hey, you two, put the barricade round the well and cover it up – oh, hello. This is Dr Sage Westfield, county archaeologist. I understand one of my students found some uranium?'

The head of the chemistry department remembered Elliott's sample, which had caused a 'minor evacuation' of the lab but not the building. All Sage could do was apologise, but the chemist was amused rather than annoyed, and was able to reassure her. The amount of actual radioactive material was minimal. He was surprised to see uranium, but even more so the amount of thorium. He promised to look into the anomaly when he had time and run further tests.

She thanked him and hung up before turning to the waiting students. 'All right, you can carry on with the spoil. We need to hurry up the process; we probably have all the intact bones.'

Steph stepped a little toward the edge of the well carrying a plastic hazard barrier, and bent to look down into the depths. 'It sort of draws you in, doesn't it? Like standing at the top of a cliff, it makes you lean towards it.'

'Don't fall in, for God's sake.' Sage glanced at the house, seeing a shadowy movement inside. 'We'll replace the deposits once we've looked at what we can in the time. We'll just take the sieved-out materials and the pottery. I'd like another few weeks but I'd have to clear it with the Bassetts, and I don't think they would agree to any more than a fortnight.'

Steph chewed her lower lip. 'I have exams coming up. I can't promise I can keep coming over.'

'Fair enough. Elliott?'

He cleared his throat. 'I'd love to keep helping – and I do live on the Island, so it's easier for me – but I do have part one of my dissertation to get in by the end of June. I'll still help when I can; you know you can rely on me.'

'Thank you. I'll see if I can round up a few volunteers from the community, or second-year students.'

Elliott shuffled his feet, studying his trainers. 'The alembic side fascinates me. I was thinking about refocusing the topic for my PhD. The experiments and practices of alchemy are really interesting.'

Sage thought for a moment, trying to remember who was supervising his PhD. 'How about I try and negotiate you a small extension with Dr Borrow and you can do one more week here? We could brainstorm the findings, see if it's a viable change.'

'That would be great.' He smiled, locking eyes with

Sage. 'Maybe we could brainstorm over a pizza, and then I could do some basic training for your volunteers.'

Sage wondered if she had time to fit it in. He had worked hard; the least she could do was buy him a pizza and help him modify his research proposal. 'Sounds good. You might even be able to look into funding; I think alchemy is a fascinating subject. It reveals so much of the Elizabethan ideas about the world.' She smiled at the crestfallen Steph. 'And I'll give you lab time with the artefacts, after your exams, and I'll make sure both your names are on the report. This is going to make a terrific paper.'

Steph smiled, then tilted her head towards the house. 'Mrs Bassett is waving to you.'

Sage turned and attempted a smile. 'Cover me, I'm going in.' She was only half joking.

Judith was, if anything, even thinner. 'James wants to speak to you.' Her hostility crept through the twitch of a smile, and she turned away the moment she had shown Sage into the living room.

James was dressed in a bright jumper that made him look paper-white.

'Sage.' He smiled warmly. 'I was wondering if I could get an update on your investigation, if you have time.' He waved at the sofa. 'Ju's put the kettle on. Is tea all right?'

As the tea ritual worked its way to a conclusion, and

Judith brought in three mugs, Sage looked around the room. It was still cold, although there were logs crackling in rolling flames in the woodburner, and a hand extended to the radiator suggested it was on.

'It's always cold here,' James said. 'It seems to be getting colder, not warmer. I think it's the chimney. How did the school talk go?'

Sage drew a deep breath. 'I'm afraid I have to apologise to you. One of the people who dug out the well for us has told people in the village about the bones. Chloe was a bit upset. I'm surprised she didn't mention it.'

Judith lifted her hand to her mouth but didn't say anything.

James shrugged, his smile slipping. 'We guessed something was up, but she didn't tell us. It had to happen eventually. We can't protect children from the realities for long, can we?'

Sage took in his grey lips, and was sad for Chloe, sad for the hostile woman standing by the window blowing on her tea. 'We do think we've found out some more about Solomon Seabourne, who rented this house.'

'Seabourne? We had a thought.' James turned to Judith. 'Do you know where the deeds are, love?'

'I'll get them.'

He turned to Sage. 'When we bought the house, they came with a redundant record of the previous owners, most of them just photocopies, but they go back ages. We weren't sure they were even of this house. To be honest, we couldn't read most of them. But one stood out, you might be able to decipher it.'

Judith returned and dropped a heavy folder on the coffee table. 'I'm going down to the school to pick up Chloe.'

Sage spread the documents out. Most were Victorian or Georgian, selling off parcels of land. One was bigger and older, a faint copy of an agreement. James got up with difficulty, walked across the room leaning on a stick, and sank onto the sofa beside her.

'That's the one,' he said. 'Doesn't that say Seabourne?'

Sage read slowly. *"Indenture made on the last day of July, in the seconde and twentieth yeare of the reign of our soveryne lady Queene Elizabeth, between Sir Solomon Seabourne of the county of Sussex, and Lord Anthonie Banstock, Baron of said manoir. Being the lease of the Well House, one garden, one orchard, six acres of good pasture in nine fields, let to Richard Arnesley of Newport, and fourteen acres of woods."* He paid thirty pounds per annum, a reasonable rent, I think.' She counted the years in her head. 'The twenty-second year of Elizabeth's reign makes it 1580.'

'It doesn't seem much.'

'I think that was probably a good price for land as well, especially with a tenant for the fields paying an income. And he was the fiancé.'

'So this Solomon was really here, then. When the well was filled in?'

Sage thought through the information she had. 'It's too soon to be sure, but there's evidence that Seabourne could have been here around the time the well was filled in. Seabourne was what they called a "natural scientist", a mixture of a philosopher, chemist and occultist, who was trying to understand the nature of the universe. We found some glass, which Elliott thinks is an alembic, laboratory glass. It was deep in the well, around the bones.'

'Occultist?' James's tone was flat. 'I just thought we were haunted.'

'What makes you say that? I mean, Judith mentioned something before.'

His long hands stretched over the bones of his knees, outlined under the baggy cotton. 'The wailing, mostly. It started the day we moved in. The dog went crazy; he ran out into the road and was hit by a van, Ju probably told you.'

Sage shivered, the air running down the nape of her neck. 'Maeve, who used to live here, said she heard something too.' She fastened the top button of her plaid shirt over a thermal T-shirt. 'Would it be a good idea to move out for a few days, get a break? We can finish up here and restore the garden a bit before you come back.'

He smiled, a sad twist of one side of his mouth. 'I've suggested it, but Chloe's just settling in at school. I don't want to believe in ghosts but Judith is right, there is something odd about this place. I've heard more than just the howling. A couple of times I've heard noises downstairs, at night.' He shut his eyes for a moment, then turned his head and looked straight at her. 'I'm leaving Judith here to care for my child, you understand? I want to be sure they are both – safe.'

'I understand.'

He stood and limped to the fireplace. On the mantelpiece was a wooden box, which he opened, and took out a small spherical wireless camera. 'I set this up, though I don't know if there's anything on it. It's a nanny cam, activated by movement.'

'OK.' Sage wasn't quite sure what response James was expecting.

'Can you have a look at the footage? If there was anyone else in the house… I'm too scared to look at it.'

Sage took the camera he put into her hand. 'I'm sure it's nothing, but I'm happy to check it out.'

'Thank you.' James smiled, looking weary. 'Maybe we have a photogenic ghost and can make a fortune doing tours of the house.'

Sage grinned and placed the camera in her bag. 'I'd like to find a way to talk to the local people about the finds. We're hoping they'll be less spooked about the bones if we put them in historical context.'

'I'd like to come to that,' James said, eyelids drooping. 'Give me plenty of warning, though.'

'Of course. Thank you.'

He was already asleep.

Sage gathered up her bag and jacket and crept towards the front door. The sound of the door creaking on its hinges made her jump as Chloe bounced in.

'Oh, hello, Chloe. Feeling better about the excavation?' Sage said. Judith followed the child indoors.

'My friends want to see the haunted well.' She took off her coat and stood on tiptoes to hang it up. 'Where the dead baby was.'

'I promise it's not haunted. And it's really not safe—' Sage met Judith's eyes. 'Perhaps we could organise something? But you mustn't go into the garden without a grown-up until the well is filled in.'

'I won't.' Chloe reached out with one hand, brushing Sage's pregnant belly, which made her flinch and smile to cover her discomfort. 'You wouldn't put your baby in a well, would you?'

'No, of course not.'

'And no one would steal it, would they?' Chloe's mouth started to tremble.

Sage crouched down to look Chloe in the eye. 'No one's going to do anything bad to my baby. That was all in the past, OK?'

Judith was holding the door open. 'Thank you, Dr Westfield.' The syllables clinked in the air, like ice cubes knocking together in an empty glass.

26

10th September 1580

In settlement of bill presented by Michael Stratton, the baker ———————— *twenty shillings*

Accounts of Banstock Manor, 1576–1582

I sleep well, confident we can keep the news from Viola, and the Frenchwoman can be got away. The morning brings disappointment and Mistress Agness is before me with the news that a washerwoman in the laundry has noticed the seamstress's shift has been eased to allow for her increasing girth. This is relayed to the men servants of the hall and kitchens, who tell the stable men. Overnight the whole estate and probably most of the village know that Isabeau has been a harlot with someone and is fat with child. If *I* guessed it must be Seabourne – for who else has the freedom and the access to Banstock's seamstress – then so will they.

Viola is to visit an outlying farm where one of the lads was injured by a falling wall. I step into the stableyard to see her off. I am distracted by a concern about one of the farm horse's hocks, when I hear a screeching from the yard.

The woman Agness Waldren has stopped Viola before she has mounted her palfrey. She is haranguing the girl, her red face lowered to Viola's, who, though she looks afeared, stands her ground.

'I shall listen to neither rumour nor lies,' she says calmly, moving around the angry woman to step onto the mounting block.

''Tis proven truth,' hisses the woman, her face twisted with a kind of righteous hatred. 'The papist has seduced Master Seabourne by her wiles, and carries his bastard.'

Viola falters, then pushes herself onto Coral's broad saddle, hooking her knee over the pommel. 'I am sure it is no business of yours, Mistress Waldren.' Her voice is flat and polite, where she could have just commanded Agness be silent. 'I am to visit one of my father's tenants, which is my duty. You should attend to yours.'

She kicks her pony, which breaks into a trot, and rides off through the gate. Viola's groom follows, the fellow leaning back to listen to Agness Waldren's outburst. Much of her ramble is muddled, and for a moment I wonder if she is cup-shotten rather than mad. But it seems the woman is incoherent with rage, and her screeches of hysteria build.

I turn to one of the hall men and bid him fetch me a vessel

of clean water. When he returns with it, Mistress Waldren is red-faced and shouting hoarsely at me about the French whore and her sluttish ways. I step forward and empty the ewer over her, stopping the screaming in a second.

While she fights for breath, I speak sternly. 'You will return to the rectory or I will have you taken there. Have you lost all sense of your place and duty?'

Finally she manages to speak. 'I have not. I see sin and condemn it, as you should. You will let your Viola sleep under the same roof as her betrothed husband's mistress?'

'That is none of your business,' I say, 'nor should you talk about your betters. Return to your duties as a good sister, subject to your brother's governance, and stay away from the manor.' I frown at her. 'Do you understand me?'

'I understand well,' she replies. 'I know that the French witch enchanted Master Seabourne, and that the whore uses her wiles to enchant you also. Those who consort with witches will be condemned with them,' she spits at me.

I am perturbed, for I know how such accusations grow. 'There is no witchcraft in Banstock.' I turn to the grooms listening with interest to our exchange. 'Escort Mistress Waldren to her brother's house. I will send a letter this morning, charging him with control over you, Mistress. I can only hope that reflection and prayer will make you retract your foolish accusations.' But I am uneasy, for once uttered, the word 'witch' cannot be easily retrieved.

Vincent Garland, Steward to Lord Banstock, His Memoir

27

Tuesday 9th April

The morning had started sunny, and Sage decided to let the students get on with work at the site while she spent a morning at her office in Newport. Elliott had offered to help but she wanted him to have as much time at the excavation as possible.

Her room in the adapted Victorian building that housed the county archaeologist's office was lined with bookcases full of folders, maps and blueprints. Paperwork had reached avalanche proportions, and she spent a couple of hours opening letters, returning phone calls and answering emails. She was fairly sure the weekly newspaper would lead with 'Dead Baby Found Down Well', since she had three phone messages from the feature editor on the office line, and one from the local TV station.

There were more planning issues; one application for a home extension was overconfident given that the previous owner had brought in a carrier bag of Roman tesserae from his rose bed. The chance that the bungalow was at least partly built over a Roman building was high, so Sage drafted a response and included an offer to quote for a proper archaeological survey. She granted a couple of reasonable extensions, then took a few minutes to look through a late assignment. Teaching one module a semester at South Solent University had sounded like a good idea until she tried to timetable it in. Even getting on and off the Island added hours of travel time she didn't have, and now she had to fit the dig in as well.

Her phone beeped. Nick had sent her a text thanking her for her support the other night, and to suggest they met up one evening to talk about the situation. It didn't sound like a date, but she could feel a flutter in her chest. She was finding herself looking out for his dark hair when she walked or drove around the village, jumping when the phone rang in case it was him. She texted back a businesslike reply, agreeing to meet and suggesting he decide when and where.

Next she dialled the number for Banstock Manor, and recognised the cultured voice of Lady George immediately. After an exchange of how-are-yous, she asked if the Banstocks could host an information session for the village. She found herself apologising. 'I'm afraid we wouldn't be able to pay you anything. I don't have a budget for that.'

Lady George brushed her apology away. 'Oh, don't

worry, Sage. It would give the manor a terrific boost at the beginning of the season. Of course, we wouldn't charge for the meeting itself. But if you use the great hall, we could then offer the visitors a tour around the house and grounds for our usual fee.' She sounded enthusiastic.

Sage sighed appreciatively. Perfect. The manor was within reasonably easy reach for the villagers, had loads of parking and would cost the county archaeology department nothing. Her university department's research budget for the rest of the financial year would be tight after digging out the well. 'I can answer any questions the local people have, and reassure them that it's a historical burial.'

'You know, the Banstock Historical Society and the East Wight Genealogical Society may have information for you. About Viola and Isabeau, I mean.'

'Well, that would be helpful.' Sage felt overwhelmed by Lady George's enthusiasm.

'And my ladies will do tea and cakes. How's that?'

'I don't have a budget for that either, I'm afraid.'

Lady George laughed. 'Oh, it will be their pleasure, I'm sure. You only have to ask one to make a cake and they all join in. Having a group of volunteers is all strategy and politics – they can get very competitive. We'll cover the cost of ingredients and we can open the coffee shop, offer tea for free and charge for the cakes.'

'That would be great.' Sage hesitated for a second before broaching the next subject. 'I've been in contact with a leading forensic anthropologist, Dr Yousuf Sayeed. He *has* advised that I apply to activate an existing exhumation order for the gravestone in the woods.'

There was a moment of silence. 'Oh. Well, I suppose that would confirm whether someone is actually buried there. It has a nasty sound, "exhumation", but it might be good for us.' She paused again. 'Look, I'm sure it would be fine, but it would be… private, wouldn't it? I would hate crowds of people turning up to gawp. Just in case there's a body.'

'It would all be very respectful.'

'Then you can count on us to co-operate. You won't mention it at the meeting, though, will you?'

Sage smiled to herself. 'We won't need to. We might not get permission, anyway. I have a dozen forms to submit first.'

'For this meeting, how would Sunday do? We could open the manor early, we're nearly ready. Say, two in the afternoon?'

'You can get ready that quickly?'

'Easily. We're set up for school parties out of season anyway. And we can get the local paper involved. I'm sure a lot of history buffs will want to be there.'

Sage felt dizzy. *I'm tired, I should take it easy.* 'Of course. That's very kind of you.'

She put the phone down and took a deep breath, closing her eyes until the light-headedness wore off. The idea of inviting Nick to the meeting crept into her brain. It gave her an excuse to call him.

'Hello, vicarage.' The voice sounded like a young woman, maybe the one she had seen on Friday morning.

'Is the vicar there, please? This is Sage Westfield, the archaeologist.'

'He's rather busy at the moment. What's it about?'

Sage was amused by the defensive tone. 'It's business. Please tell him I'm calling about the irregular burial.'

There was some muffled speech before Nick came on the line.

'Hi there.' His voice was warm and sounded like there was a smile in it. 'What can I do for you?'

'Two things. First, I wondered if you were free on Sunday afternoon.'

'I'll probably be free after one. What did you have in mind?'

'I'm going to speak to the locals about the excavation. I wondered if you would be able to present the information we have from the church records and reassure people the bones are being treated with respect.' She waited for a response, and when she didn't get one, she added: 'Two o'clock, at Banstock Manor.'

'I'll be there.' He sounded like he was moving to another room, and then she heard him shut the door. 'What was the second thing?'

'I was wondering when you wanted to have dinner.'

'One evening this week? It would be nice to meet away from Banstock, and we could sort out some things about the burial.'

The room suddenly seemed warmer. 'That would be lovely.' She could hear him breathing but he didn't speak. 'Nick? How are you getting on with the phone calls?'

'It's strange, it's better now you've heard them too. I don't feel like I'm exaggerating it now. They've slowed down, too.'

'I saw Judith and James yesterday.' She paused, not wanting to sound even more paranoid than she already felt. 'James gave me a nanny cam he set up in the living room; he thinks there might be something on it.' She pulled the camera out of her bag, turned it over in her hands, looking for the hard drive. She'd forgotten about it, but talking to Nick had reminded her.

'Nanny cam?'

'One of those hidden cameras you keep an eye on children with.' There was a tiny hatch on one side. 'James said he's heard noises at night, like someone moving around, so he put it on the mantelpiece.'

Nick's voice sounded deeper than usual. 'Maybe you should tell the police, they might be interested. In the meantime I'll spread the news about the meeting on Sunday. The church team will probably have everyone from the village there.'

'Could we get Maeve to come, do you think?' Sage said. 'She seemed so interested.'

'I'll do my best. She's always said the house was haunted.'

Sage fell silent, thinking of the ghost of the woman still haunting him. 'I'll see you on Sunday, at the manor.'

She put the phone down, then examined the camera — there, a groove that, on a bit of pressure from a fingernail, flipped up to reveal a small memory card. She plugged it into an adaptor and waited for the computer to find it, then opened the video file.

There was grainy black and white footage of Judith, half in frame, doing some ironing. Pressing the forward button brought stills every few seconds, making a jerky animation out of the chore. Chloe came in, bounced on the sofa, Judith turned... It was such an invasion of their privacy that Sage fast-forwarded. Skipping through the evening in blocks of images, the recorder was only activated by movement so many hours were unaccounted for.

The figure of a man came as a shock. A dark shadow, filling the whole screen as it walked past the camera, the time stamp 00:06. The next footage was at 00:26, a hooded shape distorting as it moved, as if there was a dark cloud around the man, like smoke. The figure paused in front of the camera, dense darkness coalescing into the shape of a nose and a mouth, but no more. There was definitely someone in the house.

28

11th September 1580

Money to almshouses •————————— *fifteen shillings*

Accounts of Banstock Manor, 1576–1582

I could not keep my concerns from my brother, Lord Anthonie. His anger at hearing of Seabourne's behaviour is great. He is the first to declare that Viola should be free of him, and the betrothal shall be broken.

I remind him of the advantages of the match, and that Viola herself wishes the marriage, but his concerns for Viola are more than simply the sin of adultery, which commandment he has many times broken. They are compounded by unease at the association with sorcery in the man's study of science. He summons Viola, who is almost ready for her bed, her hair already braided, her feet in felt slippers.

'My father?' she asks, sleepy-eyed.

He looks at me, as if I can say the heavy words in such a way that they will not wound our dear child. I am unable to find them, faced with her inquiring look.

He blunders on. 'I am of a mind to break this betrothal to Seabourne,' he says, and Viola stares at me.

'How can this be?' she asks.

Her father raises his voice. ''Twas I who made this betrothal, and having come to know the man Seabourne, it is for me to break it.'

Viola stands her ground, and addresses us both. 'I took my betrothal vows in good faith, and will not break them. We are already man and wife in the eyes of God.'

Her father looks at me, his face becoming redder.

'It is for a good child,' I say, 'to obey her father.'

'When I took the vows of betrothal I left childhood and became a woman, Master Vincent,' she says, though her voice is trembling and she moves a step closer to me. 'I have plighted my troth to Master Seabourne and I wish to be his wife.'

For a few moments, my brother breathes like a bull, huffing, the words choked from him.

I turn to her and hold out my hand. After a moment, she places her cold fingers in mine. 'My dear Viola, who will always be a child to me.' I smile at her uncertainty. 'There are things about Seabourne... things he has done.'

'I do not wish to know them.' Her voice is very decided,

and she pulls her hand from my grasp. 'When I cross his threshold as a bride we are reborn, and our past is past.'

'But he has lied to all of us, behaved badly,' her father rages, 'and is a sorcerer to boot. What kind of father would I be—'

She interrupts him with a quiet voice I find more convincing. 'He has not lied to me.'

As her father gapes I ask her, 'He has told you about Isabeau Duchamp?'

'He fell in love with her in the spring, when he came here for the betrothal to Elizabeth. His family coerced him into marriage with my sister, for the connections we have with the Earl of Leicester and Lord Burghley.' Her little slippers are tight together on the cold stone, and her hands are clasped together at her breast. 'He told me all. How they had met, discussed marriage which was impossible, and how they had lain together in sin in the old abbey.'

I shake my head at her, amazed that she had kept so much from her father and uncle.

She turns to me. 'He is truly repentant. He says he will be a good and loving husband, and that the time with Isabeau is past.'

'But the time cannot be past,' her father says, in his gruffest voice. 'She admits she bears his child. You have heard the story from his own lips.'

The light outside has almost gone, the light from the candles flickering over her face in the draught from the empty fireplace. Swallows have been replaced by bats that cross the windows in the pink and purple sky. Viola stares at me for a long moment, her face first hurt, then defiant.

'Then she bears his child. You of all people, Uncle, must see that the child is well cared for.'

It stings that she touches on my illegitimacy, a wound my whole life. Viola is frozen in an attitude of boldness that I feel a night of reflection might soften.

'Perhaps you should go to bed and allow your elders to consider the case. My Lord Anthonie?'

'Yes, yes, go to bed. And tomorrow your uncle and I, *we*, mark you, will decide your future.'

She opens her mouth but then catches my eye, and closes her lips tight.

I reach for her hand again, and after a moment, she takes it. I kiss her on her cheek, feeling her tremble like a bird. A brave sparrow to stand between two hawks.

'God bless your sleep, and bring you wisdom, child,' I murmur, and she smiles though her eyes are wet with tears.

She kisses me back, but does not answer, as she always does: *what do I need of wisdom when I have you?*

Vincent Garland, Steward to Lord Banstock, His Memoir

29

Wednesday 10th April

Wednesday was grey, mizzle drifting over the esplanade to Sage's flat. She looked out at the sea while cleaning her teeth, watching the gulls try and balance on the streetlights opposite her window. The hovercraft from the mainland, though noisy, was obscured by mist and the pier extended into the fog as if going nowhere. Portsmouth was lost in the drizzle and rain.

Sage's to-do list included an antenatal appointment at the hospital and arranging for an osteoarchaeologist to look at the skulls. The shape and weight of the adult skull confused her. Even on the scanned images, it seemed to jut out of the screen; heavy teeth in a prominent lower jaw looked as if they were about to shout something. They had estimated the woman as around five-nine, very tall for a woman in the era. Sage didn't like looking at the baby's skull, with its huge eyes and tiny, slashed jawbone. Infants always looked like tiny aliens anyway, there was nothing to say what he or she would have looked like. She rubbed her belly, to quiet her own somersaulting baby. Thirty weeks, so the books said he or she was nearly three pounds in weight. It felt more like ten, as it squirmed into her bladder.

She had given the nanny-cam footage to the police but there was no way to be sure the time stamps were correct, or who had been fleetingly caught by the camera. They took the memory card and gave her back the nanny cam, but she was concerned about worrying James further. The police had reassured her and as they couldn't rule out James as the person on the footage there was nothing they could do. Nothing had gone missing, nothing was disturbed. Because the family were vulnerable and had a child, they promised to check in from time to time, but couldn't offer any more help.

The parking lot at the hospital was more crowded than usual, and Sage struggled to park the van. Sitting in the antenatal clinic, she was relieved at the excuse just to stop, and she was relaxed when she went in for the ultrasound.

The normally chatty sonographer wasn't so chatty. The baby looped the loop, forcing a mouthful of stomach acid up Sage's throat, but she started to feel cold as the woman pressed a button and another woman – a doctor – came in. They turned the screen away from Sage.

'Is everything all right?' Sage asked.

The doctor smiled in the dim light, the glow from the screen making her teeth gleam. 'Don't worry.' She pointed to something, and the sonographer typed away on the keyboard.

'I wasn't. Now I'm starting to get nervous.'

The two women swapped places. The doctor turned the screen towards Sage. 'Here is your baby – perfect size, healthy heartbeat, looks just right.'

'OK.' It was hard not to get gooey about the shadowy imp on the screen, caught as it rested a hand by an ear, the hatched ribs around the heart. 'So…?'

The doctor clicked her keyboard and ground the transponder against her overloaded bladder. 'At your first appointment, we noticed your placenta was a bit low. Which is why we recommended this extra scan.'

The baby squirmed in and out of focus. 'They said it would probably come up as my womb grows.'

'Well, it did, to a degree. But it's still lower than we like.'

A wave of cold adrenaline shot through Sage, making her heart beat faster, less regularly. 'What does that mean?'

'Possibly nothing. You might deliver normally, if you go to full term. But if you experience any bleeding, at all, you must come in.' There was an authority in the doctor's voice that scared Sage more than anything.

'OK.'

The doctor clicked for a final still, and pointed out a

grey blob amongst other grey blobs. 'This is your uterine wall. This,' she indicated a line, 'is the edge of your placenta, lying low, possibly over the cervix. It's called placenta praevia.'

'I know. It's one of those complications you skip over in the books.'

The doctor smiled at her, and switched the light on, then pulled off a swathe of blue tissue from a roll on the wall and wiped some of the gel from Sage's stomach. 'It's borderline, and we're not worried just yet. But I'd like to see you again in a few weeks to see how it's going. Any bleeding, even spotting, is serious. You would need to be seen, and if the bleeding didn't resolve, I'm afraid you would be on bed rest.'

Sage stood up, and pushed her feet into her shoes. She was shaking, and the doctor touched her shoulder with a warm hand.

'It's just—' Sage could feel tears prickling behind her eyelids and thickening her voice. 'I'm being silly.'

'No, it's fine. This is your baby; you're allowed to be emotional. But unless you have a bleed, I wouldn't be too worried. Most of these cases resolve by forty weeks. We'll just keep an eye on it. We'll make you another appointment for a month's time.'

Waiting in outpatients, Sage let the noise of children, mothers and midwives wash over her. The pregnancy had been unplanned, unwanted, then just a part of everyday life.

The reality of the baby's existence was somehow brought into focus by a threat to its survival. The pathetic face of the infant in the well crept into her memory, somehow mixing with the grey shadow on the screen.

Sage phoned Elliott to say she wouldn't be back all day, and took to her sofa to watch TV and huddle under a throw with a box of sweets. After Steph left three messages, she picked up her phone to call back. Somewhere between meaning to return Steph's call and actually dialling the number, she found herself calling Marcus's mobile.

'Hello?' he answered, his voice warm. It made Sage's eyes fill up with tears. 'Hello?' He sounded puzzled. 'Sage?'

'Yes, it's me.' Her voice was, in her own ears, unrecognisably husky.

A tinge of something sharpened his voice. 'Are you OK?'

'I'm fine, I'm just—' She swallowed hard, wiped her sleeve over her eyes. 'I had a scan this morning. The baby's fine, it's just the placenta's too low, well a bit too low, they said…' She tailed off, waiting for a reaction.

'But you're OK. You're both OK.' For a moment, she wondered if his flat tone was relief or disappointment.

'Yes. I was being silly.'

His voice dropped. 'I should come over.'

'No, no. I was just worried today. I didn't think what it would be like if something didn't go right, you know?'

He sighed, and she could imagine the wry smile on his face. 'Fliss had that with Tom – no, Ivy. It worked out fine, it just grew up or something. You can always have a caesarean.'

Sage could feel irritation settle on her like dust. 'Well, if *Fliss* had to have a caesarean section, it wouldn't be such a big deal. I mean, between her husband and the nanny and the cleaner, she would probably be fine.'

'Don't be like that.' She could hear him cupping his hand around the phone, hollowing his words. 'If you needed it, I'd get you some help over the first few weeks, you know that. Or maybe your mum would stay.' There was a note in his voice she hadn't heard before.

'You should never have tried to split up with me.' There it was again, that sharp edge.

'I did split up with you, Marcus. It really is over.'

'But you call me the second you have a problem.'

She frowned at the strange tone. 'It's your baby. I just thought you would be interested.'

She could almost hear his teeth grinding. 'I'm concerned. I may not have wanted this baby but you do. And I want you to be OK.'

She ended the call with a stab of a finger and turned her phone off. She hadn't worked out how Marcus fitted in with the baby, yet. She wondered again what life as a county archaeologist would be like with a newborn, a toddler, the school run. Each encounter with the baby seemed to make it more real. She had started to notice tiny babies, even exchange smiles with new mothers who nodded at her bump as if she was part of a club that she hadn't noticed before. She took heart from the ones that looked busy, like they still worked, like they occasionally slept.

By late afternoon, she was reviewing the measurements from the face of the adult skull in the well. The arched palate and projecting teeth, heavy features and powerful jaw made for a plain woman. Her phone rang.

'Hi. It's Nick. The vicar.'

She smiled, stretched her aching back. 'Hello, Nick the vicar.'

His voice had a soft rumble in it she was starting to like. 'You weren't at the dig today. Your male student said you were taking the day off sick.'

'Oh, that.' She stood up and went to the window, staring out at the rain-swept esplanade, cars splashing through a huge puddle by the roundabout, by the dark green sea. 'I'm not sick, I just—'

'Just what?' His voice was soft, concerned. 'Is it the baby?'

'The baby's fine. I just had a scan that suggested I have to be careful, that's all.'

'What's wrong? You can tell me, I've got three older sisters.'

She sighed. 'It's fine, really. The placenta's a bit low. It will probably be all right, but I may need a caesarean.' The tickling under her eyelids started again and she sniffed them away. 'I've been catching up with paperwork instead of fretting about it.'

There was a long silence at the end of the phone. 'I was wondering if you would like to go out for some food tonight.'

Her stomach rumbled at the thought. 'Actually, I've just realised I haven't eaten since breakfast.'

'A friend of mine runs an Italian restaurant in Ryde. Francesco's, do you know it? It's on the Esplanade. I promised him I would stop by at some point and try his sea bass special. I could pick you up.'

'I know it well, it's just around the corner from my flat. I'll meet you there.' The restaurant was so close she could smell the food in the summer, when windows and doors were left open. 'It's one of my favourites. When can you get away?'

'How about six-thirty? I'm between committee meetings and visits at the moment.'

She agreed, and rang off. She pulled her sweatshirt out from her chest to examine it. It was dotted with smudges of melted chocolate, and a splash of tea from trying to drink lying on the sofa. Her T-shirt still had a smear of ultrasound gel on its hem. Time for a shower and a change of clothes.

* * *

Francesco's was half empty but filling up as Sage and Nick made awkward small talk over their menus. The place, formerly two shops, was decorated in earth tones, and copper pans gleamed on the walls.

'What would you like to drink?' Nick nodded at her bump. 'I suppose you don't want a bottle of wine, and I'm driving back to Banstock.'

'Water's fine. Still, though.' Sparkling water gave her heartburn. In fact everything was starting to give her heartburn, and the menu was full of rich dishes. She sighed, and ran her hand over her stomach.

When she looked up, Nick was watching her, smiling. 'So, how are your investigations going?'

She had another look at the menu. 'One of my friends uses software that can estimate how someone used to look. I'm hoping to get a facial reconstruction done of the woman – if it is a woman.'

'You're still not sure?'

'The pelvis says she's more likely to be female, but it's ambiguous. She was tall, with a strong, heavily featured face. So I can only say that the evidence leans more towards female, when the pelvis ought to clinch it for us.'

'Can't you look at DNA?'

Sage grinned wryly. 'It's expensive, difficult and will take a while. I don't know if a body essentially immersed in salty mud for four hundred years would have any DNA that wasn't too degraded to test.'

Nick nodded, then waved at someone behind her. 'Francesco!'

'Nicky! Finally you come to the restaurant.' The voice stretched the vowels and lilted the words with a hint of the Mediterranean.

Nick stood, and the two men hugged before the short, heavyset restaurateur turned to Sage.

Nick waved a hand. 'This is my new friend Sage.'

'Dr Westfield, we know.' The man beamed at her. 'Ah, our Nick has good taste – wait, you not tellin' me something, Nicky?'

Sage intervened. 'Nick and I are just friends.'

Francesco turned to Nick, and then to Sage. 'OK. You tell me that story, I believe it. But she's very pretty, Nicky – maybe you need a few pointers? You know, if you're out of practice.' The Italian wore a half-sad, half-rueful smile. Clearly, he knew Nick's wife had died. Sage felt a ripple of something – jealousy? She realised how ridiculous that was: she was pregnant by a married man and had a crush on a vicar, for God's sake.

Nick sat down and worked his way through the menu with Francesco, occasionally glancing up at her. She agreed to share a starter, and chose the sea bass special. When Francesco left, she topped up her water glass.

'Are you OK?' Nick said.

'Of course. DNA might be possible if I could organise some funding and there was useable DNA in the teeth, but it's a long shot.'

He reached over the crisp tablecloth and touched her hand. 'I was really wondering if *you* are all right.'

She sighed. 'Nick, what are we doing here? Is this related to the bodies, or is it more personal?'

He withdrew his hand. 'I hoped a bit of both. I think you are—' he seemed to be struggling to find the right word '—fascinating. You're beautiful, of course, but so bright, so interesting.'

Sage held her palms in front of her, then pressed them to her bump. 'I'm in no position to have a personal relationship with anybody. Not a serious one anyway.'

'Not even the father?'

'Especially not him.' She looked down at her hands, suddenly embarrassed. 'He's a bit possessive.'

Nick took a deep breath. 'Well, let's at least enjoy the food. And we do have the well to talk about.'

The antipasti was delicious, salty and rich, and since Sage seemed to end up with most of it, satisfyingly filling. Nick kept up a flow of small talk: amusing anecdotes about the parish; his training; his three young nieces. By the time the waiter took their plates away, she felt able to tackle more taxing subjects.

'How have the phone calls been?' She nibbled on a breadstick.

'They seem to have tailed off a bit. I didn't get any last night.' His face fell. 'James took a turn for the worse yesterday. I think there are nurses going in day and night now.'

The news was a jolt. Emaciated as James Bassett was by the cancer, he had a vitality that had struck Sage.

The main course was presented to them like two works of art, to be smiled and exclaimed over by Francesco and the waiter, then explained to Nick and Sage. When they left, she concentrated on dissecting the fish. She thought of James and the sad, grey woman and her child. 'James said something odd to me.'

'Oh?' Nick was concentrating on his food.

She put her cutlery down and opened her bag. 'I checked the nanny-cam footage and it seemed to show a man in the living room. Here, I printed out a still.' She opened her bag and handed the sheet to Nick. In the low light the figure looked shocking, as if the man was made of black vapour. 'It's not James, I'm sure of it.'

'That's creepy. Have you told the police?'

'I have, but they just suggested the Bassetts change their locks. They think it could be James.'

Nick held the still up to the light. 'I don't think that's James. And who has their hood up in their own living room?'

Sage shivered. 'It's an odd house.'

'True. It is also the coldest house I've ever been in. Have

you seen the size of the fireplace? You could stand up in it and it's like being in front of an open window.'

'I wonder if we're all letting the bones in the well and the phone calls get to us.' Sage lifted her glass. 'I just keep thinking that someone must have missed her, not to mention the baby, if they accidentally fell down the well or were murdered and hidden down there. To have just disappeared like that.'

'Disappeared.' Nick put his cutlery down. 'Hang on a minute. I may know something about a missing woman: when the main road was widened twenty-odd years ago, it cut the edge of the churchyard off. They had to move a memorial to the new graveyard.'

'And?'

'There was a lot of correspondence about the importance of the monument, because it commemorated the disappearance of the rector's sister. I can't recall the details, but I have a whole folder of letters and council records about it. I didn't think of it because it's a Victorian monument, but I think it was made to replace an earlier stone.' His eyes were shadowed by long, dark lashes that distracted her momentarily. He looked up. His voice softened. 'Then you look at me like that...'

She could feel a lopsided smile creeping across her face. 'You might be onto something, that's all. This monument, do you remember the name?'

His eyes narrowed again as he tried to remember. 'The

rector's name was Matthew Waldren, he's got a plaque inside the church. The sister who went missing – Alice? No, Agness. Her name was Agness.'

30

20th September 1580

Rent for Mistress Isabeau with Eliza Dread until Christmas ——————— eight shillings and eight pence

Accounts of Banstock Manor, 1576–1582

It is my duty to substitute for my Lord Anthonie when he is away from the manor, and he travelled to London upon the dawn. The rector asks me to discuss something with him, and I sigh, thinking his sister is yet again calling for the hounding of Mistress Isabeau. The apothecary and the midwife had both advised the Frenchwoman not to travel, and she has sought refuge with an old bawd called Eliza Dread in the town of Ryde. It is a fine day, so I decide to take my lord's mare and ride through the farms. I carry the books Lord Anthonie has borrowed, and a firkin of ale for the rector from the manor, as Agness seems too much preoccupied with condemning others to perform her own duties. The rectory is only a mile from the manor.

I am made welcome by the Reverend Waldren, who takes me into his study, and calls for a Rhenish wine he has just bought from town. We are halfway through the bottle when he broaches the subject of his worries.

'I have great concern about my sister. I had hoped that she would seek a husband but she feels herself too far above the local farmers. She is the granddaughter of a baronet, you know.'

I make a noise suggesting interest but the wine is more engaging.

'Our grandfather – Sir Richard of Ensley, in Kent, you know – paid for us to have the best education. She is well read in the scriptures as well as the arts of housewifery.'

I look around the room. Ensley's coat of arms, I presume, is the one that adorns the embroidered hanging behind his chair.

'Indeed, sir.' I keep my own opinion to myself, which is that of the two, the brother is the daintier. 'And she is known to be virtuous, religious and an excellent nurse to Lady Banstock. But her opinions are harsh; she raises a storm among my lady's women.'

'I hoped that she would find occupation in marriage and would cease her suspicions and megrims. She may still bear a child or two; she is in good health and not yet forty.' He looks at me. 'I hoped that someone in a good position, who has connections with a good family, might be attracted by her dowry despite her age. Perhaps she would make an excellent consort for a man of letters, like yourself.'

I almost drop my glass. 'You might better take her to the seat of your family and introduce her to gentlemen who seek a well-bred wife.'

'For some reason, she will not leave Banstock.' The rector finishes his wine in one gulp, and fills both glasses again. 'She feels her life is here. She was happy enough until this year, until the Frenchwoman came. It was like a demon of jealousy possessed her.'

'Strong words, sir.' Strange talk of demons from a man of God. 'How does this jealousy manifest?'

'I was called out three nights ago – the widow Blackthorne was dying – and I returned at dawn, much tired. I didn't call at the front door and awaken the household, but left my horse loose in his stable and slipped in through the kitchen, where my man was already lighting a fire. As I passed my sister's room, I caught sight of her, dressing. When she saw me she slammed the chest where she keeps her clothes and bade me go, in the hardest of terms.'

I am sceptical. 'Mayhap an excess of modesty. Or concern for her appearance.'

Waldren pours most of the remaining wine into his glass and sups heavily. 'Have you ever known mine sister care about appearance? Condemn a maid for doing so, more likely.'

I drink my wine slowly. 'She is disappointed in love, perhaps. She is getting beyond the age of marriage.' Yet, I think, what are her prospects? Her looks are plain, her fortune small. All she has to offer is what all women offer a husband, but I doubt any man would find bedding her consolation for her acid tongue.

'I waited until she went up to the manor.' The rector stands, his years heavy upon him, yet two decades less than I. Too much time sat at a trencher, I think. He leads me into one of the two chambers upstairs, the one inhabited by the lady. It is unlike any woman's room, save a nun, perhaps. No brushes, no trinkets, no shawls. The bed appears as hard as a table, the blanket tucked in tight around it, no hangings or rugs to lighten it. He kneels awkwardly, dropping onto fat knees, and lifts the lid of a chest. 'Then curiosity led me to look at what she hides.'

Lying on dark grey dresses is a doll, flaxen wool for hair, a white kirtle, bound loosely in a scrap of lacy binding.

'See, Master Garland? What madness makes a woman seek a child's toy?'

I feel the chill of evil before me. 'Madness, perhaps. But it could be seen as more.'

He stares up at me, his round face looking confused. 'What do you mean?'

I wonder at the resemblance to the woman Isabeau Duchamp. 'Such dolls are used in witchcraft.'

'I know my sister would never consort with any part of

the Devil's games.' He acts shocked, but I know the thought of witchcraft might have crossed his mind. And he thought such an impious, spiteful shrew a good match for me?

'You said yourself perhaps she grows a little mad. Let us take the doll and dispose of it. It may be time to seek a doctor who can consider the case. With fasting and purging she may regain her good senses.'

He picks up the doll and passes it to me. It is, in truth, much as a child might play with, but a woman in her thirties is no child. 'My mother had spells of moon madness at the end of her life,' Waldren concedes. 'Perhaps Agness imagines a baby when she has none.'

'Then there is your answer,' I say. 'Your sister needs a child, and her madness makes her create a doll to care for. I had a hound once who would take ducklings as if to suckle when she had not been mated.'

He acts reassured but neither of us can put the fear away. I leave with the doll shoved into my saddlebag, and ride back uneasy at its presence against my leg. If it were a harmless toy, well, Mistress Agness's reason is better without it. And if it is a most foul device of witchcraft? I resolve to destroy it.

Vincent Garland, Steward to Lord Banstock, His Memoir

31

Thursday 11th April

Sage was cleaning her teeth when there was a knock at the door, and she assumed it was just her neighbour when she opened it. 'Mum!'

'Mum, yes. So, give me hug.' Pressed against Yana's coat, Sage tried not to cover her in toothpaste, but her chest tightened with tears.

'I'm glad to see you,' she mumbled, through minty foam.

'You said there was problem, I came.' The answerphone message Sage had left on impulse, immediately regretted, had obviously had an impact. 'I stopped your dad coming over, but he wants a full report.'

Sage detached herself, and padded into the bathroom to spit and rinse. 'I said I was fine,' she grumbled. 'I specifically said, "Don't come over."'

'Then you weren't at home all evening,' Yana called from the front room. 'And you haven't tidied up for what, a week?'

'I've been really busy at work.' She ran another towel over her wet hair, and walked into the main room. Her mother had opened the blinds and a window.

'Is a good day, sunny,' her mother mused, squinting down the Esplanade, her accent more vivid than usual. She turned to scrutinise Sage, looking down at her belly, prominent in her pyjamas. 'You look well. Fat.'

'I am well, really. The placenta is a little low, that's all. I'm going to have another scan next month.' Sage cleared the blanket and a handful of sweet wrappers off the sofa. 'Sit down. You must have left home at dawn.' She smiled, a little lopsidedly. 'I really am pleased to see you.'

Yana draped her coat over a chair and hugged her again. 'Of course you are.'

'But I have to work today.'

Yana waved her words away. 'I have plenty to do. Maybe I'll clean up a bit here. I have some friends to see – you remember Mary Ellis? We're meeting in Newport for lunch. Can I borrow car?'

'Of course, I'm using the van. But, Mum, I'll tidy up when I get home—'

'Shush. I don't mind doing a bit of cleaning, kill time until I run into town.'

Sage knew Yana would do her own thing anyway, so went into the bedroom to get dressed. The rainy weather had given way to a cool sunshine, so she chose a few layers. When she came out, Yana was already cooking something. 'Mum, I'm in a hurry—'

'Well, my grandchild wants oatmeal porridge cooked by his *apa*, and it won't kill you, either.'

'Yes, *Sheshe*.' Sage sat at the table and Yana smiled down at her.

'So, this placenta, they say how bad?'

'Just borderline. If I go full term, it might be right out the way. I've just got to let them know if I start bleeding.' Yana put the porridge in front of her, and added the sugar pot and a spoon. 'I would have anyway.' The porridge was creamy and rich, and the first mouthful made her feel hungry for the rest.

'Well, that's OK then. You don't mind if I stay a couple of days? Catch up with friends.'

Sage was absorbed in blowing on each spoonful of porridge, then she remembered something. 'Sure. I think I might have met one of them, actually. Kate Jordan, she's a local historian in Banstock. She says she knows you.'

'Ah. Kate.' Yana's voice dropped lower. 'I remember her. Of course. This is tiny island, full of stories. Your man, he's married, yes?'

'He's my ex, Mum, but yes. He's married.'

'His wife, does she know?'

Sage considered. Marcus thought not, but it seemed impossible that Fliss wouldn't suspect. 'I don't know. They live in Fishbourne, so maybe she doesn't.'

'Years ago, I met friend at Women's Institute, when I

give talk about herbal medicine. Caroline, remember?'
Sage had been just finishing primary school, but vaguely
remembered Yana going off with her to events that didn't
interest her father.

'I remember – wasn't she one of the gardeners at
Osborne House or something?' Yana nodded, and waited.
She folded her hands in her lap as Sage frowned.

The penny dropped with a thud, right into the pit of her
stomach. 'You mean, Caroline was more than just a friend?'

Yana shrugged. 'We were lovers, yes, two years. Your
father, he was glad I found a friend who loved plants like
me, but then it turned into this big thing. Love thing. And
Kate Jordan, she found out.'

'Oh.'

'She told Caroline's husband. She was husband's sister.'

The worst thing about living on an island, everyone
knew everything, sooner or later. Gossip spread like the
flu. Sage finished the porridge. 'Oh. No wonder she was
a bit... standoffish at first.' She stood up. 'Mum, I really
have to go, I'm so late. The car keys are in the top drawer
by the door.'

'I know, I know. See you tonight.'

Sage stopped long enough to hug her again. 'I'm glad
you came. Enjoy your lunch with your friend.'

* * *

Elliott and Steph were already at work at Bramble Cottage, the spoil pile going down and the sieved sediments pile going up. Rob Greenway, who had excavated the well, had promised to return to fill it in again over the next week. The two students had an air of urgency as if they knew they wouldn't get all the spoil processed. Sage eyed the quiet Elliott and lowered her voice. 'What's wrong with him? He's very quiet.'

Steph smiled, and glanced over at him. 'Hopefully he's trying to work up the courage to ask me out.'

'Oh.' Sage studied him. Elliott had seemed so absorbed in his work she hadn't noticed any hint of him flirting with Steph. She noticed how tired he looked; even at his young age, combining studies and full-time site work was probably a bit much. She should have insisted he take more time off. But then, for the last couple of weeks her attention had been stretched thin.

She turned back to Steph. 'Look, I was going to investigate a memorial to someone who went missing around the right time as our lady in the well. Fancy a stroll?'

'I do, actually.' Steph replaced the cover of the box containing pottery fragments. 'Let me get my rucksack.'

Nick had explained that the road by the churchyard had been widened, and a few eighteenth-century headstones and a replica of a Tudor memorial had been moved to the new village cemetery. The memorial was prominent, and village fundraising had been matched by a government grant to move it to the larger site. They walked in the bright spring sunshine along roads edged with celandine and daffodil verges. The baby moved lazily, as if he or she was getting more cramped.

'You're getting big really fast.' Steph's gaze was curious.

'This is the stage where the baby grows rapidly.' Sage rubbed her side, where an elbow or knee had grazed. 'I'm getting quite used to it, now. It's going to be strange when the baby's gone.'

'But then he'll be out. Or she.' Steph crossed the road towards the cemetery. 'I really admire you. I mean, you've got a senior job in archaeology and you're having a baby by yourself.'

Sage couldn't help a laugh that sounded a bit mocking when it came out. 'I wish it was that easy. Right now I'd love a husband to take some of the strain.' She glanced at Steph. 'How did you and Elliott get on with the pottery? I didn't mean to leave you all day yesterday.'

'We got loads done. Oh, I meant to tell you. Someone was snooping around the back garden, a man in a suit. I wondered if an estate agent was looking around, hoping they would sell the cottage. I sent him packing, what a ghoul.'

'What did he look like? Good-looking, dark blond, designer stubble?'

'I suppose so. Forties, big smile, like it wasn't in the worst taste checking out the house before Mr Bassett even dies.'

The worst possible taste. Ghoul. Definitely Marcus. Sage pushed the thought away. After all, he had already seen the house – he sold it to the Bassetts.

Steph pushed open the gate to the cemetery and Sage walked in. It was a shortcut between the school and the shops, and the neat rows of graves were well tended, many of them decorated with flowers.

Maybe Marcus was looking for me. Maybe he was worried about the baby after all.

'Mrs Bassett's already thinking of selling.' Sage stopped walking halfway down the path. 'This must be the newest bit. Where's the memorial?'

Steph turned around, scanning the graveyard, then pointed to the far corner. 'Those gravestones look older. And that must be the memorial.'

They walked up to the squat obelisk, maybe six feet tall, crafted out of limestone blocks and set on a brick plinth. One face was carved with words, difficult to read. Sage squinted at them. 'It's very worn – this looks like rainwater damage. Acid rain dissolves the surface.'

Steph pulled out her phone and started snapping. Then she reached into her rucksack. 'I did come prepared. I thought I might record some of the Banstock headstone inscriptions from the 1580s, but the earliest ones in the churchyard are much later.' She laid a piece of tracing paper over the stone. 'I'll hold it, you scribble,' she said, holding out a crayon with her free hand.

'Gravestones in churchyards became more common in the 1600s. This takes me straight back to primary school,' Sage said, gently rubbing the surface, releasing the smell of the smooth wax. It worked. With a little more pressure, incised edges of the carving caught the crayon. She remembered something from brass rubbings, and peeled the wrapper off the crayon, offering the long edge to the inscription.

The words crept out of the stone onto the paper.

> *In memory of Agness Waldren, sister to the Revd. Matthew Waldren, rector of this parish.*

'Wow.' Steph held the paper up to the light. 'There's more below, shall we try that?'

Sage started rubbing the next piece of paper, bending awkwardly to vary the direction of the crayon. It took longer to decipher the smaller words, but they told a story.

> *Said Agness disappeared in her thirty-eighth year, in a great storm 13th day of November, 1580, swept away by the sea or otherwise taken to the Lord. Requiescat in pace.*

Steph carefully folded the paper. 'That could be her, the woman in the well. If she didn't end up being "swept away" like they thought.'

Sage gazed across the cemetery. Each rectangular plot

held another body – for a moment, she was overwhelmed by the scale of it all. She, her baby, the baby's grandchildren – all destined to rot away. What had taken Agness? Suicide, plague, murder, the storm?

'What do you think?' asked Steph.

'Sorry. Miles away. I don't know. It's all a bit circumstantial, and we can't narrow the date down enough to be sure.' She managed to smile. 'So, do you think Elliott is going to ask you out?'

'I don't think he will, somehow. Though I caught him taking a picture of you and me back at the cottage, so I thought he might be interested.'

Sage looked at Steph, who had a rueful expression. 'That sounds promising.'

'Except he wouldn't show me any of the pictures he took.'

Sage started walking back to the gate. 'What will you say if he does ask you out?'

'Ha. What will *you* say to the vicar?' Steph grinned.

Sage laughed in shock. 'What makes you say that? Anyway, he's only just lost his wife.'

Steph followed her down the path. 'I'm not blind.' She swung open the gate for Sage. 'He can't take his eyes off you.'

32

23rd September 1580

Physic for Lady Flora ———— *two shillings and four pence*

Accounts of Banstock Manor, 1576–1582

Lady Flora was racked with agues and tremors all night, her groans keeping us all awake. She called for the midwife and for Agness, whose piety and prayers comfort her more than the physics given to her by the wise woman. I did not call for the rector's sister at first, lest she be mad or worse. By morning, the lady was convinced she was close to death, and we dared not refuse her. Mistress Waldren arrived in good time and calmed the lady greatly, who then voided much matter and was relieved of her griping bowels.

Agness is forbidden to speak to Viola. My lady may be comforted by the gruff voice of the rector's sister but

I am not. I am fatigued, but I make the short journey to Well House to speak to Seabourne about the doll, as his knowledge of such sorceries no doubt eclipses mine.

Kelley answers the door, and bows low, showing me into the parlour. The air stinks with some foul smoke, and he forces open a window for me. ''Tis the charring of base matters,' he apologises. 'I shall fetch Master Seabourne.'

I look around the room, as cluttered with books and equipment as before. A clay pot is filled with powdered brimstone, and a glass bottle is filled with quicksilver. Other substances are confined to small jars and bowls.

'Master Vincent.' Seabourne stands before me, in a simple shirt and hose, covered with a linen apron. 'You bring bad news? Is Viola unwell?'

'I am not the man who should speak to you,' I grumble. 'It is widely known that you have got the seamstress with child. Viola's father is of a mind to dissolve the betrothal.'

'I have not denied it.' He stands before me, bareheaded, his eyes flashing. 'Lord Banstock may decide Viola's future, as her father, but I have a duty as father to Mistress Duchamp's child.'

I shut the heavy door, mindful of Kelley's ears in the hall. 'You should have thought of that before you made a whore of an honest woman, as a betrothed man, as well. You are neither of you children. Did it not occur to you that your lusts might bear fruit?'

'I fancied myself in love.'

There is something about his voice that I take note of. 'You are still smitten.' I sit upon his high chair, favouring my stiff knee. 'You would take our sweet Viola to wife while you are still besotted with the Frenchwoman?'

'Isabeau,' he says, 'will be well cared for. Viola will not be embarrassed by my foolishness, and Isabeau will be secure and able to bring up her child in prosperity.'

'We can do better.' I look to the table where a ledger lay open, I suppose relating his experiments. Many of the symbols are unfamiliar to me. 'Viola can go to her sister's lodgings at court and will attract other suitors. She will soon forget the betrothal.'

Seabourne takes a turn about the room, stamping a little, his hands clenched behind his back. 'I love Viola, in my own way.' He returns to the table, and looks down at me. 'You know the tale of Lettice Knollys and the Earl of Leicester? Even though he loved the queen, he married his other love.'

'Who is utterly banished from court and treated badly,' I say, turning a book towards me to examine a diagram. 'She is like to hardly see her husband, as the queen demands his attention. Will you not yearn to be with your mistress and child?'

Seabourne's face is racked with some sadness. 'I shall arrange it so I never need see her again.' He looks determined, now, to follow through his plans. 'She goes to my cousin's estate, to a cottage there, and will take in sewing as she pleases. I have written to my father some days since, and asked for a pension for her.'

I am secretly impressed, but try not to show it as I examine another open book. 'Very proper,' I say. 'But Viola may still be grieved if you decide to see your child.'

'I have confessed all to Viola.' There is a tone in his voice that makes me look up. 'She is remarkable,' he says, his voice shaking a little. 'I am not worthy of her.'

I agree. 'And yet you think to bring your shame to her, as a bride gift?'

He shook his head. 'I think you do not yet know Viola the woman as well as you knew her as a child.'

I stop my reading and think on his words. Perhaps he sees something I do not. 'You must give her father time to think about it, some time to forgive.'

'He shall have it.' The man bows with grace, and as low as if I were, in fact, her father. 'And you, Master Vincent, whom I know Viola loves and trusts as a father also.'

I admit to being a little flattered when I leave, but then think of the strangeness of the summer we are having, with the unborn baby, the exotic Frenchwoman and her lover the sorcerer, and the madness that seems to afflict Mistress Agness. Master Kelley is outside, holding my horse, and I remember the doll that looks so like Isabeau.

I turn back to my host, who has accompanied me. 'Master Seabourne – there is a matter I would value your opinion upon.'

He stands with his hands behind his back. 'If I can help…'

'There is a small figure made of cloth and straw that resembles Mistress Duchamp, discovered in Banstock. I fear it was made by someone who bears her ill will.'

The man looks at Kelley, who steps forward. 'We have some writings about the magical use of such,' he says, his bright eyes darting around me, as if expecting me to produce the mannequin. 'Her Majesty was portrayed by such a doll, and her astrologer Dr Dee himself was called upon to dispose of it.'

Seabourne bows to me. 'I would be happy to safely destroy such an item, but would ask who carries such malice?'

'I cannot say.' I mount the horse, feeling somewhat stiff and old this morning. 'I shall consider the matter.'

Seabourne looks up at me. 'Please keep it safe, Master Vincent. Who knows what evil it carries?'

Vincent Garland, Steward to Lord Banstock, His Memoir

33

Friday 12th April

After a day of site visits for the planning committee, Sage got to the dig late in the afternoon. The students were starting to pack up. More than a dozen cases of plastic-wrapped finds waited to go to her office in Newport, and Steph was filling in inventories for each box. She smiled at Sage in a distracted way, and went back to her lists.

Elliott was still sieving, hoping to find more glass, probably. 'I'm almost finished,' he said, not looking up. 'I think I have most of it. We've put the big cover over the well, and cordoned it off, but we can't get it filled in until next week. When it's all finished we should celebrate with that pizza.'

'Good idea, but I'll warn the Bassetts first. Are they around?'

He dropped his voice. 'I think the doctor's there now.'

'Oh. It's probably better if we pack up and go, let them have a bit of peace.' Sage inspected the heavy cover Rob

Greenway had lent them. It was a storm drain lid, so heavy it took two people to carry safely, and completely covered the well. 'I think it's too heavy even for several kids to move. Well done, you two. We've done a great job in very little time, mostly down to your hard work. Ideally, we'd work the site for months, not a couple of weeks.'

Elliott looked pleased, although he was always hard to read, and Steph grinned.

'It's been great.' Steph glanced over at Elliott but he had turned away. Perhaps he hadn't asked her out, after all.

Sage smiled back at her. 'As long as you know digs aren't usually as good as this one. Normally it's a few tons of earth, modern bricks and pipes, and a couple of scraps of pottery.' She took her phone out of her pocket. 'Let's get a picture of the two of you. It will be good for the university website.'

Steph stepped over to Elliott, who looked more uncomfortable than normal. 'Come on, Ell. Smile.'

He looked over to Sage and managed a grin for the camera.

'One more, then we better start packing up.' She waved at them. 'Huddle up, guys.'

After Sage had taken the photo, the students started shuttling backwards and forwards with the finds boxes, packing them in the van. When everything was secured, Elliott locked the van's back doors and gave the keys back to Sage.

'So we're finished,' Steph said.

'For the moment. But we have thousands of finds to examine and identify, and the whole puzzle of the bones to solve. There's plenty for you to get involved in, when you both have more time.'

Elliott nodded. 'I'll see you at the office on Monday, Sage, if that's OK. I'd like to work on reconstructing the bowl of the alembic.'

'Go ahead. Actually, I have one more cheeky request.' They both looked at her expectantly. 'I've organised a public meeting to talk about the excavation, the bones, everything. It's Sunday, two o'clock, up at the manor.'

Elliott bit his lower lip, looking down at the floor. 'I'm busy,' he said, finally. 'Sorry.'

'That's OK. It was a long shot after all the effort you've been to already.' She turned to Steph. 'There will be cakes.'

Steph laughed, and then feigned a sigh. 'OK. You've convinced me. One more ferry ticket.'

'I will even fund the ferry ticket. You can talk about the bones, if you like, I'll do the pottery. Are you off now?'

'No. Sadly, I need to document so I'm going to be sketching and taking photos for a bit longer. I'm writing up the report for my end-of-year project. Elliott's going to show me his site plan.' Steph looked at Elliott but he was staring at Sage.

'Well, that's kind of you, Ell. Ride carefully, Steph.'

Sage gave them both a wave and walked over the village green to the vicarage.

Nick was in a T-shirt and jeans, mowing the lawn in the front of the Victorian house in the fading daylight. He switched off the mower when he saw Sage and walked over. He seemed younger with grass stains on his clothes.

She was suddenly shy. 'I came over to say the dig is finished. Greenway's going to fill the well in with the remaining soil. Do you know how James is? The doctor was with him when I left.'

'He had a bad day,' said Nick. 'I think he'll be going to the hospice tomorrow for another transfusion.'

'I'm sorry. I really like him, and it must be dreadful for Judith and Chloe. Hopefully, the well will be filled in next week and that will give them some peace.' She sat on a bench on the edge of the lawn, stretching back in the sun. 'Maybe things will settle down when the well is covered up again. Buried bodies in the garden would unsettle anyone, let alone a family going through cancer.'

'I know something of the hell they're going through.' Nick wiped his forehead on his forearm. 'I wish I could do more to help.'

'I suppose there isn't much you can do,' Sage said. 'I mean, nothing's going to change the facts.'

'No. You're right. I remember——' He seemed to shake off what he was going to say, and Sage wasn't sure whether she was relieved or disappointed. 'They seem haunted by that house.' He seemed like he was only half joking. 'Maybe there *is* a curse on the place. It's creepy enough.'

'I think there's definitely a case to be made for suggestibility, given the stress James and Judith are under. But it's time for me to take all the finds back to Newport and let them go back to their lives without strangers digging up the garden.'

Nick held her gaze. 'So, you won't be in Banstock next week.' The sadness in his expression made her catch her breath.

'I'm back on Sunday for the village meeting at the manor, remember?'

'You know what I mean. Sage… I've been thinking a lot about you.' He sighed, sat next to her on the bench. 'I know this is ridiculous timing, but when the right person comes along, you have to ask, you know?' The sun glinted off his gold wedding band.

She snorted a laugh. 'You mean the timing when I'm having an illegitimate child and you're recently widowed?'

He moved a little closer, and she could smell the cut grass, and a salty tang on his skin from the work. 'Every relationship has problems.'

That made her laugh. She looked up at him, squinting into the low sun. 'Maybe we could just be friends, until the baby. See what happens.'

A smile crept across his face. 'I'd like that. I'll see you on Sunday.'

Sage walked to the van in a daze of speculation. She got her keys out of the pocket, then saw it. It was laid out on the front seat, a splash of colour. She had left the windows open a crack to dry the van out in the spring sunshine, and whatever it was must have been shoved through the narrow gap.

She fumbled the key into the lock and wrenched open the door.

It was a doll, hair cut raggedly, eyes inked black. It was the one Chloe had made into an archaeologist. But now its body had been hacked open with a dozen cuts, and stuffed with red cloth.

34

24th September 1580

Received as bride gifts ——— eight yards of red silk, imported, and a gold-framed miniature the size of a girl's palm.

Accounts of Banstock Manor, 1576–1582

It is only after the morning's work that I recall the rector's strange story about his sister and wonder again of the wisdom of letting her see my Lady Banstock. I reach within my money chest for the doll, where I have hidden it away from meddling servants, and place it upon my desk. It looks like a child's toy save for the eyes, the stitches so deeply set into the padding that they seem buried. It is as if the eyes are gouged out. The simple body has no arms, merely empty sleeves as if it is deformed, and the face has no mouth. Yet there is a sense of Mistress Isabeau about it. The tight bodice, the scrap of embroidery, surely taken from her workbox, the white wool escaping from her cap all give a sense of the Frenchwoman.

Do they not say that if a mannequin of a person is created, the person will suffer if the doll is harmed? I examine the thing more closely, but there is no sign of damage. It gives me disquiet, however, and I resolve to destroy it even as I wonder how to do so in such a way that it harms no one. Feeling foolish, I hide it away again. Perhaps I will take it to Well House and let Seabourne deal with it, as he suggested.

I am called to the home farm in the afternoon, to see the bullocks and choose a new bull. The farmer shows me three, but I insist on seeing the rest, and certainly a fine fellow is hidden in a barn. Ned the cowman walks him home, while I ride over the park to see how many of the deer calves are stags and will be good for the hunt in the winter.

The still, hot air is heavy, and I am not surprised to see the heavy clouds above. A flash is followed by a rumble of thunder and the deer scatter into the trees. I hope the rain holds off until I reach the house. A few large drops of rain spatter onto the dusty path, but it seems just a shower. I put my heels to my horse, to make the hill to the manor gates.

Although his behaviour is poor, Seabourne's repentance seems sincere and Viola still resolves to wed him. I shall wait for her father's judgement, of course. All this is driven out of my head by the wailing in the stableyard as I ride in. Three laundrywomen are screeching as one, and the stable men look frightened.

'Witches at Banstock Manor' seems to be the message, as I order a pail of water apiece for the women, who rapidly control themselves. I question them, and the story seems to be that two of the smith's children saw signs of devilry at the abbey and were chased off by a great crash of thunder.

The children, two boys known for causing mischief mark you, are sent for. The rain is coming down harder and the sky darkening above the stables when I dismount, cast off my hat and coat, and seek out Viola.

She is overseeing the decanting of beer in the buttery, wearing an apron that dwarfs her. I tell her the rumours. 'There can be no witchcraft here,' she says, 'or we would have heard of it.'

'I wonder how long it will be before they blame the seamstress, given Mistress Waldren's words,' I answer, sampling the beer, which is potable, if a little green for my taste.

'Perhaps Master Seabourne would know more,' she says, nodding to the man standing by with the bung and mallet.

I lead her out into the quieter dining hall. 'Child, are you truly still wishful of marrying the man?'

She looks at me with the directness I have always loved. 'I am, Uncle, and I hope you will support me in this. If you do my father will agree, even if he grumbles.'

This is true, of course. My brother says he is a poor thinker, as he has me to think for him. But his anger is all his own.

'Do you not fear he will be unfaithful after the marriage?' I say, holding one of her little hands. 'Maybe he will set Isabeau up as his mistress.'

'Marriage, as you have said a hundred times, is not about love but duty.' It is irritating to have one's words thrown back at one. It may be that I frown. 'It seems Master Seabourne has an excess of love, not too little,' she adds. 'Please, Uncle, let me worry about my marriage, and let you worry about everything else.'

I sigh, but nod and change the subject. 'How fares your lady stepmother?'

She wrinkles up her nose. 'I cannot say. One minute she is insensible with tiredness or her aching bones; the next minute she wants to be sung to, or for Mistress Agness to read the psalms to her.'

'Yet the babe still moves?'

'More than ever. She complains 'tis a foal in her belly, his legs are so long.'

We share a laugh, the first since our quarrel, and she kisses my cheek. 'Worry not for me,' she says, pulls her fingers from mine and walks to the door.

As she departs, my heart asks if I shall ever stop worrying about Viola.

Vincent Garland, Steward to Lord Banstock, His Memoir

35

Saturday 13th April

'Lady George?' Sage took a step into the hall. The golden retriever padded over, wagging her tail, followed by Lord Banstock, who took a bite out of a sandwich held in one hand.

'Hello there,' he mumbled around the bread. 'She tells me you need to set up some tables?'

'I just wondered if I could put my information boards up and the pottery finds out today.' Sage stroked the dog, while Lord Banstock finished his lunch.

'We've moved the rug from the great hall. We've got some chairs that we use for weddings, we can put them out. Do you want to use the big table? It's a bugger to move without about a dozen helpers so you'll have to leave it where it is.'

Sage followed him into the great hall and inspected the wooden table, probably twenty feet long, four or five foot deep and possibly two planks from a tree felled five hundred years ago, mirror images of each other. It was almost black, and the grain tickled her fingers.

'This is *perfect*. It doesn't need moving.' She could set up her easels with the pictures from the dig behind, and there was plenty of room for finds.

'There you are!' Lady George bustled in, and to Sage's surprise, gave her a hug. 'Isn't this exciting? Olivia thinks this will really help us promote the manor.'

'Oh. Good.' She stepped back, and nodded at Olivia, who had followed Lady George in.

'We've got some things to show you.' Lady George was almost jumping with excitement, rising on her toes. 'Come up to the solar.'

The broad black stairs creaked in a hierarchy of satisfying old-house groans and scrapes. On the first floor Lady George walked to a pair of carved doors, and theatrically pushed them open.

The solar's walls were lined with linenfold carved panelling, with moulded and carved plasterwork on the ceiling. The room smelled of centuries of beeswax, woodsmoke and dog. The fireplace had a few smouldering logs in it on a heap of ash, and the oak had darkened so much the walls were almost black.

'Wow!' Even Sage, who had limited architectural knowledge, could appreciate the warmth and character of the room. One wall was lined with a block of nine narrow mullioned windows, some with stained-glass panels. The ceiling was decorated too, although the design was simple square panels with rose bosses.

'It's gorgeous, isn't it? We usually end the tours here.' Lady George was beaming, and waved her to an old sofa by the fireplace, which had an elaborate fire screen pulled to one side. Olivia sat next to her, holding something wrapped in a cloth.

'We – that is, Lady George and I – have something really exciting to show you.' Olivia unwrapped the parcel carefully. 'We wondered if it was of Lord Anthonie, the third baron. But something we read in Vincent Garland's ledgers suggests this is Solomon Seabourne. It may have been a wedding gift to Viola.'

The portrait of a young man with black curly hair was flat-faced and poorly executed, but had a strong chin and deep-set eyes that immediately drew Sage in. There were words written around the face, a motto: *caeca invidia est*, and a date.

'What makes you think it's Solomon?' She turned the case over in her hands. Paint and debris from the vellum had flaked off inside the glass cover, making it difficult to see clearly.

'An entry for Viola's wedding, that described some yards of red silk and a miniature portrait.'

'He was a good-looking man.' Sage handed it back to Olivia. 'And *caeca invidia est*, that's from Livy, the Roman historian, isn't it? "Something is blind."'

'Jealousy.' Olivia smiled slightly. 'Jealousy is blind.'

'*Sheshe*, when's your ferry?'

Yana had made dinner when she got back home, and Sage hugged her, wishing for a moment that she wouldn't go.

'Seven thirty, seven forty-five, I forget. Ages yet.' Yana ran her hand under her daughter's chin, and lifted it. 'I come back whenever you need me. Whenever you want me.'

'I know.' Sage managed a watery smile. 'I'm just tired.'

'Now, eat food. I made quiche.' Yana helped herself to some salad. 'What did you do today?'

'I was up at the manor. Oh, something else happened, I found this in my car yesterday.' She rummaged in her bag, retrieving the doll, which she had put in a specimen bag. 'I forgot about it; it's a sick joke, maybe.'

Her mother pushed her chair away from the table. 'Is cursed. You must get rid of it.'

'It's just a doll.' Sage hesitated, however; it did seem to have an evil stare. 'I was going to show a picture of it to the anthropology professor, Felix. He's looking at some carvings in the well for me. Folk beliefs are his specialism.'

'I wrap it up.' Yana collected a thick marker pen from the desk, took a piece of paper from Sage's printer and started writing in Cyrillic Kazakh. 'At least stop curse, yes?'

Sage was bemused. 'Mum! Let me get some pictures to show Felix.' She snapped a few shots with her phone. 'I don't believe in curses.'

'I do believe, we know of these back in Kazakhstan. Make *Sheshe* happy, at least.' She wrapped the doll in the paper firmly, like a fish. 'Now put in bag, then get rid of it. Burn it.'

'I think we're being overcautious.' Sage stretched her shoulders, feeling her neck crack. 'It's just a toy. That man I told you about, at the cottage? He's been going back and forth to the hospice with his wife. They have a daughter, a nine-year-old. She's been playing up.' She hesitated whether to bother Felix, but something in the deep eye sockets, the split belly stuffed with red cloth, made her press 'send'.

'You have baby, of course you're sad, dealing with bones all day. And you are upset about the doll, *iye?*'

'It was just a shock.'

'You show this to your professor, but then – burn.'

'I've sent him the pictures.' Sage sat down and took a big bite of quiche. 'But I'm mostly worried about the owners of the house,' she mumbled.

'The sick man and his wife?'

'And Chloe, the daughter.' Sage felt a squirm of disquiet run down the muscles of her back. 'She's fascinated with my baby, for a start.' She looked at her mother, seeing new lines, new grey hairs. *I'm going to look just like that in twenty years.* 'I've been thinking about it. I think maybe she planted her doll in my car. A sort of gift. Perhaps the cloth is some representation of the baby.'

Yana shrugged. 'Not something a normal child would do, no. By the way, were you ever going to tell me about your new friend? Nick the vicar?'

Sage almost dropped her fork. 'How did you—?'

'He leaves message on phone, I hear. That's all.'

'He's just… he's the vicar of Banstock, he's helping the family who live in the cottage.'

'And he enjoyed seeing you, apparently.'

Sage sat back in her chair, seeing a hint of frustration in Yana's expression. '*Sheshe*, I really wasn't keeping him a secret, we're just friends.'

'OK.' Yana rose. 'I'm going to pack the last things.' She turned and said, over her shoulder, 'I think you should listen to message.'

Yana left in a flurry of bags, hugs and promises. Yes, Sage would eat properly; she would tell her mother if anything – anything at all – happened with the baby; she would get rid of the doll; and most important of all, she would listen to the message from Nick.

Just as Sage shut the door behind her mother, her mobile rang. Her chest lurched with the thought that it might be Nick.

'Sage? Felix Guichard.'

'Oh, Felix. Thank you for getting back to me so quickly.' She curled up on the sofa.

'I was a bit concerned about those pictures you sent me.'
He seemed to be rustling papers.

'Well, the nine-year-old daughter of the family has been
acting oddly. I wondered if she mutilated her doll and put
it in my car.'

Felix paused for a moment. 'Listen. What you have in
that doll is a physical expression of a wish that is intended
to affect you. And your baby. I doubt it was made by a nine-
year-old.'

'But it's just a creepy doll. What threat can it be?'

'It's been made to look very like you. What worries me
are the cuts in the body.' He tapped something at his end.
'This was put together by someone with a knowledge of
curses. It's fairly well researched. These pictures would be
recognised across the communities that believe in witchcraft
all across the world. Can you see if there's something
personal linking you to the doll? Like hair or fingernails?'

'My mother wrapped it in paper,' Sage said, feeling
uneasy at the thought of unwrapping it. 'She wrote
something in case it was cursed. Dolls like this were known
in her community where she grew up in Kazakhstan.'

'Just unwrap it. Leave it on the paper if it makes you feel
better.'

'This is daft. It's a kid's toy, I should be—' Sage's voice
got caught somewhere in her chest when she unwrapped
the paper and looked at the thing up close. The eyes were
blackened sockets and the mouth had been coloured with

dark red pen, disturbingly the colour of blood. There was a pen line around the throat – no, she realised something was tightly wound around the neck. She picked at it, and it started to unwind. 'There's a hair tied around the neck – dark, almost black.'

'Could it be one of yours?'

Sage removed the hair and laid it on the paper then pulled out one of her own. They were about the same length, colour and thickness. 'It could be.'

'Now look at the body of the doll. What is that inside it?'

Sage fished in a drawer for her tool kit. 'I don't really want to touch it again.' She found forceps and grasped the edge of the red cloth, tugging it free. It was quite large, compressed into the waist of the figure. She spread it out on the paper, flakes of something red spitting onto the surface. 'There's a cut down the body, with some fabric packed inside. It looks like part of a scarf. It's silk and has a faint pattern of birds, I think.' It had an unpleasant odour, and she bent forward to sniff it. 'It smells a bit rank.'

'This is important. Is there anything of anyone else in there? Like nail clippings, hairs, even bloodstains?'

Slowly, the truth coalesced in Sage's brain. She pushed herself up from the chair and backed halfway across the room. 'Oh, God, Felix, it was soaked in blood. There's dry blood everywhere. Why? I don't understand.'

'You need to take it to the police. If someone is using blood to charge a curse they mean you harm.'

She was holding the phone in one hand, the other pressed against her mouth. It was a few seconds before she could speak. 'I don't think they have a witchcraft squad. Bloody hell, Felix, what's going on?'

'It's a traditional spell, the sort of thing your sixteenth-century people would have understood. I don't think it puts you in any danger, but someone's going to some lengths to intimidate you.' He paused. 'These things can... I have seen some evidence that they might have some negative effects, if only because they distract and stress the recipient. I'll come over to the Island and have a closer look at it for you. I want to see your carvings in the well in person anyway.'

Sage could feel a bubble of laughter building inside her. 'You could lift the curse, you mean?' She took a deep breath to centre herself. 'I'm fine, it's just a shock. I don't believe in magic.'

'Maybe the person who made the doll does. They certainly intended to upset you.' Felix's voice was full of concern. 'Actually, there are different methods used in making poppets – that's what they're often called. I want to see what book – or horror film – the doll's maker was drawing on. And like I said, I also want to see the well for myself. The symbols were designed to control a specific entity or influence.'

'You can't believe that a few carvings—'

'I know it sounds extraordinary, but somehow two people ended up in the well, which you have said is incredibly rare.

Is it just coincidence that the symbols in the well suggest a kind of psychic trap?'

Sage looked at the doll. It glowered back. 'Now you're scaring me.' She was only half joking.

'I'll come to the Island tomorrow, if that works for you.'

Sage stepped away from the doll, feeling foolish that she felt safer. 'That would be great. But I'm running a public meeting tomorrow afternoon for the locals, with one of my students. We're interpreting the well finds to the village.'

'Where? I'll try and get there. Keep the doll for me.'

Sage gave him directions, then rang off. The doll lay next to the stained cloth, and she got latex gloves from under the sink to scoop the whole lot into the paper and back into the specimen bag. She took it down to the outside store where she kept her bike. Tucked onto a shelf with a box of tools, it seemed less threatening.

She finally pressed the answerphone for Nick's message.

'Hi, Sage. It's Nick – Nick the vicar. I… I don't really know how to say this. I had a great time at Francesco's. A really great time. It's just… even seeing you. Oh, for goodness' sake, I should just spit it out.' There was a long silence with a few frustrated breaths. 'I don't really want to be just friends. Can we leave the possibility of more out there? See how things go. Call me back and put me out of my misery, will you?'

She smiled as she picked up the phone.

36

25th September 1580

Four linnets in a cage as a gift to your lordship's daughter
Viola upon her betrothal ———————————— *twelve shillings*

Accounts of Banstock Manor, 1576–1582

The boys who raised the alarm about witches in Banstock, when summoned, have already been chastised by their father and are no doubt still smarting from his efforts. They come before me: one Tom Brewster, eleven years old, and his brother Harry, not yet ten, with their father.

'So, tell me. What business did you have trespassing on the abbey lands?' I say, as sternly as I can manage. The younger snivels, but the elder looks up.

'We saw a light there, two nights ago,' he says. 'I thought they might be gypsies come to Banstock. We went to spy on them, no more, and warn my father that they are back.'

It was well known in Banstock that the last time vagrants camped they brought with them disease and left with two stolen lambs.

'And you did not immediately tell your father but went instead spreading rumours?'

The boy shuffles his feet and winces. 'I beg pardon, your honour.'

'Well, sirrah, since you did trespass, you had better tell me what you saw.'

They tell a simple tale of the cell that I have seen, which they marvelled at, and then they climbed through a ruined window of the chapel. There, they claim, lies an altar soaked in blood whereon lies a crucified animal, turned upside down in a terrible parody.

The story makes me shiver, as we had thought to hang or exile all the witches on the Island years ago. Wise women live among us, yes, but no one who practises those darkest of heresies. It makes me uneasy about the doll found in Agness's chest.

I tell the boys someone has played a terrible jest upon us all, and we will clean up such a nasty mess. Meanwhile, I suggest that they keep their silly tales to themselves.

As they file out, their father lifts a hand. 'Please, your honour, a word?'

'Of course.'

'It was just a bit of tittle-tattle, I didn't like to repeat it.

But there's a rumour that the Frenchwoman has been seen at the abbey, taking flowers and whatnot in some evenings. In the spring, this was.'

'I see. Yes, she did go there, but not for witchcraft.'

'It's just...' he looks away. 'They say witches use flowers in their potions. And sacrifice animals.'

'I have spoken to Mistress Duchamp, and I know why she was at the abbey. Nothing to do with witchcraft, I assure you.'

He seems to struggle with his conscience. 'There are those that say witches do consort with the Devil, your honour, and half the village is talking about how the seamstress is with his child.'

I think through what he has said. 'Then start another rumour, Master Brewster, that the woman is a lightskirt, not a witch, and she laid with her lover at the abbey. She is no more a witch than you or I, but a sinner. A few days ago, the world thought she was a papist, for goodness' sake, and now thinks she worships Satan? The woman is a woman, like others, and fell prey to carnal sin. That is all.'

He looks relieved when he leaves, but I am left wondering who has brought such disquiet to our corner of the Island. I suspect the woman Agness, and resolve again to get her removed from the estate.

Vincent Garland, Steward to Lord Banstock, His Memoir

37

Sunday 14th April

Sage arrived at Banstock Manor to find that Lady George had polished the oak table in the great hall. She ran her hands over the scarred, blackened surface, arranging the information boards and boxes of specimens.

'Thank you again, Lady George, Lord Banstock. This is very helpful of you.'

The manor's owners were already looking into the plastic boxes. Lady George lifted out a tub of corroded metal fragments. 'What are these? Buttons?'

'There are a couple of coins that we can tentatively date to the 1560s. We can't be more accurate, because coins remained in circulation for decades. There's a belt buckle and a few household nails and pins, too. That all fits with the cottage being built in the 1550s.'

Sage smiled at the first few villagers arriving, then checked her watch. She wished Steph had arrived, but the student was dependent on the ferries. 'I hope you don't mind, but I've invited an expert to listen in. He's a professor of social anthropology from the University of Exeter.'

'Oh, how exciting.' Lady George looked at her husband and then at Sage. 'What does he do? I mean, what is social—?'

'Social anthropology studies the history and influence of culture. His special area is folk beliefs, local mythologies, that sort of thing.'

Two familiar figures entered the great hall: the care assistant Nathan pushing Maeve Rowland in a wheelchair covered in a brightly coloured blanket. Sage waved them over.

'Nathan, Maeve. I'm so glad you could make it. It's lovely to see you.'

Maeve smiled with the mobile side of her face. 'Can't wait. I even got this wastrel out to something educational.' Nathan rolled his eyes.

The tall figure of Felix Guichard appeared at the door, looking upwards before joining Sage and the others. 'Hi, Sage. That ceiling is beautiful. Is it original?'

'Mid 1500s, apparently. Let me introduce you to Lord and Lady Banstock; they can tell you more. Professor Felix Guichard, Lady George, Lord Banstock. And this is Maeve Rowland, former owner of Bramble Cottage, and her helper Nathan.'

Felix shook hands with everyone, then lowered his voice as he spoke to Sage.

'And the——?'

She grimaced at him, and waved over his shoulder at Nick as he came in. 'In the shed at home.' She realised Lady George was trying to get Felix's attention, and backed away to finish setting up the laptop to show a slideshow of the exhibits. *I could really do with Steph.* She gave her a quick ring but got nothing.

It took until nearly three to get everyone seated. There were about fifty people in the audience. Sage recognised several from the school, the landlord from the pub, who waved, and a row of restless children along the front. She checked her phone again, and then sent another text to Steph. *Where are you? Getting worried.* Maybe she'd come off her bike. She couldn't wait any longer so she stood to face the audience.

'Good afternoon, everyone——' she caught sight of Nick at the back of the room, standing with Lady George. Sat down at the end of the first row was James Bassett in a wheelchair, a stick leaning against his knee. He managed a crooked smile and a wave.

The talk was easy: she outlined the excavation, introduced the finds and projected images from her laptop onto the wall behind the table. People listened in relative silence, especially when she showed the pictures of the bones. A little ripple of sighs greeted the images of the skulls.

Two representatives from the Island Historical Society

were introduced next, and Sage sat at the side of the table, glancing at her phone. No messages.

'We would like Dr Westfield, and the community, to understand the investigations in the context of what is known about the local history.' The society's chairwoman paused for dramatic effect then lowered her voice. 'There was a witchcraft investigation right here, in Banstock.'

After a satisfying ripple of reaction, the woman went on, outlining a tale – mostly apocryphal, Sage decided – of witches believed to have communed with the Devil in the ruins of the old abbey. She was mentally preparing for the question-and-answer session that would conclude the presentation, when something the chairwoman said made her look up.

'—and of course, Agness was in a good position to make accusations of witchcraft against the Frenchwoman, Isabelle. Agness was the rector's sister. If Agness hadn't disappeared, a witchcraft trial might have included Solomon as a sorcerer, or even Viola as his betrothed.'

Sage put up a hand, and the woman nodded at her. 'Dr Westfield?'

'I'm sorry, where does this information come from?'

The chairwoman held up a brightly coloured hardback titled *Tales of a Haunted Village*. 'This was originally published in the 1840s. That was before the churchyard was partly destroyed to make way for the new road.'

'What was the connection with the churchyard?'

'A memorial was put up in the churchyard to the missing sister of a rector, which described how she had gone missing.' One man passed a copy of the book to Sage. 'It's said that witches used to dance around bonfires up on Witch Hill, by the old abbey.'

There was a good illustration of the monument. Sage stood up and faced the room. 'We – my assistant and I – have managed to decipher the words on the monument, but there is no connection to witches. It said the rector's sister was lost in a storm.'

The chairwoman held up one hand. 'True enough, Dr Westfield, but when the monument was moved the original rear panel was dropped and shattered. The lost inscription was recorded and is reproduced in the book.' She held open the page and read clearly. '"May God bless this manor and relieve it of foul witchcraft and all manner of devilry." You know witches were often thought to raise storms.'

Smiling at the reaction she had achieved, she gave way to the East Wight Genealogical Society. Their spokesman rose to the heightened atmosphere by declaring he was a descendant of Lord Anthonie Banstock. He talked about the early lords of Banstock from research into his family tree, then leaned forward conspiratorially. 'I'm excited to say that we have just republished the letters between Viola and Solomon. They were left to the eleventh Lord Banstock and he originally published them in 1862; we recently found them in the library archives.'

Sage was astonished, and when he bowed and produced a booklet with a flourish, the audience gave him a round of applause. He turned and handed it to Sage, who flicked through the pages. The letters were all dated from around the late 1500s, and Sage was struck by the different tone of the two authors.

'Can I borrow this?' she asked.

'Keep it, please, it will be our pleasure to contribute to your investigation.' The genealogist smiled at the audience. 'There are more copies for sale from me and we have put a few copies in the manor bookshop.'

Sage decided it was time to wrap things up. 'Thank you all for your insights and contributions. We may never exactly know who the people in the well were, beyond that they were a baby, about newborn, and an adult, probably female. But we'll keep you informed.'

Several voices spoke up, some asking about Isabeau/ Isabelle, some about Agness, even a question about Viola. Sage raised her hands, as she caught a smile from Nick. 'I'm sure the society's investigations will continue much longer than mine and I'm really grateful for the chance to put my findings so far in the context of local history.' *And myth, and legend, and fairy tales.* She looked around the room. 'I've got time for one more question.'

A woman maybe a few years older than Sage stood up. She was slim, blonde and beautifully groomed. 'I have a question for you.'

'Yes?' Sage smiled at her, even as she registered the tension in the woman's face. She looked familiar... As recognition dawned Sage could feel herself go pale.

'How long have you been sleeping with my husband?'

'I'm sorry?' Sage gripped the table in front of her. She couldn't find any words.

'Why don't you tell the people here how you seduced my husband, the father of my children? And now you're having his bastard.'

'This— this isn't the place or time,' Sage stammered.

The woman – Fliss – folded her arms. 'It seems like the perfect time and place to me.'

Sage addressed the rest of the audience. Her face was hot now, scarlet with shame, probably. 'Well, thank you for coming, everyone. Please come and talk to me if you have any more questions relating to the excavation.'

Sage stepped away from the table as Fliss walked up to her. 'Well?'

'I don't know... I don't know what you want from me. I didn't know he was married—' Sage saw several villagers observing the exchange. She lowered her voice. 'When we met, I didn't know he was married. He told me he was separated. I'm sorry.'

Fliss's eyes were brimming with tears but her face still looked furious. 'Do you think he's going to leave you for me?'

'No. It's over, Marcus and I aren't seeing each other

anymore.' Sage was keenly aware how many people were listening. 'I'm sorry, but you'll have to talk to him.'

Felix came over. 'This isn't the time, as Sage says.' He towered over Fliss who was a little shorter than Sage. 'You should pose your questions to your husband, not Sage.'

'He just wanted a bit of fun with you,' the woman hissed. 'He'll never leave me and his kids.'

'No— I mean, I don't want him to. It's over.'

Behind the anger in Fliss's face was something else, tears in her eyes. Maybe she really loved him, maybe she was afraid she would lose him.

Felix ushered her away, saying something soothing, while Sage leaned against the table feeling sick. Sick and a bit faint. She closed her eyes for a moment to blot out the curious and disapproving faces. She surveyed the great hall for Nick but couldn't see him. There had never been a good time to tell Nick, and anyway, it was over. Over the building hum of chatter, Lady George invited everyone into the orangery for tea and cakes. Gossiping loudly, the visitors began to crowd through the double doorway at the end of the hall.

Sage and the site manager, Olivia, started to pack up the artefacts, and Felix returned to help. Nathan wheeled Maeve over in her wheelchair.

'My goodness, girl, you have got yourself in trouble.' The old woman's bright eye was fixed on her. 'And I thought the vicar was sweet on you.'

'I think he was.' Sage tried a smile, but felt it come out more as a wince.

'And the cottage is playing up, too, I hear. From Den, at the pub. He came to visit me.'

Sage shrugged. 'It has a strange atmosphere, that's all.'

Maeve shook her head. 'I'm glad I'm out of there. All those years, and there were bodies just outside the back door. Maybe that noise Ian and I heard was their ghosts, crying.'

Sage reached out a hand and Maeve took it with her good one. The old woman's fingers were shaking, the skin dry and warm.

Sage attempted a smile. 'I really don't believe in ghosts, Maeve. Some places seem to have a spooky atmosphere. I'm sure it's all down to creaky stairs and old pipes.'

She squeezed Maeve's hand, then rose and went back to packing up the well finds. Felix leaned down and spoke quickly. 'Look, Sage, you've obviously got a lot more going on here than I thought. I can stay a couple of days, until the end of reading week, anyway. I'll ask Rose to look through the Seabourne research we have. Let me help.'

Sage nodded. 'What about the doll?'

'Keep it out of the house if it worries you. I'll take a look when I can.'

Sage managed a half-smile, Marcus's wife's anger still ringing through her like electricity.

* * *

Sage spotted Nick in the orangery, making polite small talk with various locals. Before she could speak to him, James Bassett approached her, leaning heavily on a cane, looking even taller now he was thinner.

'Well, well, quite a dark horse, our county archaeologist.'

Sage flushed. 'Apparently so,' she said, trying to keep her tone light. 'You look better. I heard you had the doctor out to the cottage.'

'One blood transfusion and a change of painkillers, and I'm ten times better.' He smiled gently. 'Relatively speaking.' He looked at the crowd through the doorway. 'I wouldn't worry. Who hasn't done something that they don't want shouted out across a crowded room? There's nothing the village likes better than a scandal.'

Sage shrugged, and winced as she heard her name behind her. 'It's a *really* small island.'

'That thrives on gossip, we're starting to realise that.' He smiled at her, a little crookedly. 'The wife will suffer more than you, in the long run. At least you got to be the sexy and seductive mistress. She was just the woman betrayed by an adulterous husband.' He sat down heavily on a chair, and sighed.

'Is Judith here, or Chloe?' Sage hoped they weren't. She wasn't in Judith's good books as it was.

'They're at the cottage with Judith's mother. Pat's come to help her. Poor Ju isn't coping very well at the moment and Chloe is playing up. The police phoned about the nanny cam: they can't identify the man in the pictures, the resolution is too low. We have had the locks changed; we should have done it when we moved in but the estate agent told us we don't need to on the Island.'

'It's a very safe community.'

Olivia came over to them. 'Sage, thank you so much for coming, and giving such an informative talk. I'm sorry about that unpleasantness.'

Sage shrugged. 'Self-inflicted, I'm afraid. Oh, Olivia, this is Mr Bassett, who owns Bramble Cottage. James, Olivia is the manor's site manager and archivist.' They exchanged greetings while Sage looked over at Nick. He caught her gaze, then turned away, bending to hear what a young woman – Mel, the woman she had met at the vicarage, Sage noticed – was saying. She had her hand on Nick's arm.

Sage bowed her head, bereft of something she had hardly known she had. A warm hand cupped her elbow and Felix spoke over her shoulder.

'Mr Bassett, I presume?'

'James, please. Maeve tells me you're an anthropologist. You're here about the excavation too, I suppose?'

'Yes, specifically I'm interested in your well stones. The symbols carved into them have magical meanings, by the beliefs of the day.'

'Did she tell you there were more inside the house? Over the fireplace.'

'She did.' Felix squeezed her elbow; it was reassuring. 'I'd love to see them for real.'

'Any time. Well, any time I'm there, anyway.'

'One of my areas of interest is the symbols devised by John Dee and Edward Kelley. They were mathematicians and necromancers from the reign of Elizabeth the First, so contemporary with your well.'

'Necromancer?' James laughed nervously. 'Isn't that raising the dead?'

'Actually, Dee was the country's foremost mathematician and scientist, as he understood science. Solomon Seabourne, who lived in your house, was one of his students.' Felix smiled. 'He was also a famous and passionate scholar, trying to heal the schism between the Catholics and Protestants. He devised the symbols to communicate with angels that he believed were trying to share the system of divine magic with the world. He wanted to speak to the dead to prove there was an afterlife.'

James laughed. 'Wow. I suppose he never came here? We could put up a blue plaque. You know: *Dr Dee raised the dead here, fifteen something.*'

Sage managed a tight smile. 'I'd better pack up the van so I'll leave you to it.' Felix let go of her arm and she felt colder.

As she turned, she heard James ask Felix, with a note of anxiety in his voice, 'Do you think there's anything to this ghost idea? I mean, I have heard the wailing myself.'

'If you ask our archaeologist, she'll say no. There's no solid scientific evidence for ghosts, although there is some for the mechanism by which we see or hear manifestations that we interpret as ghosts—'

As she walked to the van, Sage dug in her pocket for her phone, but there was no message from Steph. She sat for a moment in the driver's seat, wishing she could just leave it all, the investigation, the embarrassment…

Nick tapped on the window and Sage opened the door. 'Were you just going to sneak off?'

'No!'

'Is it over? With the husband?' His tone was hard.

'It was over before I met you. Really.'

'But you are the sort of woman who has affairs with married men.'

'Yes, I fell in love with a liar who turned out to be married.' Her eyes stung with tears, more from anger than distress. 'So you can stop slumming it with fallen women, and go back to your wholesome helper.'

She pulled the rear doors of the van open and started clearing a space for the specimen boxes.

'I would, if I could,' Nick snapped, in a low voice. 'Unfortunately, I'm not attracted to her. Mel is a good friend, by the way, as well as a colleague. She runs my team of volunteers and manages the office when she can.'

Sage took a step towards the manor's portico. 'I have work to do. I have to pack everything up.'

'So that's it? You're embarrassed because you didn't tell me you'd behaved badly, so it's over?'

'What's over?' She stood up, the hair falling into her eyes. 'I slept on your sofa and we had one dinner. We hardly know each other.'

He stared down at her. 'I thought—'

'Well, you were wrong.' Her anger spilled out, at Marcus, his wife and her own stupidity. 'I'm out of your league, vicar. I like to live fast and play hard. You can't keep up with me.'

'Apparently not.' The stones under his heel crunched as Nick turned, leaving Sage, her temper evaporating, watching him walk away.

38

26th September 1580

Money for the bellringers — thirteen shillings and eight pence, to toll upon the dread news that your lordship's son George Banstock has perished a hero upon Drake's great undertaking. May the Lord rest his soul.

Accounts of Banstock Manor, 1576–1582

It is with heavy heart that I set out to clear up the mess in the ruins of the old abbey. Our last male heir is gone. George, my favourite of the boys, is dead. Now all hopes rest upon my Lady Banstock and the babe inside her. God grant that it is a boy.

I send for Master Seabourne and his servant, Kelley, to help me clear up the altar at the old abbey as I do not want the manor servants making more of it than it is. We find the cell much as I left it but the chapel is another matter.

The altar is covered with fur and dried blood from some animal, which we soon see is a cat, its body straddled upside down over a simple cross made from two boughs tied with string. It has three black paws and one white, and I recognise it as belonging to the wise woman Jennet Dawtry. Not just a wise woman but the village midwife, and as good a Christian as the rector, I say.

Also on the altar is a girdle, a simple woven thing, only recognisable by virtue of it being formed of the leftover threads of her trade.

Kelley picks it up between finger and thumb. 'Is this…?'

'I think it unlikely Mistress Isabeau would leave something of her own here,' I say. 'Such would condemn her.'

'She would not – she did not,' says Seabourne. His colour is high, whether with shame or anger, I cannot tell. 'She is a true Christian and no witch.'

'I suspect the one person we can be certain did not leave this here is Mistress Isabeau,' I say, 'but someone who wished to impeach her. Anyway, this cat is recently killed, and the seamstress has been chaperoned day and night since we returned from London.' I take the girdle and wrap it in my bag. 'Best we clean up the mess and burn the poor cat.' Its jaws, gaping wide, cry its agony endlessly.

Seabourne nods. 'Certainly, we three should clean up this abomination. And get the Reverend Waldren to speak cleansing prayers over the chapel.'

With Kelley sent off to fill his bucket from the abbey well, Seabourne speaks to me in murmurs.

'This is not witchcraft, Master Vincent, but pretence. I have studied the science of sorcery.'

'To cast suspicion upon the Frenchwoman, certainly,' I say. 'She is a sinner, but I know she didn't do this. We must ensure that the village agrees.'

'Then, who?' He examines the cross from which the carcass of the cat sags. It is tied on with twine, and a pitiful sight, its belly opened and its congealed entrails hanging loose. Kelley returns with the water.

'I have some reason to be concerned about Mistress Agness.' I take a cloth and start to wash away the bloodstains from the defiled altar.

Kelley assists me. 'She visits the laundrywoman and asks about Master Seabourne.'

'She does?' Seabourne, gathering some pieces of broken timber from the charred panelling to build a fire, looks up.

Kelley gestures to me to stand back, then sluices the altar with green well water. 'I thought at first she had a kindness for Allen Montaigne, your body servant. But I think not.'

'Agness has—' I take a deep breath and explain the doll's discovery to Kelley.

Seabourne looks across the carnage at me, wrinkling his nose at the stink. 'She is deranged. Could she have done this, as well?'

As Kelley goes for more water, I gather another handful of wood to build a fire in the fresh air, beyond the stink of death and blood.

'There is no real intent or knowledge here,' Seabourne says, as he carries the crucified cat out of the building at arm's length. 'It is the ill-informed facsimile of someone making mischief. To cast suspicion upon Isabeau.'

I build a small pyre and he lays the cat carefully on it, even though it was just a beast. I manage to catch a handful of dried grass with my tinderbox, and take the girdle from my bag to catch the flame. By a combination of blowing and adding tinder from the hedge we soon have a blaze going. The stench of burning meat drives us back into the chapel where Kelley is still scrubbing the blood from the altar.

'It is a shame about the cat,' I muse. 'Her kittens are the best ratters in the village; we were to have two for the dairy.' I sniff. I can still detect the stench of decay in the rushes below the altar. I crouch down and uncover the stiff remains of five bloodied pieces of meat. Kelley stops his work, and stands beside me, his mouth open. It takes me a moment to recognise the furled ears, shut eyes, and tiny open mouths. They are unborn kittens, ripped from their mother's belly.

Vincent Garland, Steward to Lord Banstock, His Memoir

39

Monday 15th April

Sage didn't sleep well, turning over in her mind the excruciating moment when she was exposed as Marcus's mistress to Banstock village. She dressed early, and drove over to the cottage before nine, ready to clear up the last bits of equipment. She tapped hesitantly on the front door.

'What do you want?' Judith's hair was unwashed and straggling, her face gaunt.

'I'm sorry, Mrs Bassett, I'm just waiting to hand over the well to the builder, so he can prepare for the landscaper to put the turf back down. Have you heard from him at all?'

Judith turned, and an older, shorter woman with grey hair peered through the gap.

'Oh, you must be this Sage that James and Chloe have told me about. I'm Pat Levitt, Judith's mother.' She pushed past Judith, hand outstretched.

Clasping it, Sage wondered exactly *what* Pat had heard about her. 'Nice to meet you, Pat.'

The older woman pointed in the direction of the garden. 'We were wondering if it was your bicycle in the hedge? We moved it to the shed.'

'Steph's bike?' Sage turned to look at the hedge. 'She left it here?'

'It's been there since Friday. We didn't want anyone to pinch it.'

Sage's mind started to race. She hadn't heard from Steph since— well, since before the weekend. She checked her mobile. No calls from Steph. She rang the girl's number.

The wind carried the faintest ringing from across the garden. Sage walked slowly towards the hedge, along its base, looking amongst the leaves. Steph's phone was half buried in them, the light glowing faintly. It had almost no battery left. Eighteen missed calls, twenty messages.

As she scrolled through the texts, a feeling of dread started to build inside Sage, a shiver that started in her chest and spread outwards. Steph's mother was looking everywhere, had called the police – her limbs were heavy as she turned, it felt like she was wading through cold water.

The well.

As she walked towards it, she called out to Pat and Judith.

'Has anyone been anywhere near the well?' She inspected the heavy cover, which seemed in place. A small scrape on one side suggested it had been moved a little.

'No one.' Judith came out in her slippers, wrapping her arms around herself. 'Why? What's wrong.' Her voice was as flat as if she were reading out a shopping list.

'Help me get this thing off.' Sage bent, pulled at the metal disc's recessed handle, but it weighed more than she expected. 'Please, help me!' Horror was building inside her, and she felt sick.

Pat, pulling on a coat, came to join them. 'If we do it together – towards me, then. Watch your back.'

Sage pressed her fingers into the mud underneath the edge, and heaved. With Judith suddenly helping, and Pat pulling on the handle, they managed to move it a few inches, then a few more, until the well was partially uncovered. Sage dropped to her knees and shone the light of her phone down the shaft. The water was no more than eight or ten feet down, much higher than it had been on Friday.

She could see nothing, so tried taking a photograph with the flash. Nothing but black water. But as she enlarged the photograph she could see there was something, a pale half-moon, reflecting the light.

Focusing on the area brought an incomprehensible fuzz of details that made no sense.

'Oh, dear God,' Pat whispered.

Puffy and unfamiliar, the shape was that of a face surrounded by a halo of fair hair.

* * *

The police were strict with their instructions. Sage, sat on the doorstep with her teeth chattering, was not to leave the site until the body – dear God, the body – had been identified. She leaned against the doorframe, feeling sick. She had given her phone to the police, and didn't want it back. But when it rang, an officer answered it, and held it out.

Sage took the phone gingerly, not wanting to reveal the photograph she had taken.

'Yes?' Her voice was cracked, her throat tight and dry.

'Sage?' Nick's voice was strained. 'I… I just heard from the police. Do you know who it is?'

'They—' she dragged in a breath. 'They think it might be Steph. Stephanie Beatson, my student. But how…?'

'When they told me someone had fallen down the well, I thought it might be you,' he said. 'I just… I felt sick.'

'No, not me. I thought it was odd that she didn't turn up yesterday for the meeting…' The words faded as she remembered yesterday, and its revelations.

'Do they know how she fell?'

She swallowed hard, her words trapped in her throat.

'Sage?'

Finally, she managed to croak the words out. 'They don't know. But someone had to have put the cover back on after—'

'I'm coming over.' He rang off before she could argue.

'Dr Westfield?' A man was bending over her, and she squinted into the low sun to see him. Late forties, dark-haired, nice-looking, wedding ring. *Just my sort*, she thought hysterically. 'I'm Inspector Belmont. How are you feeling? Could you answer a few questions?'

She nodded, and took the hand he held out to help her to her feet. She was shaking; her knees felt like they weren't under her control. Belmont led her into the cottage's kitchen, and pulled out one of the chairs at the table. The Aga was on but the glow of warmth didn't penetrate her shock. He wrapped a blanket around her and put a mug of tea in front of her.

'How are you feeling? The baby—'

Sage nodded, pulling the extra layer around her. 'I'm OK. It's just—'

Belmont nodded with sympathy, and sat down beside her. 'So, you found your student's phone in the hedge. What made you think of the well?'

The question took her aback. 'I... I don't really know. It's just that the whole excavation has been about the well and I was always worried someone would fall in.' Her teeth started to chatter. 'I must have told Steph a dozen times to mind the well.'

'Is there any reason she would take the cover off? Maybe she thought she had left equipment down there, had forgotten something?'

Sage shook her head. 'No, nothing like that, the well

was empty. It was starting to fill up with water after we took the pump out. Anyway, I don't think Steph could have moved the cover by herself – I couldn't and she was smaller than me.'

'And you are sure the cover was in place when you last saw it?'

'Of course. It's deep and there's a child living here. We took every precaution.'

She could hear Nick's baritone outside, and a little warmth crept in. Inspector Belmont looked up. 'Is that a friend?'

Sage nodded, although her vocal chords were paralysed.

Nick swept in, and when she staggered to her feet, took her in a bear hug. She clung to him, hearing words rumble over her head but unable to process them. All she could think about was his warmth, his hands grasping her almost painfully, his breath in her hair. He smelled of soap and laundry and damp wool. She dropped her head into his chest, wishing she could howl. *God, Steph—*

When she lifted her head, she stared straight at him. There was only concern in his eyes at first, none of the hurt of the previous day, but as she watched, it began to creep in, a distance. He slowly released her and rested his hands on her shoulders. 'Are you all right? Because you look terrible.'

'I'll be OK.' She stepped back, looking at the inspector. 'I found Steph's phone under the hedge. No way would she ever leave it deliberately, you know students and their phones. Her whole life was on it.' She cleared her throat, looking up at Nick. 'I just knew something had happened to her – she wouldn't just go, leave her phone and bike without saying anything to anyone. The well – it's so dangerous now it's empty. I just had to look.'

'I would have done the same.' Nick nodded. 'I'm so sorry, Sage, she seemed like such a nice girl.'

And that was it; tears poured out of her. Her knees buckled, and Nick lowered her into a chair. She could feel herself fold up into a ball, a small part of her watching as if outside of her body, watching the storm from afar. Her ribs hurt, the sobs were so violent. She realised distantly that the pain was about Steph, and Nick's face yesterday, and her mother's matter-of-fact rejection of a lifetime of love and marriage with her dad.

Gradually, the sobs started to soften, and she could feel a strong hand rubbing her back. She wiped her face on the blanket, past caring what she looked like, and glanced up. Inspector Belmont had gone.

'Is it definitely Steph, Nick? It didn't look like her… maybe it wasn't.' She knew the second she said it that she was clinging to fantasy.

'They think so.' His hand still stroked her back. He managed a crooked smile. 'I'm so sorry. Do you feel better for a good cry?'

'I never cry. Hardly ever, anyway. I seem to be doing it a

lot, recently.' She stood up and helped herself to a handful of kitchen towels. Blowing her nose, she felt more ready to tackle the disaster outside. 'Must be the pregnancy.'

'Sage—'

'Not now, OK? There's so much— I need to deal with Steph, right now.' She looked into his eyes. 'But, thank you, Nick.'

The police finally allowed Sage to leave the site. Nick, seeing her hands trembling as she failed to unlock the van, took her keys off her and guided her towards the vicarage. The sound of her feet crunching on the gravel of the drive suddenly halted her.

'No! Is… anyone inside?'

'You mean any of the volunteers?' He put an arm around her. 'I don't think so, but does it matter?'

'I thought – I was just worried that – that woman who was helping you overheard that spiteful remark I made yesterday.' She could feel the warmth creeping up her cheeks.

He stepped in front of her. 'Mel works for the parish, with me. Maybe she's got a little crush.' He smiled, touched the dog collar with a finger. 'The uniform does that, it's just transference. She doesn't know the real me, and probably wouldn't like me if she did.'

'Do I know the real you?'

His smile faded, and he stared into her eyes for a moment. Finally, he spoke. 'You have only known the real me, even if only for a few days. Have I ever really known you?'

'I never pretended to be an angel. Marcus and I are over. We... I was stupid, that's all. I fell in love with him.'

'And now?'

'Oh, I fell out of love with him, too.' Sage reached up with her hands, and grasped the front of Nick's coat, shook him. 'And then I met you.'

He kissed her as if he was starving, and she clung to him for a long moment, hardly knowing or caring if they were being watched.

'Right. Two sugars, lots of milk.' Nick put the tea down a little too firmly, slopping a few drops onto the vicarage kitchen table. 'Don't argue. You need the sugar after all this.'

Sage blew on the tea, wrinkling the surface and blowing the remaining bubbles around. 'I can't believe anyone would deliberately hurt Steph. But I can't see how else she ended up falling into the well.'

'We don't know much about her. Maybe someone was upset or angry with her. But it seems unlikely, doesn't it?'

'I can't believe it was an accident and the police seem to agree,' Sage said. 'Someone moved the drain cover. Maybe someone heard about the Tudor burial and it gave them the idea. It's common knowledge on the Island.'

'I don't think people naturally see a well and think "I could chuck someone down there and get away with it."'

'But someone did in the 1500s, didn't they? That's all the locals have talked about for weeks.'

'I suppose so.'

'Even if Steph fell down in some freak accident, she couldn't have moved the cover by herself. It took three of us this morning.'

'Women, one older, one pregnant,' Nick said, 'and Judith Bassett, of course, who looks thinner every time I see her. One strong person could have got the cover off and dragged it back, if they didn't have to lift it.'

She rested her head on her hand, realising how much it ached after the bout of crying. 'Yes, but *why*? Steph isn't a threat to anyone.' She rubbed her forehead, feeling it crease. 'Wasn't. Wasn't a threat.'

'Don't think about that. Keep your scientist hat on.' Nick pushed a packet of biscuits towards her. She recoiled, but he nudged them again. 'Go on, you look white as a sheet. Your blood sugar's probably in your boots.' A sound in the hall brought his head up. 'Hello?'

The door creaked open, and Felix put his head around the frame. 'I've been to the cottage but the police sent me here.'

Sage smiled up at him, her eyes misting up again. 'I'm so glad you're still here.'

'I went to look at the carvings and… well, you know what happened.'

Sage waved at Nick. 'This is Nick, he's the vicar here. Nick, this is Professor Guichard.'

The two men shook hands and Sage took a biscuit while Nick explained how she had found the body.

'Call me Felix,' Felix said to Nick. 'Sad. Very sad.' Felix nodded to the offer of tea, and then put one of his big hands over Sage's clasped fingers for a second, making her jump. 'I'm so sorry. How are you holding up?'

Sage nodded, her mouth full of crumbs. Nick had been right, she was starving. 'I'll be OK,' she mumbled. 'Talk among yourselves.'

Nick put a mug of tea on the table for Felix. 'Those symbols in the well, were they put there as part of some kind of archaic occult belief? Or was it some parody of Christianity?'

'I know this will sound strange to you, but those symbols were carefully researched and designed, and are inscribed with what's called magical intent.' Felix's hair flopped in his eyes as he sipped his tea, and he pushed it away. 'The symbols spiral down into the well like a path.'

'We know Seabourne was a writer on the occult,' Sage added. 'He believed in all this stuff.'

Felix nodded. 'And it's possible he intended the spiral to summon something or someone, and trap them in the well.'

Nick sat down beside Sage, and put his warm hand over hers. He looked over at Felix with a slightly possessive air. 'Well, the superstitious beliefs of an Elizabethan scientist hardly apply today.'

Sage put her drink down. 'The bodies could have been put there for lots of reasons,' she said. 'And covered up with whatever loose material they had available. In this case, the midden.'

Felix nodded. 'What seems strange to me is if you were concealing two bodies in a well, wouldn't you have put them in first? Then covered them with rubbish? They would be towards the bottom, not the top.'

'I suppose the well was full of water when they were put in,' Sage said. *God, they would float like Steph...* She shut her eyes for a moment.

Felix turned towards Nick. 'What do you think?'

Nick stood up and reached for the teapot. Sage smiled as he topped up her mug. She didn't even own a teapot. 'I think talking about some occult connection to that well when a girl has just been found dead in it is a bit tasteless,' he said.

'Quite right. Sorry.' Felix sounded so contrite that Sage managed a lopsided smile.

'Actually, I think it's somehow important. It would be important to Steph, too, as an archaeologist,' Sage said, and looked at the two men. 'Why would we think it's Isabeau's bones down the well? She was known, she had status as an employee of the manor.' She cupped the tea in her hands and let the warmth soothe her cramped fingers. 'This was a sophisticated culture with deeply held beliefs about Christian burial. No, this was an act of violence, cruelty, like—' She couldn't finish, swallowed the lump in her throat. 'She was hidden. Just like Steph. Rob Greenway would have just dumped a load of spoil straight onto Steph if I hadn't looked down when we found her phone.'

'A parallel act of violence and disrespect, then,' said Nick. 'So the only other obvious candidate is the rector's sister.'

Sage nodded. 'Or someone of such low status that their disappearance didn't warrant a memorial or a mention in records. But that stone in the woods puzzles me.'

There was a knock at the front door. Nick went to answer it and returned with the police inspector. 'Inspector Belmont has some questions for you.'

The policeman nodded at Sage. 'Dr Westfield. I thought you had gone home.'

'Inspector Belmont.'

Belmont nodded. 'I'm just so sorry it's turned out like this. Tragic.' When Nick waved him to a chair, he sat down with a sigh of relief. 'I've come to tell you we're having difficulty retrieving the body – the young lady – from the water. We don't think the well is stable, and the structural engineer from the council agrees.'

'So what now?' A bubble of hysteria rose up as Sage imagined Steph trapped.

'We plan to fill the well with water, and the body should float up with it.'

'What if she sinks?' Sage put her hand over her mouth

to stop herself laughing, though she also felt suddenly terrified. This was too real. 'Oh, God. Has anyone told her parents?'

'Of course.' The policeman nodded. 'We'll have her on dry land soon. Then we'll pump the well out again, to look for trace evidence. When you packed up on Friday, was there any water in the well?'

Sage thought back: they took out the ladder, the drain hose and the petrol-driven pump. 'It was starting to fill up again. A couple of feet, maybe.'

'And how deep is the well?'

'We found a rough rock base at almost seven metres. Twenty-two feet.' For some reason, perhaps the serene paleness floating in the well had led her to assume Steph had fallen into the black water and drowned. She had a sudden image of Steph falling down the maw of the well to crash onto the stone slab.

Belmont's voice softened. 'We need you to tell us what Miss Beatson was wearing on Friday, if you can remember.'

'I don't know... pale blue jacket, jeans, boots with heels, we teased her about them, because she's quite short... hang on. There's a picture of her, with my other assistant; we took it on Friday. It's on my phone— oh. I gave it to that other officer already.'

'Thank you.' The inspector turned to Felix. 'Professor, could I have a word outside?'

'Of course.'

When the two men left, Sage looked at Nick. 'About yesterday: Marcus's wife.'

He shrugged. 'I knew there must be a father somewhere.'

'I'm sorry she... no, actually, I'm not.' Sage put her pale hand over his. 'She deserved her say. And now he'll be in no doubt that it's over.'

'Was there any doubt?'

'In his mind.' She tried to smile. 'I think I might get the lock to my flat changed. He kept a copy of the original key the estate agents had. I bet he's still got it. He's a bit overbearing on occasion.'

'Is that how you met him?'

She nodded. It seemed a long time ago now. 'When I bought the flat he told me that he was recently separated, about to get a divorce. He was charming, good-looking. Then he became a bit controlling, and we split up. Quite a few times.' She looked into Nick's eyes. 'I knew he was still married by then, of course, and I got pregnant during one of our... reconciliations.'

Nick squeezed her fingers, warm and strong. 'I was a bit shocked yesterday, but mostly worried. For you.'

'Don't worry about me. I felt sorry for Fliss. They have kids, you know.'

'Do you know how she found out?'

'I have no idea.'

'Someone could have told her.'

Sage thought back over the last few weeks. 'Maybe she's known for ages.'

'I think she would have had her say before now if she had.'

She finished her tea. 'Who would even know? I mean, we were pretty discreet.'

Nick took her cup. 'Maybe someone with a grudge?'

Someone with a grudge. Someone who called her a whore for visiting Nick late at night, someone who planted a doll with a ripped belly full of bloody cloth in her van. She remembered Steph had seen someone like Marcus at the cottage, and Sage had definitely seen him in the village. Maybe he'd been at Bramble Cottage, talking to Judith for some reason? Was he following her? God, he could have had access to the cottage keys from when he sold the place. And he would easily have recognised her voice on Nick's phone.

'I need to make an appointment to see Inspector Belmont.'

40

4th October 1580

Fine hat for your daughter Mary in London
——————————————————————— *ten shillings*
To joiner for two stools of elm wood for the dairy
——————————————————————— *nine shillings*

Accounts of Banstock Manor, 1576–1582

y Lady Flora is at ease in her chamber and Viola sits reading to her, poetry I judge from the rhythm of it, in French as well as English. Sometimes Viola is found writing poetry as well. She has not seen her prospective bridegroom for some days. My Lord Anthonie has yet to make his ruling on the wedding, and the man stays at Well House with his experiments. Still unsettled by the discovery at the abbey, I ride over to see him.

I find him not in the house but behind it, beside the old

well with Kelley. Men still labour to finish the new one at the front of the house, their shouts ringing around the hedged garden.

'What do you do with the old well?' I say. 'It was always brackish.'

He stands from kneeling beside the uncovered ring of stones. 'I am constructing a circle that will summon a spirit to help me in my work.'

I step away. 'Is that safe?'

He laughs up at me, looking younger in his shirtsleeves. 'It will be when I construct a container for it.' He stands, wipes his hands on his hose, and bows politely. I bow back.

'What teachers have instructed you in summoning spirits?'

He opens the door for me to step ahead of him, into the house. 'I have been taught by the queen's astrologer and adviser himself, sir, and others of his circle. Edward, fetch wine for Master Garland.' He lifts from a shelf a tome so heavy it takes two hands, and all the sinews in his wrists stand out. It thuds onto the table. 'This is the *Pseudomonarchia Daemonum*, the book of Johannus Weyer, who describes the demon Berith most vividly. He holds the key to the transmutation and elevation of base metals into precious ones.'

'Daemonum? Ungodly monsters of Satan?'

He pushes the book towards me. 'The creatures from the lower reaches, demons as we call them, are created like by God, like all beings.' He opens the book and begins to read. *'Vere de præsentibus, præteritis et futuris respondet.'* He translates for me, though my Latin is rusty I can see it for myself. *'He answers truly of things present, past, and to come.'*

Kelley enters with a tray and two fine gilded goblets.

I read on. *'Virtute divina per annulum magicae artis ad horam scilicet cogitur.* He is compelled at a certain hour — through divine virtue, by a ring of magic arts. *Mendax etiam est. In aurum cuncta metallorum genera mutat.* He is also a liar, but he turns all metals into gold.'

Seabourne looks at me, smiling, as if all is explained.

'I cannot believe that summoning a demon is anything but foolhardy.' I was torn between disbelief and a natural horror of things demonic. 'If such creatures exist, they must be dangerous.'

'I assure you, the summoning circle will contain Berith's conscious essence if drawn correctly. I have devised a special snare should he prove worrisome. I can draw him into the well, where his energy will diffuse into the earth.' He pulls down a parchment covered in symbols. 'We are inscribing these symbols in a spiral path, into the stones of the old well. My men empty out the water, and Kelley and I climb down a ladder to carve the sigils within.'

I can see the shapes are arranged in a spiral but unlike any I have seen before. 'And this will draw this Berith in?'

'It will.' He hands me a cup of wine. 'We were given the power to mutate one form into another, one substance into another by Enoch's ascent into heaven to speak to the angels. I seek the wisdom of the transmutation of base metals into gold.'

I do not know what to say. It seems like a child's dream. I take my satchel from my shoulder and draw out the doll the Reverend Waldren found amongst his sister's linens. I place it upon his table. 'Here is the doll I described.'

Seabourne frowns as he examines it. 'This is definitely meant to be Isabeau.'

'I believe so.'

'This is witchcraft. The basest of all magics. This is the Devil's work.'

'The evil lies in the rumours and accusations that will fly from that thing if it is not destroyed,' I say.

He walks to the fireplace and sits upon the bench there. He rubs his hand through his hair. 'And this was in the room of the rector's sister?'

'If Agness were not a great comfort to Lady Banstock in her distress we would banish her to a relative on the mainland.'

'At first I thought her a servant. It seems the sin is in this woman, Agness. I cannot see that Isabeau would have had much opportunity to so offend her.'

I shake my head, sitting heavily in his good chair, my knees stiff. 'She has never caused any concern before. This year has brought much disruption to Banstock, and much misfortune.' The dead heir, I think, and sweet Elizabeth sleeping in her tomb. 'Perhaps it is madness. I have no doubt she desecrated the abbey to cast suspicion on Isabeau. I shall speak to her myself, and ask the rector to have his sister supervised at all times.'

'No one should suspect Isabeau of witchcraft,' Seabourne says, his gaze lowered. 'She has been almost under guard since the summer. I myself have not been able to get word to her, nor see her. Beside that, she is devout. In her own way.'

'I know that.' I pity the man, in a mire of his own creation. 'But rumour is inclined to be more interesting than truth.'

'Viola has spoken to her,' he says. 'I must advise that she does not speak further, lest she too is tainted by unfounded suspicions.'

I sigh heavily, remembering Viola's words. 'She wishes for the marriage, still.'

'I am glad.' Some of the tension seems to ease from his body. 'I would be honoured to husband her.'

'What of your love for the seamstress?'

He spreads his fingers out and stares at them. 'That was spring madness, Master Vincent. I was newly betrothed to a woman I did not know, though she seemed a gentle, kind girl. But Elizabeth did not look kindly upon me, either, so much her senior, and I the youngest son.'

'So, Isabeau—?'

'You have seen her.' He shrugged. 'She was there, and like sunlight she drowned out the stars.'

'But you no longer love her.' I pressed for an answer, for Viola's sake.

'I love her as a dream, a fairy princess that I can never have. My love for Viola is that of a man who takes a woman to wife.'

'She is young, still,' I say. He looks back at me.

'She is intelligent, she thinks like a scholar. She understands my books, nay, she takes them further than I have. She writes elegantly and maturely. She is young, yes, and perhaps unready for the full duties of a wife, but a woman withal.' He smiles a little sadly. 'Perhaps she loves Isabeau too, as the heroine of a story.'

'A sordid tale, perhaps.' I stand, and he stands also. 'I shall speak to my brother, but I doubt he will consent to a marriage until Isabeau has borne the child and gone away to the mainland.'

'Can you tell him I beg to be allowed to speak with Viola? I am happy to be chaperoned.'

'I will ask. And will you destroy this… thing?' I nudge the doll forward.

'I shall.'

I sigh, and stretch my aching knees. 'In my turn I shall confine Agness to her duties.'

'I know she is an enemy to Isabeau, and would accuse her of witchcraft. If she condemns—'

'There are always those who will say there is no smoke without fire,' I say, remembering that I thought that myself. A plague upon clucking tattlers.

Vincent Garland, Steward to Lord Banstock, His Memoir

41

Tuesday 16th April

Sage and Felix travelled over the Solent to her office at the South Solent University, after she'd given him the strange doll. Reminders of Steph were everywhere, and Sage was stopped several times by other students, shocked and upset but also curious. Felix fielded the worst of the questions. She sent him to find Professor Yousuf Sayeed while she went to the facial reconstruction laboratory.

Sage studied the computer-modelled face of the adult skull. It had a strong profile, and as Dr Cally Reynolds swept her fingers over the mouse pad the image swivelled from side to side. Her office was decorated with printouts of the reconstructed skulls she had worked on.

'Here it is with hair—' another sweep, and brown hair appeared.

'She's plain.' Sage leant in, to see the heavy jaw and large nose more clearly. 'A strong face.'

'She looks a little masculine, to be honest. Are you sure it's female?' Cally seemed to be only half joking. 'Good solid supraorbitals and masculine jaw muscle attachments. The jaw itself is quite square, too, with biggish teeth. We don't have the whole nasal bone, but we know it would be a good size.'

Sage took in the jutting teeth and heavy chin. 'Actually, we're not all that sure. The pelvis is more likely to be female but it's ambiguous. She was tall, too, about five-nine.'

Cally pressed a button, and the printer began to hum. 'On your advice we gave her long hair. Have you thought that she might be older? Post-menopausal women often develop changes in the pelvis.'

Sage was drawn by the drama of the face; even with a blank expression, it seemed filled with purpose. 'We put her at over thirty by the fusion of the skull sutures and the clavicle, but with a wide margin. There are no obvious pathological changes so I think she's probably in her middle years. Thirty to forty-five, maybe. Did you have any more luck with the teeth?'

'Given a mid-range quality diet, wear and decay suggests about the same. Do you have a name?'

'Officially, no. But a woman called Agness Waldren went missing about the right time, and was thirty-seven.'

'Agness. Good name. It means chaste, I think, from the Greek.' Cally stood and fetched the printout for Sage. On paper the woman's face was even more striking, if hard.

'Not someone you would have wanted to cross.'

'We know a bit about her brother. He was the rector of the parish church, and she kept house for him.'

Cally screwed up her face. 'Dogsbody for her brother.'

'It wasn't a bad life for a woman of that era. She had more freedom, more choice than a married woman. And not burdened with endless babies.' Sage read the data on the side of the screen. 'I see what you mean, she's borderline on several markers.'

Cally clicked a few more buttons. 'I've sent you the file. Oh, just one other thing.'

'Hmm?' Sage was fascinated by the face, trying to imagine what the woman was like as a person. Warm, funny? Clever, stupid?

'I know you said it wasn't worth doing the baby, but we did find out a lot.'

Sage suddenly felt an irrational shiver sweep through her. She really didn't want to see the face of a butchered, abandoned child.

'I don't want to see it. Is that daft?'

Cally looked at Sage's belly and smiled. 'Not daft at all. Let me give you the highlights. The baby has a small jaw and poorly ossified long bones, even for a newborn. Our best guess is the baby was just a few weeks short of full term, maybe thirty-six weeks gestation. I wasn't sure it would be useful to see our reconstruction, anyway. It's a very imprecise science – babies all look quite similar.'

When Sage didn't answer for a moment, Cally turned back to the screen. 'I've emailed you the images and the report anyway. The community always loves reconstructions, so they might come in useful.'

'Thank you.' She swallowed, feeling a bit absurd. 'I'm sure you're right.'

Cally leaned forward, and touched Sage's hand. 'How are you holding up? About Steph, I mean. We were all so shocked. Lovely girl, promising student.'

Sage looked at her hands. 'I don't think it seems real, even now. I'm meeting with the dean later. The police say we weren't negligent, the site was well secured, but that means... maybe someone killed her.'

'I heard they interviewed Elliott Robinson all last evening.'

Sage rocked back in her seat. 'What? No. Why?'

Cally shrugged. 'He was the last person to see her, and apparently he had a bit of a thing for her.'

'I can't believe Elliott—' Sage paused. Who knows what went on inside people's private thoughts? 'They worked well together, they were a good team. But I don't think he was really interested in her. She gave him enough encouragement, but he was a bit shy. Anyway, thanks, Cally.'

Sage walked along the corridor to Yousuf's office, where she found him sitting with Felix.

'Ah, there she is. Sit down, my dear. I've just been

sharing a theory with Felix on the injuries to the bones.'

'Oh?' She sank into the chair with some relief. Her neck was aching since the short ride on the ferry, and the spring sunshine made her feel too hot.

Yousuf was holding a photograph of the baby's bones. 'The baby's jawbone was cut, and its clavicle and humerus.'

'Yes. We did speculate that perhaps the baby was born by caesarean after its mother died. Maybe the knife caught the baby.'

Yousuf patted her clenched hands. 'Certainly the baby, if it were in the breech position, might receive such injury from a vertical incision. In an emergency situation, an unskilled person might attempt to save a baby from a dying mother.'

'Oh.' Sage looked at Yousuf. 'So there might be some injury to the mother. Possibly Isabeau if we ever see her bones.'

'You have the exhumation order. I can make the calls to expedite it. In all honesty, I think I should be present anyway, since I countersigned the request.' Yousuf opened his diary and flicked through the pages. 'Thursday. I could do Thursday afternoon, if you and my team start the dig in the morning. How about you, Professor? I think Sage is going to need some support on this.'

Felix nodded. 'I was going home this evening, but, yes, I can stay. What do you think, Sage?'

'I have to talk to the police tomorrow. I've cancelled

my teaching commitments for the moment so Thursday would be fine.' She swallowed hard. 'The cottage is still a crime scene.'

Felix's voice softened. 'Maybe exhuming the body in the woods would take your mind off Steph.'

Lost in dark imaginings, it took Sage a few seconds to answer. 'Yes. Let's do it.'

The dean's office was on a corner of the main building, with a view over the gardens. The dean was joined by a man looking as drawn and exhausted as Sage imagined any bereaved parent would be.

'Mr Beatson, this is Dr Sage Westfield. She was supervising Stephanie through her practicum.'

Oh, God. He was going to blame her. Sage held out a hand to Steph's father. 'Mr Beatson.'

His handshake was unsteady; he clung to her as if she could hold him up. 'I'm glad to meet you, Sage. Can I call you Sage? Steph talked about you all the time.'

'Of course. She was a lovely girl. She had a real feel for the history, and was great with the public. I loved working with her.'

She led him to a chair. The tears in his eyes spilled down his face.

'I can't believe she's gone.'

'I'm so sorry.' Sage couldn't think of anything to say.

Words seemed to thicken in her throat. 'I don't know what happened.'

Mr Beatson shook his head, wiped his eyes with a handkerchief. 'The police told us... it looks like murder. Someone killed our girl.'

Sage caught the dean's eyes. He pulled up a chair next to Mr Beatson. 'I'm sure the truth will come out over the next few weeks,' he said.

'I was wondering,' Steph's dad looked up at Sage. 'Would she have suffered? They can't tell me anything.'

There was a right answer somewhere, but Sage couldn't find it. 'I hope not.'

'Only, you found bones in the well, Steph told us all about it.'

'I don't know about them either. I'm sure any distress would have been very short.'

Mr Beatson hung his head, looking at his hands. 'I couldn't identify her, I just couldn't. My father-in-law had to in the end.'

Sage sniffed back tears. 'I saw her – just a glimpse of her – in the well.' The pale profile was burned into her memory. 'She looked very peaceful.'

Mr Beatson started to cry in earnest. 'Thank you for that,' he managed to mumble. 'I know this sounds odd, but will— will you tell us what you conclude in your final excavation report? We feel like we know the story so far, and it was so important to Stephanie.'

Sage nodded. 'Absolutely.'

'They won't release— they won't let us plan a funeral yet.' He looked up, his eyes red.

Sage fumbled in her bag for a tissue. 'I'd like to be there, if that's OK? I know many of Steph's fellow students will want to be there too.' She tried to smile. 'Steph made friends everywhere she went.'

'She did, didn't she?' Mr Beatson nodded. 'We just want you to know, we don't blame you, we don't blame any of you. I'm glad she was doing something she loved.'

Sage couldn't find more words, and just let him cry.

42

13th October 1580

Meats and eggs to be taken to M. Isabeau

six shillings and threepence

Accounts of Banstock Manor, 1576–1582

The house is upside down again, thanks to Mistress Agness. She spoke to Isabeau directly when she came to fit a bodice to Viola, and the Frenchwoman is thrown into anguish. The servants took the rector's sister out and threw her from the house. Lady Banstock is distressed, the seamstress is sobbing into her apron and Viola cannot comfort her, and the servants are so busy muttering in the hall they have burnt a haunch of pork roasted for the evening meal. I start by summoning the men and ordering them to their many posts. Viola is sent to read to her lady stepmother, and I speak to Isabeau.

'Master Seabourne hopes you are well, Mistress,' I say sternly, for I do not wish to give comfort to her sins. 'He has arranged a pension so that you and the child might live safe on one of his family's estates.'

'My husband will find me before then,' she says. She is very pale these days, and I wonder if the life she carries is draining her. Her hands tremble for a moment, then still as she bends to her embroidery. 'All this talk of me will bring him here.'

It is stitching such as I have never seen before, the cloth the green-blue of the sea upon a bright day, each line of thread laid upon the silk as if 'tis woven there, a line of gold. She stitches it onto the cloth in a lattice so fine I fear for her eyes, yet her movements are almost as if she need not look, but simply strokes it onto the cloth. Jewels glint from golden clasps in clusters like tiny flowers.

I am filled with compassion for her, even as I know her sins. On occasion I have spoken to husbands on the estate who are too rough with their wives or children, but her terror is so strong she quivers like a hart whenever I move. I sit upon the bench by the door, and shiver in the draught. The winter is racing upon us.

'Mistress Duchamp, Lord Seabourne is minded to give you the name of one of his own cooks, a Frenchwoman who made sweetmeats at one of his brother's manors and is lately died. You shall take her name.' I laid out Seabourne's father's plans, and her eyes, always large, seemed huge in the fading light. Her fingers never stilled in their work, needing only a glance down occasionally.

'I—' She sets the cloth aside before a tear stains it, and holds a linen kerchief to her eyes. 'I seem to cry from joy as well as pain,' she says, and dabs at her eyes. She smiles at me, and I see the beauty again that still astonishes me.

I point at the turquoise silk with a finger. 'This cloth, madam.' I did not recognise it, and I know all the cloths we have ordered. I dare not touch it with dirty hands from my horse, and she holds it carefully up to the last light.

'This was given to my mother by the queen,' she says, smoothing tiny creases from the skirt, the bodice stiff with decoration. 'Not her Majesty Elizabeth, you know, but Queen Catherine.' She drapes it over the linen cloth she covers her worktable with. 'It is silk from Venice, given to the queen by the Holy Roman Emperor. She misliked his religious policies, and gave the bolt to her ladies.' She smiles, looking at me sideways. 'I am glad to give it to Viola with her other bride clothes.'

The silk, though probably five and twenty years old, glows with colour and smells sweet. It is worth... I cannot imagine what it is worth.

Vincent Garland, Steward to Lord Banstock, His Memoir

43

Wednesday 17th April

The chair in Inspector Belmont's office was surprisingly comfortable, for which Sage was grateful. She hadn't slept well since Steph's body was discovered, and her neck and back ached. 'I don't really have anything to add. I got there and we found her.'

'Well there are always three people we really need to talk to. The boyfriend, the last person to see her alive, and the person who discovered the body.'

'What motive would I have for hurting—' Sage closed her eyes for a moment '—or killing Steph?'

'You aren't a suspect. It's just that you do have a lot of knowledge of both the excavation of the well and all the people concerned. For example...' he looked at his notes. 'Tell me about Mrs Bassett.'

'Judith? She's under a terrible strain, of course. Her husband is so ill.'

'I believe Reverend Haydon told you about the nuisance calls he has been receiving?'

Sage shifted. 'I've heard some of them. They sound like a man's voice, and the abuse was aimed at the vicar. Although...'

'Although?'

'Well, when I answered the phone, the caller told me to get out. As if they recognised my voice.'

'Did you recognise *their* voice?'

Sage shook her head. 'It was just an angry voice, but the anger was aimed at Nick and me, not Steph.' She looked at her hands. 'I know this sounds odd, but the father of my baby... has been a little difficult.' She told Belmont about Marcus, both about their relationship and the possibility that Steph had seen him at Bramble Cottage, about the meeting at Banstock Manor and Fliss's outburst.

'OK. I'll look into that. Is there anything else you can think of that might be significant?'

Sage considered mentioning the doll, but she felt silly suggesting that she was being targeted by someone trying to put a curse on her. 'You know about the nanny-cam footage of someone in the Bassetts' living room? They reported it to the police. Mr Bassett was certain it wasn't him, and didn't recognise the man on the video.'

Belmont checked back through his notes. 'Yes, but I think we'll look into that in more detail. How about you, Dr Westfield? Anyone in your field that might resent your work in this case, for example?'

'No one I can think of. And Elliott and Steph were volunteers.'

'Mr Robinson is a postgraduate student. What does that entail, exactly?'

'Elliott is studying for a PhD in archaeology. He's a hard worker, and I trust him. He and Steph were always friendly; there was a little banter perhaps, but Ell takes the work very seriously.' She met his gaze. 'They both did. They knew they were involved in a fantastic puzzle, and would get their names on the research paper. It was a tremendous opportunity.'

Belmont nodded. 'You appreciate that we don't think this was an accident. The well was covered up after Miss Beatson fell in, and no one has come forward to say they did replace the cover, and it would have taken considerable strength.'

'When do you think it happened?' Sage asked.

'Based on the condition of the body, we believe she entered the well some time between five and eight o'clock on Friday evening.'

Sage's heart lurched in her chest at the thought of Steph's body. 'I was there until five-fifteen.'

'And Mr Robinson claims to have left shortly afterwards, leaving Miss Beatson.'

'She was setting up to draw a site plan when I left.' Sage leaned forward. 'Was she killed before she went into the well, or did the fall kill her?'

'I can't disclose that. That's for the coroner to discuss at the inquest when all the evidence is in.' Belmont's dark eyes seemed full of sympathy. 'Will you be there?'

'I think I should be.'

'Then prepare yourself for bad news.'

It popped into her mind. *Maybe she drowned. Terribly hurt, and terrified, she died in the cold, dark water.* Sage closed her eyes. The thought was like a physical pain.

Sage walked back to her car and sat inside for a moment. There were messages on her phone: one from Nick, one from Felix. 'Call me, I have information about the doll.'

'Hi, Felix,' she said, resting her head back and closing her eyes.

'Sage. I've got good news. At least, I think it's better news than some curse on you.'

'Oh?'

'The doll. It's not a curse at all; it could be a kind of crude love spell.'

'Who would even think like that?' she said, trying to imagine someone playing around with a doll. Trying to make her fall in love with him. 'Someone deluded.'

'Possibly.'

'Well, it's not working.' She could hear the waspish tone in her own voice. 'I don't believe in all this crap, you know that.'

'But it is working. You are attracted to someone.'

The silence stretched out between them as she absorbed his words. 'I'm attracted to Nick, but that happened before anyone created a doll in my image and stuffed it with bloody rags.'

'That's the bit I'm worried about.' His voice had a reasonable, fatherly tone that made her want to shout at him.

'But the cut in the body of the doll, the cloth, the blood,' she said. 'It's so violent.'

'It's true, love spells are usually benign, but there are some voudun spells that are raw like this.' Felix shook his head. 'But I think whoever made the doll is disordered in their thinking.'

He had a point. She didn't like to even guess what the doll's maker was thinking.

'I'm not buying into any of this, but is there a way of neutralising…' *God, I'm as mad as he is.* 'I suppose we ought to show it to the police.'

'What would they do?' Felix's voice was calm, with no humour or ridicule in it. 'You may not believe in such things, but I've still seen people suffer ill effects from them. Anyway, I've already got rid of it.'

Sage felt oddly relieved. 'Thank you.'

'My pleasure. Be careful, Sage.'

* * *

When Sage got back to her flat there was a note from Marcus. It was angry, demanding she meet him, come to her senses, let him look after her. He had always been so genial and persuasive, it came as a shock to see him be so forceful. Three months ago she might even have been flattered, but now it was just unpleasant. Maybe Fliss had confronted him too.

She put her bag down and started to tidy the piles of papers and books that were scattered around the living room. She couldn't keep up with housework at the best of times. She started putting books back on the shelves as she went. *Life in Tudor Times, Osteology in Archaeology, Pregnancy: A Guide* were all on the floor at the end of the sofa. She swept a few bits of underwear off the radiator – what if Nick came over? She sat down and read the note again. It seemed so angry, the way the pen had been pressed into the paper, cutting it in places. She turned the paper over and realised there was more writing.

And tell the police to fuck off. You know I would never hurt anyone let alone that silly little bitch at Bramble Cottage.

44

20th October 1580

Two ells of taffety at nine shillings an ell — eighteen shillings

Accounts of Banstock Manor, 1576–1582

was resolved to get Agness away from the manor and its lands. Discussion with her brother informed me that she has an older sister in Southampton town, much afflicted with agues and four sickly children. There Agness's talent for nursing the sick should be appreciated. Perhaps after a year or two she might return, after Isabeau has left and when Solomon and Viola are married. The Reverend Waldren spoke to her but she raged and fought with him, until he was forced to strike her. The next day she was fled from his house and he tells me, in much agitation, that he fears for her safety. No one at the manor has seen her, and Waldren fears that she might harm herself. I set men to watch for her on the manor lands as she is certain to return.

It seems a good time to take Viola from her duties reading to Lady Banstock, who lies almost insensible, and take her for a ride over the Island to visit the lawyer in Newport to consider her marriage settlement. We take the groom Elias Courtney, who carries a sturdy stick in case of brigands, but in honesty the Island roads have become safer since Her Majesty came to the throne.

Viola looks much more her old self since her father has allowed her to write letters to Seabourne, and he is permitted to reply. I have been tasked with reading them, but they are mostly stilted politenesses or their shared passion for science. Master Seabourne says he is planning to raise the demon to give him the clues he needs to make gold. God's speed, I jest, since the rents this year are low and much of the harvest is poor. I allow such talk, since there is no such possibility. It gives them something to converse about.

Viola has taken to her sister's horse, a fine grey, much more spirited than her old pony but her seat is secure. We get a few good canters on the roads that remain dry though the sky is clouded.

'Come, Master Vincent,' she cries, and sets spur to flank. Elias and I can keep up, but both of us are blowing hard when she pulls rein. Then I see what she sees. A group of men surround a woman, standing upon a bench outside the Hawk and Hare Inn beyond Arreton.

I hear her words, the familiar cracked stridence, before

my old eyes make out her face.

'Witchcraft at Banstock, and does Lord Anthonie prevent it? His own babe, dead in its mother's womb, and they do not care that they harbour witches? They that give shelter to witches shall be condemned with them.'

I catch at Viola's bridle and pull her alongside me.

'Here come some of her followers,' cries Agness. 'They shelter and even pay her as she weaves vile spells at the old abbey and bewitches good men!'

I stand in the stirrups to shout over her ravings. 'Mistress Waldren is unwell; her own brother seeks to send her away. She is gone a little mad.'

I can see from their faces that I have not convinced the men. Elias calls out to one of them. 'James Trotter, you know me. Would I encourage witches? This is all women's foolishness. A bit of milk sours and they call it spiteful fairies or witches.'

'That's as may be, Elias, but they say there are black masses and such up at the old abbey.'

'A dead cat, no more, my master tells me. Probably caught by a fox,' Elias adds, catching my eye. 'There in't no witchcraft on *this* side of the Island. I can't speak for them folk in the West Wight.' There is general laughter, but Agness has not finished.

'How can you say that, Elias Courtney, when everyone knows that cat was tied to a cross and left on the altar,' she shouts.

I am shocked that my suspicions are so easily confirmed. 'Madam, only Master Seabourne, his servant and myself knew how that poor cat came to its end. And the wretch that killed it, of course.'

'The smith's boys told me.' She spits at me, her eyes glaring. 'You know that the only witch at Banstock is Isabeau Duchamp, a whore who has lain with the Devil and carries his child.'

The murmuring from the crowd tells me they have turned against us again. I dismount, stand among them. I have to shout to be heard. 'That is not true, Agness Waldren. The woman lay with a mortal man in no more than lust, as well you know, since you spread the rumours all over Banstock!'

'I don't believe she was with Master Solomon, and I never will!' she screeches at me in her strange voice. 'He has eyes for only one!' She touches her scrawny breast. 'He has no need of a wife in the child Viola, nor a whore in the French witch.'

I am shocked. I cannot believe he has even spoken to Agness. 'You are mad to think he has noticed you, woman.'

'Will he deny it when I show him what spells seduced him?' She jumps down from the bench and strides towards me. I am a tall man, but she can look me straight in the eye. 'The French witch lies. She convinces you with her chants.'

I grasp her wrist, looking behind me for Viola, who is

safe by Elias on her palfrey. 'We must take you home. I think you have lost your senses.'

She wrenches her arm from my grip. 'Let me go! You are as hag-mazed as the rest.' With great strides, she runs across the yard and up the hill to the woods behind. She is fast, her long legs pulling her away beyond the reach of the road.

Viola rides forward a few steps, holding her horse's bridle tight in one gloved hand. She speaks with a clear voice that silences the muttering men and the inn servants.

'Hear me,' she says. 'That poor woman has been tormented by this madness for many weeks now. Her own brother, the rector of Banstock, has tried to contain her but she escaped. She is ill of some brain fever that makes her delirious. My father will grant a reward of a gold angel for any man who can bring her, unharmed, to Banstock Manor.' She glances at me to make sure the sum is appropriate and I nod. I could probably have got the help for less, but ten shillings was just the incentive the men needed. I can see that Viola's clothes, her voice and her natural tone of command impress them, and the few remaining caps come off.

'And let there be no more talk of witchcraft where there is none,' I say loudly. 'For to falsely accuse is a crime at the assizes.' This reminder that I am also a magistrate is enough to get a party moving up the wooded path after Agness. 'Unhurt, mark you, for the reward!' I call after them. I reach up to take Viola's bridle. 'Well done, child.'

She creeps her little hand onto mine. 'If there is witchcraft in Banstock I could sooner believe it was Mistress Agness than Isabeau, whatever her sins,' she says.

I look up at her, and decide it is time she knows all the story, since in some ways it affects her. When I mount my horse, I set the servant to ride behind us. I tell her of the strange doll, and of Solomon Seabourne's promise to take away the harm in it, if indeed there is any. I even tell her of the cat, though I do not speak of the kittens to save her tender heart.

'If he can take away the harm, then let him,' she says. 'But the evil intent remains. Someone wishes harm to Mistress Isabeau by accusing her.'

'Someone who is angry and violent. How better to describe Mistress Agness?' I say, turning my mare's head for town and the lawyer.

Vincent Garland, Steward to Lord Banstock, His Memoir

45

Sage's excavation hit Isabeau's coffin at barely four feet down, the heavy oak casket penetrated by a few tree roots, and largely rotted to black, crumbled cake-like material along the sides. The students and technicians had excavated a platform in the clay each side, so Sage and Elliott had somewhere to crouch while delicately revealing the inside of the casket. The party from the university – led by Yousuf – was accompanied by a police constable to ensure the exhumation didn't exceed its warrant. It was a reminder that the excavation at Bramble Cottage was now part of a murder inquiry.

The box had partly collapsed onto the corpse, the sides bowed. Felix was by the excavation, taking his own notes. Elliott had appointed himself chief helper, and filled each bucket gently before boosting it up to people at the graveside.

'I'm amazed there is anything left at all,' Sage

murmured to Elliott. He was pale and hadn't spoken about talking to the police after Steph's death, but seemed to want to keep busy.

'It's quite a way from the stream,' he answered, his eyes downcast. 'Can I lift this bit of lid now?'

The top of the coffin came away in several carefully numbered pieces, and was handed aloft in separate specimen bags. The bones were in situ, the ribcage caved in by the coffin lid but otherwise in good condition. Sage brushed away tiny layers of dirt, of decomposed flesh fallen into dust, to reveal gold thread. The whole skeleton was decorated with designs in it, making a ghostly outline of the body that it had once covered.

'Wow.' One of the students leaned in for a closer look as Sage snapped picture after picture. 'What is that?'

'Gold embroidery thread. The fabric it was on has rotted away.' Sage beckoned for the big arc light to be shone on the body, revealing tiny flowers, knotted in places with minute purple beads. 'I think those are amethyst.'

Elliott lay down on the clay to look around the side of the body. 'You said this Isabeau might be a seamstress. You would have thought this is much more than an embroideress could afford to wear, let alone be buried in.' He pointed with a finger, careful not to make contact. 'These bigger beads are rubies set in gold clasps.' He leaned forward until his face was almost touching the rib cage. 'These are minute. Careful, it's slippery.'

He knelt up and reached a hand to steady Sage as she crouched down at the body's feet. A flash of something in the mud beside the coffin had attracted her attention, and she pointed it out to Elliott: a tiny flash of gold, a single hook of gold wire, tangled in the debris. He dropped it into a specimen pot. Further searching revealed three more wire curves, and two beads. A larger bead gleamed from a layer of silt, this one still with a thread of gold arcing through it, with a minute eye at each end to connect to the next. As Sage brushed away more sediment, a tangle of gold thread, almost invisible, was washed out, this time hooked through more beads. It was so delicate she had to lift it out with tweezers. It looked like the finest chain, a delicate tangle of wires and beads terminating in a tiny cross, carved out of what appeared to be coral.

'What's this? Elliott, give me a box will you? I think it's all one piece.'

She handed it up to one of the students, who showed it to the others. One of the first-years, who had been looking a bit green at the opening of the coffin, answered. 'It's a rosary, isn't it? I mean – the cross, the beads.' She looked down at Sage, her colour back. 'I was confirmed, my parents are Catholic.'

'I think it is,' Sage answered.

'Look at this,' Elliott said, pointing at the chest area. 'It's a ruby cabochon.'

'Get back, Ell, before you fall in.' Sage looked up to the

ring of students. 'Anyone know what a cabochon is?'

Felix stepped forward when none of the students answered. 'I do,' he said, slowly smiling at her surprise. 'A cabochon is a gem that is polished into a curved surface rather than cut into facets.'

The cloth the embroidery had been sewn onto had almost completely dissolved, leaving fragments of more resilient linen underneath. A simple shift, its rags were moulded over the pelvis and down the thigh bones. Sage lifted an edge with forceps, and Elliott recorded with the camera.

She spoke softly to him. 'I think this was cut or torn before burial, this isn't decay.'

Elliott's eyebrows almost met in the middle of his forehead. 'Cut? You mean something happened to her? This wasn't illness?'

'Remember the baby?' Sage found herself choking on the words. 'The cuts on the bones.' She raised her voice so she could be heard by those above her. 'It has been suggested that she – Isabeau – was dying, and someone may have tried to save the baby by performing a caesarean.'

Elliott nodded. 'So they may have accidentally hurt the child trying to get it out. Those cuts on the baby's bones.'

Her own baby wriggled inside her, sending tiny shocks through Sage's bladder. *Don't listen, Bean.* She stood up, stretched her back. She was getting too big for this.

Elliott pointed out the bones of the hands, crossed on her chest, mostly in situ. 'It was unusual to bury people in clothes in the Tudor period,' he said. 'I did some research last night; normally bodies were wrapped in a length of cloth.'

Sage nodded, kneeling again to peer at the seams on the remaining shift. 'The original winding sheet. Look at the fragments of bodice,' she said, distracted by the delicacy of the web of embroidery. 'I'm not sure how to get it out intact.'

She could see the heavier, intact neckline of the shift, doubled over and decorated with a line of crossed stitches. She could see the slashes in the wide skirt leading to the thigh bones.

'OK, everyone.' She looked up at the students. 'Can anyone think how we can find out whether this body is the mother of the baby?'

'DNA?' offered one of the students.

She smiled. 'Possibly. Hugely expensive and it's very likely the DNA would be too degraded in the bones, especially the baby's, to match.'

The police officer raised a hand self-consciously. 'If the baby was cut out, you could compare the blade marks if they hit bone.'

'Straight to the top of the class, Constable. Now our only problem is getting her out with the stitching intact.'

A voice floated down to Sage. 'I have an idea, I don't know if it would work...'

'Yes, Natasha?'

'Well, we could press sticky paper or cloth to the

embroidery, at least pick it up in one piece, and maintain the relationship between the threads.'

Sage thought about it. It would be prohibitively expensive to remove the whole slab of soil underneath the skeleton, and much easier to simply remove the body. 'Phone the textiles team, see if they can suggest an adhesive and mounting fabric that would be easy to remove.' She knelt up, and wiped her forehead with her sleeve. 'Take over, would you, Yousuf?' She reached up for Felix to help her out.

'You need to take it easier,' he murmured.

'I will. I'm going to the car.' She felt dizzy. 'I got up too quickly.'

'That's enough. Time to sit down.' Even though his tone was relaxed, there was something there that made her accept his help to the van, and settle her into the seat. 'Yousuf knows what he's doing, as does Elliott. You've had a stressful week.'

'I know.'

He sat in the seat next to her and shut the door. It was a relief to be out of the wind. 'So, when's the baby due?'

She leaned her head towards him. 'June. We're really going to do small talk?'

He laughed. 'I think that would be a better idea than all this talk of death. Tell me about Nick. Did you sort things out after the meeting? He seemed a bit… protective, when I saw him at the vicarage.'

'I'm interested, but it's not a good time. To start a relationship, I mean.'

'There's never a good time.' Felix stared out through the windscreen. 'I met my partner when I was investigating an unexplained death in Exeter for the police.'

'How?' Sage closed her eyes.

'Jack knew the girl was there, knew why she had died.'

'Oh?'

'Jack believes in sorcery: the sorcery of Dee and Kelley. She gave me the choice of either helping her and respecting her beliefs, or staying out of her life. We've been together ever since.'

She was silent for a moment. 'I don't know what to say.'

'What I'm saying is, you and your vicar are both single and the attraction is obvious.'

Sage could feel the blush start across her face. 'Professor of love, huh?'

Felix smiled. 'I have a professional interest in universal *and* cultural body language.'

Sage looked up the hillside, spotted here and there with yellow flowers in the grass. 'What do you think happened to Steph?'

He grimaced. 'I think she was pushed into the well. Some might say it was predicted by the symbols carved into it.'

'Someone moved the cover, then pushed Steph in.' Sage felt sick at the thought. 'And put the cover back. Someone killed her deliberately.'

'I'm not arguing with you, other than to play Devil's advocate. All I'm saying is, some places seem haunted by… misfortune, shall we say. Although…'

'Although?'

'I was wondering if the Bassetts would consider letting an acoustic engineer examine the cottage. It has a very strange atmosphere. I can see why people think it's haunted.'

'I don't even think I can go back there. When I close my eyes, I see Steph's face in the water.'

'I'm just suggesting there may be something about the cottage that affects people's behaviour.'

'There was one thing, though it's probably nothing.'

'Go on.'

'Steph said there was someone hanging around the cottage. I thought – this is going to sound stupid – but I wondered if it was my ex. You know, checking up on me.'

'Have you told the police?'

Sage sighed. 'I had to.'

46

28th October 1580

To Mistress Browne, midwife to Lady Flora, upon the safe delivery of her female child ——————————— *two pounds*
For Master Williams upon the return of the rector's sister ——————————————————— *ten shillings*

Accounts of Banstock Manor, 1576–1582

new day at Banstock, after the night was made miserable by the labours of the lady of the manor. The gossips had assembled from the surrounding manors, goodwives to cluck and fuss over the poor woman even before her travail began. Now we are blessed with a healthy girl; not the son we all prayed for, but a hope for the future. The babe, tho' small, is fat and healthy and God willing, will grow into another daughter for the manor. The lady laboured through the night but at the end the babe was born easily. Lady Flora rests and is naturally exhausted, but the sight of her living child has given her heart and my lord says it was a wonder to see a smile on her lips at last.

'Next time, brother, a son for the manor!' It is rare he acknowledges our kinship, but I am named as godfather, as is Master Seabourne. We rarely speak of the fallen sons, so hopefully reared at Banstock, only to die upon maturity; the wound is too raw. In three years Lord Anthonie has lost two sons. Two of his other daughters with Lady Marion survive. One is married to a baron in Devon, but is childless tho' she eats a barrel of spiders a year and sleeps with cockerel feathers in her mattress. The other has a husband as old as her father, and there are no children yet. Neither are a penny to a pound to our sweet Viola.

She, the proud sister, was present at the labour and was a calming influence upon her stepmother. She feels herself a proper woman now as she is initiated into the great mysteries of childbed. She is busy in the nursery arranging her new sister's accommodation, no doubt enraging the old nursemaid and the wet nurse, who will complain to me later. So it is when women rule the house.

Isabeau is still in Ryde, living with Eliza Dread. There are those who whisper already that when the witch left the manor, my lady prospered and issued forth a healthy child.

Agness was returned by a farmer, raving, to the manor this morn. She has been confined to a storeroom and made comfortable with a mattress and chair. The woman lies racked by fits of rambling speech, screaming, and crying. Sometimes she is as a child, pleading for her mother; at other times she screeches with accusations and fantastic stories of witches and demons and other horrors. No matter, her madness cannot be heard in the upper floor, where lies my lady and her new baby.

A visit to my lady's bedchamber, now made comfortable by the uncovering of the windows and the burning of fragrant pastilles, is brief. I admire the baby, carried to my arms reverently by Viola, and remember that this is a new experience for her ladyship. She rests as best she can, in a room full of exultant matrons. She has, I am told, already put the babe to suck, and means to help feed her despite her lord's preference for a wet nurse. More mouths to feed, think I, with the gossips, the nurses.

Outside, clouds gather thick and heavy, and though it is not freezing it reminds me of snow. I send men to cover haystacks in the open, and I sup sweet wine with the baby in my arms. She is as other babies, her eyes wavering in all directions, yawning and sneezing and farting, but I do not hear her cry. She seems content. She is to be named Lily as requested by Viola, in some remembrance of the last poor lamb. One dies, one is born, such is the nature of life.

Vincent Garland, Steward to Lord Banstock, His Memoir

47

Friday 19th April

In the hospital's X-ray department, the body, pathetically thin and bundled in its muslin wrappings, appeared more like an Egyptian mummy than Tudor remains. Only the naked skull, jaws open, stood out. The technician slid the tray carrying the skeleton gently along the bed, feeding it into the scanner.

'This is really kind of you, Miles,' Sage murmured, from behind the protective window. 'Professor Sayeed's going to look at the images when you've got them.'

'I'll be interested to see what he makes of them.' The radiographer swept his hair out of his eyes, and signalled to the technician to join them. 'Come over here, Tomáš, you'll see something unusual. Bones buried for nearly four hundred and fifty years.'

'What are you looking for?' Tomáš peered at the screen as the first images started coming up.

'We're looking for injuries. The faintness you can see comes from demineralisation. Rainwater's acid, it filters in and gradually washes the bones' calcium away.' Miles swivelled in his chair towards her. 'This will take a while, Sage. Why don't you go and get a drink? The canteen is open for another twenty minutes.'

Sage winced. She'd been rubbing her back for a while now. 'I think I will, if just to sit down.'

She had only just sat down with a mug of tea and a large sandwich when she heard someone saying her name. She looked up. 'Elliott?'

'Can I talk to you?'

'Of course. How are you doing?' She noticed that he was nervously moving his weight from foot to foot. Sage picked up her tea, and sighed. 'Sit down, for goodness' sake.'

'Professor Sayeed told me you were X-raying the bones tonight.' He sat, resting his elbows on his knees. 'I hope you don't mind me coming along. I didn't have a chance to really talk to you yesterday. You know the police questioned me?'

'I know. They questioned me too.' The cold awful certainty of the white face in the black water crept into her memory. 'They knew you worked with Steph on the dig.'

'We weren't friends, and I wasn't interested in Steph like that. They're saying I must have been the last person to see her, but I left before she did. This whole thing is giving me nightmares. The baby and the woman in the well, then

Steph... Plus retrieving that body yesterday. It must have upset you too.' He rubbed his face with a hand. 'When you have so much else to worry about.'

Sage sipped her tea. She rubbed the bump before she realised what she was doing. It was a satisfying curve now, and she caught Elliott looking at it. 'You must wonder why I seem so detached about the dead baby.'

He stared at her. 'I didn't think about it.'

'I'm not blind to it, but it was an event that happened so many centuries ago. Millions of babies were dying from disease, starvation, neglect, even ignorance. This is the story of just one.'

He nodded. 'It's more important to care about the living than the dead. I admire you for choosing to bring a baby up on your own.'

'I don't have much choice.' She took a bite of her sandwich.

'You don't have to be with someone just because they're the father.'

Something about his voice made her look at him. 'What?'

He shrugged. 'I mean, you're young, life is long. You don't need to rush into anything just to look after a baby.'

She put her tea down with a thud, and it seemed to startle him. The conversation was making her uncomfortable although she wasn't sure why. Time to change the subject. 'What you found with that alembic glass was ground-breaking, Elliott. You may be able to help historians fill in some more details of how sixteenth-century scientists worked, what they were thinking. Finding the metal oxides they were working with is as good as it gets, an insight into the work of someone dead hundreds of years.'

He seemed surprised. 'I suppose so. It may not be exactly related to the bones—'

'We don't know that. It may even be the reason that baby is down the well. Who can say? Professor Guichard is here to consult about the ritual aspect of the case. I think he might be able to advise you on funding for further research.'

Elliott nodded, lowering his head to avoid her gaze. 'The alembic has been a fascinating puzzle. I've been reading about chrysopoeia, the transformation of metals into gold.'

'And?' She smiled down at the top of his dark curly head. His hair was already thinning at the crown. She got a glimpse of what he might be like in a decade's time, passionate about his craft, fascinated with history. She'd got into the habit of thinking he was the same age as the other students but looking at him she remembered he was in his late twenties. Not much younger than her.

'It's done now by bombarding mercury with neutrons. It produces unstable forms of mercury which decay into thorium and gold.'

'Thorium? Didn't you find that in the glass?'

'Some. Also uranium, as you know.' He managed a shaky laugh. 'I'm not suggesting Solomon Seabourne used a particle accelerator to make gold, but there is some gold in the sample. Maybe he did it. Actually made gold.'

'Well, that would hit the tabloids,' Sage said. 'Look, Ell, you can't talk about this until all the results are back. You also need to share this with someone from analytical chemistry.'

'I know.'

Sage was trying to engage him, but he looked at his hands again. 'I know Steph's death is hard on you, it is for all of us.'

'I wish you wouldn't think there was anything between me and Steph.' His mouth twisted. 'And I don't want the police assuming a relationship where there wasn't any. I'm sorry she's dead, of course.' That at least sounded sincere. 'But I don't want to talk about it.'

'Of course.' The police must have given him a hard time. Sage swallowed. 'I can't help Steph but I'm going to distract myself with an ancient tragedy instead, and leave the police to work out what happened. Would you like to come and see the X-rays?'

He half smiled. 'I'd like that.'

Yousuf had set up in one of the offices in radiology. He had his glasses propped on his forehead and was poring over the results when they found him. 'This is remarkable. Oh, Sage, this is Dr Henderson, the head of radiography and imaging.'

A short man with a circlet of white hair grasped her hand, hard. 'Hello, Sage. This is a very interesting case.'

She leaned closer to the screen. 'What am I looking at?'

Yousuf pointed to the lowest rib, to a white line, vivid against the white threads of embroidery. 'This is the X-ray we took first. That, my dear, is the tip of a Tudor dagger. I'd put my reputation on it.' A swipe of the mouse enlarged the image and Sage saw the triangular wedge he was talking about.

'This is the skeleton of an otherwise healthy female probably in her twenties,' Dr Henderson said. 'I'm afraid she has been the victim of a particularly serious assault that almost certainly would have killed her. There is a skull fracture, broken ribs and clavicle, and some injuries to the ribs that look like stab wounds.'

That caught Sage's attention. 'Can you say what was done to her?'

Yousuf's voice was soft, soothing. 'There is a serious peri-mortem head injury; she might have been out cold before or around the time she was stabbed *here*, in the chest. If you're assuming she was pregnant, in order for the baby to have any chance, it would have to have been delivered in minutes, no longer. The abdominal injury, even if the knife avoided any major blood vessels, would have been fatal on its own. We see a nick in the pelvis *here*, and a cut on the rib up here.'

Elliott shrugged, but Sage slowly understood the sequence, imagined the frightened woman trying to save herself, save the baby. 'Why would an injured woman be cut in this way if she wasn't pregnant? She was already badly hurt.'

'In Elizabethan medicine caesareans were rarely attempted, mostly because babies didn't survive. This is incredibly rare.' Henderson pulled up an image of an X-ray on his laptop. 'This was from a case in New Mexico, nine years ago. See, the nick to the side of the breastbone, and the corresponding nick in the pelvis. This was a panicked incision; the mother was shot in the head, the baby had minutes at best. There's a lot of anatomy in the way.'

Professor Sayeed indicated the ribs. 'See, here is a similar cut a little further over. If the baby was breech, its collar bone and humerus could have been in the path of the knife. Which we saw on the bones from the well.'

Sage tried to keep her voice calm, even if her gut was squirming at the thought. 'How can you be sure she wasn't unconscious or even dead before they took the baby?'

Yousuf pointed to the shadowy hand bones on the screen. 'This is a stab wound clean through the palm, it shattered the capitate bone. It's a classic defensive wound.'

Elliott pushed a chair forward. Sage sat down without thinking. It dawned on her. 'You think Isabeau was killed *for* her baby?'

Henderson cleared his throat. 'Dr Sayeed and I can suggest a sequence of events that fits the evidence.'

'She was stunned first,' said Yousuf. He indicated a crack on the back of the skull. 'These fine lines suggest a considerable force from a blunt object. She may well have died from bleeding in the brain if she hadn't been injured further.'

'Then?' Elliott was leaning in to see the screen.

Henderson answered. 'Maybe she was rolled onto her back, and put out a hand to ward off a knife. Then she may have received the stab to the chest, which scored the ribs either side. It probably went straight through her breast.'

The image made Sage wince. She swallowed hard, to try and clear the lump in her throat at the thought of the poor woman. 'Then, the baby?'

'The mother may have been unconscious or even already dead.'

She spoke slowly. 'But you don't think that, do you?'

He pointed up at the screen. 'Fractured collarbone, broken second and third rib on the left side. I think someone knelt on, or otherwise restrained her. Perhaps to cut open the abdomen. Which was done from the pelvis up, in a slashing motion,' he demonstrated on himself, 'like *this*. The knife stuck in the lowest rib and broke the tip off.'

'To get the baby.' The murmur came from Elliott.

Yousuf nodded. 'I think it unlikely that she was injured then another person tried to deliver the baby. A rescuer would not kneel on a dying woman: it's counterintuitive. This scenario is unique in the historical record of the Island.'

Henderson cleared his throat. 'Foetal abductions, though incredibly rare, do occur, and are often associated with psychotic delusions in the attacker, who is almost always female. She may believe the baby will salvage a failing relationship if she claims it's hers. Some even think the baby is their own, in the wrong body.'

Sage let the thoughts whirling in her head settle. 'So Isabeau – we're fairly certain that's her – was actually pregnant. That much of the legend was true.'

'Yeah, but who was the attacker?' Elliott said.

'Well, the woman who was interred with the baby's body must be a possible suspect.' Sage stood up, suddenly needing to move. 'Think about it: who would carry a stolen baby around, unless they had just taken it?'

Yousuf's voice was heavy with scepticism. 'That's quite a jump.'

'A woman went missing on 13th November 1580. Agness Waldren, I've seen her memorial.' Sage rummaged in her bag for her tablet. 'There was some sort of storm, I think. She was never found.'

'So you think she may have been buried in the well after being killed?' Elliott asked.

Sage turned to Yousuf. 'How did the woman in the well die?'

Yousuf winced. 'The fall itself could have killed her. She was probably alive when she went in, because she hit the bottom with one leg extended, not limp; it was forced into her pelvis by the impact. A dead body would be more likely to fold up on impact. Her other femur was shattered, the leg pulled up along her body. The well must have been almost empty of water at the time.'

Sage gripped his hand with both of hers. 'Thank you, Yousuf, Dr Henderson.' She nodded to Elliott. 'That's enough drama for us today, Ell. I'll drop you home if you like.'

Sage sat at her desk at home, listening to the sounds of the town as it edged the shore. Ferries, cars, people laughing on the promenade. The massive fans that steered the hovercraft spat droplets of kerosene-flavoured spray onto the window, even three floors up.

On her computer screen, the X-ray of the skeleton was a ghostly grey against the background, the gold net embroidery and clusters of gems showing up as white tracery. The effect was the shadowy form of a woman, draped in spiders' webs and flowers. She shut down the computer, wondering if just one glass of wine would do any harm to the baby. Instead she rang Nick.

'Yes.' The voice was crisp, impatient.

She ended the call. The phone rang a moment later. She answered.

'Hello? Sage?'

'Yes.' The tears started welling up as she heard his voice, and she let them spill onto her cheeks. 'I thought— I just had a really bad day.'

'Me too. James Bassett collapsed at home today. He's

at the hospice, Judith is with him.' Nick sighed, and Sage imagined him slumping onto the sofa. 'What happened to spoil your day?'

'We dug Isabeau up. The local radiology department had a look at her body. There's little doubt it is her. She was covered with embroidery – very expensive gold thread and gemstones – which raises questions in itself.'

'And?' His voice was soft, and deep. 'Sage?'

'They – the radiologist and Yousuf – think that Isabeau may have been attacked by someone with the purpose of stealing her baby.' She could hear Nick take a breath but powered on over his reaction. 'It's called foetal abduction. It's very rare but—'

'You think the woman in the well cut Isabeau's baby out?' Nick's voice was appalled.

'Maybe. Yousuf is a forensic anthropologist, he says he could interpret the findings that way.' Sage cradled her bump with her free hand. 'It was horrible, listening to that with Bean wriggling inside me.'

'Bean?'

'The baby.' She looked at the clock: nine thirty. 'Is it too late to come and see you? I could sleep on the sofa, scandalise the village some more.'

'No, don't do that.' His voice was firm. 'I'll come to you, scandalise your neighbours instead. I may get called away to the Bassetts though. I suppose you have a sofa?'

Sage sighed with relief. 'I do.'

'So, you'd better give me your address.'

She gave it to him, then tidied up the flat. It took her mind off stolen babies and dying students. By the time she had washed up a sink full of dishes, he was at the door.

When she opened it she couldn't speak, as if all the words had been said. She could feel him smile as he kissed her.

48

13th November 1580

Four yards of linens for swaddling your lordship's daughter Lily, at one shilling and two pence a yard

———— four shillings and eight pence

Accounts of Banstock Manor, 1576–1582

Two weeks later life at the manor was torn apart by a single mistake. A man, taking a tray of food to Mistress Agness, soon to be shipped to a special house for mad gentlewomen, left the door on the latch for a moment, forgetting the bolt. He realised his error and turned to the lock, but Mistress Agness was on him like a wild animal, biting and scratching. He is not a young man and fell under her greater weight, hitting his head against the wall. He lies in bed with a palsy down one side of his body, nursed by his wife and daughter, but I doubt of his recovery.

The woman is free. The rector and his man join the searchers across the farms and along the harbour, but the sky is dark with clouds and the wind brisk. On foot, we beat our way through the woods that line the shore and are lit up by great flashes of lightning. There a man finds a cloak, caught on the branches of one of the low trees that line the sandy shore. It is long and plain like a man's cloak, but I think immediately of Agness.

The tide is sweeping in, foam blowing from the tops of rollers that break upon the stone ledges. They line our shore under the sand and bring many a sailor to grief. There, against the little remaining light as dusk is hastened in, stands the shape of Agness. Her arms are outstretched into the wind, upon the rocky shelves that push into the sea, in a parody of a crucifixion. The first of the waves are licking at her boots, and she is screeching something wordless into the tempest.

'Agness!' I shout, waving the men to try and reach her. One man slips on the weeds growing on the rocks, another hesitates.

'The waves are too strong,' he shouts to me over the crash of the sea. 'One stumble and we're lost!' Indeed, the boiling and hissing of the water surging between the rocks is getting closer, catching the light in the foaming of the waves.

'Back then,' I say, beckoning the fallen man to safety. 'She is mad indeed.'

We watch as the sea slaps her skirt with each wave, causing her to stagger. Thomas, one of the grooms, leaps forward to within reach of her flailing arms and catches her elbow. He drags her a few feet from the clutches of the sea, but she pushes him off.

'No!' she shrieks, bounding across the ledge away from him. 'Don't you see? The French witch has called up a storm!'

A sound, like a tree breaking but many times louder, cracks the air. The whole world is made white by lightning. Thomas falls to his knees and Allen Montaigne, Seabourne's man, pulls me away as the roar of thunder breaks over our heads like a thousand drums.

'God will save me,' Agness bellows, her voice cracked like a crow's. The second crack of lightning throws me onto my face on the sand, the thunder deafening me, rolling around inside my head. The flash blinds me even through closed eyelids.

When I look up, and brush the sand from my beard and spit out salty grit, Thomas is crawling towards me.

'Where is she?' cries Allen Montaigne. 'I cannot see her.' He gives me a hand, and I pull myself up. Behind us, a blazing tree close to the shore is split asunder by the force of the skyfire. When I turn to the sea, she is gone, and though we search the shoreline until dark, we can find no trace of her.

Vincent Garland, Steward to Lord Banstock, His Memoir

49

Sometime during the night, Nick must have left the sofa and stretched out beside Sage on top of the duvet. She could hear him breathing when she woke to the sunshine striping through the blinds.

He roused with a start, as if at her awareness of him. He turned over towards her, propped up on one arm.

'Hello.' He rubbed his hand through his hair, making it stand up.

'Good morning.' She adjusted her T-shirt before she sat up. 'How did you end up…?'

'You had a nightmare.'

She could remember being woken from it vaguely, a soft voice telling her everything was all right, a hand rubbing her shoulders. 'I dreamed I couldn't find the baby.'

'It's probably that horror story Felix told you yesterday.'

'It was Yousuf, the forensics professor, who told me the

horror story about stealing a baby from its mother. It was bad enough thinking someone did it to Isabeau without hearing people have done it in the modern day.' She looked across at him. 'Don't you like Felix?'

He shrugged. 'He seems OK.'

'You're jealous!' She started to laugh. 'Of Felix?'

Nick grinned at her. 'You were jealous of my volunteer, Mel, as I recall. Anyway, he's good-looking; he had Lady George and her friends batting their eyelids at the meeting at the manor.'

'He's nice, that's all. And he knows his medieval history, which is *really* sexy. I once dated someone because they knew all the dates of the War of the Roses. He's also involved with someone. Anyway, I have to get up. I've got to work on the mainland this morning, on the clothing recovered from the grave. It needs to be ready for the textiles experts to start the conservation on Monday.'

'Working on a Saturday?'

'It's the only time the lab isn't full of students and it won't take long. What about James? Have you heard anything?'

'They said they would call if he deteriorated. They think he's had a bleed into his brain, a stroke.'

Sage put her feet onto a warm patch lit up by a rectangle of sun. 'Poor man. I really like him.'

'Poor Judith and Chloe.' Nick hunched his shoulders. 'I hate these young deaths. Old people – it's sad but somehow it feels right. Timely. But James has so much life to live.'

'And Steph. Twenty years old.'

He grimaced. She remembered his own loss, and rubbed his shoulder briefly before rising heading for the bathroom. The warmth of his skin through the cotton made her hand tingle.

By the time she had showered and cleaned her teeth, she realised she was going to have to cross the bedroom in just a towel, but Nick had already gone into the kitchen. She could smell coffee and toast as she dressed.

He was in yesterday's clothes, somewhat rumpled, having slept in a T-shirt and boxers. He was texting when she walked in.

'I don't have a spare toothbrush, I'm afraid,' she said.

'I brought one with me,' he said, lifting a small bag. 'Deodorant, razor, toothbrush. You have no idea how often I end up staying in someone's house unexpectedly.'

'Part of the job?'

He shrugged. 'I also come from a big family.'

'Three sisters.' She reached for the coffee he had already poured. 'I remember. Is this decaf?'

'Definitely.'

'Thank you.' She sipped the coffee. Half-ideas flitted through her mind, but she couldn't pin them down.

Nick turned towards the window, and stretched out his legs. 'I'm called up to my parents' a lot. My dad's got dementia. He's at the stage where he occasionally doesn't recognise my mother. Gets upset, even lashes out.' His profile gave little away. 'I go over to calm him down, support Mum. She's not ready to let him go to a home, not just yet.' He turned to Sage. 'We all have our problems.'

'Yes, we do.' She took a piece of toast and buttered it. 'Your family's problems make my baby worries seem trivial.'

'Nothing about a baby is trivial.' He smiled at her. 'You wait until after he or she is born.'

Sage couldn't face using her mobile phone although the police assured her they had removed the picture of Steph's body, and had given the police her work number instead. They had left a message asking her to come to the main police station as soon as she could.

The police station was quiet. She was soon taken through to Inspector Belmont's office.

'Dr Westfield, thank you for coming in again.' He pulled out a chair for her, then sat behind his desk and swivelled his computer screen around so she could see it. 'This is the best image we could get from the camera footage taken in Bramble Cottage.'

The shadowy figure looked as indistinct as before. 'That's it. James – Mr Bassett – thought the camera might capture the person making nuisance calls. Or rather, he wanted to rule out any suspicion of it being someone living in the house.'

Belmont pressed a few keys, and the contrast between light and dark increased. 'The only features we've been able to enhance are the line of the jaw and part of the nose.'

Sage leaned closer, staring at the image. A tiny gleam of light stared back, from the glossy curve of one eye. 'I don't know. Maybe it is Mr Bassett.' The second she said it she dismissed it. 'No. No, he has a pointier chin.'

'Dr Westfield, can you think of any reason why someone would be in the Bassetts' house late at night? We know it's not the wife, the doctor, or any of their relatives.'

She shrugged. 'Why are you asking me? I hardly know Judith or James, just through the dig.' She looked back at the image.

The inspector sat back and folded his arms. 'To be honest, Dr Westfield—'

'Sage, please.'

'Sage. We think the man in the picture, who may have been in the Bassetts' home, could be Marcus Thompson, your ex-boyfriend. We aren't sure how he got in; the Bassetts have a modern alarm.'

'He sold them the house. He must have had the keys and the alarm code, I suppose, when he showed them around. Most people don't change the locks when they move, I remember him telling me that.' Sage looked down at her hands.

Belmont's voice was gentle. 'I understand he's the father of your baby.'

'Yes. We ended it a couple of months ago. Actually, I ended it.'

'He doesn't seem to realise that. He says he's giving you space to deal with the pregnancy.'

She managed a small smile. 'He's arrogant. But I haven't seen him for some weeks and—' She broke off. 'Actually, I did think I saw him in Banstock on the first, and a couple of days before that on the ferry. But he sells a lot of property in East Wight, he's often over there.'

'But to your knowledge, he never met Stephanie Beatson.'

'Steph said there was a man hanging around the cottage. He spoke to her, I think, about whether the house would be for sale. She sent him away. She called him a ghoul.'

'She never mentioned a boyfriend, anyone she might have been involved with?'

Sage thought back to the day they saw Agness Waldren's memorial. 'She was hoping Elliott Robinson would ask her out. He wasn't interested though.' She looked up. 'You know, he was deeply involved in the excavation. I took up most of his time and attention.'

Belmont looked at her intensely, and she felt her colour rise. Talking to a policeman always made her feel a bit guilty.

He cleared his throat. 'We'll clear the garden as a crime scene shortly. I'll let you know when you can get back there. I understand you were having the well filled in.'

'We just have to make sure the garden is left tidy, reseed the ground.' Unexpected, irrational tears filled her eyes.

Belmont looked sympathetic. 'I'm sorry. It's always hard when someone that age dies.'

Sage pulled out a tissue and dabbed her eyes. 'You are absolutely sure someone did this deliberately?'

'Yes. And at the moment, everyone who knew Stephanie has to be eliminated as a suspect. Are you going off the Island for any reason?'

She clutched her bag to her chest. 'Work, and then I'm going over to Hampshire to stay with my mother. Then I have an appointment on Monday on my way back to the Island. I'm hoping to find out more about the textiles we exhumed in the woods in Banstock.'

Belmont made a note. 'We'll be in touch.'

50

17th November 1580

Three dozen iron-hilted knives for the betrothal banquet
—————————————————————————— *eighteen shillings*

Accounts of Banstock Manor, 1576–1582

The manor is a quiet place now the storm has blown through. The winds have chased away the rain and lightning, but left the first hard frosts, dusting the stone walls and wooden fences with white. The Reverend Matthew Waldren seems caught between relief and guilt at his sister's disappearance. We can give him no comfort; anyone in that maelstrom was surely dashed to death against the rocks or drowned. Her heavy skirts at least would have made her struggles short.

Viola is strangely affected, sad for the loss of someone who, though troublesome, was part of the life of the manor.

She gathers the last of the frost-faded flowers and comes down to the shore with me and Elias. She casts the blossoms onto the edge of the tide, just lapping the sand, quiet again.

We climb the low ridge so she can inspect the shattered tree, cleaved in two by a single bolt from heaven. The scent of charring still hangs in the air. On the ground lies a patch of sand fused into a lump.

'This must be where the lightning hit,' she says, touching a finger to it cautiously. 'Look, Master Vincent.'

I inspect it, but my attention is drawn to figures walking along the shore. Viola recognises them first, with her young eyes.

''Tis Master Seabourne and his man,' she says.

'Perhaps they seek the—' my tongue stalls over the word.

'Body?' she smiles at me, her mouth a little crooked. 'Hers is not the first.'

She speaks of a time when a fishing boat, driven off the shores of Portsmouth by high winds, was wrecked upon the ledges. Three men drowned and only one found shelter upon the shore. Viola and her sister Elizabeth were amongst a party that came upon the bodies.

I turn to greet the newcomers. 'Good morrow, Master Seabourne, Kelley,' I say, and Viola smiles so widely he cannot but respond.

'I am sorry to see you upon such a melancholy task,' says he, looking at her. I see then, as the breeze takes a strand of her fox hair escaped from her hood, and it reaches for him. He is bareheaded, in his shirtsleeves despite the cold, and looks like a young man again. They only have eyes for each other, and I look away as her hand touches his.

'Viola has found some rock where the lightning struck the ground,' I say, and she pulls away to lead us to the tree.

Kelley examines the ground, digging around the strange stone, until he pulls out a stick of it. 'See?' he says, showing it to Viola. 'The great heat and light of the storm has made a crude glass from the sand.' He hefts it, feeling its nature, sniffing at it. It does smell as if it were forged metal. 'So much heat and light infused into the glass,' he mused. 'That force might be of use to your work, Master.'

'But who can command a storm?' Viola laughs, touching the thing.

Elias leans over to see it. 'There's them that say that witches call up storms. They say Reverend Matthew's sister summoned a tempest and it blew her away.' He looks at me, and shrugs. 'Ignorant people say it's so.'

It seems to me that many people think so, including our stolid Elias.

There is no news of Agness but the cold continues, freezing the pond so that the children of the village skate upon the ice to the annoyance of ducks and swans, who needs must sit upon the fields to graze and forage. The weakest of the calves has died, despite being placed in one of the barns, and the berries are shrivelling upon the thorns in the woods.

Reverend Waldren seems almost content that his sister is out of her great sorrow, and is certain that she is in heaven. Myself, I hear strange rumours of a black-faced creature, perhaps a shade, looking in at cottage windows and being snatched away by the wind.

Master Seabourne has been conducting experiments in the grounds of Well House to the disquiet of the villagers. Once he created a thunderclap of his own, and half of his eyebrows were burned, as if he had lighted gunpowder. My brother has allowed him to visit the manor and see Viola in the company of one of the women, but while Isabeau still lives on the Island he will not yet consent to a wedding. He has relented enough to plan a betrothal party, at least.

Isabeau is now resting, her belly great. We pay for her room, food and candles to finish the work of the kirtle she makes for Viola. She mourns her lover, but he is pledged not to see her. I have grown fond of her and enjoy visiting her. Growing up at the French court she is somewhat educated, and we know in common many great lords and ladies in London. Isabeau loves Viola and speaks warmly of her, and her role in the life of little Lily, who grows bonny in the nursery. She has sewn a cap for the baby, with a sprig of lily-of-the-valley flowers as fine as if the embroideries were painted on.

I journey to the port of Ryde to see if a body washed

up upon the shore there is indeed Agness. I first call at Isabeau's lodgings, but there I am greeted by bad news. The local people, much sympathetic to the legend of Agness, have taken to whispering about the 'French witch', and her magics and curses. Now, the landlady fears that she cannot protect the woman, or even her own property.

Isabeau stands to greet me, and bows less gracefully, swollen with her babe as she is now. 'They say Mistress Waldren has drowned, and is washed up on the shore.' She shudders.

'Indeed. I am going to inspect the body.'

She indicates her sewing chest. 'I have finished Viola's dresses. If I can go to the mainland now, I could escape the rumours.' She touches the neck of her gown. 'For you know, Master Vincent, that whatever I am, I am no witch.'

No witch, lady, thinks I, *but a papist.* That's the only secret the girl has left. 'You cannot risk the boat in your condition,' I answer. 'You must come back to Banstock.' I think about the washed-up body. 'Pack your things, and I will hire a cart to carry you.' There is a small cottage, dry and warm, but too small for a family on the estate. It is close to Well House, which fills me with misgivings, but at least she can bear her child in peace.

I leave the house with Isabeau's thanks still in my ears, and walk down the hill to the fisherman's chapel close to the shore. A sturdy yeoman guards the door, but when he hears my errand, he unbars it and I go inside.

The shutters have been left open for air, and I see why when the body is revealed. The white, swollen thing surely died in the summer when the waters were warmer, for there is little left of the face or the hands and feet, perhaps eroded by the sea or eaten by crabs and fish. The swollen, ragged flesh makes it hard to see whether it is man or woman, although it is naked but for a few rags. It is probably tall enough to be Mistress Agness, and the remaining hair is long, but I have no impression of it being the rector's demented sister.

'I know not this person,' I say, backing away and covering my nose. The stench is vile, and I hack and spit on the ground outside. 'The woman I seek has only gone into the sea a few days since.'

'There is a widow coming over on the packet, thinks it might be her husband, fell off the quay at Portsmouth.' He bars the door and takes a deep breath of sweet air. 'Sooner in the ground, the better, says I.'

I walk back up the hill to the small row of houses and see that the carrier has arrived and is speaking to some fellow outside the landlady's door. Isabeau seems to hide inside the open door, away from the raised voice.

'Is there some problem?' I ask, as sternly as I am able, which is much I think, for they turn to me immediately and doff their hats.

'I was just told, yer honour,' speaks the driver, 'that I'm to carry a proven witch on my cart.'

'Nothing of the kind, my man,' says I, but it takes some persuading and an extra shilling to brighten his eye with enough greed to load the girl's boxes onto his cart.

I hand Isabeau onto the wagon, where a sturdy bench sits, and resolve to ride with the vehicle until we are home at Banstock.

Vincent Garland, Steward to Lord Banstock, His Memoir

51

The University of West Sussex's textiles lab was arranged more like a design studio than any kind of laboratory that Sage had ever seen. Clothes were arranged on mannequins or hung on the wall; pin boards were covered with sketches and samples. The leader of the team was a man in a black velvet suit and a floral shirt that looked like it fell out of the sixties.

'You must be Sage, Cally told me you were coming over.' He grasped her hand warmly. 'I'm Titus Armstrong. I was so sorry to hear what happened to your student.'

'Thank you.' Sage managed a tight smile. 'So, have you been able to identify the fabric?'

'We have, and extrapolate what the dress itself looked like, partly from the embroidery. It's a real murder mystery, isn't it?'

'How does the embroidery help?'

Titus showed her a sketch of a tight bodice, highly ornamented, and a flaring skirt. 'They are separate garments,' he said, putting a pair of half-glasses on his nose. 'The decoration would only have been where it would have been seen. The base fabric was blue silk, a sort of mid-range turquoise, we think, from GC-MS. We can tell the origins from trace elements. This fabric was incredibly rare in Tudor England, very expensive, bought from Spain. Only the areas that were doubled over, like seams at the armholes, are preserved at all.'

'We think the dead woman was a seamstress. Maybe it belonged to her.'

Titus raised his eyebrows. 'I very much doubt it. As I say, the fabric was imported silk, probably from Valencia, gorgeous stuff. If it was buried, we would expect it to be on someone with massive financial clout or social status. Also, the dress was actually draped over the body, she wasn't wearing it, which is strange.'

'And the embroidery?' Sage leaned over more sketches, enchanted by the tracery of flowers.

'Well, I'm not so much of an expert there, but one of my colleagues, Dr Bashira Enwright, she's had a look at it, and thinks she recognises some of the knots. It was certainly applied at a later date. The fabric may be from as early as 1530, but the stitching is closer to 1600.'

He motioned for her to join him at a computer monitor, and brought up several photographs. In close-up, the embroidery looked like a spider's web hung with minute multi-coloured drops of dew. 'How do you know that?'

'Two things. The thread is English, polychrome silk, and it barely penetrates the fabric underneath. The gold thread design is what's called couching; it is laid on the fabric and secured by almost invisible silk stitches. Bashira recognised the workmanship.'

'Oh?'

'Queen Catherine de' Medici of France had an embroideress called Marguerite Duchamp. She came to England about 1570, employed by John Parr, the queen's embroiderer. Marguerite was employed to adapt gifts of cloth for Queen Elizabeth. Some of the silks came from Queen Mary's wardrobe, some may even be older.'

'Recycling the old?'

'These clothes were priceless, even for a queen. Queen Elizabeth's wardrobe and jewellery were her most valuable assets after her lands. Marguerite Duchamp repaired, ornamented and cared for the queen's clothes along with several seamstresses, all under the Master of the "Broderies", Parr. Marguerite was a young widow with a child, who grew up at court and also became a royal embroideress.'

'Isabeau Duchamp.'

He smiled at her. 'Exactly. Except the dress was incredibly unlikely to be in the grave of a commoner.'

'The headstone above the body says, "Damozel Isabeau".

We believe "damozel" is a corruption or an anglicisation of "mademoiselle".'

'It's still unlikely. It would be like burying fifty, sixty thousand pounds in cash in a coffin today. No way would this Isabeau ever have been able to afford anything like that.'

'Are there any records on Isabeau?'

'She was working at the court by 1576, so born about 1550 to 1560. How old is the grave?'

'We aren't sure. We don't know much. She's linked in local Island legend to a man called Solomon Seabourne, who lived in the village of Banstock. He went on to become engaged to one of the daughters of the manor in 1580.'

'So, why did you dig the poor girl up?'

Sage sketched out the sequence of events.

'And the body in the grave had been pregnant?'

'The skeleton suggests she had been pregnant, and she appeared to have injuries that suggest a caesarean.'

'Sad.' He changed the picture on the monitor. 'Maybe if the father was rich—' He gazed at her over his half-glasses. 'That helps explain the other half of the story, really, the shift. You know the petticoat was cut up the middle?'

Sage looked at the screen. 'We thought so.'

'We found a single hole in the petticoat, about here,' he indicated the front of his chest.

'There was a cut to one of her ribs, and other injuries. We originally wondered if she'd been in an accident and someone tried to save the baby.'

'Oh, I don't think so.' Titus pulled up a reconstruction diagram on the screen. 'These are the cuts in the shift.'

There was a slashing cut to the chest, then a rent up the front that had given access to the baby. Involuntarily, Sage touched her belly.

'We photographed the shift before it fell apart. Here, under an alternative light source, you can just see the blood spatter. It's like a crime scene, isn't it?' He sounded almost gleeful, but Sage felt sick. 'It could have been a caesarean except they didn't pull the clothes up.'

'We think she was still alive when they attacked her.' She looked at him. 'The forensic anthropologist thinks she was killed so someone could steal her baby. There are cuts on the bones... and the baby's bones too.'

'Oh, God.' His mouth twisted in distaste. 'That poor girl.' He paused for a moment, then handed Sage a folder. 'This is Bashira's report. She would love to chat more about it, she's running down the patterns in the weaving. Her number's in there. Let us know what you find out — this is fascinating.'

'I will.' Sage opened the folder, leafing through printed images of tiny details of the embroidery: gold twists, threaded with amethyst purples and white pearls. 'These flowers are beautiful.'

Titus leaned in. 'They are, aren't they? Bashira identified them as representing sweet violets. Violas.'

* * *

Sage checked her messages when she got back to the Island, then put a frozen dinner in the microwave. 'Sorry, Bean,' she murmured to her abdomen and the stretching baby inside. 'It does say it's a healthy version. I promise we'll have some salad with it.' She pulled a bag of what looked like seaweed out of the fridge. 'OK, tomatoes, anyway.'

Her mobile phone beeped. Nick had texted saying that James Bassett was dying. He was talking to Pat, Judith's mother, about how to give her granddaughter the news.

Her shoes, always a little tight, had left white lines where her feet had swollen. *Maybe it's time to take that maternity leave.* She pulled off her clothes with relief, and changed into the only garments that didn't pull or constrict her: maternity pyjamas. The microwave meal, eaten slumped on the sofa with her feet up in front of some inane programme, was dull but warming. Soon she had fallen into a doze.

Sage woke suddenly, not sure what had disturbed her. The television was still murmuring in the corner and she was cold. She tried to settle down again, knowing she ought to go to bed – but something was bothering her. She struggled to her feet, looking around the flat, trying to spot something different, at the same time telling herself she was still half asleep. Books piled in rambling stacks. A hairbrush left on the coffee table. Post in a tidy pile—

wait. She looked at the letters one by one. A letter from her dentist, reminding her to book a check-up, had been carefully opened. For a moment she thought of her mother; she had a key, but no one else did.

Marcus. She looked around the room more carefully. Had Marcus been snooping around, checking up on her? He had sold her the flat, that's how they met, and it was easy enough to copy a key.

The thought of Marcus coming into her home uninvited, looking through her stuff, reading her mail, maybe listening to her messages, made Sage feel sick. She sat on the edge of her bed, sliding a hand over Bean. She felt cold, and wrapped her arms around herself.

There were other things that weren't quite right. Her diary was sat squarely on her desk, on the mouse mat. Her pregnancy notes weren't shoved on the bedside table, they were on top of the book she was reading. A note from Nick; he must have written it on Saturday morning. *I like this sleepover thing. Maybe we should do it again? N x*

It was left out on the coffee table, smoothed open although there were creases where Nick must have folded it. Someone had opened it up, left it for her to find. *This was today. Someone has been in the flat today.*

For one crazy moment she wondered if that someone was still in the flat, hiding in her wardrobe, lying under the bed. Her heart started thumping in her chest, skipping beats until she felt cold and shaky. She picked up her coat, still on the chair by the door, grabbed her phone and keys and fled the flat.

She dialled Nick as she clattered down the stairs. His phone was off, of course: maybe he was at the Bassetts'. With a cold shiver that ran down her spine and made her hunch her shoulders up she realised the calls could be from Marcus. But how would he know…? Of course, the day she met Nick in the church she thought she saw Marcus going into one of the village houses. Maybe he was in Banstock doing a valuation and had seen her with Nick. Was he always that suspicious? He had always treated her diary and phone as if they were an extension of her; there was no privacy from him, no secrets. He often asked her where she was working, where she was going. God, he could be watching her right now.

52

8th December 1580

*By your lordship's commandment, repairs by the carpenter to the orchard cottage for Mistress Isabeau, in planks of oak and chestnut beams ⊶⸺⸺ twelve shillings and two pence
Also fifteen bushels of straw to repair the thatch
⊶⸺⸺ eleven pence*

Accounts of Banstock Manor, 1576–1582

It takes a few days to make ready the cottage, as birds have filled its single chimney with sticks, and the wind has swept open the door and covered the floor with leaves. In the few days since Isabeau returned to the manor estate, she speaks little to Viola and none to anyone else. She is visited every day by one or another of her ladyship's women, from her ladyship's kind heart, and they sit in prayer together. We are all relieved when Isabeau is established with a woman from the village for company and to serve her, in her new house. The woman Margery, who has a reputation for being loose in her morals herself, is also the mother of many healthy children. She seems to put confidence into Isabeau, who naturally fears the birth of her first child. The midwife, though reluctant to see Isabeau at first, tells me the baby lies badly, being on his breech and not his head as is usual.

Viola still visits, and on this cold but bright morn I walk down through the home farm with her to the river and along the path by the mill, from where we can see the cottage. Viola kicks her way through the remaining frost. The clouds gathering suggest we might see the winter's first snow shortly. She slows as we approach the house and pauses by the tumbledown wall that edges it.

'May I see Isabeau alone?'

It is a strange request, and I am reluctant, given the woman's lewd connections. 'Why, child?'

Her cheeks grow pinker. 'I would like to ask her a question. A woman's question.' She looks away, across the fields with their trails of mist dissolving before the thin sun.

'Can you not ask your stepmother?' I have an idea what she wishes to ask, but cannot think of a way to broach the subject.

'I could but… Isabeau is easier to talk to.'

'I would be derelict in my duty to your father if I agree,'

I answer. She nods, and steps to the door, where the servant Margery is waiting.

We are greeted with mulled ale as a reward for walking from the manor, with a spoonful of butter melted onto the top, and Isabeau has floated a slice of spicy apple on each. She gives me the one chair, takes the stool for herself and Viola sits on the window seat.

Isabeau greets Viola and me with grave courtesy, but Viola answers in French. I see immediately here is a way for Viola to ask those questions that any maid asks of her mother, without embarrassing me, or my leaving them alone. I understand a little of her queries. Isabeau seems mortified, though, her colour rising, and I chuckle into my beard at the strangeness of the situation: a girl asking a woman about marriage when the man they discuss is the same for each. I decide it is quite appropriate to step outside and stretch my legs in the garden. Margery, wringing out linens over a half-barrel of soapy water, tells me of her mistress.

'She's right finicky,' the woman says, in her Island accent. "As to 'ave 'ot water every day, powders and scents and whatnot, all to smell good. And the time she spends on her hair. It's pretty brushed out, but who's to see it? She covers it up like a nun.'

'But she lives quietly, and is no trouble?'

'Trouble over her food, certainly; doesn't like plain broths but they must be fresh and have no bones in. But she's good enough, waiting for her baby.'

'Do you think it will come soon?'

Margery shakes her head. 'I think a few weeks yet; first babes keep their mothers waiting. Maybe he'll have time to turn. The midwife's got her eating sorrel from the hedge, and scrubbing the floor. Which,' she pauses, 'she does do, every day, like it was a feast day. Funny, these Frenchies.'

'And no trouble from them?' I nod in the direction of the village.

'She's no witch, I'll tell you that and I'll tell any of them that asks. Wouldn't be in so much trouble if she was, would she? If she were a witch she could magic the young man to marry her. Or magic away her baby. They say there's a woman in Newchurch can just charm a baby out of its mother's womb.'

'Yes, well,' I say, misliking this talk. 'We do not allow such things at Banstock.'

She gives me a look as if she knows otherwise, but bows, just the same. 'Yes, your honour.'

It is late evening at the manor, and I am in a mood to sleep, when Viola disturbs me getting ready for my bed.

'Master Vincent!' she says, in a loud whisper through the door. 'There is someone in the apple store.'

'What?' I say, rubbing my head and yawning. 'It is late, child…' I open the door.

'I saw a light from the roof. Between the slates, a light.'

She is anxious, clutching at my sleeve. 'Please, come and see.'

'I should send a man over,' I grumble, but I am already lacing my boots. ''Tis probably a thief. The cook will say it is elves stealing apples.'

'Or a priest,' whispers Viola. 'Maybe here to help Isabeau.'

That is a sobering thought. For a priest to be caught on Banstock land... I pull on the rough jacket I use for visiting the farms. 'I will go alone, then,' I say, but Viola is already ahead of me.

The moonlight is as bright as dawn, and we set out into the chill air. Many a clear night precedes a frost, and I shiver as the cold air reaches down my collar. 'It's a fool's errand,' I grumble, but my young lady is a dozen paces ahead.

I can see what she has spotted: the glow of a lantern shining between the ramshackle slates on the apple shed. I hiss at Viola and she turns, her hair and eyes silvered by the cold light.

'Wait! Let me go first. If it is robbers—' I say. What thieves would want with apples I could not imagine; the harvest has been such a good one we have given bushels away for cider.

As we creep up to the door, we hear the sound of a low voice, praying. I know then that I have not surprised a papist priest: the words are in English. Nor, in fact, is it a man at all. I recognise the voice immediately, as does Viola, and I open the door.

'Come down, Mistress Waldren!' called Viola, anger in her voice. 'Your brother has been afeared for your safety! He has even sent men to the shore to look for you, and has mourned you as dead these many weeks.'

The woman's face appears through the loft hatch. Her voice is cracked with emotion, though I cannot divine whether she is angry or frightened, or perhaps both.

'Demons stalk us in the night, because we harbour a witch.' Her voice is harsh. She turns to climb down the rude ladder, awkward in her skirts and cloak. She wears man's boots. 'And my brother colludes with her.'

I attempt reason. 'Mistress, your brother is concerned for your health – we all are. He will be greatly relieved that you are alive. Come to the rectory and talk to him.'

'He would have me locked up in a Bethlem house.' She stands in front of me, swaying.

'He only seeks your safety, madam.' I stand between her and the door, but truly, I am not sure I can stop her.

'My brother is enchanted, cursed by that French succubus, like the rest of you men.'

I am aware of Viola's young ears as I continue to argue with the woman, her arguments as rabid and incomprehensible as a radical. Some of her speech is of men lying with demons, and Satan coming to Banstock to take back his child from his leman, his paramour. Viola stands against the wall watching the harpy screeching at us both, her fingers stabbing at my chest to hammer home her points.

'Enough,' I cry, and hold up my hand. The woman at last pauses for breath. 'If you will not come quietly, I shall have men come from the manor and restrain you. Perhaps a night spent locked in the dairy will bring you to your senses.' Before she starts again, I take a deep breath. 'Now, Mistress, come with me and the Lady Viola to the care and love of your brother. We will examine your accusations in the morning.' *When whatever madness you suffer has worn off,* I think.

'Tomorrow may be too late.' She is hoarse, pleading with me now, her hands held in supplication. 'Tomorrow he may already be here. With all his demons, to take his child.'

'Who, madam?' Viola reaches a hand towards the woman, who stares at her.

Agness speaks as if terrified. 'The Devil himself,' she says.

I shiver a little at the tone of her voice. I wonder that the Devil would come here, to Banstock, but the woman's conviction chills my back.

'Then seek shelter within the church,' says Viola, her hand outstretched. 'Let your brother offer you sanctuary there.'

The woman springs away as if Viola was cursed. 'You,' she splutters at her. 'You who seek to marry *him*.'

'If her father arranges it—' I say, but the woman throws herself past me, and I can only snatch at an arm, spinning us both around. She tears herself out of my grasp and stands, shaking, her face twisted like a gargoyle with her rage.

'He shall see the truth,' she shouts. 'Rather he is dead than married to any but his true wife.' She bounds into the night, her cloak flapping like a bat as she disappears into the shadows of the trees.

Vincent Garland, Steward to Lord Banstock, His Memoir

53

Monday 22nd April

Sage flattened her hand against the heavy wooden door of the vicarage, banging again with some force, until her palm was stinging.

'Please be there, please…'

A light yellowed the semi-circular window above the door, and she could hear Nick calling. 'I'm coming, I'm coming.' The door was pulled open so fast she stumbled forward a step.

She was only conscious of his arms reaching for her, pulling her against him, his warmth and strength. 'Oh, thank God you were here,' she said, into his chest.

'Are you— you're frozen. Sage, come in.'

'I'm all right, I'm just cold.' She shut the door behind her. 'Is the phone on? I mean, have you had any calls?'

'Not one. For two days.'

A noise from the darkened living room made her jump.

'Who's that?' she asked, grabbing his dressing gown with both hands.

'It's Felix, he's staying here. He wants to find out more about the carvings in the well.' Nick reached for her again, deliberately, and she rested her forehead against his shoulder. His smell was already familiar, somewhere between his spicy soap and fresh bread, with a hint of minty toothpaste. 'What happened?'

'I think…' It seemed less threatening at a safe distance. 'I think someone's been in my flat.'

Felix walked into the hall. 'Are you all right?'

Sage nodded but couldn't get the words out.

Nick guided her into the living room to sit on the sofa, still warm from Felix's body. Sage pulled off her gloves; her hands were still tingling with cold.

'You're shaking.' Felix draped a blanket around her shoulders.

'It's adrenaline,' she said. 'I realised… I think someone was in my flat, reading my letters, moving things around. I think it might have been Marcus. The baby's father,' she added to Felix. When Nick sat beside her she huddled into him. 'He could have made a copy of the key.'

Felix sat in an armchair opposite her, his hands clasped between his knees. 'Try and engage your objective head for a moment. When did you realise something was different?'

She thought about it, feeling Nick's warmth creeping into her. His hand stroked her back, curving over her ribs and down her spine. She had to shake off the spell he was weaving.

'I was so tired when I came in I fell asleep on the settee. When I woke up I realised something wasn't right. I know how I left things this morning. A letter had been opened, and my pregnancy notes and diary looked like they'd been read.' She struggled at the idea. 'Things were just different. I'm not a very tidy person.' She sighed as her body relaxed. 'He might have read that note you wrote me, Nick. Maybe he's been following me since we broke up. He might even have made those phone calls to you. Although I didn't recognise the voice, I've never heard Marcus shout and the voice was so strained. And the police… God, I told them he'd talked to Steph.'

'He could have disguised his voice, we know that.' Nick squeezed her around the waist. 'And the note was innocent enough.'

Felix frowned. 'So the calls to Nick could be from someone who's obsessed with you? There are weird parallels here.' He narrowed his eyes. 'Obsession is a motive for stalking, even murder. Maybe enough for someone to take Isabeau's baby.'

That triggered some memory of Sage's visit to the manor. She rummaged in her abandoned bag, snatched up out of habit when she fled the flat. She turned her tablet on. 'I was shown a picture of Solomon Seabourne at the manor. I took a picture.' She found the image, and held it out for

Felix and Nick to look at, pointing at the caption. '*Caeca invidia est.* Jealousy is blind. It may have been done as a gift for Viola, since it's still at the manor.'

The men leaned over the image. 'Jealousy,' Nick said slowly. 'Is that what's causing the phone calls, someone being in your flat?'

'And the doll,' Felix said. 'If it was designed to frighten you, it worked. It's a powerful motive.'

'I mean, if Marcus could be stalking me because he wants me back, it means he's irrational.' Sage shook her head. 'I don't even want to think about it. I have to change my locks.' She rested back against Nick. 'Is it possible that this Agness wanted Seabourne? I mean, was she stalking him, and mad with jealousy at Isabeau?'

Felix nodded slowly. 'Maybe she was. It would give a motive to the brutality done to Isabeau, if she took the baby.'

'Jealousy: who was jealous of whom?' Nick studied the image. 'He was engaged to Viola. Surely if Agness was obsessed with anyone it would be her, not Isabeau.'

'Isabeau was pregnant by someone, we know that.' Felix held her gaze, his eyes dark green in the low light. 'Terrible violence was done to that young woman. We can't be sure who the father was, but maybe if Agness believed it was Seabourne she could have attacked Isabeau for the baby.'

She frowned. 'Even if Isabeau was targeted because it was Seabourne's child, wouldn't he have arranged a

Christian burial for the mother of his child rather than putting her in the woods?'

'Not just any burial,' Felix said. 'She was covered in gold embroidery and gemstones.'

Nick put one arm around her as he sat back. 'She was denied a Christian burial but she was recognised. You said she was buried in an expensive dress. A headstone, the bells in the church, the rosary. If she was a Catholic, she might have been denied a church burial.'

Sage snuggled into him for warmth, feeling the baby wriggle inside her. 'Attacking a pregnant woman... I don't even want to imagine it.'

'I've looked up a few recent cases,' Felix said. 'Imagine a woman is obsessed with a man who isn't interested in her. She believes that he's secretly in love with her, everything he does confirms that. Most cases of foetal abduction involve erotomania: the sort of obsession that stalkers have, that overrides normal emotions.' He grimaced. 'The sort that leads them to do violent, terrible things like steal a baby.'

Sage touched her belly softly. 'But killing a woman to steal a child?' She shivered. 'I suppose that is the extreme of obsession.' She thought of Steph but couldn't frame the words. She couldn't believe Marcus would hurt anyone, but she couldn't think of anyone else who had access to her flat. Her thoughts seemed to spin around in circles.

Felix continued. 'Some women believe that their rival's

baby actually belongs to them, or that they would be a better mother than the biological mother. Obviously, we don't know the sort of cultural influences in the 1500s. It could be a class thing or a religious dispute.'

Sage settled into the curve of Nick's arm. 'This is all speculation. We don't know it was Agness, or that it was Seabourne's baby.'

'It was.' Felix reached in his bag and took out a booklet: the book of letters between Viola and Seabourne republished by the historical society. 'I don't know if you've read this yet, but there are hints in the letters that survive – the originals, not the translations.' He started to read. 'Listen to this, from Viola to Solomon: "I grieve that your son is lost, but agree that darkness should lie undisturbed." Is she talking about the grave of Solomon's child and the woman who took him, in the well?'

'She did say "your child",' Sage said.

'"Your son is lost", she says. I suppose the well would have been very difficult to excavate to get the woman and child out again.' He turned over the booklet, looking at the reproduced portrait of Viola on the cover. 'Am I the only one who's impressed by this girl? She was a teenager when she wrote this letter.'

Sage squinted at the antique clock, its hands in shade. 'Is it really one o'clock?'

Nick heaved himself off the sofa. 'Ten past. We've got a busy day tomorrow.'

'Oh?' She took the hand proffered and let Nick pull her to her feet.

'Felix wants to look at the county records, maybe find some more background on them all. And you're staying here. Tomorrow we'll go back to your flat and sort it out. We'll get the locks changed and you can talk to the police.'

Sage managed a half-laugh. 'I don't want to go back.'

'You can't stay there. If this Marcus is stalking you, he may be dangerous.'

Even thinking of Marcus as a stalker didn't make sense; he had always been so genial. *When he was getting his own way*, an inner voice whispered. And she remembered the pale face down the well. Someone had pushed Steph to her death. 'And to you. You were the one getting the threatening phone calls, remember?'

'So stay here to protect me, then.' Nick smiled, and turned to Felix. 'Night, Felix.'

Felix smiled at the two of them. 'Go to bed, children.'

Sage found herself pushed up the stairs by Nick. He paused at the door to what was clearly his bedroom. 'Do you want the spare room?'

'No.' She kissed him quickly. 'I'm too tired and cold and spooked to sleep alone.'

He smiled, and ran a thumb down the side of her face. 'Me too.'

54

16th December 1580

Saltpetre for the making of bacons and hams, one small barrel ⟶ thirteen shillings and sixpence

Accounts of Banstock Manor, 1576–1582

We tell no one but her brother and Lord Banstock about Agness Waldren's survival. It seems to me that the reverend is disappointed that his sister still lives, as he now needs to find her a home. First find her, I say. I keep my concerns about her madness to myself. She is obsessed with Isabeau and I fear for the Frenchwoman's safety. I send a man to ride over once or twice a day to check on her. Seabourne gives me his solemn word that he will not communicate with his mistress.

As the days shorten we have slaughtered pigs and made puddings, hams and bacons until the ground by the butcher's is black with frozen blood. With Christmas approaching, we prepare for our guests: Lord Anthonie's (and my) sister and her husband and daughters. Lord Seabourne comes with his eldest sons, at least in part to haggle over Viola's bride dowry and the monies to be settled upon her should her husband die before her. Two neighbours, both old widows, also come to us at Christmas, so the manor is in a storm of cooking, baking, salting, smoking. Then we shall have Viola's wedding, which fills me with disquiet. My strongbox, just recently fattened by the autumn stock sales and harvests, is becoming depleted again as I buy in geese, sugar, wines and sweetmeats.

I get up before dawn to enjoy the quiet as I tally figures and prepare for the day. I am just lighting my fire and a stick of candles against the dark, when Viola flies into my office, much perturbed. The servant Margery, set to watch over Isabeau, has walked over the dark fields to say the Frenchwoman is missing from the cottage.

I fear no woman so close to her confinement would go far. We walk out through the early frost, towards the grounds of Well House on the way to the village. The sky is barely lightening in the east, the sky a royal shade of blue dotted with a few of the brightest stars, so I take a lantern.

We walk through the orchard looking for footprints or signs that someone has passed that way. The frost, as clear as snow, has left marks of the passage of feet: a fox or dog, trotting under the apple trees afore the pigs are let out, rabbits criss-crossing his path, and the heavy feet of a badger. Then we spot the partially frosted-over signs of small shoes.

We find the seamstress's cloak, tangled in a knot of brambles. Viola recognises it; the lining is fashioned from brightly coloured scraps left over from her work. It is torn down one side, as if a great struggle has occurred, and the cloth is lightly dusted with rime. It has clearly lain here for some time. I take it up, examining it. There is blood splattered on one edge, and my heart quickens.

We see her path beyond, her footsteps pressed into the soft ground, mixed with larger ones. One seems to be chasing the other. Viola runs ahead, and I, puffing behind holding the cloak, can spare no breath to command her to wait for me.

Her scream cuts through the still air, so shrill I think for a moment that it issues from a wounded animal.

'Uncle!' she shrieks again, and as I round the last oak I see her, cowering on the ground beyond the stream. I blunder down the slope towards the water and plough through it, the mud frozen hard on the surface and clutching at my boots beneath.

Blood in low light looks black, and such is the scene that it looks as if the thicket has been painted with darkness. The body before me, for at first I have no doubt it is a corpse, is hardly recognisable as Isabeau. Then I hear a pitiful hiss of air, and I realise the poor girl still lives.

I drop to my knees, smelling rather than seeing the woman's torn entrails, and the horror forms within my mind slowly. Her body has been cruelly opened, and her babe removed. She mewls a moment, then turns her head. Her cap hangs from her long hair, spread with frost, and she looks like a ghastly parody of a Madonna.

I reach for the hand wavering towards me. 'My child, who did this?'

'*Mon enfant—*' she murmurs, her face no less white than the ground she lies upon.

It sounds as if Viola gags, but then she kneels on the other side, and Isabeau turns her head slowly towards her. Viola speaks, her breath misting her face. 'She wants us to find her child. Isabeau, you must tell me, who has taken it? Who has stolen your baby?'

'A— Agness. *Mon enfant—*' the word drifts out on the mist of a sigh. I fear it is her last. But her hand clutches mine with a spasm, then tries to lift it towards her head. I hold my hand up as hers falls away, divining her need. Like most men of my age, I remember the papist rites, as they were drummed into me as a boy.

'I am no priest...' I try to object, but then bow my head. Tracing the sign of the cross upon her forehead, my tongue finds the last rites as I had heard them spoken over my mother. '*Salvam fac ancillam tuam—*'

I have no idea if the words will help her, but send a silent prayer to a loving God that he will find her tormented soul and keep it safe. When I look down I see she is dead, her eyes glistening in pools of tears, which wet my fingers when I close them.

Viola stumbles away from me when I would have comforted her. 'We have to save the baby!'

"Tis likely dead. Born in such a way…' I shudder. I have seen shepherds hack open dead ewes to save the lambs, but few survive.

'But he was stolen from a living mother – he might be alive! We have to do something. Where would Agness have taken him?'

I ease Isabeau's cloak over her corpse. As the light brightens I can see the footprints better: a single track leading towards Well House and the sorcerer.

Vincent Garland, Steward to Lord Banstock, His Memoir

55

Tuesday 23rd April

It was strange to return to Bramble Cottage. The police had released the crime scene, having drained the well and processed the evidence as fast as they could out of respect for the Bassetts. Sage leaned in to get a better look at the deep carving in the beam above the fireplace while Felix made notes. Bramble Cottage seemed quite innocuous by day, and Pat, Judith's mother, was very welcoming.

'If you can banish the ghosts, I'm all for it,' Pat said, bustling about with a tray of tea, and a jigsaw puzzle for Chloe. 'I made you a hot chocolate, lovey, with marshmallows. I'll help you with the sky pieces, if you like.'

The child was quiet and pale, staring at Sage with unblinking blue eyes. Pat appeared to be on edge, but seemed to be glad for the company, as they waited for what could only be bad news about James Bassett.

It was only after what felt like an hour of work that Felix

seemed to come to a conclusion. 'These marks are different from the ones in the well,' he announced. 'These are still about alchemy, but more for good luck than trapping anything.' He stepped into the inglenook, avoiding the lit woodburner sitting in the middle, and peered up the chimney. 'This is a strange chimney. It echoes. You know I said it might be worth having a sound engineer check it out? Ultrasonics can be caused by certain types of voids; they can trick people into imagining ghosts.'

'Really?' Sage lifted a finger to trace one of the worn carvings.

'Air movements are perceptible to the human senses but don't register as sound. The mind can fill in the gap with auditory and visual hallucinations. The metal flue from the woodburner might have amplified it.'

'Which might explain the spooky atmosphere and wailing sounds, perhaps.' Sage looked at him. 'Elliott, the other student helping me with the excavation, found an alembic in the well. Maybe that was used for alchemy? The glass was fused with all sorts of metals.'

'What metals?' Felix was still examining the chimney.

'Mercury, gold, uranium… and another radioactive metal, thorium.'

'Thorium?'

'Yes. That's it, why?'

Felix looked as excited as she had yet seen him. 'Alchemists were trying to convert flasks of mercury into gold. Modern chemists have tried to do it by bombarding mercury with sub-atomic particles, but the process makes radioactive metals, some of which decay into thorium and uranium, some into gold. It's been done. One Soviet reactor laboratory even noticed their lead shielding was being slowly turned into gold by the loose particles.'

'You sound like you believe in alchemy.'

His smile was a bit lopsided. 'One day I'll tell you why I believe in some of it. But you have found a little bit of that evidence yourself, in the alembic.'

'Well, Elliott did.'

The house phone rang, making her jump, and Pat left the room to answer it. Sage could hear the low murmur of Pat's voice. A moment later, she bustled in, carrying her coat and car keys. 'James has just—' She sniffed back tears, and lowered her voice. 'My sister is arriving soon, she just missed a ferry unfortunately. Can you keep an eye on Chloe for me until she gets here?'

Sage stammered, 'Uh, would Chloe be OK with that?'

'I don't mind.' The child looked up from her jigsaw, her face expressionless. 'I like Sage.' Her voice was flat, her eyes burning in dark smudges, reminding Sage momentarily of the doll.

Pat was already half out of the front door. 'It will only be a few minutes. Thank you. I called the vicar, he'll be along as soon as he can.'

Five minutes later there was a knock on the front

door. Felix brushed past Sage to answer it. 'Maybe she's already here— oh, Nick!' He stepped outside, and the door swung closed.

Sage went into the kitchen and filled the kettle. As it bumped into action, she began to realise the room seemed very quiet, as if the sound was being trapped. A quick glance across the hall into the living room showed Chloe's narrow shoulders, bowed over the puzzle again.

She leaned against the granite worktop, and let a sigh out. The baby lurched, and she rubbed her bump with the heel of her hand. *It's OK, Bean, I'll find some time for you later.*

When she raised her head she shivered, and wrapped her arms momentarily around herself. A sound behind her made her jump. Standing in the doorway was Elliott. He looked dishevelled, in a shirt with the top button undone, under a grey hoodie.

Sage froze. 'Elliott?' she stammered, spooked. She managed a shaky laugh. 'You made me jump.'

'I didn't mean to.' His face was blank, his eyes so dark they looked black.

She rubbed her belly to comfort the baby, herself. Something hovered around her memory. 'Aren't you finished here?' She was babbling. She could feel her pulse bounding in her neck. 'Back to the university for you, I suppose.'

'You sound like you want to get rid of me.' He wasn't joking; he never joked, she realised. He stared at her face, then down at her stomach. 'You want to get on with your life. And *his* baby.'

'His? You mean Marcus, my ex-boyfriend?' It was strange: here was Elliott, good, dependable Ell, and yet it felt like the ghosts of the cottage were ranged up behind him, hissing at her. The hairs on her neck stood up.

His voice was low with a strange tone, his face twisted with anger. He jabbed a finger in the direction of her belly. 'You should have got rid of it. You'll always be involved with him while you have it.' There was a strange expression in his eyes, as if he was listening to someone else. He tilted his head on one side.

'Elliott.' It was her teacher voice, and it seemed to reach him a little bit. 'Let's go outside and talk to Nick and Felix.'

He reached out a hand; his wrist was bony as it extended from his sleeve. He seemed taller indoors. He touched a wooden block on the work surface, his hand hovering over the silver handles of the knives. She watched him touch one after another before he drew out a long carving knife. It made a metallic hiss as it came out, and the shiny blade seemed to hold his attention even as Sage shuffled back half a step. His face was calm, and he stared at the blade in his hand and squeezed the handle until his knuckles whitened.

'Elliott, put that down, it's—' her voice faded as he took a step nearer, shaking his head. 'Ell, you don't want to hurt me, you know you don't.'

He twisted the blade in the light from the low window.

He was almost within arm's reach of Sage. '*Hurt* you? No, I don't want to hurt you. I just think it's time to get rid of the baby.' He made a small stabbing movement. 'Surely it's possible to hit the baby and not kill the mother.' He looked up. 'I could be careful, not like whoever butchered Isabeau. There has to be somewhere that would kill the baby and not you.' The knife stabbed forward a few inches, as if he were imagining it. 'How could you even touch him? That sleazy old man.'

'Elliott, you're scaring me. That's enough, put it down.' Sage managed to turn and stumble into the hall. A few feet to her left was the door to the living room. *God, Chloe.* She stopped and turned. 'We're friends, Elliott, colleagues. This isn't you, this is madness. Losing Steph—'

'Steph?' His face twisted into an expression of disgust that made her flinch back. 'Steph didn't give me a choice. She thought I was interested in *her*?'

'A choice in what?' God, where were Felix and Nick? Her mind flew to the silent child bowed over her jigsaw. She needed to get him outside.

'She knew. She saw the pictures on my phone, pictures of you. She found out I had copied your keys. I saw the vicar going into your building and stay all night. Did he fuck you, with that estate agent's baby right there in your stomach?'

Sage felt cold at the tone in his voice. Steph must have confronted him. What had he done? She could feel a draught from the open front door behind her, could hear the low murmur of Nick and Felix's voices beyond. 'What happened with Stephanie?' There was a shrill note in her voice, and she could only hope it reached the men outside.

Elliott walked closer, until she had to look up even as she fumbled for the edge of the door. 'You can't believe I ever wanted Steph,' he said, his face moving closer, angling this way, then that. *God, he's going to try and kiss me.* He pushed his body against hers, the knife pressed flat between them.

'Please, Elliott, don't—'

He touched his lips to her cheek, slid down to her mouth. His kiss was cold, dry, emotionless. When he pulled back, his eyes seemed enormous, black and as unblinking as a lizard. His breath smelled of stale tea. She could feel the fingers on the hilt of the knife pressing against her stomach. 'Ell, please—'

'It's like you're still full of him.' He moved back half a pace, his mouth twisted with disgust. 'You're full up with his filth.'

He angled the point of the knife towards her again. She cried out involuntarily. 'Elliott!' She fumbled behind her for the edge of the door. Thank God, it was on the latch. Her fingers caught in the door chain. 'But, why kill Steph? She hadn't hurt anyone.'

'I didn't think she would die. She hit her head on the drain cover.' He pulled her closer. 'She knew how I felt about you. I didn't mean to hurt her, not at first. But then she found out about the doll. Chloe told her I'd taken it.'

Sage's mind raced back to the disgusting thing in her car. 'The doll? But... why?'

'I started reading about the sorcerer that lived here, about spells and witchcraft.'

'You can't take that seriously.' Sage backed away a few more inches.

'But you saw the lab results – the alchemy was working. I did some research; the kid had already connected you to the doll. All I had to do was make it into a love spell.' He looked less certain for a second. 'I know you can love me. I've seen you look at me – you chose me for this project. Everything I did was for you, for us.'

'But you hurt Steph. Ell, how could you?' Sage felt sick, her chest tight with fear for the baby.

'She was going to tell you, she was going to warn you. Like I said, she knew I had the keys to your van, your flat.' He grimaced. 'She was jealous.' His eyes dropped again to her belly.

'Elliott,' Sage said, breathless with fear, 'I know you wouldn't hurt anyone intentionally, I've known you for three years. It must have been an accident.'

'I could see she was dead, so I dragged the cover off. It was easy to drop her in: no one was indoors, they were at the hospice.' His voice hissed. 'I heard her body hit the bottom of the well.'

'Oh, God.' For a moment Sage saw the white face in the

dark water. Elliott lifted the blade again and she put her arm up to defend herself. *He's going to do it.*

'Sage?' Chloe was standing in the living-room doorway.

'Chloe, get inside and lock the door!'

Sage was relieved to see the living-room door immediately slam shut. Elliott's head turned at the noise, and she found a wave of strength to push him away, her hands flat against his chest. He was thin, and she managed to push him a couple of steps back, but he recovered quickly, raising the weapon. He stepped forward and stabbed straight at the top of her belly. She put her hand up to fend him off, the blade slicing between her thumb and finger as she deflected it. She cried out with the pain but he seemed lost in the study of her belly. *This is what happened to Isabeau.* She finally managed to pull the front door open as he lunged forward with deadly speed, burying the knife in the doorframe just beside her. He wrenched it out as she turned and stumbled down the broad front step.

Sage screamed involuntarily, and staggered onto the garden path, almost falling. She turned to fend him off which made his second strike miss her, his wrist jarring her shoulder as she ducked under his arm. As the knife flashed after her, she put out her uninjured hand to protect her belly, then turned and staggered to the corner of the house and pulled open the gate to the back garden. 'Ell, you have to stop this!'

Elliott was like a robot, immersed in whatever nightmare

of jealous obsession he was inhabiting. Sage slammed the gate in his face and heard the knife crunch into the wood. She lurched into the garden, cradling her injured hand against her. Nick and Felix were standing by the well; the cover was discarded on the grass. Felix looked startled. Nick took a step towards her. 'Sage?'

She fought to get her breath back. 'It's Elliott!' She looked down at her hand, at the blood streaking down her shirt. 'He's got a knife, he killed Steph—'

'Watch out!' Nick stepped in front of her as she swung around to see Elliott pacing towards her through the gateway, knife outstretched.

'Elliott, stop!' The command came from Felix, and even Sage involuntarily glanced at him. The student stopped, standing between the two men, then turned to Nick.

'She's mine.' The words were spat.

'What?' Nick stared at Sage.

Elliott's contorted face barely looked like the young man she had known. '*You* can't have her!'

'Let her come with me then,' said Felix. His voice was calm, fatherly. 'It's all right, but she's scared and she's cut her hand.'

Elliott twisted his head around to stare at him. 'That bastard's brat has to go.' His voice had cracked into a growl, and then Sage knew for certain that it was the voice she had heard down the phone at the vicarage. 'It's not a real baby. *You* know that.'

Sage stumbled backwards, away from the hatred in his voice. Felix stepped between them and Elliott. 'Elliott, you care about Sage. You don't want to hurt her.' He glanced at Nick, who started to edge around to Elliott's side.

Elliott's face was dark red and sweaty. 'She's filthy, whoring with that estate agent and now with *him*.' Spittle dropped from his lips. 'I'll cut it out and throw it down that fucking well. I should have done it weeks ago.'

Felix's voice was even. 'That would kill Sage. You don't want to lose her.'

'He's taken her from me!' Elliott lunged forward, and Sage fell back. Her foot stumbled on the ring of stones, and she grabbed Felix to keep her balance. The well was uncovered, just surrounded by a few scraps of fluttering blue tape. She circled around it, putting the black hole between her and Elliott.

A flash of yellow caught Sage's eye – a child's T-shirt – and she saw Chloe standing by the garden gate. 'Chloe! Get inside!'

'Sage?' The child looked confused. 'Why is the scary man here?'

Nick darted towards her, but Elliott had already grabbed Chloe, who squealed in protest as he pulled her by one wrist, swinging her almost off her feet.

'Chloe, stay still!' Sage's words were breathless, sobbed. 'Please don't hurt her, Elliott, she hasn't done anything. She's just a little girl.'

'Come here and I'll let her go.'

Even as Sage took a step towards him involuntarily, Felix pulled her back. Only the ring of muddy stones and the black opening of the well was between her and Elliott, the musty stink in her nostrils. She saw Nick turn a little, move out of Elliott's line of sight.

'I'll do it!' Elliott had the child almost on tiptoes, lifted by one arm. 'Come here or I'll drop the kid down the well.'

Chloe whimpered, locking eyes with Sage. Her slippers were right over the ring of stones.

'You wouldn't hurt a child.' Sage's breath was coming in little sobs. 'I know you, Elliott.'

'I threw Steph down there,' he said, his face twisted, his voice mocking. 'It was easy.'

Felix squeezed Sage's arm. 'You can't reason with him. He isn't thinking rationally.'

She wrenched herself away. 'Elliott, please. Look, it's just me. I know you. We can go somewhere and talk. Just let Chloe go and put the knife down. We all know you've been under a lot of stress.'

'Stress, because of you!' He spat. Chloe's dangling foot was hanging over the edge of the well, her eyes wide with fear. 'You wouldn't get rid of the baby, you ignored me, you fucked *him*...' Nick froze, a few feet away from Elliott, and stared at the knife jabbed in his direction.

Sage glanced at Nick. 'Nick is a friend. That's all.'

Elliott's grip seemed to loosen and Chloe slipped a few

inches towards the shadow of the well. The child screamed, the sound cutting through the wind.

Nick shouted. 'No! Let the child go, this has nothing to do with her.' He edged forward, his hand open, reaching towards Chloe. 'You're angry at me, not Sage. Let her take the child indoors.'

Elliott's head swivelled. Chloe twisted in his grip, her wrist clamped in his fingers, her breath sobbing in her throat. 'Mummy, *Mummy…*'

'I know you were with her. In her flat. In her *bed*.'

'Nothing happened, I swear. Look at the child, she's terrified. Let her go to Sage at least.' Nick stepped closer, forming a triangle between Elliott, Sage and himself, the well in the middle. 'Come and talk to me, it's me you're angry at.'

Sage clung to Felix's arm as Nick continued to try and reason with Elliott, the other hand clenched against her stomach, dripping blood. She had the strangest feeling, like this had happened before, like a story was reaching for her and the baby. 'He's beyond reason,' she whispered to Felix, 'but maybe he'll follow me away from the well and Nick and you can grab Chloe.'

Felix shook his head. 'He'll go for the baby. Do you have your phone?'

She knew where it was, uselessly sat in the glove compartment of her car. She shook her head. 'You?'

'In the cottage, in my bag. If we can distract him and

get Chloe to you, lock yourselves in the house and call from there.'

Sage nodded. Elliott and Nick were now in a silent standoff, Nick's hands twitching as if to take Chloe but repelled by the bloodstained blade.

Elliott stared at Nick. 'Sage could love me. She just doesn't realise it yet.' He looked over at her. 'We're meant to be together.'

Sage reached her bloodied hand out to him. 'Then let her go, please let Chloe go.' She took one step closer. 'I could never love someone who hurt a child.'

'Sage!' Nick put out a hand. 'Don't trust him.'

'You would never hurt me deliberately, would you, Ell? Tell him, Nick, we're just friends.'

'Of course, we're friends…' He stared at Sage, his eyes wide with emotion. She had a flash of memory, of his sleeping body pressed against hers when she woke.

The point of the knife wavered slightly. Elliott took a step around the well towards Sage and he frowned. His expression changed. 'But the baby has to go.' He swung his hand and Sage lurched back, her ankle twisting beneath her. The raised knife caught the light.

'No!' Nick leapt forward and Elliott dropped Chloe on the grass and turned to meet him. The blade came down. Nick put up his forearm; the knife glanced off it, then buried itself up to the handle in his chest.

Sage screamed, Chloe screamed, Elliott screamed. Even

Felix shouted something, but Nick fell back without a word.

Felix strode towards the child, now sobbing in a heap, and snatched her up in his arms. Sage huddled on the grass as Elliott, now empty-handed, walked towards her. There was blood on his shirt. Her blood, Nick's blood.

'If I can't have you, no one will.' His voice was calm again, although his face was twisted into a grimace. He grabbed her wrist with both hands and dragged her a step, two steps towards the well. Although she was tall, he was taller and stronger. He hauled her closer to the open mouth. Cracks had opened up around it, dark scars in the earth.

'No, no!' She fell to her knees.

He pulled her back up and put his face close to hers. 'I heard her hit the bottom of the well,' he hissed. 'I'll throw you down there too.'

'Elliott, please.' Sage heaved against him, pulling him half a pace back.

He wrested her back against him. 'You'll be conscious all the way down,' he snarled, his face scarlet with effort, with rage. 'You'll drown in the water, you and the baby.'

One of her feet slid half into the well. '*Elliott!*'

'Sage!' Elliott turned at the sound of Felix's voice. Sage strained to look over his shoulder. Chloe was nowhere to be seen, and Felix had both hands pressing on Nick's chest either side of the knife. As she watched, he started to stand up, to come towards her and Elliott. Terrified he was leaving Nick to die, Sage found a last surge of energy. She kicked out and twisted, swinging Elliott towards the edge. His mouth was wide open, his hand gripping her wrist—

He fell backwards into the well. His weight dragged Sage forward onto her knees as simultaneously someone grabbed her around the waist, knocking the scream out of her. Felix's forearm was around her, the tendons standing out as he struggled to stop her tumbling after Elliott. She felt pulled in half, her other hand braced on the ring of stones.

She looked down to see Elliott, one elbow crooked over the edge of the well, his free hand biting into her wrist. His fingers were slipping and he shouted something, his voice high and garbled with rage. Elliott stared up at Sage with white-rimmed eyes. It wasn't even fear, it was hate, and it made her recoil, jerking his fingers from her wrist.

He screamed as he dropped and Sage fell backwards against Felix. She waited for a splash, but instead there was a horrible thud. The stones at the top of the well shifted and shook. The earth dropped underneath her as the well collapsed, and she slid towards the black mouth as darkness took her.

56

16th December 1580

I am a man of almost fifty summers yet I race across the spinney towards Well House barely three paces behind the girl, not heeding obstacles in my way. All my thoughts are on Viola ahead of me. I must be there when she confronts – as I believe she must – the demented woman that Isabeau charged with stealing her baby. I barely think what has happened is credible, yet I have seen it with my own eyes, seen the butchered body of Isabeau.

The garden gate stands ajar, and as if Agness's guilt was not proven enough it is confirmed by a bloodied handprint upon the frame. The sky casts a blue light over the frost, the last stars melt into the beginning of day. My Viola barely checks, but throws herself through and into the garden beyond, her skirts caught above her knees. Past an orchard of gnarled ancients, she sets to flight a dozen rooks in the low branches. Near the house she finally pauses, giving me a moment to catch her, to stand with my flanks heaving like a plough horse. A figure stands, side on to us, wrapped in a rough cloth, her hair unbound, a mass of wiry curls. She spares us no glances, but is rapt in the gaze of the man. He stands bareheaded, in simple shirt and hose, his boots unlaced, and stares back at her.

Viola would have gone forward, but I catch her arm, murmuring in what breath I can spare: 'Wait, my child.'

She nods, and leans against me. Agness and Solomon stare like fighting cats.

'Your French whore is dead.' Agness's voice is strident, deep like a man's, triumphant. 'I have saved your child from her filthy body.' She holds up a silent bundle to him. He glances at us, his face distorted with agony.

'Master Vincent. Tell me: does she speak truth or lie?'

I could not dissemble. 'Mistress Isabeau lies slain. Her babe is gone from her belly.'

'No!' The man's shout is harsh with his anguish, and Viola flinches in my arms. 'You are a murderess! A monster!'

Agness shook her head, cradling the bundle in her arms. 'Nay, sir, it was a French witch that had you in her spell. See – your babe. We will raise him as *our* son.' She reaches out with the bundle, as if to show him, but I hear no sounds from the infant, not even after all the shouting.

Viola steps towards them and calls out; her young voice cuts like birdsong through the rough voices. 'Let me see him, Mistress. Mayhap he is cold in this air. Let me warm him.'

'You?' the woman spits at Viola and the girl halts. 'You think to wed a man like Solomon Seabourne? Back to your books and music, child. A man needs a woman and a babe a mother.'

Seabourne has covered his face in his hands, but looks up at this. We behold Agness draw a dagger from her cloak with one bloodied hand, crushing the infant against her with the other. 'You have no claim on him.'

'Nor you, Mistress.' Viola lifts her chin, ignores the knife, and walks forward. I make a grab for her arm, but her sleeve slides through my fingers.

Solomon's man Kelley steps from the shadow of the house. 'Mistress, let us get the lamb within, by the fire.'

Viola holds out her hand. 'Yes, let us help the babe. It cannot be good for him to be in this cold, unswaddled, Mistress Agness. I will go into the house with him, then you and Master Seabourne can talk.' Her young voice is pleading, and Agness glances down at the bundle, at once uncertain, perhaps.

'He is pale,' she muses.

Solomon gathers himself, and says with his natural authority: 'Give the child to Viola, Mistress, and Kelley shall take both indoors. And you may say what you wish to say to me.'

'Solomon, my love.' Such is the woman's voice altered at this, I barely recognise it.

While she is momentarily distracted, Viola reaches her,

ignoring the wicked blade and its vile stains. She stands at her elbow like any woman admiring another's child. I hold my breath for fear.

'He is bonny,' she says, in a gentle voice, like her mother's. 'But he looks pale and cold. Poor boy. Let me get him by the kitchen fire.'

'Give the maid the child,' I add, 'and we will resolve this.'

Agness turns upon me with a snarl, and great hatred contorts her features. 'Give the child to her, the bastard child of a bastard?' She spits at my feet, then. 'You think the whole manor does not know that you are Viola's true father?'

Viola spins around, staring at me. 'It is not true.'

I answer loudly, 'It is not true, though, God forgive me, I loved the lady truly. Nothing passed between us but words. Viola is my brother's child, born in wedlock. Give her the babe. She will keep him well by the fire, Mistress Agness, and we will fetch the rector to your aid.'

The woman hesitates, then kicks aside the wooden cover that lies over the old well. I gaze across the garden at Solomon, and see that he is not trying to cozen the woman, but walking closer to her.

'Better he drowns than be given to her,' says Agness, but I see uncertainty in her expression.

Viola steps forward, her voice gentle. 'Mistress, I have seen that I should not marry Master Solomon and I will break off my betrothal. But God will never forgive you if you harm that baby.'

For a moment the woman hesitates. She unfolds the bloodstained cloth, an apron I realise, and I see the inside is wet with scarlet. The baby's face is white, his eyes closed, his budded lips blue. A slash down his chin tells of some injury, perhaps gained when his mother was butchered.

'He does not move,' the woman wonders, and Viola reaches a hand towards him, though her fingers are shaking.

'Come, Mistress,' she offers, but the woman turns to me, meets my eyes over Viola's shoulder, and her lips turn into a sneer.

'If I cannot have his child, none will.' She turns towards the well, and as I leap forward to grab Viola, Agness throws the child into its black mouth.

My fingertips catch the back of Viola's cloak as she screams and dives towards the edge, falling to her knees, sobbing something incoherent. Agness's face is a mask of triumph.

Viola falls half across the well's mouth and I see her scrabble at the stone edge to brace herself, staring into its black depths. I stumble over to her, catching one arm, seeing deep below the white of the apron and its lost burden. I pull Viola towards the shelter of the hedge and cradle her as she sobs in my arms.

I look up at Solomon. His finger is outstretched at Agness, who has stopped not a half-dozen steps from the well.

'Master Vincent, get Viola away.' His voice is strained, hoarse with his rage, his grief. 'There is the witch. For she is possessed by the Devil. Who else would slaughter a babe, and a woman who has done her no wrong? You are the villain here, Mistress Agness!'

The woman totters a step backwards. 'But you smiled at me! That day, outside the church, upon your betrothal to the Lady Elizabeth.'

'Perhaps I did smile at his lordship's servants and tenants! For I was betrothed to a gentle girl and had not yet met Isabeau Duchamp.'

'Solomon, my love!' Agness cries, her words screeched.

'No love, indifference.' He steps closer to her and his hand shoots out to clamp her knife arm. 'I did not know you existed.'

'Master, no!' Kelley darts closer and stands between the pair and the well, a brave move. 'Do not compound one black murder with another.'

'One murder? She has slaughtered both mother and child, and would no doubt take Viola as well.' He shoulders Kelley aside, dragging the now silent Agness closer to the ring of stones.

Viola shudders in my arms like a bird. 'Go, Uncle,' she whispers. 'Do not let my husband be a murderer. Let Agness come to justice.'

I watch Agness fight in Seabourne's hands but every movement brings her closer to the edge, until it lies not two paces from her feet. She drops to her knees, somehow losing half a pace, and digs her fingers into the frozen grass.

'Mercy!' she cries.

Seabourne stares down at her. 'Mercy? What do you know of the word, madam? You have killed a fine woman and a helpless baby.'

I stride towards the pair, holding one hand out to stop this, as Agness bends her head, her shoulders shaking. 'I have loved you since the day I saw you, since we saw each other.'

'I did not see you. You are no one to me.' Seabourne's words are harsh, but I see his hand waver.

In a bound, she shakes him off. I stand between the madwoman and Viola as she screeches at me, pointing the knife at my chest. 'You! You have done this – you brought the French witch here, you tried to marry Solomon to Banstock's bastard—' She stabs at me, as Solomon's arms sweep her off her feet. The knife grazes my arm and she struggles wildly as he spins around. The circle of stones seem to reach for her faltering boots as she fights free of his arms. She falls backwards, screams once and then disappears into the blackness.

Vincent Garland, Steward to Lord Banstock, His Memoir

57

Tuesday 23rd April

Sage could see blue sky overhead. She could hear her own sobbing breath, and Chloe crying. She could feel some knot of pain in her belly, and smoothed it with one hand, dreading feeling a cut or blood. But there was no injury there, just the burning pain of her cut palm. There was a wide hole where the well had been, a bowl shaped depression in the mud made as it collapsed.

'He hurt my arm!' Chloe wailed, crawling over to Sage, rubbing her small chest and wiping her face with her sleeve. 'And the bad man fell down.'

Sage became aware of Felix's voice as if a radio had been turned up. 'That's right: Bramble Cottage on the High Street, Banstock. Yes, he's been stabbed. No, no, I won't. Hurry!'

She glanced over at Nick, who lay unmoving, Felix kneeling over him. She pushed herself up with her good hand to kneel, then stood, shaking. She held out her uninjured hand to the crying child. 'It's all right, Chloe. Stay with me.' Chloe huddled against her. She looked over the blonde head to Felix. 'Is he...?' *Please, please let him not be dead.*

Nick's eyes were open, and he was looking straight at her. Just when she'd convinced herself he *was* dead, he blinked, and managed to croak a word.

'Sage?'

She let go of Chloe and knelt beside him, her good hand cradling one of his. 'Don't die.'

'The... the baby,' he whispered.

She glanced down at her bump, smudged with blood.

'It's fine, it was just a cut on my hand.'

Felix looked at her belly, then looked down further. 'Sage, you're bleeding. Lie down.' His voice had a quiet authority, even though panic had added an octave.

Sage dropped a hand to a wet patch on her jeans, lifted bloodied fingers. *Bean.* She looked back at the terrified girl. 'It's all right, Chloe. Help is coming.' She sat down, her limbs shaking.

Chloe ran to her, hunched into her side. 'I want my mummy!' Sage realised Felix's hands were bracing either side of the knife in Nick's chest, applying pressure. She lay on her back, and the child cuddled against her side. She could feel slow surges of liquid pulsing out of her, feel the world become simpler. It became about in and out, breathing in the quiet air, feeling the cold rain spit on her face, watching clouds scud overhead. Nothing seemed real, just Nick, Bean.

The paramedics arrived a few minutes later, and divided their attention between Nick and Sage. Then the police, some firemen testing the ground where the well had been with poles, and finally Judith and Pat. Judith didn't speak, just scooped up Chloe and rocked her. The child's crying slowed and stopped. Finally Judith put Chloe down, then crouched next to Sage as a paramedic took Sage's pulse.

'Are you OK? Oh, God, the baby.'

'I think... I think I'm OK.' Sage felt as if she was thinning, becoming transparent. Only Nick kept a part of her anchored. 'Is Nick—?'

'They're working on him.'

Suddenly the pain returned, gripping Sage's belly, and a gush of hot fluid was forced out. Sage could feel rivulets of tears streaming from her eyes without the energy to sob. 'Elliott tried to kill my baby.'

The next few moments seemed stretched apart, like knots in elastic. The siren of the ambulance in the dimmed interior, a voice speaking to someone else. The banging of doors as the trolley was pushed through. The pain of a needle 'just a scratch', squirming and burning into a vein in her arm, then peace came, with death, or sleep. She slowly emerged into sounds, lights, voices.

'There you are.' A woman's face was suspended over Sage. 'You're going to be a bit dopey, you've had a lot of painkillers. But you are going to be fine, and your baby is doing well. He's small but he's strong, just premature.' The woman smiled as Sage tried to untangle syllables that didn't make sense. 'It's OK. Go back to sleep.'

Sage felt herself relax. She did as she was told.

She woke in a quiet room, darkened but with a nightlight over the bed. A nurse was beside her.

'What happened?'

'You had to have an emergency section and a transfusion, but you'll be fine, and your baby's a little bruiser. NICU sent down a picture.' Sage lifted a hand to take the proffered photograph, and was surprised to find the back of her hand stuck with tape and bearing a drip. The picture was fuzzy, printed out on an office printer, and hard to see in the low light, but the nurse turned on the reading lamp. The baby's creased features burned into Sage's brain like a laser, never to be erased. He looked like her, he looked like Marcus, damn it, he looked like Nick. He was a real baby, not Bean, not a bump, he was a tiny person. Suddenly her gut tightened with the thought that he was too young, too small. She turned her face to the nurse, but the woman pre-empted her.

'He's four pounds, two ounces, and very strong. He came out yelling, which is always a good sign. He's going to need a few weeks to fatten up and get more independent, but he looks like he's going to be fine.'

'Nick.' The word cut through her thoughts. 'The man that was stabbed. Do you know——?'

The woman's face fell. 'I don't. But there's a very nice policeman who wants to talk to you, and he probably does. He'll be back in the morning. Is Nick the baby's dad?'

'No. He's…' Words faded away. Sage held the picture, and her life came back into focus. 'Can I have a phone?'

'Who are you going to call? It's four thirty in the morning.'

'Oh.'

'I'll be back before I go off shift, and I'll help you call whoever it is that's so important. OK?'

She was as good as her word, helping Sage call Felix just after seven.

'Sage?'

'Is Nick——' the breath ran out.

'He's doing well. He had to have the knife removed in surgery, and his lung collapsed, but he's going to be fine. The baby?'

'I haven't seen him yet, but they say he's OK. They gave me a picture.' She could hear the sigh at his end.

'I tried to explain to the police about Elliott,' he said. 'I said he accidentally fell down the well while in a psychotic state, trying to kill you. I'm afraid he's dead, Sage. The well caved on him.'

She settled back into her pillow. 'I didn't even think about him. He killed Steph.' She swallowed. 'Is his body out of the well?'

Felix fell silent for a minute. 'I don't know. I expect so, by now. Can I come and see you? The police are keeping me on the Island for a few days as a witness.'

'Try and see Nick first, OK?'

They rang off and Sage tried to shift up in the bed, a burning pinch across her groin reminding her of the incision from the caesarean. The nurse took the phone from her and put a blood pressure cuff on her arm. 'Was that the father?'

'Oh, no.' Sage suddenly felt a bubble of laughter float up at the idea. 'No, the father is someone else.'

The cuff squeezed Sage's arm for a long moment. 'Your blood pressure's still a bit low. You lost a lot of blood yesterday.'

'I don't feel too bad.' Sage moved her shoulders, feeling the stiff muscles and a sharp pain in her neck. She looked at the skin on the inside of her wrist, where Elliott had hung on. It was purple and red with bruises and cuts. 'Actually, I don't feel great. I ache like I've been in a fight.'

The nurse smiled. 'The police will be back shortly. I diverted them with the promise of toast, but only while I checked you over. Can I just have a quick look at your tummy?' She folded the sheet down, and skimmed up the surgical gown Sage was wearing. Sage looked down at her puffy, half-deflated stomach. Above the surgical dressing her belly was covered with bruises and abrasions, red splotches as if blood had been drawn almost through the skin.

'Ow,' she whispered. The nightmare of yesterday came into focus. Elliott grabbing her arm, dragging her across the ground, Felix catching her around the waist.

'They did say you were bruised.' The nurse half laughed. 'You can rest now, get better.' She tucked the sheets in protectively. 'Here come the police. I'll give them ten minutes, then you really need to sleep before we take you downstairs to see your baby.'

The policeman that came in was a stranger, with an older female officer, but Sage hardly registered them beside the woman who barged between them.

'*Sheshe!*'

58

16th December 1580

There will be no funeral for Agness, for none else know she is dead. Solomon, Kelley, Viola and I stand over the well and agree that it would serve none to tell the dreadful tale. Instead, we will say the storm snatched her to her death. The babe, well, it had been unborn and as Solomon says, a papist's child might as well lie near its father than be rejected from Banstock's graveyard. Only Viola begs to have the child buried with its mother, but none of us has the stomach to go into that hellish hole and retrieve the bodies.

Seabourne cannot meet Viola's eyes, and turns to me instead. 'Master Vincent, Isabeau. Where is her body? I must... see to her.'

Viola steps forward, her body still shaking but her voice calm. 'Isabeau is in the spinney, I will take you to her. She deserves a Christian burial.'

'She was a Catholic. She will be denied her place in the churchyard.'

Viola speaks with the tone of an older woman. 'Then she shall be buried where she died, with the prayers and blessings of a minister.'

Perhaps some motherly tone touches Solomon, for tears come and he looks hardly older than Viola. She reaches for him and supports him, while I send a white-faced Kelley to fetch the rector and the sexton from the church, and to send Allen Montaigne to fetch my brother.

When we reach it, the body is frozen to the ground by the blood that has seeped underneath. The rector is distraught when he arrives, I believe at the fear that his sister may have been involved. The sexton is puzzled by the terrible injuries, even though I had pulled her gown together to hide the worst of the wounds.

'Reverend Matthew,' I begin. 'Perhaps if we were to take the body to Well House, which is closest, we could confer about the poor girl's burial.'

'But we must find the monster that did this!' His eyes are wild. 'A madman, perhaps.'

Kelley intervenes. 'Or as you yourself say, a beast. Maybe a wild dog, or a pack of them. Maybe a performing bear has escaped from a travelling show.' He hesitates before leaning forward and suggesting, 'Or a wolf, perhaps?'

The sexton is adamant. 'There have never been wolves on the Island. Maybe wild dogs, though – I heard tell of some savaged sheep up on Ashey in the summer.' He looks to me.

I shrug, letting the thought sink in, meeting Kelley's sharp eyes. Better they think of natural threats than such violence.

The rector turns away as if sick, and coughs. 'That poor, misguided girl. And her innocent babe, dead inside its mother.' For I have not told him of the excision of the child.

The sexton, tapping the ground with the long pole he travels with, shakes his head. 'That ground's rock 'ard, your honour.' He pressed it into the soil a few inches. 'Froze solid. We got the Widow Archer in her son's barn, hard as iron, waiting five days for decent burial.'

I hear the familiar sound of Lord Anthonie's horse, a destrier he and I had bred some ten years before, in lighter days. The animal, perhaps scenting the great violence in the metallic stink of blood and death in the air, stamps and shies. My brother dismounts, ties his animal up, and strides over to look down at the body.

'God's breath,' he murmurs to me. 'Can we stifle the scandal, Vincent?'

'I know not. But I believe her innocent of witchcraft and any sin but the venal sin of adultery. But to die like this must be punishment enough. The poor girl, she deserved better, whatever her sins.'

'Viola, my child! What business do you have here?' My brother was distressed to see his daughter there, but it was no child who answered him.

'I am here, Father, to make sure this lady gets a Christian burial.' She reaches a pale hand to Seabourne's shoulder, and he turns to her and covers his face. 'This should go no further than us, Father,' she says. I see the tears caught in her eyes, as if frosted there. She gathers Seabourne into her arms. He rests there, shaking.

Before my brother or the rector can interject, I hold up my hand. 'This poor woman has been abused enough. We have all played a part in her downfall, and those who should have protected her have failed.' I crouch down to cover her body again, with the gaily patchworked cloak that so well represented the woman. 'It is time to let her go to a merciful God.'

Vincent Garland, Steward to Lord Banstock, His Memoir

59

Monday 20th May

A few weeks later, Sage was finally comfortable enough to walk down to the seafront from her flat and meet Nick and Felix. The summer was starting to kick in, and a few mothers with young children already dotted the sand.

Nick reached for her and kissed her. Their relationship had moved on since Elliott's death. When she was able to leave her own hospital bed, she had sat by Nick's and cried into his hand before he woke up. They were too bruised and battered to meet after that, Nick staying with his parents on the mainland when he was released from hospital while Sage was driven backwards and forwards across the Island by friends and her parents to see baby Max. Yet somehow she knew that the nights in each other's arms had created a family.

'You look good. You look great.' He beamed at her, looking up and down. 'You even have some colour.'

She leaned in to hug Felix, who kissed her cheek, his tanned skin wrinkling around his eyes as he smiled. 'You do look good,' he said.

'I feel good. Until I bend or try and lift something.' Sage sat on a bench, sandwiched between the men. 'But I want to know what happened at the cottage. That day – Elliott acted so strangely.'

Felix turned towards the sea, suddenly frowning. 'Elliott had been obsessed with you for quite a while. Didn't you get any sense of how he felt?'

'No.' She thought back over the last few months. 'He just became very helpful, driving the van back to the office, helping me sort out a backlog of paperwork, that sort of thing. That's why I made sure he did the excavation. I wanted him to do something that would be good for his PhD.' She looked at her hand, at the scar raised and pink. 'I don't think he ever even touched me until that day. He was very distant.' Nick put his arm around her.

'What did the police say?' Felix asked.

'He had every paper I've ever helped write. He even had a copy of my PhD thesis, stolen from the university library, and press cuttings from the projects I've been involved in. He'd cloned my phone, had copies of all my keys after I gave him my spare set for a day.' Sage leaned back, Nick's shoulder warm against hers. 'His neighbours complained he had changed in the last few weeks – since he started work at the cottage. I think something triggered his behaviour from stalking to action.' She remembered his face when they excavated the first bones and realised they were those of a human baby not a cat. 'The horror of a baby and a woman down a well. It cast a shadow over all of us.'

'What about the footage on the nanny cam?' Nick asked. 'Someone was in the cottage. How could that have been Elliott?'

'He was onsite for weeks, watching people come and go. Judith often left the house unlocked; she must have felt safe with us all there. It would have been easy to borrow her key.' Sage shivered for a moment at the memory. 'I can't believe I didn't see it coming, didn't realise he was so ill. Psychotic.'

Nick took her hand, and she looked down at the entwined fingers. 'Felix has come up with a couple of theories. I just want you to know I think one of them is pretty strange.'

'OK.' Sage turned to Felix. 'Tell me your strange theory.'

He hesitated. 'It seems like an odd coincidence, doesn't it? Agness may have cut Isabeau's baby out with a knife, then ends up dying in the well. Elliott attacks you with a knife to kill your baby – and he falls down the same well.'

'What are you saying?'

'That the carvings in the well were designed as a trap. Maybe it exerted some sort of psychic pressure on Elliott and drew him into the well, to repeat the story of the first deaths.' Felix grinned. 'Just a crazy thought. It's the way a sorcerer like Solomon would have understood it.'

Nick shook his head. 'Tell her the other theory.'

Felix stood and leaned back on the railing overlooking the beach. 'This is the scientific theory. I borrowed some equipment and recruited a couple of acoustic engineering students from my university. There is something very odd about the cottage's fireplace. It produces a range of ultrasonic sounds, inaudible to us, when the wind blows in some directions. It also produces a few weird notes that could be confused with wailing.' He smiled. 'It also makes the cottage bloody cold. Elliott was working a few feet from it; it was just as loud outside the chimney stack as inside.'

Sage had to shrug off a shiver as she remembered. 'That's what you mentioned before, wasn't it? Just creepy sounds we can't hear making us feel haunted.'

'People repeatedly report seeing "ghosts" in the London Underground after hours. When the daytime noises are gone, the movement of air creates ultrasonic sounds that can induce mood changes, even visual and audible hallucinations. Most people just have a change of mood or imagine things. But perhaps Elliott already had a problem.' Felix leaned back further and tipped his head into the sunlight. 'Maybe it brought out, or exaggerated his extreme behaviour, especially as he started to understand the story of the bodies in the well. A baby cut out of its mother? It might have planted a seed of resentment towards your baby. And he did know the bodies were thrown down the well.'

'Open wells are dangerous things.' Sage glanced at both

men. 'Actually, I have a theory about Agness of my own.'

'You do?' Nick said.

'Yousuf sent off the DNA from the teeth of the body in the well. Agness Waldren, if it was her, was genetically male.'

Felix spoke first. 'Is that why you weren't sure at first that the skeleton was female?'

'Probably. Although the pelvis was ambiguous it was more likely to be female. But the height, the face, just bugged me. It seemed unusual for a woman.'

Nick shook his head. 'How can that even be?'

'My theory,' Sage said, 'was that Agness was partly androgen-resistant. She should have responded to testosterone in utero, but didn't so she grew to look superficially like a female. Her male genes still affected her height and features but her genitals would appear female.'

'What made you test for it?' said Nick, his hand still in hers. She noticed he had taken his wedding ring off.

'Yousuf suggested it. Her bones were so androgynous. Five-nine was tall for a man; for an Elizabethan woman it would have been very unusual. She may have been genetically male but she was brought up to be female. She must have felt she didn't fit in anywhere. She wouldn't have menstruated, which was the signal that she was ready to marry. It's rare, but about one in twenty to fifty thousand people are born with complete androgen insensitivity. More have the partial type.'

'She wouldn't have menstruated so it would have been known she couldn't have children. Marriage would have been difficult.' Felix turned to look out to sea, squinting in the light sparkling off the choppy water. 'She must have grown up feeling like a woman, but was never able – or allowed – to be one.'

'So she fell in love with Solomon.' Sage leaned back in the seat, favouring her tender incision. 'Or rather, became obsessed with him, enough to take Isabeau's baby.'

'I have some new information, too. Rose has a friend at the British Library, and got this copied for you.' Felix fished around in his holdall for a rather shabby folder, which he handed to Sage. 'Here. I'm on the four o'clock hovercraft, so I'll leave you two.' He smiled down at them, stooping slightly. 'Invite me to the burials, would you? I'd like to see Isabeau and her baby laid to rest. After all she went through.'

Sage watched him walk away, then opened the folder to reveal several photocopies of an old book. The first page was the frontispiece, ornate and fussy, but the text on the next page was crisp and easy to decipher.

BEING THE POETTRIES AND RHYMES
of the
LADY VIOLA SEABOURNE
OF BANSTOCK

REBECCA ALEXANDER

Composed in her Youth
Deddicated always to her dear sister and friend,
Isabeau Duchamp, cruelly slain.

60

31st December 1580

To dig the hole commissioned by your lordship, though the ground be frozen — four shillings for Wm. Grove, sexton To Edward Marshall, for three gammons, two baskets of trout and several of cockles, for your daughter's wedding — eighteen shillings and four pence

Accounts of Banstock Manor, 1576–1582

Our story that Isabeau died in the delivery of her child has not sufficed. With the absence of Agness, the local people are whispering that Isabeau consorted with the Devil and that he took her and the child to hell. No matter: what is important now is that the woman is buried with dignity. Despite my arguments, Viola insisted the seamstress be buried draped in the dress she was making for the wedding, worth twice her own dowry. In truth, I could not have borne to see Viola wear it.

We found the Frenchwoman's rosary at the bottom of her workbox, protected in a square of linen, guarded by a ball of needles and beaded pins. Poor child, it cost me nothing to cast it into the coffin, or for the rector to cast his eyes away.

No one questions that Agness was taken by the storm; it is only Viola and I that saw her in the apple store. Seabourne and his servants know the truth, but none will tell what transpired. I am still haunted by the slaughtered Frenchwoman. What was done in revenge was perhaps forgivable. Master Seabourne will bear it on his conscience; I feel no stain on my own. That knife to Viola absolves me of any regret that I did not try to save Agness.

Now, with Christmas gone and us all spending hours on our knees in church, I think we have reflected upon and repented our own parts in the disaster. On the eve of the wedding, with our guests held over from the festivities, I return to my office after the evening meal. I find Viola there, and she seems subdued.

'Ho, child, you should be abed,' I say, and admit that too many glasses of good wine may be swaying my tongue. 'Your last night of childhood.'

'I cannot sleep.' She sits upon the high stool, and uncovers my accounts. '"To Edward Marshall, for three gammons, two baskets of trout and several of cockles, for your daughter's wedding, eighteen shillings and four pence." Will you account every part of my wedding?'

She sounds melancholy. I kiss her cheek. 'I cannot account what it costs me, child. I will miss you when you are at your sister's estate, and then in London and Sussex with your husband's family.'

She leans her cheek against mine. 'I will write to you.' She looks at her hands, and I move to light a few candles from the single one that burns on the wall. 'I will write to you every day.'

'You will be too busy,' I say, with some attempt at jollity, but the last day I can hold her is fast dying. 'You will be busy learning to be a wife and mother with your sister. And growing up ready to be bedded.' We have agreed that Viola should not consummate her marriage until she is better grown, and Solomon is still deep in his grief for his mistress and his child. We have had glad news from Devonshire. Viola's sister, after eleven years of fruitless marriage, is to have her first child, and Viola will be welcome to support her and learn to keep house.

'I have been thinking—' she hesitates, and turns over the page in the ledger to a blank one. 'I am to marry a man who loved another so much. How can I ever be sure he loves me?'

'Great people do not marry for love, child, and if love comes — well, it is a turbulent storm rather than a calm crossing.'

'Mayhap he will love another.'

I grunt in agreement, for who can know the future. 'Mayhap he grows great boils or falls from his horse. Mayhap he turns all the iron in the house to solid gold. Who knows, child? We must live each day at our best, to serve each other and our house.'

'My father was married to my mother, and she loved another.' She dares to glance at me, looking so like Lady Marion in the candlelight that I catch my breath.

'That love became a friendship, a strength for us both.' I cannot speak above a mumble. 'That man would not betray his brother, nor she her husband.'

She nods slowly. 'Perhaps that is the greater love.'

I put out my hands and she takes them, slipping down off the stool. Her head just tucks under my chin as I hold her in my arms. 'Perhaps it is. Write the love down, as I did.'

She pulls away from me, the better to see my face. 'You wrote poetry?'

I chuckle at that, and pat the ledger that takes up the whole of the desk. 'This is the story of my love, Viola, every entry. Duty, commerce, birth, death.'

She starts to smile at that. 'I prefer my poetry to yours.'

And so I let her leave, to bed and marriage upon the morrow. As is my duty and my love, I send her into her new world. But think not that I am detached; no, I shall have an eye upon my fair child wherever she goes.

Vincent Garland, Steward to Lord Banstock, His Memoir

61

Thursday 18th July

Sage tried to park on the vicarage drive, but the number of cars already there forced her to pull up on the grass verge. She opened the door to disentangle baby Max from the car seat's various straps and buckles, before walking towards the house.

It still daunted her, the idea of one day moving in with Nick, being in the eyes of the community 'the vicar's wife'. The sun glowed off the warm brick and gilded the many windows. A crunch on the gravel alerted her to the approach of Mel, Nick's assistant. Sage lifted the baby and settled him on her shoulder.

'Oh, he's adorable!' Any stiffness in Mel's manner melted at the tiny face peering around at her. 'Can I hold him?'

'Of course.' She lifted him into the other woman's hands, and Mel cradled him. Sage still tensed. That traumatic afternoon had left her overprotective. There was nothing like the insanity of Agness about Mel, she had to tell herself. She was just a lonely woman with a bit of a crush on the vicar. She wasn't going to snatch a baby.

'My kids are so old now, it's hard to remember them when they were this small,' Mel said.

'How old are they?' Sage asked as they walked towards the house. 'You make it look easy. I still feel like I'm juggling a stack of tennis balls when I hold him.'

Mel rolled her eyes. 'Hours and *hours* of practice; neither of mine slept through the night until they were a year old.' She pushed the big front door open. 'They're seven and nine, now, and football-mad. Especially Rosalind.'

The idea that Max, still to get to ten pounds, would ever play football was ridiculous to Sage.

Mel handed the baby back. 'I'd better go and sort out the sandwiches.'

Before Sage could follow her she caught a flash of colour out of the corner of her eye. She turned to see a tall woman in a flowery dress, watching her. 'Oh.' *Fliss.* She glanced around for Marcus but there was no one else in front of the vicarage.

Fliss walked towards her, unsmiling. 'The vicar said you would be here.' Her eyes moved to the baby and her expression softened. 'He looks well.'

'He is. He's been home a month now.' Sage scanned Fliss for any emotion, but could only see a warmth towards the baby.

'We have two children, you know. I expect Marcus talked about them.'

'He mentioned them.' It was strange to think Marcus's children were Max's half-siblings.

'He looks a bit like Ivy did, when she was little.' Fliss looked up, stared into Sage's face. Her eyes were very blue. 'I'm not going to apologise for saying what I did, that day at Banstock Manor.'

That made Sage smile ruefully. 'You had every right. For the record, I didn't know. He said he was separated when we met. But later, I worked out the truth and we carried on. I'm sorry, I truly am. I was selfish. And it's so over.'

Fliss held a hand to the baby but pulled it back. 'I know it's really cheeky to ask...'

'No, it's fine.' Sage handed the baby over, a little reluctantly. But Max's magic did its work.

'Oh, he's lovely. He's so little. Enjoy him, it goes so fast.' Fliss looked at Sage. 'Marcus wants you to keep in touch, just distantly. He thinks it's not fair that Max doesn't know his brother and sister.'

Sage was surprised. She had only had one phone call from Marcus, just to check that the baby was OK. 'I didn't think he'd want to be involved. He wanted me to get an abortion when I first found out.'

Fliss snorted a laugh. 'Typical Marcus. He's such a bastard.'

'But you stay with him.' Max twitched in his sleep and she smiled. He didn't look like Marcus, or even Sage, now; he was his own creature.

'I always think, until someone better turns up. But I did love him, I suppose I still do. Our lives are so entwined with the house, the kids.' Fliss handed the baby back. 'He's beautiful, Sage. Perhaps the kids could meet him?'

'I'd like that.' Actually, the thought made Sage feel awkward. 'What will you tell them?'

Fliss sighed, turned away a little. 'God knows.' She looked back at Sage. 'That vicar is pretty keen on you. Did you know?'

Sage grinned, and rocked the baby a little. 'I do.'

When Fliss had walked away Sage turned back to the vicarage. She followed the sound of voices into the kitchen and stopped.

Judith Bassett was leaning over a tray of cakes in a summer dress and oven gloves, speaking to an elderly woman who was filling a teapot. 'I think she misses her old friends, but the new school is good—' she looked up and stared at Sage.

'Hello, Judith,' Sage said.

Max sneezed, breaking the tension.

'Oh, let me see.' It was amazing, the effect a small baby had on people. Judith didn't touch Max, but leaned over him, starting to smile. 'He's lovely. How's he doing?'

'He's great. He's doing really well, putting on weight.'

The unspoken tension between them was painful. 'How are you?'

'Some days are OK. Nick Haydon has been lovely, he even phoned from the hospital. I'm staying with my mother on the mainland; the cottage is up for sale.' She breathed out with a sigh. 'I couldn't go back. I'm just here for the funeral.'

'I understand.' Sage wasn't sure she could go to the house again, either.

'Nick organised some people from the village to clean it up for me, and the removers took everything out.'

'Great. Good.'

'And landscapers have sorted out the garden and filled in – you know. The foundations were all right but the earth collapsed right up to the wall.'

Sage nodded, a faint shiver wandering down her neck at the memories. 'I've put a protected notice on the well – it can't be excavated again.'

'We decided – Reverend Haydon and I – to put a patio over the whole area. Out of respect for that poor girl Stephanie, as much as anything.'

'Good. How's Chloe doing?' Sage hesitated before mentioning her. The baby snuffled into her neck. When she glanced up, Judith looked sad.

'She's having some counselling. During those weeks before James died, she behaved really badly. She attacked me a few times, she had tantrums and nightmares. I don't think she understood what was going on when— She is more focused on losing her daddy than what happened to you. She's missing James terribly of course...' She smiled. 'She's young, she'll move on, and just getting out of the house has helped. She's already making friends at her new school. My mother's looking after her today – I didn't want to bring her back so close to the cottage.'

'So you just came for the funeral?'

'I felt I had to. After all, we were there for so much of the story. I want to see poor Isabeau and her baby reunited. And Agness laid to some rest, at least.'

'It sounds like Nick told you the whole story.'

'Professor Guichard did. He was so kind, he even came to see us on the mainland. It was lovely to understand how those bones ended up under my lawn, even if it was such a brutal story. I want to watch that poor girl laid to rest and to let go of the cottage forever. I know Felix says it was all sound waves or something but – I felt a really evil presence at the house. We all were overshadowed by it.'

'Me too.' Sage smiled at Judith. 'Shall we go?'

They walked over to the church together. Nick was already at the doorway, greeting the people as they came in. Maeve, looking even more birdlike, was hunched like an owl in her wheelchair. The landlord of the pub, Den, in a natty suit and a porkpie hat, was ready with a big smile for Sage and a present for 'the nipper'. People she had started to really get to know were there: the florist, who had provided the flowers for free; George Banstock looking lost without his dogs being towed by Lady George into the ornate family pew; and the local historian Kate Jordan chatting with Olivia, the archivist. Nick was flanked by a dark-haired lady she recognised from photographs as his mother, and her heart jumped in her chest. At least he'd met Yana, who was beaming from a front pew, arms already out for her grandson. And her dad was there, looking sheepish beside his new girlfriend, Karen. Rob Greenway the builder and his assistant Harry had come with their families, and Professor Yousuf Sayeed was sat at the back. The church was packed.

Nick took his place at the lectern and tapped his microphone. 'Welcome. We haven't seen this many people since midnight mass last Christmas. At least you are all sober this time.'

There was a ripple of laughter from the congregation, and a few cheers. Nick's expression changed as he looked at Sage, his eyes meeting hers for a long moment. 'Before we start the service, I want to tell you the story of what happened one winter's day, four hundred and thirty-odd years ago. In the woods beyond the common is a gravestone with three words on it: DAMOZEL ISABEAU DESCHASSEE. Damozel is short for mademoiselle, Isabeau is the name of a French seamstress, and *deschassee* is the old French word for "driven away".'

As he spoke four village men carried a coffin in down

the aisle, topped with a teddy bear made of white flowers. It contained, Sage knew, Isabeau and her lost baby, and tears tickled her eyes. She touched Max's tiny hand, as he lay in Yana's arms, dozing. The doors of the church creaked again, and a second coffin covered with flowers was brought in.

'It's also the story of another woman, who was born with a condition that nowadays would be treated and understood. Agness Waldren, who lived here with her brother, the rector of this church...'

A slight scuff of shoes behind her alerted Sage to a newcomer, but she still jumped when a hand squeezed her shoulder. She turned to see Felix, in a rumpled suit, smiling at her. She squeezed up to make room for him.

Nick told the congregation all they knew, building the best narrative out of the evidence. He became quite choked up when he spoke of Isabeau and her terrible injuries. Sage wondered if in some way, he had been a little overshadowed by the parallels of Sage's baby being threatened in the same way.

The funeral service for Agness was simple. Nick explained that the words would have been familiar to her, written as they were in her century.

'MAN that is born of a woman hath but a short time to live, and is full of misery. He cometh up, and is cut down, like a flower; he fleeth as it were a shadow, and never continueth in one stay. In the midst of life we are in death:

of whom may we seek for succour, but of thee, O Lord, who for our sins art justly displeased? Yet, O Lord God most holy, O Lord most mighty, O holy and most merciful Saviour, deliver us not into the bitter pains of eternal death.'

Nick bowed his head for a moment, and Sage envied him his complete faith. Yana squeezed her hand as Nick continued.

'ALMIGHTY God, with whom do live the spirits of them that depart hence in the Lord, and with whom the souls of the faithful, after they are delivered from the burden of the flesh, are in joy and felicity: we give thee hearty thanks, for that it hath pleased thee to deliver this our sister Agness out of the miseries of this sinful world; beseeching thee that it may please thee, of thy gracious goodness, shortly to accomplish the number of thine elect, and to hasten thy kingdom; that we, with all those that are departed in the true faith of thy holy Name, may have our perfect consummation and bliss, both in body and soul, in thy eternal and everlasting glory; through Jesus Christ our Lord. Amen.'

The people around her murmured 'Amen' in reply, but Sage found her chest tight and her eyes flooding with tears. The awful story suddenly crushed her with the sadness, the waste. Then Nick took Felix's place beside her. When she looked up a Catholic priest was completing his prayers for Isabeau and her baby.

* * *

Yana and Nick's mother seemed to have cooked for the whole village, and Sage started to wonder whether their smiles covered a rivalry that would intensify once Theresa Haydon got her hands on the baby. About fifty people were wandering around the garden or the ground floor of the vicarage. Sage sat in the corner of the kitchen, blouse open, trying to feed a restless baby without too many interruptions.

'Do you mind if I…?' he gestured to an empty chair beside her. Sage nodded, and Felix hung his jacket on the back of a kitchen chair, and sat next to her.

'How are you two doing?' he asked quietly.

'OK,' she murmured back. 'It's an emotional day. I didn't realise how upset I would be. I remember that day – and knowing Isabeau's baby was thrown down the well was too close to home. And Steph, poor Steph. It all came back to me.'

'How about the father? Has he seen Max?'

'Not yet, but I just ran into his wife outside. Fliss was kind, she even held the baby.' Max had settled into feeding, and she relaxed a little into the chair. 'She's behaved better than any of us.'

Nick put his head around the door. 'There you are.' He sat on the chair beside her, and rubbed his chest gently. 'What a first day back at work. I hope it's all over now. I know the police are still making their investigations about Elliott's death.'

Felix seemed to hesitate just for a moment. 'I'm sorry he died, but he was a threat to Sage's life. We'll have to give evidence at the inquest, but I have no doubt it was a tragic accident after Elliott suffered a psychotic break.'

Sage spoke quietly, staring at the baby's eyelashes fanned over his fat cheek. 'He did try to drag me in with him.'

'I think it's impossible to know what was going through his mind. At the inquest I'll say he fell in when the well collapsed in on itself. I can't testify as to his state of mind at that moment.' Felix's words were comforting. She wasn't clear herself what had happened that day. But the well had felt like it demanded at least one sacrifice. The mental picture of Nick lying on the muddy grass made her grateful it wasn't him.

'I agree,' she said. 'Maybe the ultrasonics did make him mad.'

'And I feel better now the well's been covered up.' Felix smiled down at Max. 'So, what's next for you two? Or three?'

Sage glanced at a grinning Nick. 'We're going to gently and slowly work towards moving in together.'

Nick laughed. 'I'm thinking about a wedding before Christmas. It's one of my busy times. Oh, I've just got to say goodbye to Father McCready.'

Sage shook her head, watching him go. She turned to Felix. 'He doesn't think it's appropriate for us to live together unless we're married, but I'm still getting used to having Max home. I haven't even thought about going back to work yet, let alone getting married. Give me a year or two.' The baby had fallen off the nipple, a drop of milk still on his lips, and she was suddenly embarrassed. She pulled her shirt together, and patted Max's back.

'You take all the time you need. He'll wait.' Felix reached out a hand to touch the baby, but paused.

'He's not fragile. Here, you take him while I button everything up.' She put the baby in his arms. Felix sat stiffly, looking very uncomfortable.

'He's so small.'

'He's amazing. To have survived all that—' Max sneezed, making Felix jump.

'He's tiny.' A half-smile creased his face as the baby started hiccoughing. 'Here. You'd better have him back.'

'I still have one puzzle,' Sage said, taking Max.

'Let me guess. The alembic. You've been approached by a company who want to fund further research.'

'How—? Yes, actually. How did you know?'

'The same way you did. There are companies in a race – technologically speaking – to use the chemistry the alchemists discovered to recreate the making of gold. The stakes are high. Anything to do with Solomon Seabourne is interesting in that field.'

'There are modern alchemists?'

Felix stood up and went to stand at the kitchen window, looking out to the garden. 'Science we don't understand yet we call magic.' He turned back, his face serious. 'But once I started researching alchemy I got a lot more research grants. Be careful. There are people out there who would be very interested in your research.' His eyes rested for a long moment on the baby, then he went to the door. 'And keep in touch.'

'I will.' Sage watched him leave, pushing through the crowd of funeral-goers. Then Nick came back into the kitchen with two glasses, and worries about the future dissolved.

Acknowledgements

Firstly, I would like to thank my editors Miranda Jewess and Jo Harwood at Titan, who have polished and sharpened the book into shape. I'm so grateful for all the work they have done, getting it ready and doing the characters justice.

Jane Willis, my agent, has been amazing, making the strange world of publishing seem easier. She is always kind, always interested, and has encouraged me to keep developing new ideas.

I would also like to thank my large and noisy family, who have always supported me, especially my son Carey. He is always willing to read and challenge my stories, which just helps them grow. My husband Russell is always willing to visit Elizabethan houses and churches, wander around museums and make shelves for my growing library.

Finally, writing is a lonely business, just the writer and a keyboard and empty pages stretching away. My refuge is a walk to The Coffee Cabin in Appledore, for a hot drink and a word with a real human being. Thanks to Martin and Richard and all the staff. You keep me sane.

About the Author

Rebecca Alexander is a psychologist and writer. Rebecca fell in love with all things sorcerous, magical and witchy as a teenager and has enjoyed reading and writing fantasy ever since. She wrote her first book aged nineteen, and since then has been runner-up in the Mslexia novel writing competition and the Yeovil Literary Prize 2012. She is the author of the Jackdaw Hammond series of supernatural crime novels published by Del Rey, *The Secrets of Life and Death* (2013), *The Secrets of Blood and Bone* (2014) and *The Secrets of Time and Fate* (2016). She lives in Devon.

A BREATH AFTER DROWNING

ALICE BLANCHARD

Sixteen years ago, Kate Wolfe's young sister Savannah was brutally murdered. Forced to live with the guilt of how her own selfishness put Savannah in harm's way, Kate was at least comforted by the knowledge that the man responsible was in jail. But when she meets a retired detective who is certain that Kate's sister was only one of many victims of a serial killer, Kate must decide whether she can face the possibility that Savannah's murderer walks free. As she unearths disturbing family secrets in her search for the truth, she becomes sure that she has uncovered the depraved mind responsible for so much death. But as she hunts for a killer, a killer is hunting her…

PRAISE FOR THE AUTHOR

"[A] gale-force thriller"
New York Times

"Splendid… riveting and addictive"
Chicago Tribune

"Brilliant… a dark and stormy novel"
New York Daily News

TITANBOOKS.COM

THE BLOOD STRAND
CHRIS OULD

Having left the Faroes as a child, Jan Reyna is now a British police detective, and the islands are foreign to him. But he is drawn back when his estranged father is found unconscious with a shotgun by his side and someone else's blood at the scene. Then a man's body is washed up on an isolated beach. Is Reyna's father responsible?

Looking for answers, Reyna falls in with local detective Hjalti Hentze. But as the stakes get higher and Reyna learns more about his family and the truth behind his mother's flight from the Faroes, he must decide whether to stay, or to forsake the strange, windswept islands for good.

"A winner. For fans of Henning Mankell"
Booklist

"A tense crime thriller woven around a captivating family mystery"
Paul Finch, bestselling author of *Stalkers*

TWO LOST BOYS
L.F. ROBERTSON

Janet Moodie is a death row appeals attorney. Overworked and recently widowed, she's had her fill of hopeless cases, and this will be her last. Her client is Marion 'Andy' Hardy, convicted along with his brother Emory of the rape and murder of two women. But Emory received a life sentence while Andy got the death penalty, labeled the ringleader despite his low IQ and Emory's dominant personality.

Convinced that Andy's previous lawyers missed mitigating evidence that would have kept him off death row, Janet investigates Andy's past. She discovers a sordid and damaged upbringing, a series of errors on the part of his previous counsel, and most worrying of all, the possibility that there is far more to the murders than was first thought. Andy may be guilty, but does he deserve to die?

"This is a must-read"
Kate Moretti, *New York Times* bestseller

"Suspense at its finest"
Gayle Lynds, *New York Times* bestseller

AFTER THE ECLIPSE
FRAN DORRICOTT

Two solar eclipses. Two missing girls. Sixteen years ago
a little girl was abducted during the darkness of a solar
eclipse while her older sister Cassie was supposed to be
watching her. She was never seen again. When a local
girl goes missing just before the next big eclipse, Cassie –
who has returned to her home town to care for her ailing
grandmother – suspects the disappearance is connected to
her sister: that whoever took Olive is still out there. But she
needs to find a way to prove it, and time is running out.

COMING MARCH 2019

TITANBOOKS.COM

For more fantastic fiction, author events, exclusive
excerpts, competitions, limited editions and more

VISIT OUR WEBSITE
titanbooks.com

LIKE US ON FACEBOOK
facebook.com/titanbooks

FOLLOW US ON TWITTER
@TitanBooks

EMAIL US
readerfeedback@titanemail.com